M000224300

THE LORNEA ISLAND
DETECTIVE CLUB

GREGG DUNNETT

For Grubby
Forever 'The Best Dog In The World'
Sadly missed, fondly remembered
2007 - 2019

ONE

I KNOW I'm in trouble. I'm just not sure what for.

I'm sitting outside the school principal's office. Lined up against the wall on a hard plastic chair. Just opposite is the school secretary, sitting at her desk and glowering over her glasses which hang from a chain round her neck. It's like she's wondering if I'm the type that might make a run for it.

The thought has crossed my mind. Principal Sharpe has a super scary reputation. But there's nowhere to run. Besides, I'm curious to know why I'm here, and if I run away I won't find out. And anyway, I'm not the running away kind.

I'm serious about Principal Sharpe's reputation though, everyone's afraid of her, not just the students. Once I was doing biology with Miss Jones, and we had to label the parts of a praying mantis in our work books. And because I was sitting right at the front of the class, I heard Miss Jones muttering when she saw the picture how it reminded her of Principal Sharpe. I don't think she meant the principal looked like one, she was talking about the way the females trap and eat the males after they've mated with them.

"Excuse me Mrs. Weston," I ask the secretary. "Will I have to wait here much longer?"

Mrs. Weston stops typing and frowns at me.

"The Principal will call you when she's ready."

"It's just I was in my math class you see, and math is very important..."

"When she's ready."

She gives me a death stare so I give up. Then when she looks back at her computer I glance around at the little alcove where she's sitting. She doesn't get a proper room, but she's tried to make it nice anyway. There's a big yucca plant on the floor next to her, and as I'm looking at that I notice a gecko sitting half way up the trunk. I assume it's a gecko, it's definitely not any of the local species of lizards we have here on the island, and it has really big toes. I lean in closer, only stopping when I hear Mrs. Weston stop typing and peer at me. I wonder where it came from. Maybe someone kept it as a pet and it escaped? Maybe it lived in the plant and no one's ever noticed. Or maybe Mrs. Weston keeps it as a pet?

I'm suddenly interrupted by a loud commotion from the other end of the corridor. I look up to see Mr. Richmond marching another student towards me. He's pushing a girl, and he's got one of her arms behind her back like he's the police and she's been arrested. He looks *super* mad. But actually, if anything, the girl looks madder.

"Sit down here and don't move." Mr. Richmond hisses at the girl when they get level with me. For a moment I think she's going to disobey him, but then she drops down into a chair, leaving her legs splayed at awkward angles. Unfortunately for me it's the chair right next to mine.

It's my fault too. There's only three chairs here, and if I'd been smarter I'd have sat in one of the end ones. Then, if someone had come along, they could take the other end chair and there'd still be another chair empty in the middle. But I'm not used to coming to see Principal Sharpe, so I didn't think of that.

I do my best not to look at the girl. I watch Mr. Richmond instead, as he talks to Mrs. Weston. I suppose he's telling her what the girl's done, but I don't hear what it is because he's talking in a very quiet voice. Then he turns to go. As he does so he notices me, and he gives a little surprised start. That's probably because I'm a really good student and he wasn't expecting to see me here. I get ready to explain to him that there's been some sort of mistake, but Mr. Richmond doesn't actually ask me anything, he just gives me a disappointed look and then he goes away. Then Mrs. Weston goes into Principal Sharpe's office, presumably to tell her she's got another student to deal with as well as me. I take advantage by moving to the other end chair so that I don't have to sit right next to the girl. It's better too, as I'm closer to the yucca. Maybe I can identify what type of gecko it is.

"Do I smell or something?"

That's the girl speaking.

"What?"

"I asked if I smell."

"What? Oh. No. Well I don't know..." The truth is I didn't notice. But I'm not going to lean over and sniff her, that would be weird.

"I don't think so."

She stares at me for a long time, then flicks her head like I'm not worth her time. I feel quite relieved by this and go back to watching the gecko. I'm not sure what they eat. I suppose flies and stuff, but maybe they actually eat yucca plants. I'll have to look it up later on...

"Well this is *bullshit. Isn't it?*" The girl interrupts again.

I don't answer. I try to keep my mind on the gecko. I think I read somewhere that you can find them anywhere in the country now, because of Global Warming and also the way bananas are transported...

"So what you here for?" It's the girl again. I drag my mind back.

"I don't know."

"What do you mean *you don't know*? How can you not know?"

"I don't know."

"You don't know how you don't know?"

I think about this for a second.

"No."

She glowers at this, then flicks her head again.

"Actually I don't know either. Except it's all *fucking bullshit.*"

I turn to look at her. I get that she's mad about being dragged here, but I don't think that swearing in front of the Principal's office will help her case, whatever it is. I consider her for a second, while she's glaring at the opposite wall. She's a bit older than me, and dressed mostly in black. She's wearing massive Dr. Martens boots, and I guess her dark hair must have been dyed blue, because it doesn't look a very natural color to me. I don't get the chance to see anymore because then she turns back to look at me. I look away, but for a long time I can feel her staring at me.

"You're that kid aren't you?"

I don't answer at first, but there's no point denying it.

"Yeah."

The girl doesn't say any more, but I sense her continuing to stare at me. I'm almost relieved when Mrs. Weston comes back out.

"Billy Wheatley? Principal Sharpe will see you now."

TWO

Principal Sharpe is sat behind her desk, writing on some papers. She doesn't look up.

"Close the door." She's still not looking at me, but I do what she says, then stand there, waiting.

"Sit."

There's one hard chair in front of her desk, and then a couple of comfy chairs by the window. I take a guess and sit on the hard one. Still she doesn't look at me, she just keeps writing. Finally she stops, then puts the pen down. Then she does look at me. Right at me. It's hard but I do my best to look right back.

"I'm sure you know why you're here?" She asks, and one of her eyebrows goes up in a sharp arch. I feel a strong urge to nod, but the problem is, I really don't know. All I know is the teacher in my Math class had a message I had to see Principal Sharpe right away. It didn't say why.

"I have to say I am incredibly disappointed in you Billy. What were you thinking?"

I'm hoping these are all rhetorical questions, because I don't how to answer them. She's still looking at me so I lower my gaze to the floor. But then there's silence, and I end up glancing up again. I think Miss Jones is wrong, she's not really like a praying mantis at all. She's more like a bird of prey, settling on its favorite post.

I guess they were rhetorical questions, because then she goes on.

"Billy. I'm aware you are one of the more *unusual* personality types in this school. I understand that." She stares right at me. "But that does not give you the right to take liberties."

I blink back at her now, trying to work out what she's talking about. In the end I have to say something.

"Yes."

"And as I'm sure you're perfectly aware, there are robust and clear procedures to deal with any..." she hesitates, and for the first time she looks away, just for a moment.

"With any *issues* you feel you may have at the school." She's back to staring.

There's a very long silence.

"OK." I say.

I'm beginning to wonder if I might get through the entire conversation without knowing what it's about. She shakes her head and continues.

"And ironically, in the circumstances, some might consider that what *you* have done constitutes bullying." She tips her head on one side and falls silent again.

But this time I have a sense of what this might be about. It was that word 'bullying', and the way she said it, stressing the 'ing' part. I open my mouth to reply, but then change my mind. I bite my lip instead.

This time both her eyebrows go up.

I bite my lip again.

"Oh," I say in the end.

"Oh indeed," Principal Sharpe says, then she shakes her head.

"I'm actually confused Billy. Did you somehow think this wouldn't come to my attention? Did you think I wouldn't find out? I'm genuinely curious. Because surely you can't have thought it was a *good idea*. I give you more credit than that."

Before going any further I want to be sure I've got it right – the reason she's angry I mean – so I interrupt her, just a little bit.

"Is this about the Kickstarter idea?"

Principal Sharpe sighs sharply. "Yes Billy. This is about your *Kickstarter* idea."

There's another silence.

"In which you publicly accuse several students of this school of bullying behavior, *and* identify this school as having a significant bullying problem."

I try to remember. It was quite a few weeks ago and I've forgotten exactly what I wrote. I haven't forgotten the idea, because it was a good idea. And I wanted to act on it quickly, because sometimes when I have a good idea, a few days later I forget about it, and I didn't want that to happen this time. No, I've just forgotten the exact words I used.

"I'm probably not actually going to make it now. The invention I mean."

She opens her mouth to reply, but then closes it again. She looks a bit frustrated.

"That isn't the issue Billy. The issue is how you've named students on a public forum when they have no right to reply. And how you've attacked the reputation of this school." She lets out a slow sigh.

"I'm just grateful it was brought to my attention before one of the boys involved happened upon it. Or their parents."

I'd better explain. Especially since Principal Sharpe just called Kickstarter a forum, which it isn't. But then she's a grown-up, and lots of grown-ups don't really understand the internet very well. You see, Kickstarter is a website for making good ideas actually happen. You post your idea – like for a new invention, or a book or a film – and then if enough other people agree it's a good idea, they give you the money for the idea to get made. It's nothing like a *forum*. They're places where people talk online, though I don't think anyone uses them these days.

"I'm very disappointed in you Billy. You've a good reputation in this school. You're not a troublemaker, but to undermine the school's good name like this... To accuse your fellow pupils. It's quite outrageous."

Principal Sharpe has a computer on her desk and she angles the monitor so I can see it. To my surprise she's got my Kickstarter web page on the screen. I see the logo I made at the top, with the words 'Bully-Tracker' in red, next to a little picture of a radar tower with little circular radio waves coming out of it. I thought it explained the technology behind BullyTracker really well actually, you see the idea is to get all the bullies to wear this special tracker device – probably it would be an ankle bracelet that they can't take off – like the ones criminals wear, and then everyone who wants to keep out of the bullies' way can use their cell phones to see exactly where the bullies are *in real time*. You could even set up a little alert so people get a message when the bullies are getting too close. It's clever isn't it?

"While I appreciate the sentiment behind this idea, to name these boys is quite wrong. I just hope we can get it down before I get a call from their parents."

"I think they're probably bullies too."

"*What?*"

"Their parents. At least, they certainly look like bullies. Just grown up..."

"*Billy!* I've not called you in for a discussion on this matter!"

I hesitate for a second.

"Well why have you brought me in?"

Principal Sharpe looks away, like a small bird just flew past the window and she thought about catching it. Then she turns back to me.

"The issue is that none of these boys has any opportunity to refute your '*claims*'. And the way you're misrepresenting the school is extremely damaging."

"But it's not *mis*representing the school if it's accura..."

"*The reason I called you in Billy is because you're going to delete it. Right now.*"

She shouts loud enough that Mrs. Weston can probably hear her outside. And that girl too. It shuts me up though.

She slides the keyboard towards me now, but it's not a wireless one, and it gets stuck when the cable isn't long enough. She has to fight for a few moments, to free up more cable. Finally she gets it in front of me.

"I assume you can log in from here?"

I can feel my forehead crunching up in a frown. I told you how lots of adults don't understand the internet. I've got a copy of the whole thing at home anyway, so even if I delete it here it won't mean anything. I glance up at her, wondering if she really doesn't know that. But she stares right back at me, her face white with veins sticking out of her neck. So I don't say anything. Instead I type in my log-in details. Then she *keeps* watching me, so I have to curl my arm up over the keyboard to stop her seeing my password from the keys I press. From the other side of the desk I hear her sigh.

"I'm not actually sure how to delete it," I tell her, while the page loads. "I haven't ever deleted a Kickstarter before."

"You're a smart boy Billy, I'm sure you'll find a way."

I don't answer, but turn my attention to the screen. Actually it's really easy. Moments later the screen says:

Are you sure? This Kickstarter has been backed!

I didn't know that. I look up to tell her.

"It's actually been 4.2% funded."

I expect her to be at least a little bit impressed by this, but she doesn't say anything.

"I set it for 50,000 dollars, which means it's actually raised 2100 dollars..."

"I'm well aware of how Kickstarter operates." Principal Sharpe replies. Even though she isn't, since she just called it a forum. Her voice is ice-cold, but I persevere. After all this is important.

"So it only needs another 47,900 dollars and it will get made. You know I really think this system could help lots of people..."

She sighs again. "Billy, have you done *any* work on it? On actually creating the device? Or the software that would operate it?"

"No. But that's why I put in the bit about the school. I thought maybe if someone at Google saw it they might want to build it. And they'd want a place to test it, once it was made. So they could do it here. At Newlea High School."

"And you didn't think to check that with me first?" she snaps. "The school principal?"

I don't answer at once. Maybe I should have checked.

"I didn't think you'd mind," I say. "You're always saying how you won't tolerate bullying and everything?"

Now Principal Sharpe sighs really loudly.

"Billy. It's my job to ensure that Newlea High School is a safe and welcoming environment for all students..."

"But it *isn't*. There are bullies everywhere. And no-one ever does anything about it."

She gasps at this, like this is somehow shocking.

"Billy... Billy that's... That's simply *not the case*. There are *procedures* in place.... Rigorous procedures..." She composes herself before going on.

"Billy, if you feel you are being targeted by bullying you only need to speak to your class tutor, or to *any* teacher. Or you can come direct to me."

I don't answer. If *that* worked I wouldn't have needed to invent Bully-Tracker, would I?

"*Are* you experiencing problems with bullying? Billy?"

I take a long time to reply. I can't help but think about what Dad's always telling me. How we just have to ignore it. To keep our heads down and not make a big deal. How things will get better. Eventually. Even though they never do.

"No."

She looks exasperated and rubs her forehead. "Well. . . Well then I suggest we simply delete this and we'll put this episode behind us."

I look at the screen again. The funding amount is displayed in big green letters. $2100. I don't have a copy of *that* at home. It seems such a shame to lose it. But I don't have much choice.

I press delete.

THREE

She gives me one after-school detention. Just one. Actually I get the sense it's a token punishment, like she has to do something, but knows that I didn't really do anything wrong. Or maybe she realizes that detentions won't have much effect on someone like me who actually *likes* doing school work. It must be hard for teachers when they have extraordinary students.

I don't get my usual bus home. Instead I sneak onto the Holport bus that goes down the west side of the island. I've been doing that for a while now, since Dad got his new job down there.

When we get into Holport I run down to the harbor. Dad works near the big square basin where all the fishing boats unload their catches. There's these little cranes where they hoist up the plastic pallets of fish and load them on trolleys, before a fork-lift pulls them into the warehouse. But all the boats are finished for the day, so there's no one about right now. As I look around my feet crunch through piles of dried fish scales that look like snow. Everything smells of fuel oil and fish gone bad in the sun.

Dad doesn't work on one of the boats, though he wants to, because that's where the real money is. Dad works onshore, in the warehouse. That's the big, flat-roofed building next to me, where they take all the fish that comes in, and auction it off. Dad doesn't get involved in that either. He just washes the auction house down when all the fish have been sold. He has this big pressure hose, and he has to blast all the fish guts and scales back into the water.

When I get there, the big, double doors are open, and I stick my head inside. I'm used to the smell now, a mix of fish and the chemicals Dad uses – but it's still not very nice. I see him at once, dressed in his overalls and boots, limping along in the far corner of the warehouse.

"Hi Dad! Did you make a bag for Steven?"

In response he shuts off the hose and points to a plastic sack just behind the door.

"Thanks," I say, then add. "How long you gonna be?"

He looks around the warehouse. "Gimme an hour." He says. Then he turns the hose back on and goes back to spraying it at the floor.

"OK." I shout over the noise. "I'll see you at the truck."

I grab the sack – it's quite heavy, but that's mostly the ice. I make sure it's properly closed, then heave it over my shoulder. Then I go back outside and dump it in Dad's truck, along with my school bag.

Dad used to have a much better job. He looked after the vacation properties for Mr. Matthews, who owns the Silverlea Hotel, but he lost that a couple of years back after the whole murdered tourist thing. It's kind of a long story, but basically this teenager went missing, and the police thought that Dad killed her. Obviously he didn't, but it was the second time Dad got blamed for murder, so – well – some people thought there was no smoke without fire. I guess Mr. Matthews was one of them, because he told Dad he didn't need anyone to look after the vacation properties any more. But then, a few weeks later, we found there was someone else doing it. So we knew that wasn't the actual truth.

Then for a really long time, Dad couldn't get any other jobs at all because it seemed no one trusted him. He says he only got *this* job because it's the kind of thing no one else wants to do. And it is a bit disgusting. But it is handy for Steven.

Since I've got an hour to kill, I walk out of the commercial harbor towards the marina. I like it here too. I like looking at all the boats. There's all sizes and shapes, from stubby little yachts to massive motor cruisers. You're not allowed actually onto the floating pontoons, unless you have a boat of course, but that's OK because I know the code to open the gate. I look around to make sure no one's looking, then I quickly unlock it and step through.

I really like the way the deck moves when you walk on it. It's like you're already on a boat, even before you get to the boats. I walk out now. I do this quite a lot, looking at all the different boats and deciding which type I'm going to have when I'm older. Probably it'll be one of the little ones, with just a small cabin, because I'm going to be a scientist when I'm older, and they don't earn very much money. I was going to be a detective for a little while, after everything that happened with Dad, because I thought the police could do with some help, but then I changed my mind because I realized my science was more important. And anyway, I don't think detectives earn that much either. And they certainly don't have much time to go out on boats.

I keep walking, out to where the bigger sport-fishing boats are tied up. Some of these are really flash, with huge flying bridges and blacked out windows. I don't like these much, but they're interesting, in a funny way. You see, tourists like to rent these boats out, the ones who have lots of money. The skippers take them out and help them catch fish and give them lots of food and beer. It's something I've been thinking about a lot lately.

The boat I do like is right at the end. It's 39 foot long, or 11.8 meters, and though it's still a charter fishing boat, it's a bit older and looks nicer for it. More friendly somehow. It's called *The Blue Lady*. There's a little offshoot to the pontoon that lets you walk right out alongside it, so I do that now. And then, because there's no one looking, I reach out and touch the boat as well, running my hand along the cool steel railing. They used to be shiny, but now they've gone a bit dull from the weather and the salt water. This boat isn't being used for charters at the moment, because the man who owns it got too old. So it's just been sitting here, with no one using it, or even looking after it. Not once since Dad started work in the fish warehouse.

I look around the harbor. Some of the restaurants are putting out their tables for dinner, but no one's watching me. So very carefully I put both hands on the railings, and then I step across the little gap of clear blue water between the boat and the pontoon. Right away I feel it dip under my weight, but only very slightly, because it's quite a big boat. Then I climb down so I'm standing in the cockpit at the back. The wooden floorboards are scrubbed clean. There's a ladder leading up to the bridge, where the skipper sits with a view out over the top of the boat. And there's glass doors that let me see into the cabin. It's light and clean inside, there's a little kitchen area, and a little table for charts, and then stairs too. I've seen from the internet that there's two bedrooms and a bathroom too, but I've never actually seen it for myself. I know the door is locked, but I try it anyway, and when it doesn't open I press my face up against the window, trying to imagine how it would be, inside the cabin out at sea. Being in charge.

I stay like that for a while, then I climb up the ladder to the bridge. This is my favorite part of the whole boat. Up here you can see all around. There's a fabric roof that keeps the sun off, and a plastic screen for the wind, so it's sheltered and feels protected. I sit on the captain's seat and put my hands on the wheel. Then I look at the other controls. There's a GPS, a depth gauge, and the one I'm most excited about, the fish finder. The way it works, it sends out sound waves into the ocean below, and if there's something down there, like a shoal of fish, then the sound bounces back and you can see where it is on a little screen. But it doesn't just bounce off fish, which is why my idea is such a good one. You could use it to find anything. You could use it to find...

"Hey kid!" A sharp voice suddenly cuts in, from close nearby. I give a little jump in surprise.

"The hell you doing up there?"

A man is standing on the pontoon right beside the boat, in the blue uniform of the private security firm that patrols is harbor.

"You here with someone?"

I consider telling him about Dad working in the warehouse nearby, but I change my mind.

"No."

"Then get the hell down from there."

For a second my daydream wants to come back, to ignore this interruption. This is *my* boat and I'm far out in the ocean doing important scientific...

"Are you deaf or just plain stupid? I said get down from there. *Right now.*"

Reluctantly I let the image fade away and do what he says. I climb down the ladder, then step off *The Blue Lady* and back onto the pontoon. I don't look at the security guard, but I feel him glaring at me the whole time. Then he blocks me off from leaving by holding out his hand.

"I seen you before haven't I? Hanging around here?"

I don't answer. I try to get past again, but he's still blocking my way.

"This is private property. No public access. You can't read the signs?"

"This one isn't private. It's for sale. They want people to look at it, so they can sell it." This stops the man for a moment, but only a moment.

"And what? I'm supposed to believe a punk like you's gonna buy it? You clear off, you hear me? I ever see you climb on the boats again, I call the cops. You got that?"

At last he drops his arm, so I can walk past, but he stays standing in the middle of the walkway so I have to go close to the water to do so. And I get a weird feeling he's going to shove me in as I step by, but he doesn't.

Then, I sense him, following close behind as I walk back up the pontoon to the gate. And all the way I feel my face burning red.

Back at the fish warehouse I wait while Dad gets changed out of his overalls, and when he comes out we walk together to the truck. On the way we go past a yacht broker, it has all the ads for boats for sale in the window. I try to steer Dad a bit closer as we go past. And when we're level with it I point at one of the ads.

"Look Dad, *Blue Lady* is still for sale."

But Dad just ignores me.

FOUR

DAD GOES for a shower as soon as we get home. He takes ages because it's so hard to get the smell off. So I go up to my room and check on Steven. Before I even get to my door I can hear he's excited, and jumping up and down in his cardboard box. And the moment I open the door there's this big explosion of flapping and squawking and load of loose feathers fly around.

Steven almost bowls me over, but I manage to sit down at my desk. Then there's a noise like a helicopter and he's up there too, striding back and forth because he's so excited.

I open the plastic sack now and see what Dad's got. I pick out a little flatfish, a plaice. I hold it out and Steven steps towards me, squawks loudly, and then delicately takes it from me. When he was little I had to train him not to peck at me, because even then his beak was very sharp. Now he could easily bite my finger off if he wanted to. He swallows the plaice whole, tipping his head back and flapping it around until it curls up and goes down his throat. Then straight away he wants another one.

It was Dad who called him Steven. He thought it was funny because of someone called Steven Seagal, who is a famous actor from the old days and whose name sounds like 'seagull', although not *that* much. I'd never heard of him but Dad said I wasn't allowed to keep the chick unless I went along with the name. It's all a bit silly because there's actually no such thing as a seagull, not technically. There's just different types of gull, like Black Backed Gulls, Common Gulls, or Ring-Billed Gulls.

Steven is a Herring Gull. I've had him since he was a baby. I found him on the beach, near the cliffs. He must have fallen out of his nest, and when that happens to the chicks, the parents can't do anything, they just have to leave them to die. So that's why I had to keep him and bring him up myself. And he's not a baby anymore. Now he's about the size of a chicken – a big brown-and-white chicken, with a black beak and pink legs. And he *really* likes fish. Which is why it's helpful that Dad can get the scraps from the fish warehouse to feed him.

I give him about half the fish scraps, until he tells me he's full by shaking his head. Then he stretches out his wings, they're so big they almost touch both sides of my room at once. He flaps them a bit, then bounces around the room, and then he just goes and stands in his box and preens himself. Steven can actually fly already, but Gerry – she's from the Lomax Wild Bird Rescue centre and she's helping me to look after him – she said I should keep him inside for a bit longer so that his wings get the chance to grow stronger before he starts using them. But pretty soon he'll have to move outside, because he's quite messy now.

Once I've fed Steven I make dinner for me and Dad, then I do my homework, and after that I do some work on my new project. But I'm still feeling a bit down because of what happened with the security guard. So in the end I pick up my laptop and go down and sit with Dad in the lounge. It's a bit weird, because he isn't actually watching TV at all. He's got the sound off and it's a sitcom, and Dad doesn't usually watch stuff like that.

"You alright Dad?" I ask eventually. He doesn't look at me. He just stares at the screen.

"Dad?"

He turns round. He gives a weak smile. "Sure. Aches a bit. That's all."

Dad got shot a couple of years ago, back when the whole tourist-girl-murder thing was going on. They sort of fixed it, but his hip still aches sometimes.

He smiles again, a bit stronger this time.

"School good?" He asks. I hesitate, wondering whether to mention everything that happened with Principal Sharpe and my BullyTracker idea. In the end I just shrug.

"It's OK," I say.

Dad's smile fades away, and he turns back to the TV. So I tell him about something else, since he's in a talkative mood.

"Dad," I say. "I was kind of looking at bank loans. The other day, on the internet." I don't look at him, I know he won't like this.

"That way you wouldn't need to pay the whole fifty thousand in one go. You just need some of the money, then you pay the rest in installments. As you get the customers I mean?"

I risk a glance at him. But his expression is familiar. It's really frustrating. It's like he's totally resistant to my idea, even though it's actually a really good one.

"I'm just saying you wouldn't need to clean the fish warehouse. And it would be better for your hip."

Dad takes a deep breath, but he doesn't say anything.

"I've sort of been working on a website," I tell him. "To show you."

I'm good at making websites. It's kind of a hobby of mine. I think it's really important that children know how to do things like that. Making websites. Coding. Using the internet.

"I put all the species on it, that people could see. And then if you click the species name it takes you to a new page with more information about them. I reckon they'll like that. I really think they will."

I open my laptop to show him, and I've already got the site loaded up. There's lots of pictures of the *Blue Lady*, one taken from the yacht broker's website, and then others that I took. And then around the edge I've put all the different types of whales, and dolphins and porpoises you'd be able to see if you hired Dad to take you out.

"I thought you could call it *Blue Lady Boat Charter*."

Dad looks at the screen, and for a moment I see him smiling, but then it fades away.

"Billy. Believe me, I would love nothing more than to buy that fishing boat you're obsessing over, and run charters or track poisonous jellyfish – or whatever it is you think is gonna make us rich..."

"It's whale watching," I interrupt. "It's taking tourists out to see the whales. It's really popular in some places, but no one is doing it on Lornea Island. Even though we get lots of..."

"But it ain't gonna happen Billy. Not now. Not for a few years at least."

I don't reply. We've had this conversation before so I know what he's going to say.

"I told you. I gotta show the guys at the fish dock I can work hard, even with this goddamn hip." Dad sighs, then turns to me.

"And I tell you Bill, I'm close to getting a space on a boat. Then all I gotta do is haul nets for a few years. I can put a little aside every month. Then maybe, in a year or two..." He glances at the screen again.

"But if you get some sort of a loan?"

"Billy they ain't gonna give a guy like me a loan. OK? I told you this before. It ain't gonna happen, and even if it did..."

He lapses into silence. I guess he's tired, because sometimes he gets angry when I try to talk to him about this. And because I know it's pointless I shut my laptop and start to walk away, heading for my room. But just as I do he calls out.

"Hey Bill, I ain't saying I don't like your dream. It's a nice dream. It really is. You just gotta work out what's a dream and what's reality. You know?"

He looks so sad I don't want to make him any sadder, so I just nod.

"Sure Dad."

FIVE

I'VE NEVER HAD an actual detention before, so I'm quite looking forward to seeing how they work. But it turns out to be very boring. We just have to sit in the computer lab after school and do the exact same homework that we'd do at home anyway. It's not much of a deterrent is it? I guess that's why the bad kids get them over and over again.

Mr. Coyne is the only teacher here. He's sat at the front marking books, and he's not even very strict, so some of the students behind me are chatting to each other.

I just ignore everyone. Or at least I mean to, but then I do something silly. I glance around to see who's talking and I notice the girl who was outside Principal Sharpe's office the other day. She's sitting on her own, and she looks up at the exact same time as I do. I almost don't recognize her, because her hair isn't blue anymore, it's purple. Then when I see it is her, I can't stop myself raising my hand to wave hello. She stares back, then rolls her eyes and looks away, so I feel a bit embarrassed about that.

But then, about half way into the detention, she sneaks forward and comes to sit at the computer next to me. I look up at Mr. Coyne, a bit worried, but to my surprise he's put headphones on and doesn't notice.

"So? You figure it out?" The girl whispers to me.

"Figure what out?"

"You figure out why you're here?"

"Oh. Sort of."

I turn back to my history homework, but it's awkward, because now she's sitting right next to me.

"Well?"

"Well what?"

"You gonna tell me?"

Obviously not. But I have to tell her something.

"I was late."

"You don't get sent to see Sharpe for lateness."

"Don't you?" I ask. I didn't know that. "I was late a lot."

I feel uncomfortable with how close to me she is now. And the way she sits there staring. In silence.

"I have to do my homework now..." I start to say, but she cuts across me.

"You know there's loads of rumors about you." Then when I don't reply, she goes on.

"About when you were a baby... About how your mom went crazy and drowned your sister, and then tried to drown you..."

I don't answer. It's not really something I talk about with strangers.

"And then how the cops blamed your dad, so he kidnapped you and brought you up here in secret. Is it true?"

"It's not really something I talk about with..."

"So it isn't? I didn't think it was."

"I didn't say it wasn't true."

"So it is true?"

I don't answer that.

"Alright. You don't *have* to tell me." She looks away now, like she's suddenly bored. It annoys me a bit.

"It is true. I just don't like to talk about it with strangers."

"I'm not surprised. That's mental."

She doesn't say anything for a moment so I turn back to my homework.

"So where's your mom now?"

I put my pen down and sigh. I might as well tell her. Maybe then she'll go away.

"She's in a secure medical facility. Out in Oregon."

"Like a prison?"

"No. It's a secure medical facility. It's more like a hospital, just she's not allowed to leave. I'm allowed to visit too, if I want to, but the judge said I don't have to."

"And have you? Visited?"

"No."

"I don't blame you. *Fuck her*."

I look up at Mr. Coyne, but he didn't hear. He's still nodding his head to his music.

"I mean. I thought *my* Mom was bad but...."

She rests her fingers on the desk in front of her, and taps out a little beat with her fingers.

"So what? You just live with your dad now?"

"I really need to do my homework actually..."

"And your dad was accused of killing that tourist girl? What was her name?"

"It's due in tomorrow."

"Olivia something? Curran – Olivia Curran. But it wasn't your dad was it? It was that waitress from Silverlea. Fucking psycho waitress killed her and hid the body in some caves."

"She wasn't exactly a psycho. It was more of an accident."

"But she did hide the body in a cave? And then she tried to kill you in the cave too."

"Yeah. Sort of."

The girl laughs. But quietly.

"My dad died," she says suddenly. And then we're both silent for quite a long time, before she speaks again.

"I've been googling you. There's tons of stuff about Olivia Curran, but not much about you..."

"That's because the newspapers weren't allowed to print my name. I was under thirteen at the time it happened."

"Uh huh." She says.

"But I knew *your* name."

I look up at her. I don't understand this.

"So I did find something interesting."

There's something in her tone of voice that sounds like she's teasing me a bit.

"What?"

In response she logs onto the computer in front of her. It takes a while because the computers here are really slow. But when she finally gets online I watch as she types in the letters of a web address. And as she does so I get this horrible sinking feeling.

SIX

THE WEBSITE COMES UP. It's dominated by a large logo. A man holding a magnifying glass. There's a headline too:

The Lornea Island Detective Agency

The girl scrolls down and starts reading.

"*The Lornea Island Detective Agency is the best private investigators in Lornea Island for solving your crimes and catching murderers...*" She looks at me, one eyebrow raised up.

"*Specializing in cases too difficult or secret for the police,*" she goes on. "*Whatever your mystery, we can help.*"

I don't say anything.

"Does that sound familiar Billy?"

"No. Why would it?"

"Oh I don't know. *Catching murderers...* Didn't you do that? Didn't you help to catch the psycho waitress who killed the tourist girl?"

"She wasn't exactly a psycho... And I didn't *help* catch her. I did catch her."

"*Specializing in cases too difficult for the police.* You're pretty cocky aren't you? For a geek."

"I'm not a geek. And I've no idea what you're talking about. This has nothing to do with me."

"Oh really?" She scrolls down again. Right to the bottom of the site. Then she looks at me and smiles.

"That's odd, because it's got your name on it."

I don't have to look – I already know – but after a moment I glance at the screen, and sure enough at the bottom of the website it says this:

Website Design by Billy Wheatley

"That's probably why it came up when I searched for your name." The girl laughs again. "I thought that maybe you just did the website design, which is terrible by the way..."

I look at her, surprised by this.

"No really, it's seriously awful. My *sister* could do better and she's three years old."

I feel my forehead furrowing into a frown. The girl clicks to the '*Contact Us*' page.

"But then I saw this. The email address you've left is BWheatley1995@gmail.com. And that just has to be you."

She looks at me, triumph on her face.

"It is, isn't it? You're actually running a detective agency?"

"I'm not running..." I begin, but I stop. It's hard to explain.

"Billy Wheatley – Private Eye!"

"I'm not actually running it... I mean I don't have any..." I try to work out what to say, it's complicated.

"It's just that, after everything that happened with Dad and the murders, I had this idea that maybe I could maybe help the police again. But it never happened. I didn't even get around to finishing the website...."

She doesn't seem to be listening. She's clicked onto the 'Our Services' page, which lists surveillance, vehicle tracking, phone tapping, debugging equipment and polygraph testing.

"So how do you do all this?"

"What?"

"Phone tapping. Polygraph testing."

"Oh. I don't."

"So why does it say..."

"I just copied the text from a site in Los Angeles."

"A real detective agency? You copied the text?"

"Sort of copied it. I improved it too."

She laughs at that.

Suddenly she holds out her hand.

"Amber."

"Pardon?"

"Amber. My *name*. It's Amber."

"Oh."

She rolls her eyes. "This is where you're supposed to say *How nice to meet you Amber*."

Obviously I don't.

"It's very nice to meet you too *Billy*." She picks up my hand and shakes it for me. She's got very soft hands.

"So have you got any clients?"

"What? No. I told you, I didn't even finish the site. I'm surprised you even found it. I should take it down, I just forgot. I just like to make websites sometimes, it's like a hobby..."

"Or you could not."

"What?"

Amber looks at me. There's a strange expression on her face.

"You could not take it down."

I frown again, unsure what she means.

"No, you see, I thought for a while I wanted to be a detective, in the police, but I'm too young for that, and I didn't want to wait. That's why I made the detective agency site. But then I decided I wanted to concentrate on my science work instead."

"Science work?"

"I'm a marine biologist. Or at least I'm going to be. So I started doing a population count of grey seals on Littlelea Point, and then I must have forgotten to take the detective agency site down."

I stop. It's nearly true what I'm telling her. All except for one thing. The real reason I didn't take the site down was because it's one of the best I've ever made. I was rather proud of it.

"It really does look shit." Amber says.

"Pardon?"

"The design. Well it isn't *designed* at all. It's just thrown together. You need to think about it. Make it look professional."

It's the first time in nearly a year I've looked at the site. And now I have to admit, it's not *quite* as good as I remembered it.

"I was gonna add something else to the logo." I say, "I don't know, maybe add an eye into the magnifying glass. You know, so that it looks really big, like you're looking at it through the glass."

Right away Amber shakes her head. "No. See that's the mistake everyone makes. With designing stuff. You don't want to add things. You have to take away. You've already got way too much going on. You should strip it back. Simplify it."

Without asking me she grabs my pen and starts drawing on the cover of my folder. I'm about to tell her to stop, but the lines she sketches out stops me.

"Just choose one element. Like the eye. That's a good idea, but..." Her tongue pokes just a little bit out of the corner of her mouth as she draws. I focus on that for a moment, then look at what she's actually drawing.

"Mmmm. Maybe something like that could work."

I look up at her, and I sort of realize my mouth is hanging open.

"It's only rough. It would take a bit of time to do something decent," she says.

"That's amazing. I've never seen anyone draw that well."

She looks at me, with an expression I've not seen yet. I realize she's kind of embarrassed. And a bit pleased too.

"It's kinda my thing. I like art."

Art is my least favorite of all the subjects. I don't see the point of it.

"I don't see the point of art."

She looks at me and tips her head onto one side. "Well it takes all sorts doesn't it? That's why I'm here actually," she looks around at the detention room. "Painting on the wall of the gym. Sharpe called it 'vandalism', but it's art."

I don't answer this either. I just stare at the logo she's drawn. It really is amazingly good.

"Can I keep that?" It is on my folder after all.

She pushes it back in front of me. "I can do you a proper one if you like. Help you design the site right too. That way you might actually get a client."

I'm about to explain how that would be silly, since I'm not going to be a private detective anymore, when Mr. Coyne suddenly gets up and tells us to pack up our books. Apparently the detention's over. The room fills with noise and movement as the other students get ready to leave. All except Amber and me. We don't move at all.

"Only of course you won't. Get a client I mean. Because the only interesting thing that ever happened in Lornea Island was all that shit that happened to you. And now that's done nothing interesting is ever going to happen again." She shrugs.

"But still. It might be fun to try."

I think about this for a moment. Most of the other students have already filed out of the room.

"Come on Billy," Mr. Coyne says now. "Amber. Time to go."

"Actually the average homicide rate in the U.S. is 4.9 deaths per 100,000 head of population. And since the population of Lornea Island is 140,000, it means there's approximately six people murdered here. Every year. Statistically."

She stops and looks at me for a long time before answering.

"You *actually* know that? Off the top of your head. Without having to look it up?"

I shrug. "I looked it up, when I made the site."

She smiles at me. "You're fucking mental Billy Wheatley."

"Amber Atherton! Watch that language if you don't want to be here tomorrow night too."

She glances up and gives Mr. Coyne a sweet smile.

"Sorry sir." Then she walks back to her original seat and starts packing up her books. I do the same.

But as I'm leaving she comes close to me again.

"I'll email you something cool. Maybe we actually will get a client."

SEVEN

IT TAKES me ages to get home, since I'm too late for the school bus, and then I have to walk the last mile because the normal bus doesn't go right to our house. Then I have to feed Steven, and then cook for Dad, and all that makes me forget about Amber. But just when I'm going to bed there's an email from Amber. She's attached the logo she drew on my folder, only it's even better this time.

So obviously I have to put it on the actual website to see how it looks. And while I'm doing that Amber starts messaging me, and we end up working together on the rest of the site. She sends through suggestions for how to make the words better, and then we find pictures of people doing detective things – like stakeouts in cars and following people – to make it look more realistic. By the time we've finished it's nearly three in the morning. But the website does look better. It almost looks like a real detective agency site.

But then, the next evening after school, Amber starts messaging me again, with a whole new list of things she thinks I need to do to make the website better, so I do that. But then the next night she does the same again, and then the night after that as well. It's annoying and in the end I get a bit fed up, and just send her the log-on details so she can do it herself.

Anyway. That was all a couple of weeks ago, and it's not very important now, because something else has happened. Something really... Well, something really weird actually.

* * *

It all started last night. I was working in the kitchen, since Steven kept climbing on the keyboard if I used my room, when there was a knock at the front door.

I guess for some people that might be normal, but for us it's not. I don't get any visitors, because I'm not really keen on people, and if Dad sees friends they usually go out to a bar. So I shouted to Dad to come answer it, but he didn't answer. So I had to get up to answer the door myself.

Then it was dark outside, so the man standing there was silhouetted and I had to squint to see if I knew him. But I didn't.

"Hello?"

The man doesn't answer, but I can see he's kinda nervous.

"Can I help you?"

The guy steps forward into the light. He tries to smile, but it keeps slipping from his face.

"You don't remember me, do you?"

I stare back for a moment and try and make sense of him. The guy's about Dad's age, with greasy yellow hair, and yellow stubble too, like he hasn't shaved in a while. I'm pretty sure I'd remember him.

"No."

The man tries to smile, but he still looks nervous.

"Is your dad in?"

"Yes."

There's a long silence as we both stand there, waiting.

"Well, you wanna go get him?"

I don't answer this right away. Instead I look at him more closely. He's carrying two bags. One is a small sports holdall, the other is a plastic bag from the store in Newlea. I can see from the way they're stuck to the outside of the bag that it's got cold cans of beer in it.

"Why?"

At this the man gives a kind of nervous laugh, like I've made a joke. But I obviously didn't. I'm thinking about that when I head Dad's voice behind me.

"Billy, get away from the door." His voice is tight, anxious. The next thing he's pulling me back from the doorway. It surprises me so much I try to push him off.

"Billy, I said *get away from the door*."

It's not that I'm scared, it's just a surprise. Then there's another silence. Then the man starts laughing, but it's not a normal laugh.

"Jamie! *Fuck me*. It's really fucking you." The man drops his bags and holds out his arms, like he thinks Dad might want to hug him. But Dad doesn't move.

I just stare at them both. Then I realize something. He just called my Dad *Jamie*.

"So you gonna invite me in, or what?"

My dad's name is *Sam*. Or at least. He's been called Sam almost my whole life. But he did use to be called Jamie, back before we came to live on Lornea Island. He had to change it when the police were looking for him. With the whole murder thing.

"What the hell are you doing here?" Dad's voice breaks into my thoughts. His voice is cold.

The man at the door laughs though. Properly this time.

"That's all you got? I ain't seen you in – what? Ten years? And that's the best you got?" He shakes his head. "Fuck Jamie..."

"I don't use that name no more," Dad breaks in.

The man stops, then holds up his hands. "I saw that. It's Sam now, ain't it? Sam Wheatley?"

Dad doesn't reply. He doesn't even move.

"Come on man. You gonna let me in or leave me on the goddamn doorstep? I come a long way..."

I look at Dad. He's still like a statue. I can't tell if it's anger or fear. But then he steps aside. The man on the doorstep smiles and picks up his bags. He comes into the kitchen. He looks around.

"So. This is where you been? All these years?" He smiles. He's got really yellow teeth. "It's nice." Then he sees me again.

"So what do I call *you*?"

I don't answer.

"It used to be Ben... I remember how you were this little..."

"It's Billy," Dad says.

"*Billy*." There's a flash of teeth again, they match his stubble. And they're sharp too, like an animal's.

"You don't remember me? Not at all?"

I look at him again. At his greasy hair. His sharp yellow teeth. He's holding out a hand now, for me to shake, and I see it's got a tattoo on it. A snake that twists round his wrist and out of sight under his sleeve. I'd remember that if I saw it before.

"Tucker and me were friends," Dad says suddenly. "Back in Crab Creek. Before you came along."

I already told you, back when that girl was asking, about how I came to live here on Lornea Island because my Dad had to get away from the police back in a place called Crab Creek. They thought he'd murdered my sister, but it was actually my mom because she had something called post-partum depression. But because Mom's family were rich and Dad wasn't, they were going to blame him for everything. So he came to live here where no-one knew anything about him.

The man – I suppose his name must be Tucker – lowers his hand. Then he laughs, a bitter laugh.

"We were more than just friends Billy. We grew up together. Did every-thing together. We were like brothers."

I look to Dad to see if this is true, but he won't meet my eye.

"Then when it all kicked off, and your dad had to get the hell out of there, he came to me. I hid you in my truck, the both of you. We had to go cross country to avoid the roadblocks on the state line, then we just drove. Day and night. All the way across the country. That was a trip and a half, eh Jamie?"

I look at Dad again. There's a vein sticking out on his neck that only happens when he's super stressed.

"It's Sam." He says, quietly.

Tucker appears to consider this for a few seconds.

"Sure. *Sam*" He nods. Then he turns back to me again.

"We had you in a cardboard box on the back seat... Took turns driving. Fed you cookies... We made it all the way to New York, then... Well..." Tucker looks at Dad, and smiles again, but a different smile this time.

"That was the last I saw of you." He shrugs and shakes his head. "What happened, *Sam*? When we got to New York. Where'd ya go? What the hell happened?"

Dad folds his arms across his chest before he answers.

"You know what happened. We had to disappear. Completely. I couldn't have anyone know where we were."

The man – Tucker – is suddenly mad. "But I wasn't *anyone*! I was your best goddamn buddy. I drove you five days across the goddamn country... And you just leave me? You don't even tell me you're going?"

There's an awkward moment when neither of them speak. I look from one to the other.

"I couldn't take the risk," Dad replies, in the end. "I had to make a fresh start. Somewhere…"

"You were worried I was going turn you in? Is that it? You thought I might be tempted by that reward?"

"No, 'course not." Dad stops. Then he goes on. "But if you *knew* where I was, I'd always have that worry... Christine's family getting to you... Putting pressure somehow..."

Christine is my Mom's name. I've almost never heard Dad even say it.

"I never liked those stuck-up..." Tucker stops, glancing at me. "Christine's folks. You must've known I'd never betray you to them."

"Yeah," Dad replies at last. "But I never knew if..." He stops again.

"What?"

"If you knew where I was, I'd always have to worry about..."

"About what?"

"I don't know. About you getting loaded and shooting your mouth off in some bar."

Right away Dad looks like he wishes he hadn't said that. Tucker just stares for a long time, then he pulls out a chair and sits down.

"Oh Come on *man*," Dad goes on. "I grew up with you. I *knew* what you were like. I couldn't take that risk? I couldn't take *any* risk, not with Billy to look after."

All the anger in Tucker seems to have evaporated. He just shakes his head, and kind of mutters instead.

"I had your back man! I would've looked after you. Your best fuckin' interests." Then, when he looks up, he's smiling again.

"Well anyway. I'm here now. So you got a beer for your old buddy?"

Dad hesitates again, but not for long. Then he goes to the refrigerator and pulls out two cans of Budweiser. He hands one to Tucker, then holds on to the second himself.

Tucker opens his at once and takes a deep swig. I can see his Adam's apple bobble as the beer goes down his throat.

"You know I would never have betrayed you. *Never*."

Dad shakes his head again.

"I'm not saying you would have. I just thought... I dunno, it was hard to think straight at the time. I figured if I could disappear completely, that was my best chance." Dad still hasn't opened his beer, and he taps the top now with his fingernail.

"I didn't want it to end the way it did. I swear." He doesn't take his eyes from Tucker as he says this.

Tucker drinks more from his can. His hands are so strong he dents the sides of the beer can, I think he does it without even realizing.

"It hurt man. Fucking hell. It hurt. I looked for you. I went round every

goddamn motel and cheap hotel in the whole of New York state. But..."
Again he shrugs. "It's a big place."

Tucker glances at me and sends me a big yellow smile.

"Long fucking drive back too."

No one says anything for a moment. Then Dad does.

So how'd you find us?"

Tucker looks surprised by the question at first. But then he laughs.

"You made the news man! I mean, you were already famous, after your
earlier disappearing act, and getting accused of killing the kid..." He
smiles at me, then shrugs.

"All I know is, one night, I'm sittin' watching the TV, mindin' my business. And suddenly there's something on the news about *Jamie Stone.*" He
turns back to me.

"That's your Dad's name, or least it used to be. Until he gets accused of
drowning your sister. Trying to drown you. That's why it was news - when
he turned up again - ten years later. They were saying he'd got mixed up in
some business about a murdered tourist, in some place called *Lornea Island.*
I'd never even fucking heard of it." He stops, laughs bitterly and turns
back to Dad. "I guess that was the point, huh? Sam?"

He grins at Dad, waits for him to answer, but Dad doesn't say a word.

"I knew it was bullshit. Just like the first time. There's no way Jami... No
way *Sam* would ever do something like that. But all the same. It told me
where you were."

Tucker stops to drink more beer, and Dad just taps on the ring pull
on his.

"So for a while, you make the news every night. About how the police
on Lornea Island had you down as this psycho murderer, and then they
finally catch you and work out it wasn't you after all. And then – like
magic – all the Crab Creek shit gets cleared up too. They talk to Christine
and she admits to everything..." He stops and looks at me.

"That's your mom. You know about her?"

I don't mean to, but I give a little nod. He watches me, like he doesn't
know what to make of it. Then he goes on.

"Post-partum depression they called it. Real bad case, I guess. Anyhow.
There's my old buddy, suddenly innocent of everything, and I'm thinking,
surely this means Jamie's finally gonna put in a call to his best friend in the
whole goddamn world? Now there's nothing to stop him."

Tucker drinks again and sniffs loudly. Dad doesn't move.

"And I wait, because I ain't changed my number or nothing. But I don't
get no call. So in the end I think to myself, well – Jamie always was the

quiet type, not wanting to make a fuss. So I figure, if I want to see you, I'm gonna have to come here myself, and look you up." He tips his beer can vertical and drains the rest of it, then crushes the can in his fist and bangs it down hard on the table.

"So here I am!"

EIGHT

RIGHT AFTER THAT, Dad tells me I have to go upstairs, because of school tomorrow. But it was only 11.00, so I knew it was actually because he wanted to talk to Tucker in private. So then I try to listen to what they were saying from upstairs, but they were talking too quietly. Even when I put the toothbrush glass from the bathroom onto the floor to amplify the sound, I could only hear that they were talking lots, not what they saying. So eventually I had to go to bed.

When I came downstairs this morning, I was wondering if the whole thing might have been some weird dream, but right away I saw there were loads of beer cans left in the kitchen – much more than Dad would normally leave. From the state of it, it looked like they'd been drinking the whole night. And that made me wonder what time Tucker actually left. And *then* I saw the lounge was darker than usual, and there was this shape on the couch, with a pair of feet sticking out. So I knew it wasn't a dream. And that he hadn't left at all. He was still here.

So after that I gathered all the beers cans and put them in the recycling, because otherwise they make the kitchen smell. Then I fixed my breakfast. And then I had the idea to google Tucker, to see if I could find out anything about who he was, and why he might be sleeping in our lounge. But that was no good because he never said what his second name was. So I just searched for Crab Creek, where I was born. I've never been back there, and to be honest I haven't thought about it much, since it's such a long way away, and Dad doesn't like to talk about it and I don't know anybody from there anymore. So I was looking on Google Maps, at how it's 3159 miles or 49.8 hours (without traffic) to get there from Lornea Island (plus the ferry crossing which is four hours). When suddenly Tucker walks into the room.

He's dressed only in his underwear, and he stops and stretches right in front of me, reaching up and nearly touching the ceiling. He's got muscles all over him. They're in places where I didn't even know you could *get* muscles. And the tattoos aren't just on his hand, they're all over his body. He's got this big green dragon thing that wraps around from his stomach all the way to his back. It looks like the sort of thing that Mafia hit men have on them.

"Morning Billy," he says to me. He finishes his stretch then rolls his neck around. His joints crack like microwave popcorn. He starts poking around the kitchen.

"You got any coffee?"

I don't answer at first, but when he turns and looks at me I don't feel I have any choice.

"Yeah."

"That's nice. You wanna make some for your dad's old buddy?" He grins at me.

I hesitate for a moment, but eventually I drop my spoon and push the chair back. He smiles again, then goes over to the window.

"Whoa... That's a hell of a view you got here," he says.

I don't answer, pretending all my attention is on the coffee.

"I didn't see it last night. I heard it. I heard the sea, but it was dark...

I feel him turning to me. "You're right on the clifftop. You can see for miles."

I don't know why he's telling me this. It's not like I wouldn't have noticed.

"You surf?" he asks. "Like your old man?"

I stiffen a bit at this. I had a bad experience surfing with Dad.

"No."

He goes on like I haven't said anything. "We used to go all the time. Your dad and me. When we were kids. We used to skip school if the surf was pumping, hell even if it wasn't pumping…"

"Dad isn't good at surfing anymore," I interrupt him. "When he got shot it took away his flexibility."

Tucker stops. "Yeah. He told me 'bout that. Tough break." He turns away from the window.

"So what about you?" He asks me. "What do you do?"

I don't know what he means by this, so I don't answer. Instead I just hand him his coffee, and he winks at me.

"You got school?" he asks. This should be fairly obvious since I'm thirteen years old and it's a Thursday. What else am I going to do?

"Yeah."

"I never much liked school," Tucker says. Sipping his coffee. Then he raises it up, like he's saying it's good. "And school never much liked me neither." He nearly laughs at this but then doesn't. Instead he asks me a question, which takes me a bit by surprise.

"You mind if I borrow that computer of yours?" He points at my laptop, which I've closed so he doesn't see I've been trying to google him.

"I just have to check something onli.... Whooa! *What the fuck is that?*"

He says that because right at that moment something happens. Steven wakes up. He's sleepy in the mornings and I usually take his box down to breakfast with me. Now he squawks and raises up his wings, then flaps them really hard.

"*Jesus fucking wept!*"

"It's only Steven."

"Steven? It's got a name? Fucking hell kid. You've got a *seagull* for a pet?"

"He's not a seagull, he's a Herring Gull. And he's not a pet either. It's illegal to keep wild birds as pets in the United States. As soon as he can fly I'll let him go."

Steven settles down now, and folds his wings back up. Then Tucker leans in close to his box. With a nasty grin he reaches out as if he's going to poke him. Steven watches him with one eye, then just before Tucker actually touches him he flaps his wings really hard and takes off. He's so big now it makes quite a commotion in our small kitchen, and Tucker jumping backwards doesn't help. Steven lands on the cabinet where we keep the cups.

"Fuck me!" Tucker says again, when he recovers a bit. "Looks like he can fly already."

I don't answer him.

"Anyway," Tucker grins at me, then looks at my computer again. "You mind? I just gotta check something online."

I'd forgotten about his question, but now I have to think about it. And as I do, I'm not exactly comfortable about the idea. It's not just that I've just been googling him, there's also a lot on my computer that I wouldn't want anyone to see.

He slurps at his coffee, the steam hiding his face for a second. I try to think fast.

"Don't you have a phone you can use?" I say in the end. "We get good reception, even out here."

"Don't have one." Tucker suddenly grins broadly. "Don't trust those things. You know what I mean?"

"What?"

Then I realize it must have been a kind of joke because he puts his hands up, like he's giving up.

"Hey, sorry I even asked. Don't worry about it. I'll ask your dad when he gets up."

I'm still trying to work out what he's talking about, when he puts the coffee down with a bang.

"Say. I gotta take a piss." He sniffs loudly, then walks towards the downstairs bathroom. As he goes I hear him talking to himself.

"Steven the Seagull. I get it. Like the guy in *Under Siege*. Man I loved that movie..."

For a few moments I don't move, I'm still a bit stunned by how strange this all is, that he's still here, wandering round in his underpants and sleeping in our lounge, and I don't know anything about him. I look into the lounge now. I see his clothes draped over the chair, all messy. I'm about to look away, when I get an idea. Whenever I need to get something from Dad's wallet - like cash for groceries, or his credit card - I have to fish it out of his jeans pocket. So If Tucker's jeans are there, then maybe I can get his surname from his credit card? If I do that, then I can google him after all.

It's just an idea, and I know I probably shouldn't do it, but at the same time, where's the harm? It's not like I'm going to *take* it. And surely I've got a right to know who's in my house?

There's a sudden, quite unpleasant noise of urine hitting the toilet bowl which means I've only got seconds before he's back. But seconds are all I need, so I get up and run into the lounge. The drapes are drawn and there's a musty smell that isn't normally there. And I'm worried suddenly, because I can't actually hear the bathroom from here, so I don't know whether he's still weeing or if he's already finished. But I'm committed now, so I reach down to pick up his jeans. I can feel from the weight that there's something in the pockets. But it's awkward, because the material is twisted. And then I don't want to touch the bit around the fly, where his groin goes, because that would really be disgusting.

So very carefully I untwist the jeans, and straight away I can feel something hard and square in the back pocket. I reach in to pull it out, but then stop in surprise. Because it's not a wallet in my hand. It's a cell phone.

I stare in surprise. It's a proper one, with a touch screen and everything – not one of those ones that old people like, that can't connect to the internet. But didn't he just tell me he didn't have a phone at all? I try to rewind in my mind. Yeah. He said he didn't trust them, or something like that? If that's the case, why has he got one in his pocket?

I press the button to wake the phone. I don't know why - he'll probably have it locked with a code, but I do it anyway. But nothing at all happens. It doesn't even light up. After a moment I realize why. The phone's actually switched off. Or maybe the battery is dead. Maybe that's why he wanted to use my computer. But why wouldn't he just tell me the battery was dead on his phone? Or ask if I've got a charger, I've actually got loads. I decide I should try to switch it on to check, but then I realize I don't have time for that, since cell phones take ages to boot up. So instead I turn back to his jeans, still confused, but thinking I can still get his surname from his wallet.

But then, right above me, I hear the stairs squeak. I know the sound, I know exactly what it means. It's Dad, coming down. Normally he'd sleep later than this on a weekday. But I guess because Tucker's here, he's got up early.

Really I should give up, I've only got seconds before Dad will see me, but I don't stop. I really want to know now, and I only need one glance at Tucker's credit cards to see what his surname is. So I scrabble with the jeans again, this time pulling out his wallet. I open it up and fumble a plastic card out, all while listening for Dad's voice. The card I pull out is a driver's license. It's hard to see it in the half light of the room, but it's got a picture on it. Tucker, but in a suit and looking much smarter than he does in real life. I'm already slipping the card back into the wallet as I read the name, getting ready to shove it back into the jeans pocket. But then I stop. Because it doesn't make sense. It doesn't make sense at all.

Tucker's name is Peter Smith.

I do a double take. I check the picture again, then re-read the name. Peter Smith.

I shove everything back and drop the jeans back on the floor. I try to walk as calmly back to the kitchen as I can. But Dad's already there. He gives me a funny look, like he's wondering what I'm doing in there.

"I left my school bag," I say. Then I sit back down at the kitchen table, hoping he won't say anything.

I feel his eyes studying me.

"You know Tucker stayed over last night? You might want to give him a bit of space."

Then the toilet flushes and Tucker walks back into the room, whistling. Or at least, the man my dad is pretending is called Tucker walks back into the room.

I told you it was weird.

NINE

BEFORE I GO to school I take my computer upstairs. I use it to google whether Tucker is a nickname for people called Peter. But before I even finish typing the question, the auto-complete tells me that sometimes Tucker *is* a nickname, but for people called William or Thomas. But more usually it's just a name. It comes from old English, where it meant someone who made cloth. Or something like that. So when I go downstairs again, and Tucker's in the lounge getting dressed, I ask dad about it.

"Is Tucker's real name Peter?" I watch him carefully as I speak, but I don't let him see that I'm that interested.

"Peter?" Dad frowns at me. "No. Why do you ask that?"

"Oh, no reason. I just thought it was a nickname."

Dad keeps looking at me for a few moments but he says nothing. If he's lying he's doing it well.

"OK. Well anyway, I gotta go to school. I'll be late for the bus."

Dad's still staring at me as I walk out of the door.

I'm still trying to make sense of this at school. I hardly listen to my morning classes which would matter if I wasn't a good student and already way ahead of the class. And I'm still thinking about it at lunchtime. But then I check my phone, and there's an email that does totally distract me. In fact it changes everything. This is what it says:

Dear Sirs,

I found your agency on the internet and have decided to engage your services. I would like you to investigate the disappearance of my dear husband, Henry

Jacobs. I have lived half my life praying that the mystery of what happened to him would be solved. And as I am now nearing my own end, I would like to know I have done everything I can to find out.

I trust you are more used to getting this type of letter than I am in writing it, and that you will know how to proceed from here. Certainly you seem to be a very trustworthy and professional looking company which gives me great confidence that you will succeed, even in this most difficult of cases. I shall look forward to you letting me know what happens next.

Sincerely

(Mrs.) Barbara Jacobs

At first I'm baffled as I read it. Then I remember about the detective agency website and how it must be to do with that. And then the text messages start pinging in.

WTF? Billy is that you jerking me around?

Then:

This is for real! No fucking way!

And finally:

Meet me in the library you retard.

These all come from Amber. I remember now that Amber added her email address to the 'contact us' page of the detective agency website. I didn't think much of it at the time, but then I never thought anyone would contact us anyway. I don't know what to think now. But I do what she says.

"Billy! Over here," she whistles at me from over by the computers. Which I don't like because you're not supposed to even talk loudly in the library, let alone whistle.

"I've tried googling 'Henry Jacobs' but there's like, six million people with that name, so that's not going to work."

I look on the screen, open on google's search results.

"Have you got any ideas?"

There's a notebook open on the desk and she's written 'Henry Jacobs' in capital letters at the top. Then she's underlined it twice. The rest of the page is empty.

"I can't believe we've actually got an actual client!" Amber says before I can answer. "This is so fucking cool!"

I sit down next to her.

"What else do detectives do?" Amber asks. "Apart from googling people I mean?"

"I don't know."

"You don't know?"

"No, why would I know?"

"You're the detective."

"No I'm not."

"You made the website."

"Well... OK but. Look have you actually replied to her?"

"Not yet. I thought we should work out what to say first."

"Oh. Good." I hesitate. "You mean about whether we should take the case or not.?"

"No," Amber looks at me. "I mean about how we're actually going to find him. We're definitely going to take the case."

I hesitate again.

"I'm not sure," I say in the end.

"I hoped we could get something from google that we could follow up on. Like a lead..."

She stops, then turns to look at me. "What did you say?"

"I said I'm not sure we should *actually* get involved. I mean, we're not *really* private detectives and if this is important to this lady, and it kind of sounds like it is, then shouldn't she go to a real detective agency?"

She frowns.

"Why?"

I'm a bit confused by Amber's attitude. I mean, isn't it obvious? I guess I'm maybe just a bit distracted with this strange business about Tucker/Peter at home. Why would Dad be calling him Tucker, or pretending his name is Tucker, if his real name is Peter? I have a few theories already – that's he's some sort of secret agent, or living a double life, or in the Witness Protection Scheme...

. . .

"*Fuck* Billy. If this is your attitude, why did you waste my time getting me to make you a private detective agency website?"

"You didn't make it, I did!"

"I made it better!"

I'm taken aback by this.

"It was alright before..."

"It was crap. And anyway, I'm the one who advertised it."

"You *advertised* it?"

"Of course I did. Otherwise no one would ever find it. We'd never get any clients."

"I didn't want to get any clients!"

"What? Why would anyone start a detective agency if they didn't want clients? You'd have to be a moron."

I open my mouth to tell her I only made it because I liked making websites. But suddenly that doesn't seem a very good reason. I close my mouth again.

Amber stares at me for a long while, then turns away.

"Fuck Billy. You really are weird you know that?"

But then she turns back.

"And anyway. It's too late now, because we've got a client now."

We don't talk to each other for a few moments. I watch her click on some of the google links in front of her. One *Henry Jacobs* is the director of a golf club in Arizona, another a doctor in Vancouver. She glances at both and then clicks away, dismissing them.

"The thing is," I say. "She's not *actually* going to want to hire us, is she? Not once she knows we're just kids. She's going to want adults."

"I already thought about that," Amber replies at once. "We'll do everything by email. We'll tell her we have to do it that way so that no one can find out our true identity. For security."

I stare at her.

"Would you hire a private detective who wouldn't even meet you?"

"Of course I would." Amber says. "It's how they all do it. It's standard practice."

I feel my face tighten into a frown. "Is it?"

"I don't know. But that's the point! You didn't know if it is or isn't. So neither will she. Besides she's already said she wants to hire us. She's already decided."

I puff out my cheeks. I suppose that might work. I feel like all my objections are being dismantled rather unfairly.

"Well how would we actually go about finding him though? It doesn't look like Google is much help."

Amber turns to me. Suddenly she looks excited again. Eager.

"That's why you're here. You're the one that found that tourist girl. You *solved* that case. How did you do that?"

I think for a moment. It is true. They even gave me a medal.

"I just kind of worked it out."

"Then just do that again." Amber's face breaks into a broad smile.

"*Come on Billy.* This is so cool. This is awesome. We've got an actual case to investigate. Just like on TV. Like in the movies. It's going to be so much fun."

I hesitate at this. One thing I know from everything that happened before is that doing detective work is nothing like they show it on TV. I suppose this doubt shows on my face.

"Look even if we can't find him, we still get paid. Two hundred dollars a day. Even if we don't find him."

"Really?"

"Yeah. That's what the terms and conditions say. Think what you could do with that money!"

I don't say anything. But I do think about it.

"Come on Billy. Don't be a dork about this!"

In the end I don't exactly say yes, but I don't exactly say no either. So then we have a go at writing an email we can send to Mrs. Jacobs. But it's really hard to know what to say. There's a ton of questions we need to ask about her husband if there's any chance of us finding him, but it's almost impossible to ask by email because the questions we need to ask all depend upon what her answers to the questions before were. And even worse than that, it's really hard to work with Amber because she keeps suggesting really stupid questions in the first place. So by the time the bell for afternoon class starts, we've hardly got anywhere. In the end I tell Amber that I'll work on our reply to Mrs. Jacobs tonight.

But even as I walk out of the library, I'm not sure if that's true. I think it might be better to reply to Mrs. Jacobs and tell her to go to a proper detective agency, because it sounds like this is something really important to her, and not just a game that we should be playing.

And that's what I've just done, this evening. I told her I was sorry about her husband, and I lied a little bit and said I had worked with the other agency and they were really good, and I was sure if anyone could find her husband they would. I know you're not supposed to lie, but I think in the circumstances that's OK.

I copied Amber into the email, so she knows too. I expect she'll be mad tomorrow, when I see her at school. But that's just too bad. I can't just do everything that people want me to do.

Oh. I almost forgot to mention. Tucker/Peter (whatever his name is) is still here. He was in the lounge with Dad when I got home from school. They were drinking beer and watching a ball game. Dad told me to come in and watch it with them, but I said I had homework to do. Then later on Dad called me down for dinner, but I said I wasn't hungry. That was a lie too, because actually I'm starving. But I didn't want to sit with him. He's made the lounge smell funny and I just don't trust him.

TEN

I ASSUMED THAT TUCKER/PETER would be gone by the time I got home from school on Friday, but he was still here. Then, when I woke on Saturday morning, he was still here. There was a huge pile of beer cans and the kitchen was a mess which I had to clear up. When he finally got up him and Dad went surfing. Dad hasn't been surfing for ages. He used to go all the time but then he got shot and like I said, it messed up his flexibility. But somehow Tucker/Peter persuaded him, and they dug a couple of Dad's old boards from the shed in the yard. Tucker/Peter even asked if I wanted to go, but I told him I was busy. It's true as well. I had to teach Steven how to fly.

Then Tucker/Peter and Dad went out drinking on Saturday night, and he stayed all Sunday as well. And then this morning, when I got up for school, he was *still* here.

And what with everything I've found out about him – how he lied about not having a phone, and how he's lying about his name, I'm obviously not delighted about leaving him in the house. I don't have a lock on my bedroom door, so I've come to school with my laptop computer, which makes my school bag really heavy. That's the most important thing, but I've still had to leave my binoculars, my camera traps and all my other equipment unsecured at home. I tried to hide it, but what with Steven following me around and uncovering everything I tried to hide, it wasn't very easy. I did have one good idea though. I remembered something I once saw in an old James Bond movie, about how you can stick a hair over the gap between the door frame and the door. It doesn't stop people going in, but at least you find out *if* they have broken in. If the hair's not there when you come back it means the door has been opened.

And anyway I'm still thinking about all this when I bump into Amber in the corridor. She's got her head down looking at the screen of her phone. And when she looks up I see a strange look on her face. Like she is pleased to see me, but then she isn't pleased to see me. That doesn't make any sense because I thought she'd be mad with me for saying no to Mrs. Jacobs.

"Hi Amber," I say. She kind of slides the phone away so that I can't see what she was looking at.

"Hey Billy," she says. Then she looks past me, like she doesn't want to stop and talk.

I'm a bit confused because of her not being mad and everything.

"Are you still mad about that email I sent?"

Again she looks past me, but then she seems to change her mind. There's an open classroom door next to us, and she pokes her head in, checking that it's empty. We're not allowed to go into classrooms when we don't actually have classes in them.

"Come in here," she says. "We need to talk."

"We're not allowed to go into..." I begin to tell her, but she just grabs me by the straps of my backpack and pulls me inside.

She shuts the door behind her, and I can tell she's excited about something, but she doesn't know how to say it.

"I got another email," she says at last. "I was just reading it."

I frown at her, not understanding.

"From Mrs. Jacobs. The old woman."

I still don't understand.

"I emailed her back, last week. Asking for more information about what happened to her husband."

"No," I correct her, after some thought. "*I* emailed her back, telling her that we couldn't help her. I told her she should go to that agency on the mainland."

"Yeah, you copied me in," Amber looks annoyed for a moment. "But she doesn't want an agency on the mainland. She wants *us* to investigate."

"How do you know that?"

The look on Amber's face changes from annoyed to awkward.

"Because she told me. I sent her an email right after you did, explaining how you thought we were too busy, but that we could move things around and still fit her in. And she said how important it was for her to have someone on the island to investigate her case."

"Oh," I say.

"And it's a *proper* mystery. She told me all about it. How her husband went to the store forty years ago and just disappeared. She has no idea what happened to him. He just vanished. Wouldn't it be cool to solve that?"

I think for a second. "I guess... But how? We tried to find out more by email before, and it's just impossible..."

"That's why I arranged to see her. Today, after school. Why don't you come with me?"

My mouth drops open. Amber is two years above me in school, you'd think she'd be smarter than this.

"But... You *can't* meet her. She's gonna see straight away how old you are?"

"I know," Amber concedes. "It *is* a bit awkward. I thought that I could put on different make up. You know, make myself look older. Then if that doesn't work, we could tell her how we've got a boss who's older, but who has to keep his identity a secret. You know, so that he can work incognito."

I just stare at her. So that eventually she looks a bit embarrassed.

"Yeah OK, forget that. But you know, the weird thing is," Amber goes on. "I actually get the sense it doesn't actually matter."

"What doesn't?"

"How old we are. I just get the idea she's a bit crazy. Like, mad enough that she won't even notice how old we are."

That's ridiculous, so I don't say anything.

"And it might mean *the case* isn't that hard either. You know, her whole problem could be that she just doesn't have a grip on modern life. The internet and everything. So we might be able to solve the case just because we understand all that. You know, because we're young."

This all sounds highly unlikely to me.

"And anyway, why *shouldn't* we investigate it? The truth is you did find out what happened to that tourist girl that got murdered. You found her. You solved it. When the police couldn't."

That *is* true, but even so. I shake my head and go to turn away, but Amber stops me.

"So what do you think?"

"What do I think about what?"

"Do you think it's a good idea?"

"No. I think you're completely mental."

Amber's face breaks into a wide smile at this.

"I know. But will you come?"

"Come where?"

"To meet her. I was just thinking, if we go together it'll look…" Amber begins.

"I'm not going." I interrupt her. "I think you're mad. And besides. I've got other things to do. Important things."

"What things?" She says at once.

That question takes me by surprise, and I think of the true answer. I've still got work to do on the *Blue Lady* project, then I've got to do more flying lessons with Steven. I've got homework to catch up on… But then I think about home. How Tucker/Peter is probably still there, and how I'll have to hide in my room so that he won't try to talk to me. I don't want to mention any of this to Amber. Given how she's completely crazy.

"Nothing."

"Well come on then. Come with me. See what you think. You know we could actually *help* this lady. She's really worried about it. If we can find her husband it would really help her. And I know you wanna do that."

I don't reply.

"And it'd be so *cool* Billy, to have a real mystery to investigate."

Amber fixes me with big, round, sparkling eyes. She puts her hands together, like she's begging me. In the end I have to look away.

"She's just going to tell us to get lost when she sees how old we are."

Amber shakes her head. "No she's not. But even if she does, we don't lose anything." She tips her head to one side. Like the way Steven does when he wants something.

"And anyway she's *expecting* us now. We don't want to let her down."

I give up. And maybe I'm a little bit interested to see what happens too.

"OK," I say. "I'll come. But only so we can tell her we can't take the case. Like I said.

"Sure," Amber replies.

"OK, good."

Honestly, just the idea of it is crazy.

ELEVEN

AMBER DOESN'T HAVE A CAR, but she tells me she can borrow her mom's. So after school we walk to her house to get it. She makes me wait in the kitchen while she gets changed. Luckily there's no one home, so I look around a little bit. There's plastic children's toys everywhere, and it smells nasty too, like baby food and diapers.

When Amber comes back down she's wearing lots of makeup and she's in this suit thing. She definitely looks a lot older. She looks quite... well, I suppose, professional too.

"Stop staring. *Weirdo*."

"I'm not staring, you just look..."

"What?" Amber smoothes down the skirt onto her thighs and turns sideways. "Power dressing turns you on does it?"

I don't really know what she means, and I don't like the funny voice she's doing, so I'm glad when she stops.

"I borrowed it from Mom, OK? She used to work in an advertising agency. She had to dress smart for clients. Though that was all before *that thing* came along." She points at a photograph on the wall. It's a little blond baby. Actually there's loads of photos of it, everywhere in the house as far as I can see.

"My half-sister, Grace. Mom remarried after Dad died and then she came along. Mom gave up work and decided to turn herself into Parent of the fucking Year." Amber kicks a large plastic xylophone out of her way.

"Ow! Never felt the need to give up work when I was a kid. I hardly ever saw her."

I don't say anything.

"Anyway," Amber goes on after a moment. "We have to get out of here before she comes home. If we want the car that is."

That makes my head jerk up. "I thought you said you could borrow it?"

"I didn't say we could *borrow* it, I said we can *use* it."

So after that we hurry outside and she unlocks an old Toyota Corolla that's parked on the driveway. I keep looking around anxiously, expecting to see her mom turn up and start shouting at us, but there's no one around. Amber fires the motor clumsily, and backs off the drive.

"I put the address in my phone." Amber steers with one hand as she opens the maps app on her cell phone. She stares at the screen as she pulls off down the street. A van is coming towards us, I can see the driver frowning as we slowly drift into its path.

"Erm, Amber..." I begin, but I'm interrupted by the van honking its horn.

"Fucking hell!" Amber looks up just in time to swerve out the way. Then she tosses the phone to me. "Hey can you find it for me?"

* * *

I quickly realize that Amber's not a very good driver, which kind of helps me not to think about where we're going, and what we're doing. I read out the directions and we take the road that goes towards the west side of the island. I don't know it well, only that there are no beaches here – it's all tall, craggy cliffs and a long drop down to the sea, which makes Amber's driving even more scary, especially when the road goes near to the edge. But even so I can't shake a feeling we shouldn't be doing this. A couple of school kids pretending to be private detectives. As if we really have any idea how to find this poor woman's husband. But I don't say anything. It wouldn't be safe to distract her.

Eventually we make it down to the southern tip of Lornea Island. There's no town here, just a few houses dotted around. One of them is bigger than the others.

"Wow!" Amber whistles as she stops at the address marked on the phone. "Check that out!"

I see what she means. Mrs. Jacobs' house is enormous. It's set back from the top of the cliff, and there's a gravel driveway leading up to it. It looks like the kind of place you'd expect to be met by a butler.

Amber pulls forward again, and as she does so, Amber starts humming to herself. I realize she's nervous. I don't know if that makes me feel better or worse.

"You know, I really don't think this is such a good idea," I say.

"Mmmm. Me either," Amber replies. But when she's stopped the car and pulled on the parking brake she looks across at me. Her eyes are shining with excitement.

"But we're here now aren't we?"

She gets out, and after a moment I do too. I figure that Mrs. Jacobs is probably going to take one look at us and tell us to go away. And at least that'll be the end of it.

By the time I get to the front door. Amber's already pressed the bell.

TWELVE

I HEAR the buzzing noise from deep inside the house. Then, moments later a voice too. A distant 'I'm coming', and then a long silence. Eventually we hear the shuffling of feet as someone comes to the door. Then it opens, just as far as the chain allows.

"Yes?" The voice is sharp. Angry.

"Hello, Mrs. Jacobs? It's Amber. From the detective agency?"

I can see an old woman through the slot in the door, screwing up her face, like she's trying to hear better.

"The what did you say?"

"The detective agency." Amber repeats it louder. "We're here about your husband."

"My husband?" The voice changes now, incredulous. "I don't have a husband. Not had one of those for years."

Amber turns to look at me, a goofy look on her face. But then she tries again.

"I know. You contacted us about finding him. You emailed us." She pauses. "Do you remember?"

The old lady snaps back at once. "Of course I remember, I'm not senile, if that's what you're implying?"

The door suddenly slams shut, and we hear the fumbling of the chain. A moment later it opens again, properly this time.

"*Is* that what you're implying, young lady?"

Amber takes a step back. "No, I just…"

"Good, because if you were we wouldn't be getting off on the right foot. Not at all." Mrs. Jacobs glares at Amber, who looks like she wants to run away. I take the chance to examine Mrs. Jacobs. She's tall and thin, but kind of elegant. Except she seems to be wearing two blouses, and she's got the buttons mixed up so they're all in the wrong holes.

"Who's this, your little companion here?"

She turns on me so quickly it makes me jump, and I'm not able to reply before Amber talks over me.

"This is Billy. Billy Wheatley. He works for the agency too. He's one of our junior investigators." She glances over and mouths that I should go along with this, so I do. But then, when I look back at Mrs. Jacobs something weird has happened. It's like there's suddenly a different figure standing there. Or maybe I just notice more about her now. She suddenly seems much more stooped over and frail now. Her face changes too. It looks more lined, more sad. She doesn't say anything for a while. But when she does it's like we're starting all over again.

"I'm sorry, who did you say you were?"

So Amber tells her a second time. But now she nods.

"Amber. Mr Billy. From the detective agency. Yes of course. Please, won't you come in? I've been expecting you."

It's weird. It's like we've just met two completely different people in the same body.

* * *

We go inside a huge hallway. It's decorated like a museum, with portraits on the walls of men in suits. One is on horseback. The floor is made of marble and above us is a huge chandelier. I look around, and notice Amber is doing the same.

"I was in the garden enjoying this lovely sunshine. Perhaps we could talk out there?"

We follow Mrs. Jacobs' curved back through several other dark rooms, all with the drapes closed. It seems to take forever, and at one point I think I see a stuffed fox's head hanging up, but I can't be sure. Finally we come to a patio door and step back out into a large garden enclosed by a high wall. It's nice enough, with flowerbeds everywhere and a big lawn, but I can't help notice we can't get out easily if we need to.

"Would you like some iced tea?"

She has a tray of it ready, on a wrought-iron table. We sit down.

"Thank you," Amber says, and Mrs. Jacobs pours us each a glass. Her hands shake as she lifts the jug.

"It's so lovely of you to come and see me," she says, her voice frail again. "It's been such a long time."

I'm not sure what to say to this, so I just smile and look at Amber, who raises her eyebrows just a tiny bit. She turns back to the old lady.

"We're here from the detective agency Mrs. Jacobs. You contacted us about your husband?"

For a second Mrs. Jacobs' face fills with a strange look. She continues to pour the tea into her own glass, but doesn't stop even when it's full, so that it pours all over the table and then flows over the edge and onto the ground below. It takes her ages to notice and stop pouring, but eventually she does. Then she sets the jug down.

"Yes, of course. Excuse me. I forgot for a moment."

She smiles. It's a sad smile, she looks lost.

"Yes. That is quite the mystery."

"Could you tell us exactly what happened?" Amber asks. She pulls out a notebook and balances it on her knees.

But Mrs Jacobs doesn't seem to hear. She looks at me instead. "I should have baked some cookies or something. I had no idea you'd both be so young"

"We're actually older than we look..." Amber begins, and I stiffen. This is the moment I've feared and I hope Amber's not going to try her idea of saying we've got an older boss who doesn't want to reveal his identity. That's such a stupid idea.

"Oh don't worry about it dear. I expect it's like policeman."

"Excuse me?"

"Private detectives are like policemen. They get younger all the time."

Mrs. Jacobs gives me a smile, and I realize Amber was somehow right. Our age isn't an issue, because Mrs. Jacobs is completely crazy.

"I'm sorry, this is all rather difficult for me. I've been a long time thinking about this."

"That's OK Mrs. Jacobs," Amber says. "If you could just tell us what happened, in your own words."

It sounds to me as if Amber spent all of last night practicing lines like that, but it seems to work because Mrs. Jacobs nods. She takes a moment to compose herself, then she begins.

"It was December 8th. 1979. I remember we'd just put the tree up and all the decorations and the children were so excited, they were still young enough to believe in Santa and all the magic of presents." She smiles at me for a moment, almost like she's not sure if she needs to pretend Santa's real – for my sake. Then her face turns serious again.

"It was evening time, the children were in bed and Henry said he was going to the store, up in Newlea. I usually bought the groceries, but what with Christmas coming up we'd run out of a few things. So he got into his car and he drove away. And that was the last anybody ever heard of him."

She looks at me again, and shrugs as if that's all there is to it. Amber's busy writing down what she said, so I ask the next question.

"Maybe he had an accident? Did you check the hospitals?"

"Well no." Suddenly she gives me a really big smile. "That's a very astute question Mr. Billy. I can see why you're a detective. No. We checked all the hospitals and he wasn't in any of them."

I'm quite pleased to be told I'm astute, so I try again.

"Did you ever find the car?"

"Another excellent question. Yes. The car came back. But Henry didn't."

Amber seems to have decided she's going to be the one who writes things down, so I keep asking questions.

"How do you mean?"

"Like I say. The car came back from the store. Or at least – I went to bed, thinking that perhaps Henry had stopped off for a drink some-where and wouldn't be back until late - he did that sometimes. But when I woke in the morning, the car was back, but no groceries, and no Henry."

"Well perhaps he came back, and then went away again, but not in his car?"

"I suppose that's possible. But the fact remains, that no one's ever seen or heard of him since."

She watches me closely, a bit too closely, it makes me feel awkward while I try to think of another question.

"Did you go to the police? What did they say?"

I look over to Amber to make sure she's writing all this down, but then when I look back at Mrs. Jacobs, she seems changed again. Her posture is more slumped. She looks frail. It's like a cloud has slid over the sun.

"Mrs. Jacobs? What did the police say?"

She doesn't reply.

I look over at Amber and frown again. I don't understand what's happening here at all.

"Mrs. Jacobs, did you go to the police about your husband?"

"When did we last see each other?" Mrs. Jacobs asked suddenly. "I think it's slipped my mind."

Amber and I look at each other, totally confused.

"We didn't. We haven't actually met before," I tell her in the end.

"Really?" She peers at both of us, like she's struggling to recognize who were are.

"And who are you again?"

Amber steps in again, but this time her voice is different now, less confident. "We're from the detective agency," she says again. "You asked us to find out what happened to your husband."

Then Mrs. Jacobs screws up her face, like she's desperately trying to make sense of this, before she finally says.

"Yes, of course." She puts a hand to her head and leaves it there, pressing against her temple. I slide my eyes again to Amber.

"I'm so sorry. I must seem rather... muddled. You see I get so forgetful these days. I do want to know what happened, but I just... forget."

"That's OK Mrs. Jacobs," Amber says. "You were telling us whether you went to the police? What did they say?"

Mrs. Jacobs looks like she's thinking for a long time. But when she finally speaks she shakes her head.

"I'm sorry. I don't... I just can't bring it back. It's like, it's all in here, but I just can't get at it. It's so frustrating. It's why I thought you might be able to help. A professional agency like yourselves."

I look at Amber. Trying to send her the message we really shouldn't be here, since we're not really a detective agency at all.

"Coconuts!" Mrs. Jacobs says suddenly.

"What?" Amber asks.

"Coconuts. I remember something about coconuts."

"What about them?"

"I don't know. They were important. In some way."

"In what way?"

There's a pause. "I don't know. Palm trees maybe... It's difficult to remember..." Mrs. Jacobs stops. She looks frustrated.

Amber tries again. "Did you say you can't remember if you went to the police, or you can't remember what they said?"

"There was snow on the ground. Not much, not enough to go tobogganing. Do you like to toboggan Mr. Billy?"

I have no idea what to say to this so I stay quiet.

"More iced tea?" Now she pours more drink into my glass. It's already full so that it overflows like before, and runs all over the table a second time.

I've seen enough at this point. Mrs. Jacobs is completely mad, and there's no way I'm getting involved investigating a mad lady's case. I don't have time for things like that.

"Mrs. Jacobs," I begin. "The actual reason we came today was to tell you we're not able to take on the case." I feel Amber's eyes shooting towards me, but I don't care.

"We can recommend the agency on the mainland, but we're too..."

"Oh no." Mrs. Jacobs interrupts me, and there's something about her voice that makes me stop.

"Oh no, it has to be you."

There's silence.

"Why?"

"Because I have a *feeling*." She taps her nose, like this makes perfect sense, which of course it doesn't. "I had it when I found your lovely website. I had it when your colleague here arranged this meeting, and I have it now. A *feeling*, that you're the only one who can help me."

I've no idea what to say to this, so I don't say anything.

"And I won't take no for an answer."

I swallow. "Yeah well that's really nice and everything, but..."

"And if it's about the money Mr. Billy. As you can see I'm quite comfortably off."

"It's not..."

"Mr. Billy, I've read the terms and conditions on your website very carefully. I understand there's no guarantee of success, but I'm prepared to take that risk. Here..." She reaches down beside her chair and there's a purse I hadn't noticed before. She pulls it onto her lap and brings out a checkbook in a leather case. She tears off the top check and holds it out to me.

"Five thousand dollars. That should be enough to get you started. Obviously there'll be more when you find out what happened." She smiles, and wafts the check in front of me, close enough that I can read her spidery handwriting. I swallow again.

"Here. Take it."

I don't mean to, but I do what she says. It's five thousand dollars after all. More money than I've ever seen before.

"Now, I do tire easily, so I'd like to take a rest now, if you don't mind?"

I open my mouth to tell her again that we can't take the case. But no words comes out. I can't stop thinking, obviously I shouldn't take the money - the old lady is very clearly insane. But *five thousand dollars?* And all we have to do is find this lady's husband. But then how on earth are we going to do that? Anything could have happened, and it was forty years ago.

"You know I do sometimes wonder if whatever happened to Henry has just slipped my mind." Mrs Jacobs interrupts my thoughts.

I stare at her, and then move my eyes across to Amber, who's grinning in delight.

"Now if you don't mind, I must take my afternoon nap."

THIRTEEN

As WE STEP out the front door and crunch back across the gravel, I feel Mrs. Jacobs eyes on me. When she's in the car Amber starts laughing, but I wish she wouldn't.

"*Do you like to toboggan Mr. Billy!*" Amber says as she starts the engine.

"She's fucking insane. That was hilarious." She turns the car around, and I ignore her. I lock eyes with Mrs. Jacobs again, standing on the doorstep, and for my last view I feel really sorry for her. She looks really sad and lonely so I don't feel like laughing.

"So? What do you make of her?" Amber asks, when we're back on the road. Thankfully she's driving much slower this time.

"I think she's a bit mad," I say.

"A *bit* mad? She's fucking batshit crazy."

"Yeah," I say after a while. Since that probably isn't an unfair description.

"What do you think about her husband though?"

I just shrug.

"It's weird though isn't it?"

"What is?"

"That he just walked out and disappeared? I mean how can that happen?"

I think about this for a while before answering. "We don't exactly know that he *did* walk out and disappear. He could have just died normally. Or he could still be living with her, and she just hasn't noticed."

Amber thinks for a moment. She laughs again, then stops.

"Well either way, we have to find out," she goes on.

I look across at her.

"But she's mad. We can't take money from a mad person." But even as I say it, I think again what I could do with that money. How it could change Dad's life.

"Why the hell not? What's five thousand dollars to someone with a house like that?" Amber turns to me, so that she's not looking at the road anymore.

"It's not how much she's got," I say, more firmly than I actually feel. "It's whether it's right to take it when she's mad. Whether it's ethical, I mean."

Amber says nothing for a while. Then she repeats the word 'ethical' in a funny voice.

"What exactly is *ethical*?"

I don't answer her.

"Look Billy," Amber tries again. "I'm not suggesting we *don't look* for him. We'll do the work we're being paid for. And like I said, it might be easy. If she's just forgotten what happened to him, or if nothing ever did, and she's just a bit mad, then it might be easy to solve. We'll tell her what happened and she can – I dunno – write it on a post-it note and stick it next to her bed. That way she can read the truth every morning when she wakes up."

It takes me a few moments to work out why I don't like her logic here.

"Yeah but she's not just *a bit mad* though is she? She's batshit fucking crazy."

Amber laughs really hard at this.

"Come on Billy. We've got to give it a go at least? I tell you what. Don't cash the check. If we can't help her we'll just give it back. That way there's no ethical problem."

Again I think about what I could do with the money. How I could use it to put Dad back on the right path. Then I notice that Amber is still staring at me, ignoring the road that she's driving along.

"Come on Billy." She makes a thing of fluttering her eyelids at me, though I know she's doing it ironically.

"Could you keep your eyes on the road please?"

She doesn't. "Pretty please Billy," she laughs, pursing her lips. I think it's only luck we're on a straight bit of road, and Amber hasn't driven off the cliff edge already, but there is a bend coming up.

"Amber!" I say.

"Billy..." Now her eyes are almost closed and she's making a kissing face.

"OK. OK, just look at the road will you!"

And with that Amber laughs, and looks forward again.

So like that we sort of take on the case.

FOURTEEN

DAD'S not in when I get home, so I grab some food and take it up to my room.

I'm about to open my bedroom door when I remember the hair. The one I stuck across the entrance, like in the James Bond film. I almost don't bother checking, since my mind is so on the Mrs. Jacobs case now, but something makes me stop. I put down my plate and carefully I examine the door frame. For a moment I don't understand it, because I can't even find the hair that I left. And then I realize the implication of this. That's the whole point of it. It means someone's been into my room while I was out. It can't have been Dad. He knows not to, and anyway he's been at work all day. So that only leaves one possibility. Tucker. Or Peter. Or whatever his name is.

I stand, on the upstairs landing for a moment, thinking about this. Then things get worse. From inside my room I start to hear a strange noise. I don't know what it is, but it's coming from inside my room. It sounds like – I don't know – it sounds almost like a weird breathing noise. I start to get a bit worried, since I'm alone in the house. I wonder if he could *still* be in there. I think about getting some sort of weapon, I could probably find a baseball bat in the shed somewhere. Then I realize this is all ridiculous – I can't be scared to go into my own bedroom. So I tell myself not to be stupid and take hold of the door handle.

"Hello?" I call out, trying to make myself sound totally confident. The noise stops, but no one answers. Then the noise begins again.

I can feel my face frowning tightly. I grip the door handle and very quickly I turn it, and push the door open. Then I get a real shock.

For a second I don't see anything out of place, then there's a loud screeching noise and then a large fluffy football of brown feathers throws itself at me and starts pecking at my face. Two long wings beat around my ears.

"Urgh! Steven! Get off!"

I try to push him away, but he's so eager to see me he almost knocks me back into the hallway. He must have been hungry, here on his own. I get him sat on my arm and go into the room. Then I see what the noise is, he's been trying to eat the corner of my desk, scratching at it with his beak. It really is time I released him. He's going a bit crazy locked up in here all day.

I share my dinner with Steven, which kind of means he eats most of it. And while that happens I start researching Henry Jacobs. But there's so many people with that name that I don't find anything, even when I add other keywords like *Lornea Island*, or *disappeared*, or *murder.* It's a bit disappointing actually, and I'm pleased when I hear Dad coming home. I get up to see him, but then I hear Tucker's voice as well. Or whatever his name is. And I don't want to see Tucker, so I stay upstairs. Dad shouts up the stairs to see where I am, but I shout back that I've got to do homework. And then, after a bit more work, I go to bed.

* * *

I have school the next day. Actually I've been having a few issues at school. I didn't tell you, because it's not really a big deal, but since you're here, you might as well know. It's just some of the boys in my class. They're idiots, the problem is, they're quite *big* idiots. I expect you probably had kids like them when you were at school. Or if you're still in school, you probably know kids like them right now. They're the type who sit at the back of the class, messing about and complaining that school is boring. It's so ironic though, because the only reason the classes are boring is because we have to do such basic stuff so that they'll understand it.

Today one of them brought in a bag of candies – jellies shaped like little Coke bottles – and they spent the lesson sucking them to make them sticky, and then flicking bits of them at the teacher, Miss Smith, when she tried to write on the whiteboard. She didn't notice at first, just wondered why they were laughing so much, but then she did notice, and she did the worst thing possible, which was to try and pretend it wasn't happening. I don't know why they don't train teachers not to do that. It never works, it just makes the whole class laugh along with the idiots. That's what happened this morning, until more and more people were throwing the sticky bits of candy at her every time her back was turned.

Anyway, what happened next was this. I was trying to get on with my work, when I felt something hit *me* in the back of my head. And when I touched my hair to see what it was, it wasn't just one piece of jelly, it was a whole wad of half-chewed cola bottles stuck together, all slimy and tangled in with my hair. And when I turned around to see who did it, right away I saw James Drolley looking right at me. He's kinda the leader of the idiots. But then, there were also quite a few of the other boys, also looking and laughing. So there's no way I could tell Miss Smith who it was.

Actually I'm not going to say anymore. I suppose it's just one of those things, but it did kind of mess up my morning.

* * *

When lunchtime finally comes I go straight up to the school library and I see Amber sitting by the computers. For some reason I suddenly feel really pleased to see her. I don't know why. But just as I'm about to go over to her I stop myself. She didn't text me this morning, and I'm only assuming she's here working on our case, but what if she isn't? What if she's actually just doing her school work, and she's not really serious about wanting to investigate Mrs. Jacobs case at all?

So I hesitate, not sure if I should go and speak to her after all. I almost turn around to leave, but then she looks up and spots me.

"Hey Billy! Over here."

Usually I wouldn't like it when people are loud in the library, but I don't mind now. So I go over to her, and sure enough it's not school work she's doing, but research into Mrs. Jacobs. This makes me very pleased.

"What are you grinning at?" Amber asks.

"I'm not grinning."

"Yes you are."

I'm pretty sure I wasn't grinning, but just in case I was, I make sure I stop.

"Now what are you doing? Are you ill?"

"No! I'm..." I concentrate on settling my face into a serious look.

"That's better. Now sit down, we've got work to do. Lots of work." She pushes a chair out next to her, and I sit down.

"I've been searching for *Henry Jacobs...*"

I lean in and examine her screen.

"Trouble is, there's loads of people on Facebook with that name. So we're gonna have to scroll through them one by one until we..."

"That won't work."

"What? Why not?"

"I looked last night. There's seven thousand three hundred and forty seven people called Henry Jacobs. And probably more who can't use computers."

"How do you know that?"

"I found a website that tells you. You type a name in, and it counts how many Facebook profiles there are for that name. And loads of them will have their security set to private, so you won't be able to see them anyway."

"Shit." Amber says.

"*And* even if you could see them, it's hardly likely he's going to have set up a Facebook account in his old name, if he wanted to disappear."

Amber frowns. "Alright then. What do we do then?"

"You could add search terms to his name," I say.

"Like what?"

"Well, if you type in '*Henry Jacobs*' plus '*Lornea Island*' plus '*disappeared*' then it helps to narrow down the results."

Right away Amber starts to type into the computer.

"But there's no point doing that either," I tell her. She stops and sighs.

"Why not?"

"Well it's obvious isn't it?"

Amber hesitates. "Is it?"

"Yeah. It's because the internet wasn't invented then."

She frowns again, deeper this time.

"The internet wasn't invented until 1983. Well, actually some people say it didn't really exist until the 1990s when Tim Berners Lee invented the world wide web, but either way it's not going to have any information on someone who went missing in 1979."

"Alright, alright. I get the point." Amber looks despondent.

"So what do we do then?"

I reach into my bag and begin to pull out a folder.

"We might not be able to search for Henry Jacobs, but we can search for Barbara Jacobs." I open the folder and start to read.

"Barbara June Jacobs is the granddaughter of the Charles Jacobs, who opened the first silver mine at Lornea Island's Northend in 1899. While the Northend mine closed with the 1950 disaster, Northend Mining Corporation is still a major player in international ore mining around the world, particularly in Africa. Barbara Jacobs sat on the Northend Mining Corporation board of directors until 2005 when she stepped down."

"How do you know all that?" Amber asks, and I hand her the paper I'm reading. On it there's a picture of Mrs. Jacobs, only quite a bit younger, and wearing a red ball gown.

"She was on something called the Lornea Island Council. When you click on her picture, this is what comes up."

Amber spends a long time reading all the pages I've printed out. In front of her there's a packet of sandwiches. And just looking at them makes me feel quite hungry, because I didn't have time to make any lunch this morning. And also, because between Tucker and Steven, we don't have much food left in the house.

"Can I have a sandwich?" I ask."

"Huh?" Amber looks up. "Yeah sure. They're not very nice though. Tuna mayo, but the tuna was old. All I could find in the cupboard."

She goes back to her reading. And because I've already read it all, I take a sandwich and start to eat it.

"OK. So we know she's *old Lornea Island*, and she likes going to charity events. So she's rich, but we knew that already. What we don't know is anything about her husband, let alone how he went missing. Or even *if* he did. So how do we find him?"

Amber's right about the tuna. It's a bit nasty. I decide to wrap up what's left and give it to Steven later. Amber looks up.

"I did have one idea." I kind of say, with my mouth still half full of mashed up fish.

"What?"

I can't help but smile a little bit, because this is a really good idea.

"You know how I said the internet was only invented in 1983, except for people who don't regard it as the real internet until Tim Berners Lee...

"Yeah."

"Well. You also know about *The Island Times*, the biggest newspaper on Lornea Island? How you can search through old editions of the paper on the internet?"

"Yeah," Amber says, and already she's pulling up the website. I smile some more.

"Then you also know it only goes back to 2000, because they didn't do the internet before then?"

Amber stops. "Oh. *Yeah I knew that too.*" Even though I know she didn't. Not really.

"Well they still *made* the newspaper, back then. Still wrote it I mean."

"So?"

"So, you can still search it. It's just not on the internet. You have to go to the actual newspaper office and do searches there. They have a special room for it. On a microfiche machine. It says so on their website."

Amber stares at me for a moment, looking thoughtful.

"Show me." She says.

I lean across to use the keyboard, still talking while I type the address and the page loads.

"It's just like in those movies." I go on, because I'm not sure if she really understands properly.

"What movies?"

"You know the kind of movies. Where they're searching for something in files somewhere. And it always takes them forever, but then, right at the end they find it. Here you go."

Amber reads on the website about the *Island Times* reading room. And then suddenly she just gets up, brushing all her papers together.

"Come on."

"Where are we going?"

"To the newspaper office. I've got mom's car."

I'm a bit surprised by this, since we only get an hour for lunch, and we've already had fifteen minutes. We won't be able to get there and back in time.

"What about class?" I say.

"What about class?"

"Well, we might miss it..."

"So? This is way more important."

I totally don't know what to say to that, but Amber's already gone.

FIFTEEN

I STUFF my folder back in my bag. Amber hasn't put away the books she's used, so I quickly dump them onto the trolley that Mrs. Lopez uses to put the returned books back to where they go on the shelves, because you're not supposed to just leave them on the computer tables like Amber did.

Then I start to run, I can see Amber at the bottom of the stairs, and it doesn't look like she's going to wait for me at all. I just about catch her up in the lobby, and I'm about to say something when she stops.

"Wait here, I need to pee," she says, and then she disappears into the girls' bathroom. I'm starting to think that Amber is quite an annoying person.

But then something amazing happens. I start to look around the lobby – it's one of those spaces that you don't really look at much, even though you go through it every day. There's a long reception desk, empty, because the receptionists have a little room they work from. Then there's a few plants to trick parents and visitors into thinking Newlea High School is a much nicer place than it really is. And up on the wall there's all this wood paneling, with all the names of important people in the school over the years. Like an honors board. And for some reason I start to read down the names on the honors board. I'm not really paying attention, I'm just passing the time, when suddenly I notice something.

But before I can do anything about it, I'm interrupted by a voice right behind me.

"Hey Wheatley!"

I recognize the voice at once. It's James Drolley, the idiot from my class earlier. When I turn around he's with all the other boys who ruined Geography earlier.

"Hanging out by the girl's bathroom Wheatley? Why don't you just go in there?"

Drolley's friends all start laughing, as if what he said was actually a joke. Though it isn't really. I don't reply. I get a bad feeling that they're not just going to walk by. It's lunchtime after all, they've got plenty of time.

And sure enough I'm right. They all stop and gather round me in a circle. Then James steps really close to me.

"Why'd ya get in the way?" Drolley asks. He pushes me in the chest. He's one of the smallest boys in the class, not much bigger than I am. I think it bothers him a bit.

"In the way of what?" I ask.

"In class you *fucktard!* I was aiming for Smith. Until you got in the way." He shoves me again, harder this time. The others laugh again.

"Go on James," one of his friends says. "Hit him." The boy's name is Paul. I used to be sort of friends with Paul, but then he got in with James Drolley and his gang instead.

There's no point answering any of them, so I turn away from Drolley, and look back at the wooden honors board again, not quite believing what I saw before. But then I get pushed really hard from behind, and I nearly fall over.

"*Don't fucking ignore me Wheatley.*" Drolley says. I only just manage to stay on my feet, and somehow my bag comes off my shoulder. Then suddenly Drolley is holding it. I realize it hurts where he pulled it from me.

"Hey," I say. I sense I need to concentrate now or things are going to turn bad.

"Give it back."

"Why?" James challenges. "You gonna make me?" He shakes my bag.

"You got any food for me Wheatley? I'm kinda hungry."

"No," I say. "I haven't got anything."

Drolley stares at me for a second. "Let's check shall we? Make sure you're telling the truth." Then he unzips my bag and looks inside. As he does so I remember the tuna mayo sandwich I wrapped up for Steven.

"Well lookie here..." Drolley pulls it out and opens the packet. "Mmmm. Tuna sandwich. My favorite. So you *were* lying Wheatley. You little fucking *shit*. You think you can lie to me?" He throws the sandwich to one of his friends, but with the packet open the two bits of bread separate and it all falls to the floor where Paul stamps on it.

"Awww fuck." Drolley says. "I can't eat that now Wheatley. You got any more?" He looks again in the bag, pulling out my books and folders to check if anything else is there. Then he pulls out the folder I made last night. I get a sudden, sinking feeling in my stomach.

"Hey, what's the fuck is this?"

On the front of the folder that Drolley is holding is a the logo Amber drew for the detective agency, only I've colored it in, and made it better. Arranged around the drawing are words, in a circle around the image of the magnifying glass. Drolley turns his head as he tries to read them.

"Newlea Island... Detective Agency?" His face lights up in delight, because – even though he's stupid – he knows when he's hit upon something he can use.

"Is that you Wheatley? Are you the *Newlea Island fucking Detective Agency*?" He opens it, letting some pages waft to the floor, and starts reading out my notes. I sense this is about to get really out of control when there's a sudden scream from across the lobby.

"*Fucking leave him alone you fucking gobshite faggots.*"

Before I know what's happening, Amber is amongst us, like some kind of wild cat. She shoves James in the chest so hard that he falls over on his butt. Then, before he can get up she makes like she's going to kick him with her massive boots. He scuttles away, looking a bit like a beetle, so in the end she doesn't actually kick him. Instead she turns to his friends. There's a sudden, stunned silence, but then the boys re-group, because it's still five against two, even though Amber is older than them.

"The fuck has this got to do with you, *Goth*?" Paul asks, but he kind of mutters it, and he's a long way back from her. Except she then turns on him.

"*Fuck you! You motherfucking dumbass dipshit,*" she steps towards him, and he almost stumbles, he backs away so quick.

"You want me to rip your tiny dick off and stuff it up your ass?"

I take advantage of the sudden silence to gather together my notes and slip them back in the folder. When I look again Drolley is back on his feet. He's trying to make himself look brave.

"Are you part of it too, *Goth*?" Drolley says, now he's surrounded again by his friends. "Billy Wheatley's fucking detective *club*?"

"I said fuck off maggot-dick." Then Amber actually spits at him, but because Drolley is hiding behind his friends, it lands on Paul's bag. It looks for a second like he might have to react to that, but then she lunges forward like she really wants to kill them all, and they scatter out of her way. Then the others realize they can turn on Paul and laugh at him, now he's got Amber's spit on his bag. That way they can still be bullying, and pretend to themselves that they're not scared of Amber. Paul looks pretty miserable about it, but at least they're leaving now. As they do Drolley shouts over his shoulder.

"See you in class Wheatley. You can't always have a *vampire* to protect you."

There's an awkward silence as Amber and me watch them disappear, jostling each other and laughing loudly, as if there were never worried.

"I hate assholes like that," Amber tells me. "Really fucking hate them."

I wonder for a moment about explaining my idea for BullyTracker but decide it's not a good time.

"Come on. Let's get out of here," Amber goes on.

"Hang on," I put my hand on her arm to stop her, and she turns in surprise. But then I point to the honors board I noticed before.

"What?"

Newlea High School is really old. I didn't tell you that, but it is. It's been here for maybe a hundred years, or maybe longer. So the list of important people in the school goes way back too. And the honors board lists them all out, in gold letters. And one of those names, the gold glowing where a shaft of sunlight hits it from the skylight, is the name we've been looking for.

"Look at the honors board."

"*What?* Why?"

"Look at the list of school principals."

Amber frowns at me again, but I see her eyes begin to scan the list. And then she gets to 1972-1979, where the principal is listed as "Henry Arthur Jacobs."

"*Shit,*" Amber says. "He was the school principal?"

SIXTEEN

IT'S NOT FAR into town but it's quite scary because of how bad Amber is at driving in traffic. She nearly kills three people, then a dog, then parks half on and half off the sidewalk. I don't know if I feel more worried about being out of school at lunchtime, or dying in a car wreck.

The *Island Times'* office is one of the big stone buildings in the centre of Newlea. I've never been in it, but I've seen it loads of times. It has that look of somewhere that used to be really important, but isn't anymore. It does still have a revolving door though, which is quite fun to walk through.

Inside we find two ladies behind a long reception desk. There are copies of this week's edition of the paper laid out all neatly, and an old man is giving some listing for the second hand section. I don't know why, you can just do it online.

"We want to search old editions of the paper," Amber says, when one of the receptionists turns to us.

"It says on your website you can do it here. You've some kind of reading room?"

"Sure." She studies us for a moment, quite suspicious. "School project is it?"

"Not exactly." Amber replies, with a smile. The woman doesn't smile back.

"Only if it's for commercial purposes I have to charge you."

"Oh. It's definitely a school project then," Amber says, and I feel her foot pressing into my leg.

I don't say anything. Honestly, sometimes I wonder if Amber thinks I'm stupid.

The woman comes out from behind her desk and leads us to a door in the corner of the room, it leads to a very small room where there's just a computer terminal and a couple of chairs.

"Where's the microfiche machine?" I ask.

"All the records have been digitized. We wouldn't be able to trust the original records with children." She wiggles the mouse to bring the computer to life.

"You put your search terms in there." She points at the screen. "You sure this is for a school project?"

"No it definitely is," Amber replies, and after a moment the woman leaves us to it. I'm still a bit disappointed we don't actually get to use the microfiche machine, but Amber sits right down and begins typing. She puts in the words:

Henry Jacobs

After a few moments the computer loads up results and we scan them. There's lots of mentions of 'Henry', and quite a few of 'Jacobs', but none mentioning them together. So I tell her to put them together properly, like this:

Henry + Jacobs

This cuts down the results to just three articles.

The first, from February 1979 has the headline:

Roadworks causing pupils to miss up to an hour's education a week, head teacher says.

We click to see the story, but it's not like a normal website. It takes us to an actual copy of the newspaper, laid out just like it was in 1979. There's only one mention of Henry Jacobs, and it takes a while to find it. When we do it says this:

School Principal Henry Jacobs warned that school buses are not able to get pupils to school due to the upgrading work on the main Silverlea to Newlea link.

We scan read the whole thing, but it doesn't seem very relevant.

"Go back," Amber says. "What's the next one?"

I click back and try the next link.

State-of-the-art building project to bring world-class gymnasium to Newlea High School.

This time the article is a bit more interesting.

Building work has commenced on a new project to construct a world-class gymnasium at Newlea High School. Henry Jacobs, School Principal, commented that students would now be able to play a range of sports in the new indoor facility.

There's a picture too, only instead of being a photograph, it's an artists' impression of all these children in a gym, dressed in old fashioned gym shorts. It's interesting because it's not just *a* gym. It's *our* gym. It's the *actual gym* we have to use at school.

"World-class facilities? Fucking hell, he was hopeful wasn't he?" Amber says. "Go back. Go to the next one."

I do what she says, and click the final link.

New Principal starts at Newlea High School

Dated February 1980, the article only briefly mentions Henry Jacobs, where it says this:

Mrs. Clarke steps into the vacancy left when Henry Jacobs quit his position of Principal in Christmas last year.

I get an excited feeling as I read on, expecting it to say what happened to him, but it doesn't. It just says how the new principal wants to move the school forward and prepare the students for the world, and things like that.

"Is that it?" Amber asks. "Isn't there anything more?"

We search for a while longer, trying different keywords. But nothing comes up. It's a bit disappointing after such a promising start. After another half-hour of searching we give up.

"I can't believe there's nothing more. How can someone disappear – how can the *school principal* disappear – and there's no mention of it in the newspaper?"

"I don't know," I say. "But at least it matches what Mrs. Jacobs said. How her husband went missing in Christmas 1979. At least we know she remembered that part right."

"Yeah, I suppose so," Amber replies, but she's clearly not satisfied. I've been getting worried about something else though.

"Hey, do you think we should maybe get back? We're going to get in trouble otherwise, for skipping class."

If Amber hears me she doesn't answer.

"It's just I already had to see Principal Sharpe once this month already...." I don't actually mean to say this, since Amber obviously already knows, but it just slips out. But it's OK because Amber just ignores me anyway.

"What do we know?" She says instead. She grabs her notebook and turns to a fresh page. "What do we actually *know* about what happened?"

I don't answer her, but again she ignores me. She answers her own question.

"We know Mrs. Jacobs says he went missing in 1979. At Christmas time. She said they were putting up the decorations, when he just walked out and never came back."

Amber writes on her pad *Christmas 1979* and then circles it. "And we know from the school honors board that Henry was school principal from 1973 to 1979. And from the *Island Times* that a new school principal started in 1980." She looks to me, as if it's my turn to add to the list of facts.

"And we know Mrs. Jacobs is crazy. So he might not have gone missing at all. He might have just... left."

Amber gives me a warning glance.

"Then why does she think he went missing? She wouldn't have hired us if there was no mystery."

I don't have an answer to this, so I think about it instead. I suppose it must count as some sort of evidence. At least a little bit.

"Well, maybe, but we don't know anything else."

"Actually we do," Amber says, and slowly she starts to smile.

"We do what?"

"We do know something else."

I frown and try to work out what she means. I don't much like the look of satisfaction on her face.

"Come on Billy. We've searched the newspaper right? For anything about him disappearing? And we've not found anything?"

"Yeah."

"So that does that mean?"

I really want to work it out, before she tells me, and I think I nearly do, but just not quite in time.

"It tells us that whatever happened wasn't a big thing. If he was – I don't know – murdered by a serial killer, or died in a big car wreck, it would have been all over the paper and we'd have found it. So because it *wasn't* there, we know that when he disappeared, it wasn't a big thing. It wasn't *news*."

I open my mouth to object to this, but I can't. It's quite clever actually.

SEVENTEEN

IT'S the middle of afternoon classes when we get back to school. I kind of expect to get into trouble walking into the lobby, but all the receptionists are back in their little room and they don't come out. It's strange though, standing in the empty lobby and looking up at the honors board. I stare at Henry Jacobs' name up there, picked out in gold letters. For a moment it's like I'm in the school, all those years ago. Someone who stood right here must know what happened to him, why he left...

"Hey Billy," Amber interrupts my thoughts. "Don't just stand there? Someone'll see you."

"Oh sorry,"

"When you get to class say you had a doctor's appointment. Say it's for something personal. That way they can't ask you about it."

I nod, and Amber leaves, to whatever class she has, and I go to Math. I decide to tell Mr. Duncan I had a dentist's appointment, and I'm all ready to pretend I've got toothache, but he doesn't really care, he just tells me to sit down. After that it's PD. And after that I get on the bus home. But all the time I'm thinking about how we can find out more about Henry Jacobs. I start to get some ideas too. But then, when I get home, everything changes.

It feels like an ambush. As I walk in the kitchen Dad and Tucker are there waiting for me.

"Billy," Dad begins. "Can you take a seat? We need to have chat."

From the sound of his voice I think I'm in trouble. For a second I wonder if he's found out about me skipping class, but how? Did Mr Duncan know I was lying about the dentist after all? And then I think that maybe it's *Tucker* who's in trouble. Maybe Dad's figured out about him lying about his name. Or not having a phone. But then from the way Tucker's smiling at me, sipping on a beer, it can't be that either.

"Come on Billy, take a seat."

I still haven't taken my backpack off, but I do so now, and slip behind the kitchen table. Dad sits down opposite me. He smiles at me, but it's not a real smile. It's fake.

"What it is?" I ask.

Dad's smile falls away. "I need to tell you something. Some news. Some good news."

"What?" I ask again.

Dad looks away, and rubs a hand over the stubble on his face, so I know it's not really good news after all.

"What news?"

"You know I said Tucker would be staying here a few days?" He begins.

"Yes. That was last Thursday, so he's supposed to go two days ago..."

"Sure." Dad holds up a hand to cut me off. "Sure, I know. The point is he still needs..." Dad stops and rubs his chin again. When he continues he's changed the subject.

"Look, I got a call from Frank earlier. You know Frank, down at the harbor?"

I wait. I guess I must frown too, since Dad explains.

"You know Frank? The skipper of *Ocean Harvest*?"

For a second I don't know what he's on about, but then I remember. *Ocean Harvest* is one of the fishing boats. The big ones. I don't *really know* Frank though. It's just one time he did let me on board one time to do a species count of the fish in the hold.

"A space has come up. For a job."

I blink.

"It's just a try out, but it's good money. Real good money. If we get a good catch, it'd be enough to start saving. Putting something away, for... well for whatever."

Both him and Tucker are staring at me really intently now. I slide my eyes from one to the other.

"But *Ocean Harvest* is an offshore boat?"

"She goes out a bit further." Dad nods. "Sure she does. But that's where the money is. It's a modern boat Billy. It's totally safe. It just means I'll be away a bit longer." Dad lets his voice fade away. So I have to work out what he means.

"How long?"

Dad makes a face, like this is an awkward bit.

"Frank reckons it's a day and a half to get out to the fishing grounds. Then the same back. So it depends on the catch. Could be four nights. A week tops."

"A *week*? So who's going to look after me?"

Straight away I'm pissed at myself for saying this. I don't *need* anyone to look after me. Most of the time it's me looking after Dad. But a week is a long time.

And then I turn to Tucker. Or Peter. Or whatever his real name is. I see he's looking right back at me. Watching my reaction.

"It's what I was saying about Tucker," Dad goes on, but I hardly hear him. "How he needs a place to crash. Just for a little bit longer."

"But you said he was only going to be here a few days," I interrupt. "He should have gone home three days ago..."

"*Billy.* It's a good solution. He can keep an eye on you while he gets himself set up. I can show Frank he can rely on me. It's the opportunity we've been waiting for."

"Set up?"

"Sure. Tuck's gonna give it a go here on Lornea. Look for work."

"*Look for work*?" I can feel my voice go high again. It feels like it's betraying me.

"Come on Billy, I know this is a surprise. But you know I've been trying to get a place on a boat? We've talked about it."

"Yeah, but not on one of the big boats. You talked about the inshore ones."

"There's no fish inshore no more Billy. You know that."

I don't reply. I suddenly realize I'm breathing super hard.

"Come on Billy, we *need* this. I've gotta have some real money coming in. We got bills to pay. And if I can save a bit we can..." Dad doesn't finish his sentence. But I sense what he was going to say. It's to do with my idea for buying *Blue Lady*, and running whale watching trips for tourists.

I try to think fast. Maybe it *is* a good idea. But then I think about Tucker again. Or Peter. About how I'm going to be left alone with him, when I don't even know which is his real name. How can Dad think that's OK? I *have* to say something.

But I don't.

"When are you going?" I ask instead.

And this time Dad doesn't answer at once. He takes a deep breath and puffs it out. Like this bit's going to be difficult.

"We're leaving on the next high tide."

At once my eyes flick to the window. Because I'm sitting down at the table, I can't see the beach, but I don't even need to. I always know what the tide is doing.

"The *next* high? Tonight's high?" My voice has risen again.

"I know it's short notice Bill. One of the other crew phoned in sick. That's why Frank rang me. That's why I wanted to have this talk now. As soon as you got back from school. I wanted to speak to you before I go."

I calculate in my head. Next high tide is in two hours. It's a half hour drive to Holport, where *Ocean Harvest* comes in. He'll have to go in an hour and a half.

"I gotta help load up too." Dad goes on, like he's reading my mind. "I gotta leave now."

"*Now?*"

Why does my voice keep going so high?

I look out the window again. I can see the sky as it hangs over the sea. The light is fading now, and it highlights the clouds building into towering thunderheads. Mottled grey, studded with showers of rain. I think of Dad heading out there. Hundreds of miles out there.

"There's a storm coming." I say. I don't know why I say it, because it's not really true. It's just a bit of rain. At least, it is here. I don't actually know what it'll be like miles out to sea.

"She's a new boat Billy. She's safe. And... efficient. You get a place on *Ocean Harvest*, it's a safe income."

Suddenly Tucker joins in the conversation. So far he hasn't spoken a word, just stood there, drinking his beer.

"We'll be alright Billy," his voice sounds weird. Creepy. "We'll get to know each other." He grins at me, and I notice his incisors are really long. Yellow, but brown at the gums where he doesn't clean them properly. He takes a swig of his beer. I can feel tears forming behind my eyes, and I don't want Tucker to see them. I really don't want that. I turn back to Dad.

"I'm gonna go to my room. I've got homework."

Dad strokes his chin again a couple of times, then he just nods.

"OK."

I wasn't expecting that. I thought he'd stop me, but now he isn't I don't have a choice. I pick up my bag and go to the stairs. As I climb up I'm still hoping Dad's going to call me back. But he doesn't. So in the end I go into my room and I have to deal with Steven hopping all over me and pecking at my face. And then I haven't even taken his fish from downstairs, and I can't really go and get it right now.

So I wait. I'm still pretty sure Dad will come and see me before he leaves. So I listen out for the squeak of the floorboards in the stairs, the sound that tells me Dad's coming up. And I decide that when he does, I'm just going to tell him. I'm going to tell him about how Tucker isn't really called Tucker at all, and how he lied to me about not having a cell phone, when he does have one really. And when I think about that, I remember how I stuck that hair across my door, and how it wasn't there when I came back, which proves that he's been searching in my room.

And I know that when I tell Dad all this, he'll realize he can't leave me alone with Tucker. He'll sort it out. He'll work out who he really is, and he'll make sure he's not in our house anymore. I know he's been trying to get a place on a boat for a long time. I know he needs the money. But he'll realize he can't do it this way.

But instead of the squeak of the stairs, I hear another noise – the bang of the front door. So I creep to my window, and I peek out of it, since it might just be Tucker outside, and I don't want him to see me.

But it's not Tucker. It's Dad. He's throwing his kit bag into the back of the truck, and then climbing behind the wheel. And then Tucker gets in the other side, laughing as he does so. And then there's the noise of the engine firing up. I think I see Dad glancing up at my window as he begins turning around, but I pull back out of sight. And when I next look they're driving off down the lane.

EIGHTEEN

IT's the next morning now. I feel a little better about things. Well, as better as it's possible to feel, given the circumstances.

I ended up staying up really late last night. Working. First of all I downloaded a new app to my computer. It's called *VesselTrack*, and you can use it to show where all the ships are in the world, in real time. So I've set it up to show me exactly where Dad is. At the moment this is where he is:

lat: 42.25495 lon: -68.13995

He's heading 077 degrees, and they're going at ten knots. That means they're about sixty miles away and still heading out. The weather isn't too rough though. The wind is force four and forecast to drop. That's hardly anything. It's worse than that here.

So I decided the more urgent problem is me being left alone in the house with Tucker. Or whatever his real name is.

I think about this first. I try to use logic to work it out, starting from what I definitely know. For example. I know that Dad thinks his name is Tucker. But I also know he has identification in his wallet where he's called Peter Smith. He can't be called both names, so one must be fake. You might think that the official identification - his driver's license - is the most likely to be the real one, but you're forgetting something. You see, Dad *grew up with him*, back in Crab Creek. So if Dad thinks he's called Tucker that must be true. Which means *Peter Smith* must be either a new name, or an alias.

I make a list of why people might use an alias. This is what I write:

Because he's a spy.
Because he an undercover policeman.
Because he's in the witness protection scheme.

Then I use google and find some more possibilities. I add the following:

Because he's an author and it's a pen name.
Because he's a celebrity and wants to travel incognito.
Because he's a criminal and wants to hide his identity.

Then I cross out the ideas that are impossible, or really unlikely. And the only one left is the last one. So Tucker is a criminal who wants to hide his identity.

Next I have a really good look around my room, to see if anything was missing from when he broke in. I don't think anything is. I do get the feeling that a few things were out of place – my desk drawers not quite closed as I'd left them, that sort of thing, but to be honest, it could have been Steven. But then, I have a good idea. I start to think about *why* Tucker might have tried to break into my room in the first place. The obvious answer is that he was looking for things to steal, because I already know he's a criminal. But since he's currently living in our lounge, it doesn't exactly make sense to steal things from my room, and just take them downstairs. So maybe he wasn't looking to steal something, but doing something else? But if that's the case, then what?

And then I work it out. Do you remember how he asked me, the morning after he got here, if he could use my computer? And then he said he wanted it to access the internet, because he didn't have a phone? But then I discovered he was lying about not having a phone. He *did* have one, only he was hiding it. I didn't understand why anyone would do that at the time. But I think I do now. It's all to do with how cell phones work.

I saw a documentary on it. And it's quite technical but this is the basic point: Cell phones connect to base stations by sending radio waves back-and-forth. Whenever your cell phone is switched on, it's constantly sending out messages, called handshakes, to the nearest base station, kind of like it's saying 'Hi, I'm over here'. It does this so the telephone company knows where to send all the calls and actual messages you get. Otherwise they'd have to send *every* call and *every* message to *every* base station, just in case all their customers happened to be standing next to it. And that would be crazy, because all the base stations would fill up, and they'd probably explode. But what this means is, when you have your cell phone switched on, your telephone company knows where you are. *And so do the police.* The police have access to the same system, and they use it to track down where criminals are. They do it all the time. And the thing is, it's not even a big secret – the criminals know about too. Probably because they saw the same documentary that I did.

The reason why this is important is this. When criminals are on the run from the police they have to leave their phones switched off. They can't even use the internet on them, because just having the phone on means it'll send a handshake message to the nearest base station, saying 'here I am!'

That's why Tucker/Peter lied about not having a phone – because he couldn't switch it on to use it. It also explains why he wanted to get into my room. He must have needed to use the internet again. So he broke into my room to try to find my computer. Luckily I had it with me at the time.

And then – because I find with me, good ideas often come in threes or fours – I have another good idea. I realize that, if Tucker doesn't want to turn his phone on because the police are using it to look for him, then there's a really easy way to get rid of him. All I need to do is find his phone and switch it on. It'll send a handshake to the nearest base station, and the police will see that and know exactly where he is. They'll come and arrest him. And because he won't even know about it, he won't be expecting them. And best of all, no one will ever know it was me.

I can't do it right now though. There's two reasons for that. First of all I don't want to get Dad into trouble. I'm not sure if it's illegal or not, but I don't expect they'll be very impressed he's gone off for a week and left me with a violent criminal. But there's another reason too – I don't know where Tucker's phone is. I haven't seen it since that time I searched his jeans. So I'll have to watch him carefully to see if I can get any clues where he might be hiding it.

And then I get *another* idea. Even better than just turning Tucker's phone on.

I wasn't sure at first if it would work, so I had to do some checking on the internet, and it was already nearly midnight by then. I know it was, because that's when I heard Dad's truck come back, and I looked out of the window to see Tucker getting out. He must have gone to a bar after dropping Dad off. I watched him with the light off, to see if he was drunk. But it was hard to tell.

Then I went back to work. I found some software that had a trial period, so it wasn't going to cost me any money. Then I took everything that was really important off my computer, just in case. I have it all backed up anyway. Then I did some testing, and checked it all worked. And then, at about two in the morning, I finally went to bed.

So when I go to school today I'm not taking my laptop. I'm going to 'accidentally' forget it. I'm going to leave it right here on the kitchen table, switched on, with the password disabled. Like I *meant* to put it in my bag, but forgot it at the last minute.

But I'm not really forgetting it.

It's a trap.

NINETEEN

IT'S REALLY hard to concentrate at school because of wondering whether Tucker/Peter has fallen for it or not. The first lesson seems to take forever, and then in morning break I have a little bit of bother with James Drolley and his little gang. But then Mr. Stewart comes along. He's one of the gym teachers, and they always act like they're perfect students around him because they love gym, so they leave me alone.

At lunchtime I go and see if Amber is in the library. But she isn't there. I look out the window to see if her mom's car is in the parking lot, but that's not there either. Although that doesn't mean anything, because some days Amber isn't allowed to use it.

And then we have history class all afternoon, and we finish up with a test. At least that's quite fun.

Eventually the bell rings for the end of the day, and I get on the bus. And then just like normal I have to wait while everyone else gets dropped off, since my stop is the very last one on the route.

But finally the bus gets to the Littlelea stop, and the doors wheeze open. I get off and hurry down the little lane to our house. But then, when I see Dad's truck, and see how Tucker's parked it differently to how Dad does, suddenly I start to feel less excited and more – well, nervous I suppose. After all, Dad's hundreds of miles out to sea and I'm alone with a dangerous, violent criminal. And the thing is, last night when I was setting up my trap, I assumed he was just a *normal* criminal. But what if that's wrong? What if he's actually a computer-expert criminal? You know, the type in those movies who can disable alarms and open safes electronically. He doesn't look like one, I know, but then maybe that's a kind of disguise.

And then I remember the photograph in his wallet – where it showed his real name was Peter Smith. He actually *did look* like a computer expert in that photo. If Tucker/Peter is a computer-expert criminal, then he's going to know I tried to trap him.

I start to feel short of breath. What if he's in there now, knowing I know who he really is? Knowing I know the police are looking for him? I think of those muscles he has all over him. I'm getting quite strong, but I'm nowhere near as strong as that.

But then I tell myself to be rational. He's not a computer expert, he can't be. People with muscles like that are never computer experts, even if they are in disguise. If Tucker/Peter is a criminal, and I remind myself that I don't know this for 100% yet, then he's the type who's good at fighting and violence. Or even the type who's not very good at anything much, given the police are looking for him.

So, even though there's no way I can know for sure, I decide it's unlikely that Tucker will have realized the computer is a trap. So I take a deep breath, and I unlock the front door.

* * *

Tucker is in the kitchen. I didn't expect that. He's standing next to the stove stirring something in a big saucepan. He turns around to look at me, his face impassive. I can't tell anything from it.

My computer is still on the kitchen table, but it's not where I left it. It's been moved to the end. The space where it was has been laid for dinner.

"Finally," Tucker says. "I was going to eat without you." He ladles up a spoonful of something red and lets it slop back down. If he's angry at me trying to trap him, he's hiding it well.

"I hope you like spicy shit." He flashes a smile, but it's only a half smile, just a flash of those yellow incisors and he goes back to looking – I dunno, it's a funny look. I don't know what it means.

I still haven't moved from the front door.

"Come on Billy. Take a goddamn pew. I wanna eat."

I don't move, except to look at my computer again. The lid is shut – I left it open, to look as inviting as possible, with the screen unlocked and the power plugged in, so that it would sit there, tempting him to use it.

"Tell me something. You have a good day at school? You giving the teachers shit? Talk to me."

I glance up at him, and notice how he was following my gaze. I'm not 100% sure, but I think he looks guilty for a moment.

"Come on kid. Sit down."

I don't have a choice, so I do what he says. Then I watch him as he goes to the refrigerator.

"You wanna beer? I won't tell your old man."

"I don't like beer."

Tucker shrugs and takes one for himself. Then he kicks the refrigerator door shut, grabs two plates and serves up two enormous portions of rice and the stuff he was stirring. It turns out to be beans with tomatoes. He sets one down in front of me, and then sits down opposite me. I wonder if he's going to try and make small talk, but instead he just starts eating, shoveling the food in fast. I try a little bit of the sauce, and though it's really spicy, it is actually quite nice. So I start to eat properly. Though what I really want to do is get my computer upstairs and see if my trap's worked.

"You hear anything from your old man?" Tucker asks after a few minutes. I look up and see he's finished already.

"No."

"You know whereabouts he is?"

This question could be a kind of test. I left the *VesselTrack* app on my laptop. Is this his way of letting me know he's seen it?

"No. Not really." I go back to my food. It's actually very nice. You wouldn't think someone like Tucker could cook so well.

"He told me where he was going. It sounds a long way, but it ain't really. And the weather's good. Better out there than here." I don't answer him. But I glance up at his face, and he gives me another half smile. I look back down again.

"You like sports?" He says suddenly.

"Pardon?"

"Sports. Football? Basketball? I dunno, *badminton*? You like it?"

"Oh. No. Not much."

Tucker chuckles.

"You're not such big talker are you Billy?" Tucker says, and again I don't say anything.

"Like your Dad I guess. He was always the strong silent type. Maybe that's what your mom saw in him. She came from a family of big talkers. Real flash bunch. You're lucky you take after him, you ask me."

I move another forkful of the food up to my mouth, but this time I don't taste it. I've never met anyone, other than Dad, who actually *knew* my mom. In a way I'd like to find out more about her. But this is hardly the time to ask.

Then there's a beep from my phone. It's the noise it makes when a message comes in. I slip it out and look at the screen, and straight away I see it's from Amber. Obviously I can't read it at the table with Tucker looking on.

"This is important," I say to Tucker, making sure he can't see the screen. "I need to..."

"Sure," he says. He inclines his head, like he's telling me it's OK to leave.

"It's just something from..." I stop quickly, annoyed at myself. I don't need to tell Tucker who it is, but now I've started I have to finish the sentence.

"From school," I say. It sounds a bit lame.

"No bother. You go. I'll clean up here." He leans back in his chair and beats his chest with his fists, like he's a gorilla or something. Quickly I take another couple of mouthfuls, and then put the fork down. I stuff my phone back into my pocket and pick up my computer. I'm about to head upstairs when I remember my manners.

"Thanks," I say. "For the food."

"Anytime kid. I told your old man I'd look after you didn't I?"

* * *

As soon as I get into my room I open my laptop. It doesn't ask for a password, but I type one in anyway. It's a secret password. It stops the software I installed last night from working. Then I get to work, opening the programs and scanning down the results.

Right away I can tell that I've got some results. My computer was used while I was at school. My trap worked.

TWENTY

THINGS CHANGE PRETTY FAST after that.

I put two different types of software onto my laptop. The first was something called *SpyCatch*. What it does is secretly record everything that happens to your computer. Every time someone uses the keyboard, it turns on the webcam and starts recording. Only there's nothing to tell the person using it that the webcam is on. It does it secretly. It doesn't even turn on the little red light. If you're using the computer, you'd never know that you're being recorded the whole time.

That's what I look at first. I open *Spycatch,* and it has a list of the videos it's made during the day, along with the time it made them. The first is at 08:47. I have to catch the school bus at 08:30. That means Tucker must have got up and used my laptop less than fifteen minutes after I went to school.

I *knew* it.

I click the file, and wait while the video player loads. Then there's a sudden image of Tucker, leaning in close to the computer. Actually seeing him there takes my breath away too. He *really did steal* my computer. And if I'm right about that, then maybe I'm right about everything else as well. I suddenly feel exposed, with him downstairs, and no lock on my bedroom door. So before I hit play I get up and drag my wooden chest in front of the door of my bedroom, just so there no chance that he can surprise me by walking into my room, and see what I'm doing. Then I plug in some head-phones, so he can't hear me either, and I sit back down to watch.

Tucker doesn't have a top on, I can see his tattoos and his muscles. He's sitting down at the breakfast table, frowning at something just below the screen. It takes me a while to figure out that he's frowning at the keyboard. He must be trying to type, only he has to look at the keys when he does so. This makes me a lot more confident that whatever type of criminal he is, it's not the computer expert type.

I don't know what he's typing from looking at *SpyCatch,* but I've got that covered for later. Now I just keep watching, and for a long while he stares back at me through the screen. I can see his eyes moving left to right, so I guess he's reading something. I can see his lips move too.

Then suddenly he gets up. It's hard to tell, but he looks angry when he does it. Something about the way he pushes himself back from the table. Then he's out of the frame for a long time, and I'm about to fast forward the file when he comes back. He sits again, but he keeps shaking his head. Then there's this really long section of the recording where he's got his head in his hands. And then he's rubbing his face all over, covering his eyes. When I next see them, there's a moment when it looks like he's actually crying.

But then things go crazy. He starts swearing. I can hear it so loud I panic, but then I remember it's only in the headphones. I won't say the word, but he uses it over and over and over. It's the one beginning with F. He shouts it really loud.

And then there's a couple of minutes where he leaves the chair again. And then when he's back I see right away he's holding his cell phone. I snap to attention.

He's calmed down now. He just sits there, staring at the phone – not like he's using it, more like he's thinking about using it, because I can see it's still switched off. Every now and then his thumb hovers over the button, like he wants to turn it on, but something's stopping him.

Bang!

Then there's a moment that makes me literally jump. Real suddenly he slams the phone down against the edge of the table. It must have made the laptop jump too, because the image suddenly changes, like the screen got knocked and the angle of the camera changed. Now it shows the door of the kitchen, and I can't see Tucker. But then I can. Because the next thing I see is Tucker walking through the door, outside.

I'm baffled by this. He's still got no top on, just a pair of jeans, so he can't be going out for the day. I'm about to fast forward again, but then he comes back in. The next thing is the laptop is suddenly slammed shut, and the recording ends.

I rewind a bit and watch it again. This time I try to focus on whether he's carrying anything as he walks out of the kitchen. It's hard to tell for sure, but it looks as though he has something black in his hand – the cell phone. And it's definitely clear when he comes back that he's not holding it – I get a clear view of his hands as he walks up to the laptop to close it.

So then I minimize SpyCatch and think. For years now I've had a weather station mounted outside my bedroom window. It also has a camera that pointed down at the beach, and everything was linked to the internet so that people could actually find out the weather and actually see the surfing conditions on Silverlea beach, before they drove down from Newlea. But it wasn't a very good camera, it only took one picture every hour, and then some water got into the lens after a storm, so that the image was all misty. So about a year ago I bought a better camera on eBay, one that records actual video. You're supposed to be able to log in from anywhere in the world and see the view from outside my bedroom window, in real time, and high definition. The problem is, the camera was second hand, and I couldn't find any instructions for how to set it up, so I never managed to get it to connect to the internet. I did set it up though, the camera had the same bracket as the previous one, so it's outside, actually recording right now.

So I go onto my other computer and I log in, then I rewind the recording all the way to 08:47 yesterday, and I'm a little bit surprised to see there's an image there. Nothing happens for a while, it's just the normal view of the clifftop, Dad's truck, and the beach below. But then, at 08:56:12 Tucker suddenly emerges into the frame. He's quite small, since the camera is zoomed out, but it's obviously him. He goes out to the front, by the cliff edge. He stands there for a second or two, and then he pulls his shoulder back, and throws something far out over the edge of the cliff.

You can't see what he throws from the image – it's too small. But I already know what it is from the laptop footage inside.

TWENTY-ONE

THE SECOND PIECE of software I installed is called *Keylogger Free*. It's something that logs your keystrokes – that's everything you type into the keyboard – and again it does it secretly so that whoever is typing doesn't know that they're being recorded. If you don't know about key loggers then you definitely should. They're used all the time by computer hackers and cyber criminals. They use them to get people's passwords or bank card numbers. There's a good chance your computer might have one on it right now. You should definitely check. People think that anti-virus software only protects them from viruses, but they also work against key loggers. That's one of the reasons it took me so long time to get everything set up the other night. I had to work out how to stop my own anti-virus system popping up. You do have a good anti-virus don't you? You really should.

Anyway, I look through the results now. It gives me another list of files, and I can click into the box titled 'keystrokes' and I can see exactly what Tucker has typed.

At 08:47 twelve seconds Tucker typed this:

Hounds Beach Classics Jewelry Store secrity guard

Then he deleted the word *'secrity'* and changed it to *'security'*.

Then he didn't type anything for a long time. I guess this was when he was reading. When he next typed it was this:

"Adam Smith security guard Classics Jewelry"

Keylogger doesn't have any pictures or anything, and I can't see where he typed it – in what program I mean. I would be able to if I had the full

Keylogger software, but this is only the free trial version, and some of the features are restricted. But it's pretty obvious that he was searching online. So I copy what he typed and then go to Google and paste it.

I hit search. There's over 3 million search results. For a moment I think I'm going to have the same problem as before, not knowing which page to load. But then I notice something, right there on the first page of the search results, a few of the links are in a different color. You know the color that internet links change to when you've already looked at them? So it turns out I can see exactly which links Tucker clicked. The first one he looked at is from the *Western Enquirer* newspaper. I've never heard of it, but when I click it this is what it says:

Security Guard Killed in Armed Raid

A father of two died tonight after being shot three times during an armed raid on a Hounds Beach jewelry store. The raid took place on Tuesday morning, at Classics Jewelers, a family owned store which has been trading over 50 years. It's believed a masked man holding a pistol entered the store and demanded items from the display cabinets. It's believed Adam Smith, who was employed as the store's security guard, then challenged the raider, who opened fire. Mr. Smith was shot three times, dying later in hospital. The store has issued a statement confirming it was attacked this morning, and that it will be closed until further notice. It also offers its condolences to Mr. Smith and his family, and states that everyone involved is praying for him.

I stop reading. I check the date. The robbery happened two weeks ago. I think for a minute, then I read the whole thing again.

It all fits. It's pretty clear.

I do another google search, this time for *Hounds Beach*. I've never heard of it, but it turns out to be a little town about thirty miles up the coast from Crab Creek. That's the town where Dad comes from. And where Tucker comes from too. Where he was living until two weeks ago, when he turned up here.

I go back to Tucker's search, and read the rest of the links – they're all newspapers or news sites, and the only thing he reads on them are articles about that robbery.

I think about calling the police. I could add my bed to the barricade of the door, so that there's no way Tucker can get in before they arrive. But then I realize I can't call them. Because of Dad. The police will want to know how come he's away, and how come he left me alone in the house with a murderer. So instead I make sure I've got all the evidence saved and backed up, and I think about what to do next. Pretty quickly I get an idea.

TWENTY-TWO

Obviously I spend the rest of the evening in my room, it's not safe to go downstairs with Tucker.

Slowly it dawns on me that I'm going to need proper evidence. I can prove that Tucker read a newspaper article about a robbery, but that doesn't prove he was the robber. And even my video of him throwing his phone off the cliff doesn't *prove* anything. It's not illegal to throw away a cell phone. Except for littering.

But if I could find his phone. Then I'd have evidence. Real evidence.

The cliff here at Littlelea is 60 meters high, but it's only the bottom part that's completely vertical. At the top, you can climb down a little way and there's lots of little ledges where bits of grass grow and birds nest. You shouldn't though, because it gets steeper and steeper, and if you slip there's nothing to stop you falling all the way down to the beach. Sometimes it happens to sheep. You never see them fall, but I find them on the beach, dead with all their bones broken.

I watch the video of Tucker throwing his phone, and I try to work out exactly where it might have landed. You'd think he'd have a good throw, but he doesn't stand right by the edge, presumably because he's worried about falling over. And he throws it at an angle, maybe to get it more out to sea. So after he releases it there's a moment when he leans forward – as if he's waiting for the splash – but it doesn't come.

Then I notice it's two in the morning, and I decide I had better go to bed.

* * *

In the morning, I have a really good idea.

I go downstairs like any normal morning. Tucker is still asleep in the lounge, and it feels weird to know he's a murderer and I'm alone in the house with him. But I try not to think about it. I have breakfast, I feed Steven and then I make it look as if I'm going to catch the school bus, just like a normal morning. But instead of putting Steven back in my room, I take his box outside. Tucker is awake by now, so I shout to him that I'm going to school, but instead of going down the lane to get the bus, I grab Steven and carry him in the opposite direction, along the coast path to the beach. When I'm well out of sight from the house, I open the box and lift him out.

Steven is quite tame now, so there's no danger of him flying off and not coming back. In fact I'm more worried that when he does have to fly away he won't want too. Right now he just stands in front of me, stretching his wings and waiting for me to throw pieces of fish up in the air for him to catch. But I don't do that.

Instead I pull my cell phone out of my pocket, and show it to Steven. I let him have a good look, tipping his brown head onto one side, and inspecting it with one eye. He pecks at it gently.

"*That's it Steven,*" I tell him.

Then, when he starts to lose interest, I pick up the phone, and I pretend to throw it. And then quickly I hide the phone behind my back, so that Steven doesn't know where it is. He looks a bit confused for a second, but then he goes back to staring at me and squawking a little bit.

"*Find it!*" I say. But Steven ignores me. So I try again. Getting him interested in the phone, and then pretending to throw it along the cliff. This time Steven just holds his head on one side and watches me, like he thinks I've gone mad.

I try again, this time smearing a little of fish paste onto the back of my phone. We keep some for when Dad isn't able to get fresh fish from the harbor. This makes Steven a lot more interested. At first he pecks at the phone enthusiastically, and then he looks affronted at me when I throw it away.

It lands a couple of meters away, on a tuft of grass. Steven continues looking at me for a moment, then walks over to the phone and starts pecking it again, scraping little beak-fulls of paste every time.

"*Bring it here, come on Steven. Bring it back.*" I pull out a small fish from the Tupperware box in my bag, and hold it out to Steven. At once he flies back to me to take it, but I shake my head.

"*Uh huh. Bring the phone.*" Steven tries to prize his beak into my closed fist, but I don't let him, and instead I go to the phone and point at it.

"*First the phone. Then the fish.*"

I don't know if you've ever trained a herring gull, but you do need a lot of patience. It takes me an hour of this before he does what I want, picking up the phone in his beak and flying it back to me. I give him loads of praise, and he hops up and down squawking, and flapping a fish up and down in his beak before tipping his head back and swallowing it. And maybe an hour after that, I've got him reliably flying after my phone when I toss it away, then bringing it back, and dropping it, before I feed him a fish.

So then I move onto the next part of my plan. I pick up my phone, and this time I *pretend* to throw it. But I don't really. I just pretend that it's gone in the direction that I saw Tucker throw his phone on the video. And this time I hide my phone properly, slipping it into my jacket pocket and zipping it closed.

"Come on Steven! Find it. *Find it!*" I call, and I shoo him away up into the air. For a few moments he just beats at the air around my head, but I keep waving him away with my arms. Eventually he gets the idea and takes off properly, but he just starts to glide back and forth above me, riding the air currents rising up the cliff face. Again I wave towards where Tucker's phone must be, out on the steeper part of the cliff. But Steven won't go there. He just circles above me, and then after a while he lands and watches me.

After another hour I give up. Apart from anything else, I've run out of fish. So I walk back up the cliff path. I slow near the top, but as soon as I can see the house I can see that Dad's truck's gone. That's good, because it means Tucker must have gone out somewhere. So that means I'm able to go to the top of the cliff, at the spot where Tucker threw his phone from, and get a better sense of where it might have landed.

I stand there for a while. I consider throwing my phone down, trying to recreate Tucker's throw, this time with Steven watching? But I've kind of lost faith in Steven a bit, so I don't do that.

Instead I go to the storage shed we have in the yard, and I dig around until I find some rope. There's a length I salvaged a few years ago, after some fishing tackle got washed up on the rocks at the other side of the headland. It took ages, but I managed to recover about forty meters of it, only I haven't known what to do with it since, so it just sat in the shed.

Now I tie one end carefully around our gatepost, giving it a good tug to make sure it's solid. Then I put knots in the rest of the rope so it's easier to climb. Then I toss the open end down the cliff so that it disappears out of sight. And then, with Steven still watching me, I begin to climb down towards where Tucker must have thrown the phone.

I get about five meters down when I wish I had some sort of harness. It's not the effort of holding my weight, it's because my hands start to get sweaty from nerves, and I realize that, if they slip on the rope, there would be nothing to stop me falling, and I'd end up like one of those sheep. But I force myself to go on, because I've started now.

Slowly I lower myself down, stepping on the ledges in the cliff face, or just leaning back against the earth. A few times I dislodge loose bits of mud and stones, and they tumble away below me, some getting caught on other ledges and some disappearing over the edge. It makes my hands feel even more sweaty.

There's a big ledge about five meters below me, and I aim to get there, thinking it might be where the phone ended up. I pay out more and more rope, telling myself to keep gripping it, because my hands are getting more slippery all the time. Eventually I get there, and I can relax a little. I look around at my feet, searching for the black plastic of a phone, embedded somewhere in the grass, but I can't see it. Eventually I know I'll have to go lower.

But as I do, stepping off the ledge, I realize I've been stupid. Looking above me I can't see anything except the cliff, so I can't keep check on the house and when Tucker is coming back. It's a horrible thought. He could be there already, at the top of the cliff looking at this rope stretching out from the gatepost and leading out over the cliff edge. If he is, he's gonna know right away that it's me, because no one else ever comes to this part of the cliff, not since the footpath was closed. And he's gonna know exactly what I'm doing too, because obviously he knows he threw his phone down, and he knows it got stuck in the cliff, so he'll work out I'm looking for it.

And if he works that out, he'll know I know he's a criminal. And worst of all, I'm giving a really easy way to stop me. All he has to do is cut the rope.

I try to convince myself this is crazy – if he cuts the rope I'll fall and I'll die. And surely he wouldn't actually murder me? But the more I think about it, the more worrying the answer is. He was prepared to murder a security guard to get away when he robbed the jeweler's, so what's the difference between that and murdering me? And my death wouldn't even look like murder. People would think I was counting nest sites or something like that, and just slipped.

I get this sudden strong urge that all I want to do is pull myself back up the cliff face *right away*, and get away from the drop that's hanging beneath me. My hands sweat more, and the feel the rope slippery under my fingers. I try to calm myself, and move a few steps up, to a another mini ledge where I can take some of the weight off my hands. I try to slow my breathing. I look down at my feet, I scan the ledge, hoping against hope that maybe I'll find the phone here, so I can get off the cliff face. But there's nothing there but the scrappy rock-nests of terns and a few tufts of grass. I don't really care. I just want to get out of here.

Then I feel the rope move, like someone has grabbed it higher up.

TWENTY-THREE

Right away I start to panic. I can feel the vibrations from the serrated blade Tucker's using to saw through the rope. The ledge I'm standing on isn't wide enough for me to cling on to without the rope, and I flail around a bit pulling myself back up to the wider one, just above my head. But as I do so, I see what the real problem is. It's Steven, he's flown down to see what I'm doing and he's actually landed on the rope. The vibrations are him moving his wings up and down to keep his balance. I freeze, and feel it for a while. Steven settles, and pecks at the rope a couple of times. I feel how it makes the rope move. It's not Tucker at the top, the movement on the rope is just Steven.

I flick the rope, to dislodge him, and when he's flying around me again, skimming along the cliff face in the air, I feel the rope very carefully, just to be sure. It's not moving any more.

"Stupid bird," I call out. "If you want to be helpful, why don't you go and check Dad's truck's not there?" But he just peeps at me, and glides past my head with his wings outstretched.

But after my scare I start to gain a bit more confidence. Now I'm near the bottom of the rope I work out that I can wrap it around my body, and it works as a kind of harness. As long as I don't let go, it takes my weight quite well. I discover I can even traverse to the left and right, moving in little arcs, and covering more of the cliff face as I do it. And doing that I lower myself right to the limit of the rope, right before where the cliff goes fully vertical. And that's when I see it. On the final ledge before the cliff drops away to the rocks below I can see a Samsung Galaxy S9. It's the right way up, with the screen totally shattered.

I go to lower myself the last few steps to pick it up, but I can't quite get there. I've run out of rope. I try unwinding it from my body, but even holding the very end of the rope, I can't reach the phone. I'd have to let go completely, and if I did that there would be nothing to prevent me tumbling the rest of the way down. The tide is in below me, but I wouldn't hit the water, I'd fall straight onto rocks.

I look down now, seeing the jagged fringe of granite, like teeth, and then the blue of the calm ocean. I swallow.

I wonder if I can hold on with just one hand, and reach below me to pick up the phone. I don't want to, my hands are sweaty again now, but I force myself to do it. I bend down and slide my other hand along the cliff face, feeling my way down the rock and earth. But it's no good. I'm still too high.

I try to reach with my foot instead, and this time I get within a couple of meters of the phone, but no closer. I'm beginning to feel super frustrated when Steven suddenly comes in to land on the same ledge as the phone. I guess he got bored flying around watching me.

Effortlessly he steps over to Tucker's phone. He pecks at the screen a couple of times, and then looks at me. I hold my breath, hardly able to watch.

"*Come on Stevie. Get it boy.*"

He pecks at it again. With his beak he carefully lifts it up, and turns it over. As he does so he pushes it almost to the edge.

"*Careful boy. Just pick it up.*"

But then he seems to lose interest. Instead he lifts up one of his legs, pulls it into the softer feathers around his belly, and closes one eye.

"*Steven!*" I shout at him, and he wakes again. And then I pretend I've got fish on me. I pat the pocket of my jacket. Steven looks interested.

"Come on boy, get the phone."

All that training definitely taught him to do something, but he's not sure what it is I want him to do. I wish I could speak better Herring Gull. I pat my pocket again. I point at the phone, and eventually he moves back to it, and paws at it with one claw.

"*Grab it!*"

Then Steven fianally does what I've asked. He gently grips the phone in his beak, it nearly slides out at first, but he gets it balanced, then tips his head back. Then he stretches out his wings, and before I can stop him, he takes off, right out away from the cliff edge.

He gets about five meters before it slips out from his beak and tumbles down. Steven arcs down after it at once, trying to snatch it out of the air, but he just ends up clattering into it. The phone spins further out from the cliff face and moments later splashes into the sea. For a second I hope Steven might dive in after it. Or it might float, but neither of those things happens. Instead there's nothing left except the mirror calm surface of the water, interrupted only by a small, growing ring of ripples where the phone disappeared.

TWENTY-FOUR

I CLIMB BACK up the rope to find Steven waiting for me at the top. I feel like shouting at him, but there's no point. And at least there's still no sign of Tucker. I pull up all the rope and put it back in my shed. And I find my goggles.

Then I climb all the way down the old cliff path to the sea. The tide's high, but it's a totally calm day. I clamber out on the rocks along the edge of the cliff base until I'm right below where I was just climbing. Then I strip off my clothes, and I slip into the sea.

I used to be really scared of the water. I could swim – Dad made sure of that – but I didn't much like it. I wouldn't go into any water except the swimming pool, and only then because there were lifeguards and I could touch the bottom the whole time. And it all got made worse when Dad was trying to teach me to surf, and I got confused, and thought he was actually trying to murder me. I had these therapy sessions after that, and they told me it was all linked to what happened when I was a baby, when my mom tried to drown me. I don't think the therapist helped much, but even so, I like the water now – swimming and diving. You can't really be a marine biologist and *not* like the water. It's kind of where it all happens.

I swim out now, with my goggles in my hair. I try to put myself right at the spot where the phone hit the water. It's hard to be exact, even though I took bearings, and even though I know the rocks really well. When I get to where I think the phone will be I put the goggles down over my eyes and duck my head under the water.

I'm lucky it's such a clear day. When there's a swell it churns up the sand and you can't see more than a few meters under the water, but now it's been flat for a couple of days, and the visibility is good. I can see all the way to the bottom, four or five meters down. The rocks and the sand are bathed in greeny blue sunlight. I take a deep breath and kick down for the bottom.

A couple of bass watch me as I descend. I reach out and grab hold of a rock. I didn't use to like touching things underwater, I felt like they were going to grab me and hold me down, but now I'm OK about it. Even long strands of seaweed that look like they're going to wrap around your feet, I know it's just plants. Underwater plants.

I hold onto the rock now. I look around. The water is cold down here, different to how it feels at the surface, where it's warmed by the sun. I feel my hair caught in the water as I look from side to side. I spot something on the sea floor, on a patch of sand. I swim over to it, but I run out of air, and I have to surface again before I can get to it.

My lungs hurt when I get to the top, and I have to float for a little while, getting my breath back before I'm ready to dive again. But then I take another big breath, and I push my head back under the water. I pull myself down with strong strokes. I have to hold my nose half way down and blow out hard, to equalize the pressure in my ears.

But this time I make it all the way to the bottom, and there in front of me is Tucker's Samsung Galaxy S9 phone. I grip it in my hands, making sure I'm not going to drop it like Steven did. And then I kick off from the bottom and leave a stream of bubbles flowing out of my nose as I coast back to the surface.

* * *

I swim back to the rocks, and clamber slowly out. I dry myself with a towel. I'm kinda frustrated with how much effort that took, but at the same time I'm quite pleased with my day's work. Then I carry the phone back to my bedroom.

The glass back and screen are totally shattered, and there's a couple of scuffs in the aluminum part too. I don't even bother trying to turn it on. There's no way it's going to work. Instead I pull open the drawer and rummage around until I find a paper clip. Then I press in the button to release the SIM card tray, and it pops out right away. And then I give a really broad smile.

Do you remember I told you I saw a documentary on cell phones? It talked about how most US cell phones don't use SIM cards because they use the CDMA network. That means all the data gets stored on the phone itself. So if the phone gets broken – like, for example, smashed against a table and thrown down a cliff into the sea – then all the data on the phone would be lost. But some phones, notably T-Mobile and AT&T use a different cell network called GSM. GSM phones store all the information on a little electronic chip that you slot into the phone called a SIM card. And on these phones it doesn't matter how damaged the phone gets, because all the information is on the SIM.

Tucker's phone is T-Mobile. And the SIM is still there.

TWENTY-FIVE

"BILLY! Where the hell have you been?"

I'm just stepping off the bus, outside school and I can't actually *get* off because Amber is standing there at the stop, yelling at me. There's something different about her too. I takes me a moment to work out what. Then I see it. Her hair isn't blue anymore. It's a kind of rich, dark red. I quite like it actually.

"I've been calling, messaging. Trying to get you on Skype. You wouldn't answer anything." She stares at me. I open my mouth to reply but don't know what to say. Eventually she moves enough so that I can climb down off the bus.

"Where were you yesterday?" she follows me now. "You weren't at school."

I didn't tell you, but I had to switch my cell phone off yesterday, when I was trying to train Steven, because Amber kept messaging me and making the phone beep. It was putting Steven off. I try to walk past her, but she falls into step beside me.

"Did you even get my messages?"

I try to keep looking dead ahead, but there's no way to escape her.

"I've been busy..."

"*Busy?* Doing what? How can you be *busy*?" Suddenly she stops, and when I don't do the same she grabs my shoulder so I have to.

"Hey, you didn't get another case did you? One you're not telling me about?"

"What do you mean?"

"From the agency. You didn't take my email off the website? You didn't get someone else to give you a case?"

"No." I screw up my eyes. It's actually quite a good idea, to remove her email. Just in case another email does come in. I thought about taking the whole site down, but Amber would see that and she'd go mental about it.

"Course not."

Amber stares at me suspiciously for a few moments. "You better not. We're partners, you know that?"

I kind of half-nod my head.

"I have to go to class."

"Fuck class, we have to go to work."

It's really hard to get used to the language Amber uses.

"I can't... I can't *not go* to class."

"Yes you can. What class is it?"

"Geography. With Mr. Parker."

"Mr. Parker's a fucking moron. You can skip it. Come on."

And so, without me really meaning to, I find myself turning around and following Amber in the complete opposite direction to the school. There's quite a few other students still arriving, and I feel like they all must be staring at me. But no one says anything, and soon we're around the corner and out of sight.

"Where are we going?"

"Smithsons."

I wait for her to explain further, but she doesn't.

"What's Smithsons?"

"I told you. I messaged you." Amber replies, and then she doesn't say anymore, she just walks really fast so that I can't keep up with her.

"Well can you remind me?" I ask, when I've caught up.

"You did read them didn't you?"

"Of course."

"Well then."

She's still walking really fast.

"Could you maybe remind me? Just a little bit."

Amber stops, but just for a second. Then she sighs.

"You're unbelievable Wheatley. Smithsons is the auto garage at the end of Main Street. It's been there for years." Amber turns to start walking again. But I stop her.

"So why are we going there?" I wonder if maybe she's crashed her mom's car. I wouldn't be surprised.

"We're going to speak to Gerry Smithson."

"OK. Why?"

"I thought you said you read my messages?"

"I maybe missed one. Or two. I've had some... Issues."

This causes Amber to stop for a second time.

"What does that mean?" She cocks her head to one side. It kind of reminds me of Steven, when he thinks I might be holding a fish behind my back.

"Nothing."

She keeps looking at me.

"Do you want me to read them now?" I ask this just to stop her looking at me like that.

"Fuck it. Read 'em later. For now just listen." Then she starts walking again, just as fast as before.

I have to half run to keep up with her.

"I figured something. If Henry Jacobs was the headmaster of Newlea High School back in 1979, then there must be plenty of people who were *in* the school at the time. Students I mean. And they might remember him, and what happened to him."

I think about this for a moment. It makes sense.

"So I worked it out, we need people who were aged between 13 and 17, forty years ago. So that would make them 53 to 57 today. And then I searched on Facebook for people who've put down their school as Newlea High School, and with a date of birth between 1963 and 1967." She looks at me and waits, like she knows I'm going to check the math. I quickly work it out, then I nod.

"Only, you can't *actually* do that, as you probably know – since Facebook doesn't show you people's ages." She gives me a smug grin.

"But even so, you can get a pretty good idea from how old people look. So then I started messaging everyone I could find who looked the right age and attended Newlea High School. I asked them if they remembered their school principal Henry Jacobs, or knew anyone who did. And Gerry Smithson, from the garage on Main Street, got back to me and said he remembered him. So that's why we're going to see him. OK?"

I do my best to process all this.

"OK."

"Good."

The garage isn't far, so even though I've got a bunch of other questions to ask Amber, I don't get the chance to ask them.

· · ·

Smithson's garage is just off the road, behind a set of bright blue gates. There's a double-width opening to the workshop itself, through bright blue doors, where a couple of cars are lifted up in the air. There's music playing from a radio somewhere, and a man in greasy blue overalls is leaning into the engine bay of a battered looking sedan. Since this is Amber's idea, I let her take the lead.

"Are you Gerry Smithson?" She asks.

"Yeah." He's got his hands deep in the engine, but somehow also a roll up between his lips. "What you want?"

"I'm Amber. I sent you the Facebook message."

Mr. Smithson narrows his eyes. He looks confused.

"The detective?"

"That's right."

His frown deepens.

"You look older. On the computer."

Amber smiles at this, but the man doesn't. "Thanks," she says.

Mr. Smithson doesn't move. I'm not sure he meant it as a compliment.

"You said you remembered Henry Jacobs, from when you were at school? You said you wouldn't mind meeting? To speak about it."

Still Mr. Smithson hasn't moved, his hands are still in the engine.

"What the hell is this? Some kind of kid's project?"

Amber glances at me, then swings her bag off her shoulder. She roots around for a moment and then pulls out a small rectangular card. She glances at me again, and then holds it up so that Mr. Smithson can see. I have to lean forward to see what's on it.

"Not at all. As I said, we work for the Lornea Island Detective Agency. We're investigating the disappearance of one Henry Jacobs in 1979. You said you might be able to help."

It's a proper business card, and she's put the logo from the website in the middle. Below that is her name. It says:

Amber Atherton
Senior Investigator

Gerry Smithson looks from the card to Amber and then back again. Then he looks at me as well and I can tell how confused he is. I'm quite confused as well, but I try to keep it off my face.

"You said you remember Henry Jacobs?" Amber goes on. "He would have been the principal of Newlea High School from 1973 to 1979. You said you were a student there at the time?"

Finally Mr. Smithson takes his hands out of the engine and walks away to a bench. It's littered with oily tools and bits of car engines. He picks up a rag and wipes his hand. Then he turns back to Amber.

"Yeah I remember him."

Amber bites her lip and tries not to look excited.

"Could you tell us what happened to him?" She asks. But Mr. Smithson just frowns for a bit, then shrugs.

"Far as I know, nothing happened to him."

"But he stopped being the principal? A woman took over instead. She was called Mrs. Clarke?"

Still Mr. Smithson wipes his hands. Finally he shrugs again. "If you say so. I don't remember her. It was a long time ago." He stops, and I think that's all he has to say, but then he continues. "But I do remember Jacobs." He doesn't go on, doesn't explain the look he gives us.

"What do you remember about him? Was there something... memorable?" Amber asks.

I still haven't said a single word since we got here, and maybe Mr. Smithson wonders about this now, since he looks at me again. He's still holding Amber's card and he studies it again.

"So are you two like..." He hesitates, sounding really unsure now. "Look what's this about? This kid is way too young to work for any detective agency."

Without hesitation Amber replies. "Do you remember the case of Olivia Curran, the tourist girl who was murdered two years ago?"

He looks at Amber, confused. "Yeah, I remember."

"My colleague here may look immature, he I can assure you he was absolutely instrumental in solving that case." Amber pauses and looks to me, like maybe I should say something. But I don't know what to say, so I just nod in what I hope is a meaningful way.

"And since then he has solved many crimes. He is a most able investigator."

I look very serious and do some more nodding.

Now Mr. Smithson looks like he thinks he doesn't know if Amber is being serious or pranking him. But in the end he settles on the former, or maybe he just decides he wants to get rid of us as quickly as possible.

"How old would the guy be now?"

"Who?"

"Jacobs."

Amber takes an age to work it out, so I tell him.

"Seventy two."

At first I'm not sure if Mr. Smithson hears me, because he doesn't reply at once. And when he does it's to Amber again.

"And is he... Look is this..." He drops his voice, I suppose trying to make it so that only Amber hears him.

"Is he still *doing it*? At that age? Is that why the kid's here?"

Me and Amber look at each other.

"What do you mean? Doing what?" Amber says at last.

Mr. Smithson stares at us.

"Nothing." He turns away.

"Mr. Smithson, whatever it is you're trying to tell us, we need to know." Amber sounds really anxious now, like she's dying to hear him say something. But Mr. Smithson just looks from one of us to the other. I have to admit, I don't really know what's going on.

Finally Mr. Smithson speaks again.

"You swear you're nothing to do with the police? I don't want no trouble with this."

"No." Amber shakes her head firmly. "Absolutely not. You can tell us anything in the strictest confidence. We'll just use it for deep background." She gives him another smile, but it doesn't seem to settle him much.

"Look I ain't sure I wanna say this. It was a long time ago..."

"*What* was a long time ago Mr. Smithson?" Amber's eyes have gone really wide, her whole face pleading with him.

"Tell us Mr. Smithson. Please. What you have to say could be incredibly important."

He looks around again. Like he's hoping there's some way he can get away from this girl who's staring at him with her big doleful eyes, but she's leaning in close, hanging on every word.

"It didn't happen to me, right? Nothing happened to me. I just knew about it. *Everyone* knew about it."

"Knew about what?" Amber asks. "What did everyone know about?"

He puffs out his cheeks, than shakes his head.

"Jesus. I can't believe I'm saying this. It was forty years ago. What you want to go digging all this up for?" He takes a deep breath, but Amber is relentless.

"Please Mr. Smithson. It's important. We're working for someone connected to Henry Jacobs. They're desperate to discover what happened to him. Telling us is the right thing to do. Whatever you're still feeling, it'll help."

He laughs at this, but it comes out more of a cough.

"I don't need no *help*. I ain't even thought about school in forty years.

And I sure don't see why I should be bringing it up now. Specially not to a pair who look like they should still be in school themselves..." He glances over at me as he says this. I get the sense he's not going to say anything now.

Mr. Smithson looks away and exhales slowly. But then he seems to come to a decision.

"Alright. But you didn't hear any of this from me, OK?"

"Absolutely. Of course." She makes a zipping sign across her lips, and he watches her, blank faced.

"Whatever." He starts to walk back to the car he was fixing when we came in.

"When I was in high school, Principal Jacobs had a reputation. That's what I remember. People said he liked his students a bit too much. The boys."

"What do you mean?" I'm really surprised to hear that it's me who's asked this question. And I think Mr. Smithson is too because he looks up at me for a moment. Then he continues.

"You say you're detectives. They used to call him 'Handsy Henry'. You fucking figure it out."

TWENTY-SIX

"Wow I wasn't expecting *that*!" Amber says as soon as we're far enough from the garage so that Mr. Smithson can't hear us.

"You know what he means don't you? By liking boys. It means he *messed around* with them. Interfered with them. Fucking hell! This is *massive*."

I don't answer.

"It means he was a pedophile Billy. This changes everything."

Still I don't reply.

"So what do we do now? Do we go back to Mrs. Jacobs and tell her? That her husband was a kiddie-fiddler? Do you reckon she'll still pay us?" She's walking fast again, and we're half way back to school already.

"I mean we've still got the check right? The 5000 dollars? We can still cash that?"

I don't reply.

"Billy? What do you think?"

Reluctantly I answer her.

"I think we have to be careful."

She spins to look at me. "What do you mean by that." But I hesitate. I don't know how to say this.

"We don't *know* he was a pedophile. We only know Mr. Smithson *heard* that he was. It's not the same thing."

"Course we do. Why would Smithson say so otherwise?"

I screw up my face, trying to make sense of this. I can't work out why I'm feeling anxious about this. Then I remember.

"I made a mistake. Once before." I begin.

Amber waits, her face screwed up into a deep frown.

"When I started investigating that murdered girl, there was this guy that used to hang around in Silverlea. He had a limp, and people thought he was a pedophile. And I just assumed he was too. And I thought that meant he was the murderer too. But it turned out he wasn't. And he wasn't even a pedophile. People just thought he was because of how he looked. So we have to be careful. That's all."

Amber doesn't reply to this, but I can see her thinking it over.

"OK." She nods, and we start walking again, in silence this time.

"Did you like the card?" Amber says after a while.

I shrug.

"I got them printed on the internet. I thought they might help convince people we're serious."

"It's alright." I can feel my face is still tight where I'm scowling.

"It was a good idea wasn't it?"

I shrug again.

"Did you like the design? Did you think it was alright?"

Honestly, I don't know why she doesn't just drop it.

Suddenly Amber stops dead on the sidewalk, and I take a couple of steps further on before I realize she's not beside me anymore. I turn around to see her rooting around in her bag. Then she pulls out a small box.

"Here you go." She hands it to me, and hesitantly I take it. I pull off the lid, and inside is another stack of business cards. But this time they have a different name on the front.

William Wheatley
Private Investigator

I look up at her. "William?"

"I thought it sounded more serious than Billy."

Amber grins at me, and I realize from my face I'm smiling too.

"You really think I'd forget you?"

I feel quite happy for a few moments, just looking at it. You couldn't tell, that it's not real I mean, because Amber is really good at design.

"They cost $35 dollars. We'll have to take it out of what Mrs. Jacobs pays us. When we've found out what happened to Henry. Which we will."

· · ·

We set off again, and soon we're at the school gate. The only way back in is through the reception hall. Amber sticks her head round the gate to have a look, then pulls back.

"*Shit.* The receptionists are there. We'll have to wait till they go back to their office."

I feel a stab of anxiety, but Amber just leans back on the wall, waiting. She looks totally relaxed.

"Have you ever been caught? Doing this?" I ask after a while.

"Doing what?"

"Skipping class?"

"Not so much these days." She shrugs. I get a strange sense, that maybe she wants me to ask more. But I don't ask.

"Say," Amber says a few moments later. "If Henry *was* messing with kids, isn't that a pretty strong motive for someone to do away with him?" She looks at me and tips her head onto one side.

"I suppose."

"Like an angry parent who discovered what he was up to? Don't you think they might lose control? When they found he was abusing their kid? Maybe *they* killed him?" The light in Amber's eyes is dancing as she says this, and I can tell she half believes it already. I take a deep breath, and try to keep my thoughts clearer.

"Maybe."

I guess that doesn't sound enthusiastic enough for her.

"Come on Billy, you have to admit it's pretty likely?"

"I suppose it's possible," I accept. "But even so. There were hundreds of pupils in the school, and it was forty years ago. I don't see how we can know which ones he was abusing, and who might have found out about it."

Amber looks away, considering. "I suppose we could go to the police," she muses, and right away I start thinking about that too, since I've been considering it to solve my Tucker problem. But that's kinda complicated too, what with Dad still away on the boat...

"But what would we tell them?" Amber goes on. "We don't even know *for sure* that he disappeared. We need more evidence. Something concrete."

Then Amber suddenly reaches over and picks up my hand. I don't have any idea what she's doing, but then she turns my wrist over, and reads the time on my watch. It's weird to be touched like that. I don't like it, but then also, as soon as she lets my wrist go, I wish she was still holding it.

"Come on. It's break time. Let's risk it. Message me if you figure out what to do next."

Without another word she pushes herself off the wall, and strides confidently through the gate. I don't feel anything like so confident, but I follow her anyway.

We get about halfway through the lobby, almost joining the flow of students streaming past towards their next class. But at that moment there's a call from inside the receptionist's office.

"Miss Atherton?"

Amber freezes, but her voice is calm and clear. Unbothered. "Yes?"

One of the receptionists comes out, and I get the sense she's actually been hiding in there, where she knew she couldn't be seen.

"Principal Sharpe has been looking for you. You're to go to her office straight away."

"What for?" Amber doesn't sound so confident now, and the receptionist ignores the question. Instead she turns to me.

"And it's Billy Wheatley isn't it? The Principal would like to speak with you as well."

I glance at Amber, as if I'm somehow expecting she has some secret trick to get us out of this. But of course there isn't anything.

"Well go on then. Now please. She's waiting in her office."

TWENTY-SEVEN

"*Sit down both of you!*" Principal Sharpe says when we get in her office. We didn't have to wait outside this time, we got sent straight in.

She waits until Amber and I have taken a seat each in front of her desk, and then she sits as well, in the much bigger chair on her side. She looks calm, sort of. But when she puts her hands together, resting on the desk, I can see they're shaking.

"Miss Atherton. I came to look for you this morning. In your history class earlier, but you weren't there. Quite ironic, in the circumstances wouldn't you say?

I look up, not getting the reference. The receptionist wouldn't tell us why Principal Sharpe wanted to speak to us. I assumed it was for skipping class, but I can't see how that would be ironic.

Amber doesn't reply, she just studies the floor, and Principal Sharpe stares at her for a really long time. Then she slides her eyes over to me.

"And Billy. It seems you had something more important to attend to than your Geography class this morning, would you care to explain what that was?" She waits, and I try to think of something to say, but I can't tell her what we've been doing, so I don't say anything.

Principal Sharpe sighs. "I thought not."

She stares at us both for a few more seconds, then opens one of her drawers, and pulls out a sheet of paper.

"I was contacted last night by a concerned friend. Someone who thought there was something I should be aware of. Billy, this is beginning to get a little repetitive don't you think?

I try to work out what she means. This can't be about *BullyTracker*. She saw me take it down, and I haven't done anything on it since.

"I really didn't know what to think when I saw it. I can honestly say that. In all my time in teaching, I've never had a situation like this one." She glances at the window, and when she looks back she's smiling.

"So well done – for that at least."

I guess, like me, Amber has decided we're not supposed to say anything. It seems Principal Sharpe is just really into rhetorical questions.

"Miss Atherton, I understand you've been sending messages to former pupils of this school on social media sites, posing as some kind of investigator, and asking for information on former principals. Specifically Henry Jacobs? Is that correct?"

Amber looks up sharply mid way through the question. And when Principal Sharpe finishes, Amber hesitates for a while, but then shrugs and nods. Principal Sharpe waits to see if Amber is going to say any more, then when she doesn't she pours herself some water from a jug on her desk.

"I was forwarded one of these messages this morning. Would you like me to read it out to you?"

Amber shrugs again.

"Would you like me to read it to you?"

It turns out that question wasn't rhetorical after all.

"Not really." Amber says.

In response Principal Sharpe picks up the paper and begins to read.

"I'm a private detective and I'm looking for Henry Jacobs who was principal of Newlea High School who disappeared – *there's two 'p's in disappeared by the way* – in 1979. It says on your Facebook profile you went to Newlea High School then, so I thought you might remember him. If so please contact, blah blah." Principal Sharpe drops the paper on her desk.

"Blah."

There's silence for a moment.

"A private detective? I know many 10th graders take on part time jobs," she gives a cold smile. "I encourage it. But I've never heard of any working as private detectives before."

Principal Sharpe waits in silence, until finally Amber starts to say something, but I don't hear what it is, because she cuts her off immediately.

"And then I wondered, what *possible* interest could you have in a man who was the principal of this school *forty years ago*. So would you care to enlighten me?" She sits back in her chair and waits.

Amber's more cautious this time, but finally she replies.

"I don't mean this the wrong way, Principal Sharpe, but we can't talk about it."

"You can't talk about it?"

"No. Because we have a client and..."

There's a bang as Principal Sharpe slams her palm down on her desk. It makes Amber stop. It makes me nearly jump out of my chair.

"You have a *client*," Principal Sharpe repeats. "And who, pray, might that be?"

"We can't say that either."

"Of course not. Of course not. Because that would be a breach of confidentiality wouldn't it?" She leans forward again.

"Well perhaps I could ask you this – did your *client* contact you about this matter? Or did you approach her?" Principal Sharpe watches us carefully.

"She did." Amber answers in the end. "She wanted to find out what happened to him. She's been wondering all these years, and now she's getting old..." Amber stops and she stares open mouthed for a moment.

"How did you know it was a she?" she asks.

"How indeed? I have to say you're not particularly impressing me as a detective Miss Atherton. Neither of you." She looks to me for a second.

"Tell me, when were you planning on interviewing *me* about this matter?"

Amber looks up. "You? Why?"

Principal Sharpe's eyebrows go even higher. "Well I thought I would have been an obvious place to start. As the current principal of the school." She pauses, then goes on.

"And of course, given that Henry Jacobs was my father."

TWENTY-EIGHT

It's as if all the air in the room is suddenly sucked out, and replaced by new air that's colder, like it's from a freezer.

"Father?" Amber says after a long while. "What do you mean?"

"Well, it shouldn't be that difficult to understand, not for a *detective*. Your 'client' as you call her, is my mother, who I should point out is a very frail and confused old woman. So I was extremely concerned when I spoke to her last night, and discovered she is under the impression she had contracted a *professional agency* to locate my father."

Amber turns to me. Her eyes are as round as dollar coins. Then she turns back.

"Father? Henry Jacobs was your *father*?"

"I know, it's amazing. Even school principals have parents. I know this must come as a huge shock to you."

Amber turns to me again, her mouth hanging open. Then she turns back to Principal Sharpe.

"Well... Well what happened to him?" Amber asks. "Do *you* know?"

"*Of course I know.*"

Suddenly Principal Sharpe gets up from behind the desk and goes to a side table at the edge of the room. On it there's a tray with more glasses.

"Would you like a drink?" she asks us both, but doesn't wait for a reply. Instead she comes back, standing over us now, and pours us both a glass of water. While she's distracted doing so, Amber mouths to me:

She's Henry Jacob's fucking daughter!

Which obviously, I've already realized.

Then Principal Sharpe is talking again. "In normal circumstances I would say this is absolutely none of your business. But since my mother appears to have played her part in creating this *situation*, I feel bound to give you enough information to settle your curiosity. But after that this matter shall be closed, and it shall go no further than this room. Do we have that clear?"

Neither me nor Amber really say anything to this, so Principal Sharpe says it again.

"Do I have your agreement on that?"

I quickly nod, and then look at Amber to see if she does the same, but if she did I missed it.

Principal Sharpe takes a deep breath. "Good." She sits down again behind the desk.

"My mother is seventy five years old, and unfortunately she's suffering from a rare form of dementia. Her memory is the most obvious symptom, but it also affects her personality. She can shift from one version of herself to another. I don't know if you noticed?"

I nod again. Principal Sharpe looks annoyed at the interruption. But then she smiles at me.

"People with her condition tend to lose their older, or more traumatic, memories first. And it's not uncommon that they become quite distressed and put time and effort into trying to recover those memories. They feel there's a significant gap, that needs to be filled." She laughs suddenly. "The irony is, there's often another part of their personality that still recalls those memories. So at times she knows what happened. At other times she doesn't. But the two parts of her no longer join up."

Amber and I wait in silence.

"My mother has always lived a very active life, she's certainly not one to sit around being distressed. And it seems that, when part of her lost her memory of what happened to my father that same part concluded it was a big mystery. And so she looked for help solving it. And then somehow got mixed up with the two of you, pretending to be detectives..."

She look levelly at me. I don't know what she's thinking.

"So what did happen to him?" Amber asks.

She glances at her, she seems annoyed.

"Nothing."

"Well where is he then?"

"There is no mystery, Miss Atherton. I'm very sorry to disappoint you."

"But... We found out he was principal here until 1979, then he disappeared and no one knows what happened to him." Amber pauses, maybe she realized that might not be quite right. "At least, we couldn't find anything about what happened to him. There was nothing in the *Island Times* about him."

A slight frown creases Principal Sharpe's face.

"Why would there be anything in the *Island Times*?"

"I don't know... We just thought... Well if something did happen it would be news."

The frown deepens.

"So what *did* happen to him?" Amber says in the end.

"I told you. Nothing happened. At least nothing dramatic. He and my mother separated, and he moved off the island."

For a moment it feels like Principal Sharpe is going to say more, but she doesn't. There's a few moments of silence before Amber speaks again.

"But... Mr. Jacobs, she said he disappeared. That he went out one night and never came back."

"No. That's not how it happened." Principal Sharpe drums her fingers on the desk. "Perhaps that's the dementia..." She stops and watches us. A few moments later she goes on.

"There's an element of truth in it. Perhaps that's why..." But then she stops again and sighs.

"My father did walk out. And it was at Christmas. It could have been 1979, I'm not sure without working it out." She takes a deep breath. "I can't believe I am explaining my childhood to two of my *students*." She takes a sip of her water.

"I was nine years old, and yes, for a few weeks we didn't know where he was. But it wasn't the first time he'd gone away like that. My mother thought he'd come back, like he always did, but this time he didn't. Then we got a postcard. From Hawaii. My father explained how he had met someone else, and moved in with her on the island of Maui. He continued to send letters, and birthdays cards for a few years. But then they dried up. It was very hard on my mother. It was very hard on all of us. But there's no mystery. And there never was."

There's silence for a while. Then Amber speaks.

"Palm trees," she says.

"I beg your pardon?"

"Mrs. Jaco... Your mother said she remembered something about palm trees. How they were important."

"Hmmm. Perhaps. They may well have featured on the postcards."

I zone out for a while. I'm getting this really weird feeling watching Principal Sharpe. All the time I've known her she's been this scary authority figure, but now it's as if I can see beyond this. That she wasn't always that way. Once she was just a kid, and bad things happened to her. But Amber doesn't seem to be thinking the same.

"Do you know if he's still there now?" She asks.

It takes Principal Sharpe a long time to answer.

"Excuse me?"

"Your dad. Is he still there now? In Hawaii?"

"I don't know. His communications dried up a few years after he left. And to be honest with you, after the way he treated us, I wasn't minded to care much either way."

There's a long silence while she takes another sip of water, and I see how much her hands are shaking. As she sets the glass down it spills and a drop falls on the paper she read from earlier. The surface tension holds it up like a translucent blob before finally it collapses, being absorbed and sucked into the paper.

I can't take my eyes of it.

TWENTY-NINE

WE EACH HAVE to go to class after that, but we arrange to meet up at lunch in the school canteen. There's nowhere to sit though, not where we can talk in private. That is until Amber asks a couple of first graders to move.

"Well? What do you make of all that?" she asks, when they've skulked away saying how they're going to tell a teacher. I think for a moment how to answer.

"She's actually alright isn't she? Principal Sharpe. Underneath all that..." I reach for the right word. "Fierceness."

"Yeah but," Amber interrupts. "Do you actually *believe* her?"

"Believe her?"

"Yeah. Cos I'm not sure I do." Amber takes a bite of her hot dog and ketchup squirts onto her plate.

"Why not?"

She chews for a minute, fast, because she wants to keep talking. "Because of what the guy in the garage told us." She takes another bite.

I think back to what the mechanic said. About how Henry Jacobs had a reputation for liking the boys.

"What's that got to do with it?"

"Like I said before. It's a motive. It's a reason why someone might want to kill him."

"But we know now that no one *did* kill him. He didn't disappear, he just left the island."

"That might be what Sharpe told us. But it doesn't make it true. What if he was actually murdered because of what he was doing to the students, and then whoever did it, sent a letter to Mrs. Jacobs, pretending it was from him and saying how he'd met someone else?" Amber opens her mouth wide and pushes all the rest of the hot dog in. Then she keeps talking, even though her mouth is totally full.

"Or, what if *she* did it? Mrs. Jacobs I mean. We already knew she's mental, and now Sharpe's confirmed it. But what if she's *really* mental. What if she actually murdered him, and then pretended to her daughter that he'd gone with the other woman? Isn't that possible?"

I think about this for a second. I'm not even sure that it is.

"Well? Isn't it?"

"I suppose it *might* be. But isn't it more likely he went off to live on Maui, like she said?"

Amber looks annoyed and turns away. Feeling a bit awkward, I take a bite of my own hotdog. I chew it carefully and swallow it down. Then I open my mouth.

"I saw a documentary on Maui..."

"*He didn't go to fucking Maui!*"

"What?" I almost choke on my mouthful.

"He didn't go to Maui. I can't believe you're being so dumb about this. He was a pedophile who *disappeared*. Doesn't that strike you as a hell of a coincidence?"

"But he send postcards. And birthday cards."

"It's easy to fake a birthday card Billy," Amber says, like she's some kind of expert in it.

"Is it?" I ask. "Wouldn't it be really hard? Wouldn't you need to go to actually Maui to post it, to get the right postmark..."

"*Oh come on Billy!* What the fuck's wrong with you?" Amber interrupts again. "Aren't you supposed to be the expert in all this? Didn't your dad lie to you about your mom for years? Didn't he tell you she was dead, when all the time she was locked up in some mental institution? I don't get how that can happen to you, and you can't accept this could have happened to Sharpe?"

I don't say anything to this. In fact I freeze a little bit, my hot dog quivering over my plate. Amber looks at me for a while then sighs.

"I'm sorry, I didn't mean to say it like that. It must be hard to have that much shit in your family history." She offers me a smile. "But don't you see? If it can happen to you, why can't it happen to someone else too?"

I still don't reply. But she's got it wrong. I don't mind her talking about everything that happened in the past. The problem is, there's so much going on *now*, with Dad hundreds of miles out in the ocean, and me living with a murderer. Maybe she's right, and I've just been too distracted to see this case for what it really is.

"Do you really not believe Principal Sharpe?"

She watches me for a long time before answering.

"I don't know what to believe. But I think we should keep on investigating. It's possible that Henry Jacobs never left the island. Or at least, never left the island alive."

I puff out my cheeks. Leaving Principal Sharpe's office I really thought this stuff with Mrs. Jacobs was over. That I could just concentrate on sorting out the Tucker issue. And then everything else that I have to do. Suddenly everything feels overwhelming.

Then I can't stop myself. I reach into my pocket and I bring out the SIM card I found in Tucker's phone yesterday. It feels like weeks ago.

"What's that?" Amber asks.

"It's a SIM card."

"I can see that. What are you doing with it?"

Then I tell her. I just blurt it all out. I explain how this old friend of dad's turned up at our house a couple of weeks ago, completely unexpected, and how he won't leave. And how I suspected he was a criminal, so I tricked him into using my computer when I was at school and recorded how he'd murdered the security guard in the jewelry store he was robbing. And then how Dad's gone out on the *Ocean Harvest*, and left me alone with him. And then how he smashed his phone up and threw it down the cliff, and then how I found it. And when I'm finished, and the remains of my hotdog are left on the plate completely forgotten, and Amber's mouth is open in amazement. Then she laughs.

"Fucking hell Billy. There was me thinking you were useless at this detective stuff, when all the time you've got that going on at the same time. No wonder you've been distracted."

This cheers me up quite a lot.

"So what are you going to do?"

So I tell her about how the police will be monitoring his phone, so if I put his card into *my* phone it'll look like his phone is switched on. And then the police will see that he's here, on Lornea Island. And then they'll come and arrest him.

"Fucking hell," Amber says again. Then she thinks a bit.

"Well go on then," she says. "Put it in."

Her eyes are shining bright with excitement.

"I can't *here*."

She frowns. "Why not?"

"Because then the police will come *here*. I've got to do it at home, later on. So the police know that's where he is."

"So when you gonna do it?"

"Tonight I guess. I'll swap it over when I get home. Put Tucker's SIM in my phone. It doesn't matter what phone you use, as long as it's unlocked, it'll send out the same signal to the base station."

"OK." Amber looks thoughtful. Then she speaks again.

"I've got an idea," Amber's eyes shine brighter still. "I've got Mom's car today. Why don't I give you a lift home? Then I can help you do it. And I'll get to meet a proper murderer..."

THIRTY

HOOOOOOOoooooNK. The white panel van goes shooting past the windscreen, the driver leaning on the horn, alarm on his face at the way Amber has veered into his lane.

"Asshole," Amber says, giving him the finger.

The good thing about going home with Amber is that I don't have to sit on the school bus and drop off half the school before I get home. The bad thing is I figure I've about a fifty-fifty chance of making it alive

"You have to be careful with the turn off the Silverlea road to Littlelea," I say, trying not to sound as nervous as I feel. "It's a left, and Dad always says..."

"I can drive you know." Amber shoots me a look.

Actually it's not just Amber's driving that's making me unsettled. Obviously I'm nervous about the whole plan to alert the police to where Tucker is. But there's more to it than that. The thing is, I've never actually had anyone from school come to my house. Not ever. It's not that I'm ashamed of where I live. It's just... Well, I'm a bit worried there's some things she might think are a bit odd. That's all.

I feel tense for the rest of the journey, and make a vague plan to try to keep her out of my room at least. And somehow we do make it alive. She stops behind Dad's truck. I notice again the way Tucker's parked it wrong, he doesn't turn it around, ready to go the way that Dad does.

"Jesus Billy, you live on the edge of the fucking cliff!" Amber is already out of the car and standing looking out over the beach below "It's amazing. You can see for miles!"

I don't really answer her. "He's here." I say instead. "Dad's letting him borrow his truck, so he must be in."

Amber spins around, and seems to notice the truck for the first time. Then she takes in the house and the yard.

"What's that?" she asks.

I frown, not sure what she means, then I follow where she's pointing. "Oh. It's the jaw bone of a sperm whale. It's not really..."

"Where the hell did you get that?"

"On the beach, but it's not relevant. We need to go inside."

Amber eyes linger on the bone for a moment, but then she spins around.

"Right." Then she looks at me and gives a grin. Her eyes are sparkling with excitement. Honestly, I don't know why she's so excited to meet a murderer.

We go inside, Tucker's not in the kitchen, but I can see the TV's on in the next room.

"That you *Billy boy*?" Tucker calls from the lounge. Me and Amber look at each other.

"Yeah," I call back, but not too loud.

"I made veggie lasagna. Figured you boys been eating too much red..." He appears in the kitchen. Straight away he notices Amber.

"...Meat. *Hi there.*"

His eyes take her in. They don't focus on her hair, which by the way, is dark green now. Instead they run up and down her body.

"Say Billy, you didn't say you were bringing a *friend*."

I don't like the way Amber is looking at him either, like he's a white tiger in a zoo. Dangerous and rare, but beautiful.

"So? Aren't you going to introduce us?" Tucker's grin widens.

While I'm thinking what to say, Amber steps forward.

"I'm Amber. I'm a friend of Billy." She pushes a strand of hair out of her face and tucks it behind her ear. Her eyes are sparkling bright.

"Tucker."

"Billy's told me about you."

"Has he?" Tucker's eyebrows go up. "Nothing bad I hope?"

Amber half shrugs, but smiles to show she's kidding. Then the two of them just watch each other, like I'm not even here.

"Amber needed some help with her homework," I say, just to break the weird silence. "So we're going to go upstairs..." I know I said I didn't want her in my room. But when a plan goes wrong, you have to change it.

"Sure." Tucker glances at me, but then turns back. "Say Amber. You'll stay for dinner right? I made plenty." Tucker laughs. "You wouldn't think it, looking at the kid, but he eats like a goddamn horse."

"No, she's got to..." I start to say, but Amber talks over me quickly.

"That would be great. I love veggie lasagna."

"*Alright then.* Girl after my own heart." He smiles. He looks a bit like a tiger now. Or a cat, purring about something.

"I'll set up another place at the table. Give you a shout when it's ready."

They watch each other some more.

"Come on Amber," I say. Then when she doesn't move, I grab her sleeve and pull her towards the stairs, so hard she nearly stumbles.

We walk upstairs, and I sense how Amber is checking out everything in our house. She sticks her head into the bathroom, and then into Dad's room. I pause before I finally let her into mine.

"You might be a bit surprised," I say, "looking in here..."

"Why? What's in there? Is it like a museum filled with dinosaur bones? Or have you got a massive porn collection? That wouldn't surprise me Billy. Nothing about you would surprise..."

She doesn't finish what she's saying because at that moment Steven wakes up. There's a loud mewing sound, and then a big *thump* on the door.

"No. It's not that."

I open the door, and all at once I'm set upon by an overjoyed juvenile herring gull, flapping his wings and trying to rub his neck against mine. I catch him and smooth his feathers down to calm him, and tell him I'll get some food in a minute. Eventually I get him sitting on my forearm, mewing noisily. Then I look up at Amber. Her mouth is open, staring at Steven.

"You've got... A *seagull* as a pet?"

"He's not a seagull. And he's not a pet. You're not allowed to keep wild birds as pets. I'm just looking after him until he's ready to be released."

Amber looks around the room. I see her take in my collection of dried starfish, my fish posters, and then settle on Steven's nest, it sits in a plastic dog bed, his name written in black marker pen on the top.

"*Steven?*" She says. "Is that its name?"

"His name. Yeah."

"Why?" Amber asks.

"It was my Dad's idea. There's some actor called Steven Seagal and he thought it was funny."

Amber looks at me, screwing up her nose. "Jeez. Parents are so fucking lame sometimes."

At least we can agree on that.

"Does he bite? Can I pet him?"

"He won't if you're gentle."

I hold Steven out to her, and Amber gingerly puts her hands around him and lifts him up.

"He's heavy. *Hello Steven!*" She says to him. "I love his eyes! Big brown eyes. You're a handsome boy aren't you?"

Suddenly I feel a bit weird. I can't really explain it. It's like – It's not jealousy, or anything like that. It's just, the way she's going all soft over Steven. I kind of wish she was saying that to me. I shake the thought away, it's ridiculous. I sit down at my desk.

"What were you doing? Downstairs? Didn't I tell you he's a murderer? He's *dangerous,* and you want to have dinner with him?"

"Yeah but you didn't tell me he was hot."

I feel that strange thought again. Steven picks up on it, and shuffles awkwardly.

"Hey, it's alright baby," Amber soothes him.

I look away, then turn to my stereo. I switch it on, then I turn it up loud even though the song is some rapper or another. Amber looks up, questioningly.

"I never had you down as a hip hop fan."

"I'm not. I just don't want Tucker to hear what we're talking about."

"Oh. OK. Well anyway, *you're* having dinner with him."

"Yeah but I *have* to."

"Well?" She shrugs. "And anyway, what kind of a murderer makes veggie lasagna?" She asks the question in her cutesy voice, but more to Steven than to me.

"Hey little birdy man? Not a very scary murderer that's what..." So I have to talk to her quite sharply to get her attention back.

"Amber. It is possible for someone to be a murderer and also a good cook. The two attributes are not mutually exclusive."

Amber ignores me, stroking Steven's plumage. But then she very carefully she puts him down so that he stands on the carpet watching her and offering up one of his feet like I taught him.

Amber plays with him for a while, taking his foot and shaking it like she's saying hello.

"So anyway, *Sherlock*," She says at last. "What's gonna happen now with your SIM card?"

THIRTY-ONE

I REACH into my pocket and pull it out, folded into a square of paper so I
don't lose it. I put it on the desk and look at it for a moment.

Amber watches me. Anticipation etched into her face. Her eyes shining
with the thrill of it.

I reach into my other pocket and pull out my phone. I check it for
messages, then when there aren't any, I press the button to power it down.
While I'm waiting for that I open my drawer and root around for a bit until
I find an electrical screwdriver. As soon as the phone screen has gone black
I carefully prize the back of my phone, then slide my SIM card out of the
slot. I replace it with Tucker's, then fit the phone's back case into place
again.

"Is that it? That's all you have to do?"

"It's because he's on T-Mobile," I start to explain, even though I told her
all this at school. "All the phone's data gets stored on the card, so the
network will think it's his phone."

"OK, OK. How long do you reckon the police will take to start tracking
it?"

I hesitate, because I don't actually know this.

"They might have some sort of alert set up, so that they know the
moment it gets switched on." I consider this for a second. "Or they might
not. I'm not sure."

I still have the phone in my hand, but I don't turn it on. I'm not sure
why I don't.

"Seems a shame in a way. He's quite a cool guy. And, you know, he's pretty buff." Amber gives me a look to tell me she's joking. Or at least I think she's joking.

"Well go on then. Aren't you gonna turn it on?"

I swallow carefully. And then I press the button to power on the phone.

Nothing happens at first. The phone loads, and it's weird because it still *looks* like my phone. The photo it shows is my usual one, a dead oarfish I found on the beach the other day, but when I go to contacts, all my numbers aren't there, and instead there's lots of names I don't recognize. Amber is leaning in close to me, so that she can see the screen too. I can smell her too, and feel her hair brushing soft against my face. I hold the phone a bit further away, so she doesn't need to lean so close.

"Check the messages," Amber says, moving closer again.

"OK."

This time I don't lean away.

But when I check what she says, they're all my messages. A couple from Dad, and then lots from Amber herself.

"How come..." Amber begins, but I know what she's going to say.

"It's because the messages get stored on the phone once they've been delivered." I tell her. "They wait on the network until they get delivered, but then they just stay on the phone. Otherwise the telephone base stations would fill up. They might even explode."

"Oh." She sounds confused by this, but then she brightens. "How about the photos?"

I shake my head at once. I'm not actually sure of the answer, but I'm definitely not showing Amber my photos.

"So what do we do then? Just wait?" She sits back on my bed and crosses her legs.

It's funny really. I've never had anyone else in this room. Obviously Dad has been in here, and I suppose Tucker has too, but not when I wanted him too. And maybe when the police searched the house, when they were looking for Dad, they must have been in there. But other than that, there's never been anyone else in my room. And now there's *a girl*. A girl who's sixteen years old. I don't know why, but that thought keeps coming into my head. I risk a glance at Amber, I don't know why it feels like a risk suddenly. She's leaning over my bedside table, poking at my starfishes.

"Urgh," she says, and screws up her nose. I'd never noticed before, but there's something really interesting about the shape of her nose. I can't stop staring at it.

Then suddenly she moves away from me and goes to the window. It's a relief, at least, I think it is.

"I wish I had a view like this," she says. "You can see all the way to the end of the beach." She pushes the drapes out of the way so she can see better.

She half turns to me, still facing the window, but twisting her head and neck towards me. It means her chest is side on to me, and I can't help but notice how her blouse is pulled taut over her boobs. I hadn't really noticed that she really had boobs before, I mean I had, but I hadn't thought about them. I don't know why I'm thinking about them now.

I try to stop thinking about them.

"Did they?" She says.

"Did they what?"

"Did they close off the caves? Because of what happened to you?"

"Oh." I shrug. "I don't know."

She gives me a funny look, a kind of half smile, and again I notice how it makes her face look interesting. Kind of *pretty*.

"Billy? Are you alright? You look *weird* again."

"No, I'm not… I'm fine."

I turn away at once, but I notice I can still see her in the reflection of my computer screen. She turns away from the window, a bounce in her step. Her boobs bounce too. I wish I could stop looking.

"Well come on then."

"Come on where?"

"Downstairs. Lasagna will be ready. Bring the phone."

THIRTY-TWO

DINNER IS REALLY ODD. Tucker has set three places, and put glasses and a jug of water on the table. Then he offers us beer again, and Amber says yes, and gives me this innocent look as he gets it for her from the refrigerator. When we're both sitting down he pulls out a big tray of lasagna from the oven, and I have to admit it looks really good, all the cheese on the top is bubbling and crispy from the heat. He sets it in the middle of the table and then serves some to Amber first, then me, and then to himself.

It *is* really good. It's probably the best vegetable lasagna I've ever had, and that's a bit annoying, because it's one of the things I cook sometimes too.

"Mmmmm, this is, like, this is just amazing! Mr..." Amber says when she's tried it, not saying his second name even though she knows what it is, because I told her.

"It's just Tucker." He says. "The secret is you gotta pre-bake the eggplant. Get it good and tender."

"It's delicious. I wish my step dad could cook like this."

Tucker's eyes flick onto Amber.

"Step dad?"

"Yeah, my real dad died."

I remember Amber mentioned this once before. I don't know why she's bringing it up again.

"I'm sorry," Tucker says. Then he goes on.

"What happened?"

Amber doesn't answer right away. She actually sounds a bit strange when she does answer.

"Pancreatic cancer. Four years ago. Then my mom remarried, and they've had a new baby, so they don't have much time for me."

"Shit," Tucker says. Then he thinks for a little while.

"Cancer's a fucking bitch."

This time Amber doesn't reply, but after a moment she nods.

I don't say anything all this time. I'm thinking that we can maybe eat and then go outside. I could tell Tucker we need to fly Steven, or that we have to finish the work we were doing, but then Amber opens her mouth again.

"So you're like... You're like Billy's *uncle* or something?" She looks up into his face, her eyes round. She even flutters her eyelids a little bid.

"Kinda. Billy's dad and me were buddies growing up." He hesitates a moment. "You know anything about what happened to Billy?"

"Yeah, he's told me." Amber says, like she wants him to go on. But he doesn't.

"Well then you know it ain't so easy to talk about." Tucker sucks air through his teeth, like he wishes he could say more. Then he gives her a smile. There's a silence for a moment.

"What about you? You're not in his classes or nothing? You look a lot older..."

Amber seems delighted by this. "No I just... I decided to help him out, a few weeks back, with this project."

"Uh huh?"

"Yeah, we're working on it together." She turns to me. "Aren't we Billy?"

I wonder what she expects me to say to this, it's probably not a great idea to explain to a murderer on the run that we're actually private detectives. But in the end I'm saved from saying anything when there's a loud beeping sound from my pocket. It's a message coming into my phone. Only it isn't *my* phone anymore. Both Amber and Tucker look at me, expectantly, but I guess for different reasons.

I decide I'm best off pretending I haven't heard anything. "Yeah, it's for biology," I say, a bit too loudly, and then to cover that I quickly make something up.

"We're doing a count of grey seals out by the headland. Their numbers keep falling so we're gonna monitor them." I actually did do this, so I can talk for ages on it if I need to.

Tucker finishes chewing a mouthful of food. "Uh huh." He says when he's finished.

"Yeah. There's about a hundred at the moment. Or fifty breeding pairs," I go on. And that's true as well. "They have their pups later in the year, in October usually, so maybe the numbers will go back up again. I hope so because they're a sign of the overall health of the oceans."

Tucker nods seriously, then his face brightens. "Say. I saw a whale earlier today. Out in the bay."

"Really?" This is actually quite interesting. "Do you know what type?"

"I dunno, it was a way out. I just saw the spout and maybe half its tail."

"Fluke."

"What?"

"If you saw only half its tail, then that's a fluke," I explain.

"What you saying?" Tucker sounds a little bit angry, like I'm accusing him of something, so I have to explain again.

"Whale's tails are made up of two halves. Each is called a fluke." People are always getting that wrong.

"Oh," Tucker says. And then my phone with his SIM card beeps again. And as soon as it finishes it beeps again. So I guess two more messages have come in. Putting the new SIM in must have reset the phone to its standard message settings, because the notification message is super loud.

"You're popular tonight ain't you Billy?" Tucker says.

I don't reply, it's just occurred to me that maybe Tucker's SIM card holds the notification that Tucker has chosen for his messages. If so he might recognize the noise my phone keeps making.

Before I finish that thought another message comes in.

There's another silence.

"You sure you don't want to look at that? Could be your old man," Tucker says. So obviously then I *do* have to look. I slide my eyes over to Amber, hoping she can think of some excuse, but she's just smiling at me brightly.

So I have to pull the phone out of my pocket, and really carefully using my other hand to shield the screen so there's no way Tucker can see it, I glance at it. You don't get to see the whole messages, but it tells me four messages received, all of them from the same person. And what I can see of them, they're pretty weird.

"It's not Dad, I say, and slip the phone back, and as I do so it beeps again.

I eat the rest of my food as quickly as I can, but I can't go upstairs until Amber stops talking. She's on about her dad again with Tucker, and they keep talking right up till all the plates are washed and dried.

THIRTY-THREE

What the hell happened? Where are you?

THAT'S THE FIRST MESSAGE. It comes from a guy called *Vinny*. It was sent a week ago. It doesn't look like Tucker answered it.

We need to talk. Call me.

That's the second message. Sent a day later. Then the next one says

I ain't mad. I just need to know where you are.

Then there's a whole load more, all saying the same sort of thing. I show them to Amber, who's super excited.

"Who's *Vinny*?"

"I don't know."

"Why did all the messages come in now?"

"I told you. They get stored on the network until they can get delivered.

"That's so awesome. Do you think the police will have tracked the phone by now?"

"I don't know."

"What are you going to do now?"

"I don't know."

We wait for a few moments, and then Amber gets up and goes to the window, like she's expecting the police might turn up at any second, but of course they don't.

"Is there any way you can tell if the police have tracked the phone yet?"

I think for a moment.

"No."

"So is there anything you can do, now, to alert them?"

Again I shake my head. "I don't think so."

"Do you even still want to?" Amber asks then. "I mean. Are you sure he's definitely a murderer? He seems a really cool guy."

I look at her, a bit annoyed by this.

"Do you want to read the articles about the man he killed?" This shuts her up a bit and she comes back to the bed and sits down. Then she looks at her watch.

"I probably have to get back soon."

I don't reply to this. I'm still a bit annoyed.

"Why don't you phone him? He could probably tell you."

"Phone who?"

"This Vinny guy. He seems to want to contact Tucker pretty bad. Hey -" she hesitates, and turns around to face me. "Maybe he actually *is* the police. Or his probation officer or something. That would make sense, from how the messages sound."

I read them again, trying to see what she means. I'm not convinced.

"*I'll* call him, if you like,"

This is such a stupid idea I don't even consider it. But I do think of something else.

"We could *text* him back. Ask him what he wants? Maybe he'd tell us something more that way?"

Amber bites her lip, thinking this over.

"Go on then," she says.

"What do we say?"

It takes a bit of discussion, but in the end we settle on writing this:

What do you want?

I know that looks simple, but it's actually deceptively clever. It doesn't reveal anything about who we are, but it forces Vinny, whoever he is, to tell us something about what he wants. And just in case Vinny *is* Tucker's probation officer, which still seems unlikely, it will also alert him to noticing that his phone is back on, so that the police can track where he is.

I explain all this to Amber while she fiddles with the phone, but as I do so I begin to wonder if it's such a good idea after all. We actually don't know *anything* about who this Vinny guy is, or what he wants, and we're kind of messing in Tucker's business, and maybe we shouldn't do that. I'm wondering how to say all this to Amber interrupts me.

"Done. Message sent."

"What?"

She throws the phone down on the bed and shrugs.

"It's done."

So that's kind of that.

Then Amber stares at the phone, like she's waiting for something to happen right away, which obviously it isn't. I turn away and open my laptop, which I took upstairs with me this time. I turn it on, and type the password again, to stop it recording, then pull up the list of keywords Tucker has used.

"What you doing now?" Amber asks, leaning in close again.

I start to explain how it all works, how I downloaded *SpyCatch* and *Keylogger Free*, but I can sense Amber losing interest. "So it's just like spying on someone's internet search history?"

I hesitate. "Not exactly no..."

"I do that with my step dad all the time. He's so bad at deleting his search history. He gambles on this poker site. And sometimes he browses porn sites, he really likes Asian girls. So I've no idea why he's with my mom."

I don't know what to say to this, so I show Amber the newspaper pages on the robbery at the jewelry store in Hounds Beach.

"Shit," she says when she's finished reading them. "That *is* pretty bad."

I feel a bit better at this. Downstairs she was acting like he was Bruce Willis in *Die Hard*.

"Has he looked at anything else since then?"

"Hmmm?"

"Has he used your computer since then? Have you recorded him looking at anything else?"

"Oh." It's quite hard to answer this. I've used my laptop myself since installing the spyware, as well as leaving it out as a trap for Tucker, so his pages are mixed up with mine. Even so, I go to the list and we both lean in to look. I sort the results by time of day, selecting only the times when I was at school.

That narrows it down to about fifteen results on the screen. Fifteen separate webpages that Tucker's visited. But even then there's a problem. Most of them are impossible to read. You can see there's something there, but the program has blurred the words so you can't actually read them.

"Why can't you see what it says?" Amber asks.

"It's because I only installed the free trial version of the software. They only work for a few days then you have to pay."

"And you can't click them either? To see where they go?"

"Only the ones you can read."

Amber goes quiet for a moment, looking at the list more carefully. She puts her hand onto the track pad, and places the mouse pointer on the first legible name on the list. It expands to show the whole web address. Then she moves down, and goes to the second legible name, and then the third.

"Billy, these are all jewelry stores..."

"Are they?" I say. And then she clicks the link she's resting on.

The internet window opens and slowly a page loads. A video starts playing, showing a happy couple spinning around on Silverlea beach, and then a close up of their hands, with rings on the fingers. It's a store called Carter's.

"That's the jewelry store in Newlea. At the end on Main Street."

Amber frowns. She clicks back, and checks the next website on the list. Straight away I can see it's another jewelry store, also on the island. Then she clicks the third legible search on the list, and a third jewelry store website opens.

"Why is he looking at other jewelry stores?"

"Dad said," I begin, thinking back. "Before he went out on the boat, he said that Tucker was looking to give it a go here on Lornea Island."

Amber turns to look at me, her brow deeply furrowed.

"Like get a job?"

"That's what he said but..."

"... Maybe what he meant was, actually *do* a job. Like another robbery."

THIRTY-FOUR

THERE'S silence for a long while, then Amber stands up.

"I dunno. Maybe he's just looking for a necklace?"

"Look at him. Why would he want a necklace? And Dad told me he was *looking for work* here. This *is* his work."

Still she looks doubtful, but after a while she laughs.

"What's funny?" I ask, confused.

"You are. Everyone at school thinks you're this weird, nerdy geek, but then you've got the most full-on fucked-up home life that no one knows about. It's hilarious!"

Strangely enough, I don't laugh at that.

"You really think he's planning to rob a jewelry store here?" She asks a few moments later.

I shrug. "I'm not thinking anything. I'm just looking at the evidence. We know he robbed a jeweler's in that Hounds Beach place. And now he's looking at all the jeweler's stores on the island?"

"Maybe he's..." But her voice faces away. In the end she just stares at me.

"Fucking hell Billy. This is so fucked up."

* * *

Amber has to go home soon after that, so we don't get a chance to talk about what to do next. But she promises she's going to help me, with whatever it is. Like if we need to get more evidence that Tucker is planning to rob jewelry stores. Or if we just need to tell the police what we already know. Whatever we decide, she's going to help.

And then she goes downstairs. I watch for her out of the window. She takes a while, and I hear her laughing downstairs for a bit. But then she appears outside, gets into her car and drives away. Then I make sure the desk is securely in front of my bedroom door and go to bed.

I guess I must be getting a bit more used to living with a criminal, or maybe I'm just exhausted. But either way I get to sleep quite easily, and the next morning I wake up and I'm in quite a good mood. Maybe it's because I get woken up naturally for a change, instead of by the alarm on my phone, which obviously doesn't work because it doesn't have my SIM in it.

So I turn on my radio. It's tuned to Lornea Island 104FM. It's a music station, and I used to listen to it all the time when I was younger, but recently I've forgotten about it, until last night, when I needed it to make sure Tucker couldn't overhear what we were saying. But actually it's nice to listen to music, and some people say it's good for your brain too, it's something about helping the neurons to connect to each other. I don't think the evidence is clear, but it does feel nice sometimes.

After a while I get up and have a look at *VesselTrack*, and then my mood gets even better, because I see that Dad's boat is heading back from the fishing grounds. I work out he'll be back sometime tonight, which is earlier than he said. That's double good news because the boats only ever come back early if they're totally full of fish, so he'll have earned a lot.

Then I start to very quickly do my homework, because I've been so busy with all the Tucker stuff, and the Mrs. Jacobs stuff, that I haven't had a chance to do it, and there's two pieces I have to hand in this morning. So I'm doing all that when suddenly my phone rings.

I know what you're thinking, but I guess I'm still half-thinking about Dad, because I just assume it must be him on the phone, that maybe he's come back into range now he's getting closer to land. So without realizing what I'm doing, I answer my phone.

"Hi Dad!"

"Who's that?" The voice is all wrong. Right away I realize what I've done.

I lower the phone to look at the screen. The caller ID says 'Vinny'.

"I said who's that?" The voice says again. He sounds gruff, a bit angry.

"No one." I reply, desperately trying to work out what to do.

"Well it's definitely someone. And it's someone with Tucker's phone." The man goes on. "You know where he is?"

I don't answer, but I can't help thinking the answer. That's he's downstairs on the sofa, asleep. Then I have another thought. He might not actually be downstairs by now. I've been doing homework for a while now, and sometimes Tucker does get up early, and he's in the habit now of just coming upstairs and using the shower without being asked. And if he does that he'll hear me speaking on the phone, and wonder who I'm speaking to. So just in case I twist the volume knob to make the radio louder.

"Well? You know where he is?" The man on the phone repeats.

"No," I lie. "He's not here."

The man – I suppose I should call him Vinny, since I know that's his name - doesn't reply, and I wonder if I could just hang up. But I spend too long thinking about it and miss my chance.

"So where's 'here'?"

"Erm. I don't know."

For a stupid moment I wonder if Vinny might actually be Tucker's probation officer, like Amber thought last night, but I know he isn't. He doesn't sound anything like a probation officer would sound.

"How'd you get hold of Tucker's phone son?"

But then I'm not quite so sure. Suddenly he sounds a bit more friendly. So what if he *is* a probation officer. Or a policeman. How would you actually tell?

"Listen kid. I only want to speak to him. He don't have nothing to worry about, not from me."

I swallow at this because the way he says it, it kind of makes me think the exact opposite.

"Where are you kid? You don't sound like you're from round here. You got an accent. Tell me where Tucker is..."

Still I don't hang up, and I begin to understand why. I start to feel a bit braver. I work out that, whoever he is, there's no way he can tell where I am, just from a phone call. That's why he keeps asking me. Because he *needs* me to tell him. So I'm safe, as long as I watch what I say. And that means I'm able to start asking *him* questions. It might help when I speak to the police.

"Who are you? And why are you looking for Tucker?"

There's a long pause, and at the end of it Vinny laughs.

"Who am *I*? You got a nerve kid. And who says I'm looking for Tucker? I'm just looking *out for* him, you know what I'm saying?"

I don't answer.

"Tell me where you are you kid? Where's that accent from?"

I don't reply. I know what he's trying to do.

"Is that East Coast?"

Again I stay silent. I'm not going to be tricked into revealing anything.

"Tucker's a friend of yours is he?"

"*No.* He just knows my Dad, that's all." Straight away I realize I shouldn't have said that. I know it from the way he replies, sharp and fast.

"And who's your dad?"

I try not to answer, but Vinny just waits for me to speak, and it's weird how hard it is not to tell him, with the question just hanging there. And I can feel myself about to reply, even though I don't want to, when he speaks again.

"Who's your dad kid? What's his name?"

And somehow that makes it easier to not answer him. I shouldn't have let slip about Dad, but it's not enough for Vinny to know where we are, and now I'm not going to make a second mistake.

"Where's that accent son? You don't sound like you're from around here..." His voice has changed now. He doesn't sound mean, more like someone offering candy to a kid.

I decide the best thing to do it hang up, to be on the safe side. But then something really bad happens. Something really super unlucky. Just before I press the button to end the call, the song on the radio ends, and the DJ starts calling something out. And right away I know what he's gonna say, because I've heard it before, when I used to listen to *Lornea Island 104* a lot. There's this really old movie, you might have seen it. It's about the war in Vietnam, and a DJ in the army played by the an old actor called Robin Williams has this catchphrase. I reckon the *Lornea Island 104* DJ must have watched the movie a lot because he's always doing it too.

"Goooooooooood Moooooorning..." I panic. I should just kill the call, but instead I dive across the room to switch the radio off. But I don't get there in time. "... Lorneeeeeee Issssssland!"

The room is suddenly silent. The phone has fallen to the floor, and I stoop down to pick it up, praying that it broke or stopped the call when it fell. But then I realise Vinny is saying something.

"What was that kid? What's goin' on..."

I don't wait long enough to hear it all. I fumble with the buttons until the phone's screen goes blank.

I stare at the phone for a few moments, and then the screen lights up, and the caller ID shows he's rung back. Hurriedly, and fumbling even more now, because my hands are really shaking, I manage to slide the back off and rip out the battery. Then I pull out the SIM card out too, and throw it away, it cuts through the air, like when you throw a playing card, but then it hits the wall, then drops down to the floor like a dead insect.

THIRTY-FIVE

AMBER CORNERS me as I get off the school bus, and asks if Vinny replied to the text, That's good, because it means I don't have to lie to her. I tell her that he hasn't sent any texts, and she looks disappointed, but then she starts talking about something else.

"I had an idea," she tells me. "About Mrs. Jacobs."

I have to get to class, so it's not really the time to talk.

"You remember how Sharpe told us about Henry Jacobs running off with another woman? But we know he was more interested in little boys."

"So?"

"So I figured that kinda proves how he didn't go off with a woman. You see what I mean?"

I try to follow her logic, but it isn't actual logic. As in anything actually logical.

"Why not?"

"Because he liked *boys*. So he wouldn't go off with a woman would he? Think about it..."

"Maybe he liked boys *and* women."

She gives me a look.

"That's how it works Billy," Amber says, then she drops into step with me, so we're both walking together down the corridor.

"What are you interested in?"

"What?"

"Girls? Boys? What do you like?"

Straight away I feel my face begins to heat up.

"What do you mean?"

"What I said. Handsy Henry liked little boys. So he's not going to like women as well. What are you into? Are there any girls you like?"

I don't look at her. I make a real point of it.

"No."

"Why not? Are you into boys?"

"*No!*"

"It's alright. I don't mind either way."

"I'm not..."

"Look my point is, people usually like one or the other. Except for bisexuals I suppose. And people that like to stick it into sheep. Maybe they like goats just as much, I don't know."

I open my mouth to reply, but she's off on one now.

"*Henry Jacobs.* If he was into boys, then I reckon it *proves* he didn't run off with another woman. Or if it doesn't prove it, then it pretty nearly does. Because he didn't *like* women! Not in a sexual way."

I don't know what to say. I think I just want this conversation to end. And then it does, but not quite how I wanted it to.

"Anyway." Amber says. "I gotta get to class. I had this great idea what we should do with Mrs. Jacobs. I'll tell you at lunch." And then she disappears.

* * *

I've had a bit of bullying to deal with recently. Ever since what happened in the reception hall, when Amber attacked James Drolley. It's not been anything too serious. But that kind of changes, in mid-morning break, when I'm going from one class to the next. Most of the classrooms in our school are in the main block, but there's also an annex, where the science labs are. To get there you have to go down this long corridor. And I'm walking down there when I hear someone calling my name. I turn around and see Drolley and a couple of others. Right away I know it's going to be bad. You can always tell.

"Wheatley. Where d'ya think you're going?"

I think about making a run for the classroom. But it's still break time. The teacher won't be there yet so I'll be trapped, and they'll be wound up from chasing me. So I wait for them, hoping to get it over with. Drolley's gang stop a few steps away, but Drolley himself doesn't stop. He keeps walking till he's almost on top of me, and then without slowing down or hesitating he punches me in the stomach. He punches me really hard.

It hurts twice as much because I wasn't expecting it. I double up. I'm still on my feet but it's knocked all the breath out of me and I can't get any new air in. I start to panic, trying to draw a breath, but it's like my lungs have broken.

"No vampire protector today Wheatley?" Drolley asks, then there's a fresh wave of pain as he hits me again. Then a third time. This time I don't stay on my feet, though I don't know how I go down. I just find myself on the floor, gritty against my cheek.

"Fucking little freak." I hear him mutter above me. And then there's a blow on my back, I think where's he's kicking me. I curl up into a ball, the kicks don't hurt as much as the punches, and now, finally, I'm getting some air in again.

It's bad, but at least it's quick, because then they're gone, laughing as they carry on down the corridor, and into the classroom. And slowly the pain recedes, and eventually I can get enough air in. I push against the wall of the corridor with my feet, and after a while I get to a sitting position. Quite a few of the other kids from my class have come by now, but none of them have done anything. They can't really, because Drolley will only pick on them if they do, so they just step by, like they're pretending they didn't see. And I know I have to get up too, before the teacher comes to take the class, because he'd ask what I'm doing here on the floor. And then if I told him what happened, Drolley would know I sneaked on him, and then he'd just do it again.

I'm sort of on my feet by the time Mr. Edwards comes by. He just gives me a strange look.

"Everything OK Wheatley?"

I still can't speak, so I nod, and he pulls a face. I've never got on with Mr. Edwards.

"Well don't hang around here looking *odd*. Get into class." And he waits so that I have to walk in front of him into the classroom. Normally I get in early, so I can get a desk at the front, but because I'm late there's none left, and I have to take one right at the back, right next to where Drolley is sitting, smirking at me.

So that's not very nice.

* * *

"You what?" I ask Amber, at lunchtime.

"It *has* to be her. It all fits."

I stare at Amber in amazement. "You actually think Mrs. Jacobs killed Henry Jacobs?"

"I'm sure of it."

"Why?"

"She found out he was a pedophile. She didn't like it. So *boom*." She mimes the action of a handgun against the side of my head.

"But what about the letters? The birthday cards Principal Sharpe received from her dad, who was living with another woman in Maui?"

"Faked."

I'm still staring at her.

"But why would she hire *us*? To find him, if *she* killed him."

"I know, it's crazy right? But what if she forgot? What if her mental state, whatever it's called, made her forget, but she really wants to know?"

"Her senile dementia?"

"Yep, that's the thing."

I realize I'm shaking my head.

"Look Billy, I'm only saying it's a possibility. This is how you investigate things. You make a hypothesis, then you test it."

"So how are you gonna test it?"

"We, partner, are going to go back to see her, and we're going to tell her we know the truth – that she killed him. And if that *is* true, it'll make her remember. She won't be able to hide it. And we'll record what she says, so we have the evidence."

"But..." There's so many reasons why this is crazy that I don't know where to start. "Principal Sharpe told us we're not allowed to speak to her again."

"She also lied about Henry Jacobs moving to Maui. You really gonna listen to her?"

"We don't know she lied, and she's the school princip..."

"Cos I'm not. Can't you see? She was covering for her mom. That's the reason she doesn't want us speaking to her. Because she knows what really happened to Henry Jacobs. She doesn't want us finding out."

"Or she just doesn't want her mother getting disturbed because she's got – what did you call it?"

Amber shakes her head to dismiss this at once, but then she stops.

"Actually it's a pretty big problem for her isn't it? Here's her mom with this dark secret, who's now going mental, and she could spill it out to anyone."

I open my mouth to protest again, how Principal Sharpe has letters from her dad which prove her mom didn't kill him, but I can tell I'm not going to get anywhere. Amber has convinced herself. So I try a different issue.

"How are you going to do it? We don't have any secret recording equipment."

And then Amber leans down to her bag, with a broad grin.

"Oh yes we do." She pulls out a tangle of black cables. "I borrowed this from the music department. All we have to do is tape this under your clothes and plug it into a phone. She's never going to search us is she?"

As she speaks I can't help but picture a miniature, secret microphone, like the type you see in spy movies. But the microphone she pulls out isn't one of those. It's like of those ones you clip onto a shirt, that the news-readers wear. I guess you could call it discreet maybe, but it's definitely not secret.

"Why me? Why do I have to wear it?"

"Because I'm gonna be the one asking all the questions, so she'll be looking at me more, and she might see it."

"I don't know." I say, after considering all this.

"What do you mean you don't know? What is there to know?"

"I don't know if we should. I mean, after what Principal Sharpe said. What if Mrs. Jacobs tells her that we tried to speak to her again?"

"She can't stop us speaking to her. She's our client. Besides, you saw what a lonely old lady she is. She'll be pleased to see us. And, if we're wrong, it'll give us the chance to report back what we found out. We can tell her we discovered her husband moved away to Maui. If it is true, we should tell her that at least."

I think about this for a while. I guess it makes sense when she puts it like that.

"I can't go tonight." I tell her. "Dad's back and I want to see him."

"OK." For the first time Amber looks reasonable. "Are you gonna tell him about Tucker? About how he's casing out jewelry shops?"

I nod. I don't know *how* I'm going to tell him. But I know I do have to.

* * *

But then when I get home and look on *VesselTrack*, Dad's boat is still quite a long way out from the island, and I realize I misjudged how slowly it goes. I discover you can measure the actual distance on the screen, and since I know the boat's speed, I do my calculations properly this time, and I work out that *Ocean Harvest* will dock at about 10 tonight. I guess he'll have to help unload too, so probably won't get back here till midnight. I won't be able to tell him about Tucker then, so it will have to be in the morning, before I go to school. Then Dad can throw him out and I don't have to be part of it.

At least Tucker isn't here this evening. There's still half of the vegetable lasagna in the refrigerator, and he's left a note on the table saying he had to go out, and I should eat it.

So I catch up a bit more on my homework and tidy the house a bit, for Dad. It's not going to be easy to tell him about Tucker. Dad'll ask how I know about him, and he'll think I've been snooping, which he hates. I've just got to hope he'll understand it was the right thing to do, because of what I ended up finding out. But you never know with Dad.

I'm still thinking about this when, just before I go to bed, I break into Dad's emails. I actually do this from time to time, not because I'm being nosy, or snooping or anything, but just to keep an eye on things. A lot of the bills for the house come in by email, and I need to know if Dad's on top of them. So I scan his inbox a bit absently, and I'm about to click away when I see something that stops me dead. It's an email from Tucker, sitting in Dad's inbox. It's already been opened, I guess Dad in range of the shore now and he's seen it on his phone. So I click the message to see what it says. and after a moment it opens.

It's really short, just an email link and four words:

How about this one?

Confused, I click the link, and then my screen fills with a familiar looking website. It's the one with the couple spinning around on the beach, showing off the diamonds on their fingers. Carter's Jewelry. Tucker's sent it to Dad. Which means...

Which means I don't need to tell Dad that Tucker is looking for a jewelry store to hold up.

Because Dad already knows.

THIRTY-SIX

MY DAD ISN'T a bad person, I just want to take a moment to say that. It's just he's had a really tough life. When he was growing up his mom and dad had no money at all. So Dad couldn't afford to go to college, or even finish high school because he had to get a job or they wouldn't have been able to eat. Then he must have thought his life was going to get better when he met my mom, because she came from a family that had loads of money, and lived in this big house. But then my Mom went mad and murdered my sister, and tried to kill me, and her family blamed it all on Dad, so he had no choice but to run away here with me, in secret. So it didn't really.

And if that wasn't bad enough, then Dad got involved in all the stuff that happened here. But that was just bad luck. He started dating this girl who seemed really nice on the outside, but turned out to be a murderer, and then Dad got blamed for the girl *she* killed. And even now, half the town doesn't really believe he was completely innocent even though she's in prison for it. So if he's involved in Tucker's idea to rob a jewelry store then it's only because he's desperate. He just wants to earn enough money so we can both live here and have folk leave us in peace.

Even so I can't get to sleep for worrying. I keep trying to work out what to actually *do*. There's no point me telling Dad about Tucker, because obviously Dad already knows.

And I can't go to the police now either. Because if they came to arrest

Tucker, they'll also look into his emails, and they'll work out that Dad is part of the plan too.

I can't even tell *Amber* about it, because... Well, because Amber's basically insane.

And I know that things like this always seem worse in the night, and not so bad in the morning. But even so I can't stop myself crying. Just a little bit. And once I start crying, pretty soon my pillow is all wet, because I'm crying quite a lot.

But after that I do feel a bit better. And just in time, because then I hear the noise of an engine outside, and I peek out the window, and I see Dad and Tucker getting out of Dad's truck. And I see how they're laughing and joking with each other, and Dad looks really happy. And I don't know what to feel about that. I'm pleased to see Dad again, and I want him to be happy. But I'm terrified about what he's going to do.

Quickly I wipe my eyes and get back into bed. I pretend to be reading a book, so that when Dad comes in, to tell me he's back and he's safe, he can't tell that I've been crying. I hear them both, still laughing downstairs, for quite a long time, but eventually I hear the squeak of footsteps on the stairs. I wipe my face again, and get ready for Dad to come in.

But then he doesn't. I hear the sounds of him in the bathroom. And then his bedroom door opening, and then shutting again. And then nothing. So I'm left there, holding the book I'm not really reading.

So eventually I just put it down, and try and go to sleep.

THIRTY-SEVEN

I'M a bit vacant in school the next morning, so when Amber catches up with me and tells me we're sneaking off for the afternoon to see Mrs. Jacobs, I don't even try to argue with her. It's easy to leave. There's a teacher by the gate, but she's only checking students who are walking in, and we're in Amber's mom's car, driving out.

Once we're out of Newlea she stops and tells me to take off my shirt. Again I do what she says without arguing. She's got some of that silver sticky tape that sticks to anything, and she pulls off long strips of it, and uses it to tape the microphone leads around my body and to my back. We put the actual microphone just below the neckline at the front of my t-shirt. When I put it all back on I can't move because the tape pulls and rips at my skin.

"Has that Vinny guy replied yet?" Amber asks as she's pressing the tape back down on my chest. "To the message we sent?"

I sense my body tensing up, and force it to relax. I'd forgotten about that.

"No."

"How about your Dad? Did he get back last night? Have you told him about Tucker planning to hit the jewelry store?"

"No."

"*Relax will you?* You'll put the tape off."

"I am relaxed. Just stop picking on me."

Amber doesn't mention it again.

I know why, it's because *she's* distracted. She's super excited about what we're doing. I've figured out how to tell with Amber. It's in the way her eyes go really shiny. She totally believes that Mrs. Jacobs murdered Mr. Jacobs, instead of him just going away like Principal Sharpe told us. And she really seems to believe she's going to persuade Mrs. Jacobs to confess to it. It's ridiculous. But then so is Amber half the time. But I suppose she *is* right about telling Mrs. Jacobs what we've learnt. Probably Mrs. Jacobs is too mad to understand, but just maybe she won't be, and maybe it'll even help her. And if that's the case then maybe we could hold onto the $5000 check. I still haven't quite decided what we should do about that.

We pull up outside Mrs. Jacobs' house and Amber fusses about with my wires again before we get out of the car. Until I knock her hand away, because Mrs. Jacobs will have heard us arrive, and might be looking out of the window.

"*Alright*. Easy Billy," Amber says. Then she presses record on her iPhone, and slips it into my pocket. And then she gives me an excited look, then we get out of the car and walk to the front door.

Amber rings the bell and we wait for a while, but nothing happens. I start to feel a bit relieved, because I don't really want to do this, now that I'm here. I think it's stupid, and I think we could get into a lot of trouble.

"Come on. Let's go back to school." I say. "She's not in. Even if she was, she wouldn't tell us anything."

Amber presses the doorbell again. And then she uses her fist to bang on the door.

"Shit," she murmurs.

"Come on," I say again. "Let's get back before we're missed..." But then the door suddenly opens. Just a crack, only as far as the security chain allows it. There's a rustling sound from inside, and we can see a strip of Mrs. Jacob's face. Just wide enough to see her eyes looking back, milky and a bit scared.

"Mrs. Jacobs? It's Amber. From the detective agency. We said we'd come to meet you?"

The eyes blink slowly. They look confused.

"Detective agency?" I didn't remember from before how old she sounds.

"The one you hired, Mrs. Jacobs." Amber is speaking really loudly now, and the poor old lady winces away from the sound, like it hurts her ears.

"To find out what happened to your husband."

The eyes come back again, blinking. Even though I can't see much I feel sorry for her, and I hope she won't let us in, because I'm worried about what Amber wants to do to her.

"To Henry, Mrs. Jacobs. Remember? Your husband Henry? He disappeared that Christmas. You asked us to find out what happened to him."

Then Mrs. Jacob's eyes rotate in their sockets as they inspect first Amber and then me. I feel awkward standing so close, it's like I can feel the wires of the microphone standing out through the thin fabric of my shirt.

"My husband?"

"That's right Mrs. Jacobs. We've got some news." Amber bites her lip hopefully. "Can we come in please?"

Suddenly the door shuts, and I feel slightly hopeful for a second that maybe she won't let us in. But of course she's just taking the security chain off. It rattles for ages, like she's struggling with it, and then the door slowly opens again, but all the way this time.

I'd forgotten how stooped over she is. And how crazy. She's only wearing one blouse today, but it's two buttons out of alignment. It makes her look lopsided. Amber slides a quick look at me.

"Thanks you Mrs. Jacobs. We appreciate it."

Mrs. Jacobs does a sort of smile, and then she stands back from the door. Amber walks in, and then I don't have any choice but to follow her in.

I remember the big hallway, the oil paintings. It all seems darker this time. Then I get a weird thought. I can suddenly imagine Principal Sharpe running around here as a nine year old who just lost her dad. But she's not like a real nine year old, she's like a miniature Principal Sharpe, just scaled down to be the same size as a child.

Then Mrs. Jacobs shuts the front door, making it even darker. She puts the security chain back on. It takes her ages again, and while she does it Amber and I just stand there waiting. But eventually she gets it, and that's a relief in itself. I wonder if she's going to take us somewhere crazy to talk this time, like into her bathroom. But again she leads us out into the garden, just like before.

"Could I get you a drink? Some coffee perhaps? Or some iced tea?" Mrs. Jacobs asks, and we both say no straight away, but she doesn't seem to hear.

"I'm sure I've got a soda somewhere. I won't be a moment." She waves her hand, and Amber and me are left there for a moment, looking around her garden again.

"What are you going to tell her?" I ask. The truth is I've been a bit distracted all day, with all the Tucker and Dad stuff, and I haven't really thought through what we're doing here.

"I told you," Amber say. "We're gonna tell her what we've found out and get her to confess ."

"But what about..." I don't finish what I'm saying because then Mrs. Jacobs returns with two cans of 7 UP on a tray. She sets it down and makes a big thing about giving us both coasters.

"I know what you young people are like with spillages," she says and winks at me.

I pick up my 7 UP and notice the tab is already open. I sniff it, a bit suspicious. But it seems alright, I get a nose full of fizz, so I take a sip.

"Now dear," Mrs. Jacobs says to Amber. "You said you found out something about Henry?"

I'm glad she asks Amber, because I don't have a plan for what we're supposed to say. I don't see how we can say how Principal Sharpe – her own daughter – told us about Mr. Jacobs running off with another woman. Nor how she – Mrs. Jacobs – must have *known* this, only now she's forgotten because she's gone mad. How's that going to make her feel? As it happens, I don't think Amber knows what to say either, because she starts off by explaining how we discovered Henry was the Principal of Newlea High School when he went missing, and how we searched the newspaper archives for information about it. And all the time Mrs. Jacobs sits there with a whole series of looks on her face, from confused, to nodding, to angry.

"But I know all this!" She says, when Amber finally stops. Then she looks at me.

And that makes Amber look at me too. So I have to say something.

"We spoke to your daughter. Or rather, she spoke to us. She's our school Principal."

There's a moment when Mrs. Jacobs smiles, I suppose at the mention of her daughter, but then she looks totally baffled.

"*Your* school principal?"

"We go to Newlea High School. You know she's the principal there now?"

"Well yes. Of course. But..." she lifts a frail hand and points at me. "You're a student at Wendy's school?"

"We both are."

There's a moment of silence, then I try to smile. Amber isn't looking very happy. But what am I supposed to say?

"She told us..."

"But you're *detectives*. She told me you were detectives." Mrs. Jacobs spins in her chair and stares at Amber again, but she's more confused than angry.

"We *are* detectives. We're just students as well."

There's an odd moment when I don't know how Mrs. Jacobs is going to take it, but then she laughs.

"My my. Good heavens. I did think you were rather young." Mrs. Jacobs pauses, her face screws up again, like something's just occurred to her.

"But Wendy doesn't know what happened to Henry."

I'm not sure what she means by that, so I decide to correct her.

"Actually Mrs. Jacobs, that's what we need to..." But I don't get to finish my sentence because there's a sudden change in Mrs. Jacobs. She suddenly sits up straighter in her chair, appears less frail. And her voice hardens. It's like what happened the first time we were here.

"She doesn't know anything that girl. Never bloody did!"

It's like someone has magically just made Mrs. Jacobs vanish, and replaced her with someone else. Everything about her is different. Even the dullness has gone from her eyes.

"What did she tell you?" Mrs. Jacobs demands. "What did that *stupid girl* say?"

I look at Amber, trying to get her to take over again, but her eyes are wide and she just nods, urging me on. And I can feel Mrs. Jacobs eyes too. Piercing and sharp. Suddenly *mean*. I go on, as carefully as I can.

"She said your husband left the island with another lady. That he started a new life with her. In Hawaii. He wrote letters. To Principal Sharpe. That's how she knows."

Mrs. Jacobs eyes flare with something, surprise, perhaps. But she doesn't speak.

"I'm really sorry," I start to say, but then she interrupts me.

"*The goddamn hell he did!*" She suddenly explodes. "There's no way that man was ever going to leave *me*. I made damn sure of that."

There's a long silence. All I can hear is the birds tweeting, and the rolling of the surf at the bottom of the rock cliffs.

"Could you say that again Mrs. Jacobs." I hear Amber asking, but it's from a long way away.

"Say what again?" She snaps.

"What you just said. About how you made sure he wouldn't leave you? What did you mean by that?"

There's another shift in Mrs. Jacobs, and for a moment I think the sweet old lady is back. Or maybe I just hope that's what happens, because this version is scary. But I'm wrong. She's someone else again. Less angry, but more lucid.

"Henry was never going to *leave me*. I made him respectable. My family had all the money. Oh no..." her hand comes up again, even that looks somehow less frail than it did before.

"No. I killed him." She sits back and smiles, her lips drawing back to show her old, stained teeth and blood-red gums.

Amber's staring at me now, and there's all sorts in the look on her face. Like she's telling me how she told me so, and that I'd better be recording this.

"You... You did what?" She asks.

Mrs. Jacobs turns on Amber, and gives her a pitying look. It's like she doesn't have time for Amber's stupidity.

"*I killed him dear*. I warned him I would. If he kept on with that dirty fiddling he did. I told him what would happen. But he wouldn't listen. So I killed him."

She turns to me, and smiles again. I think I can feel my mouth hanging open.

"He'd have liked you, Mr. Billy. I tell you that. You'd have been one of his *special ones*, if you'd been around back then. Oh no. I couldn't let him carry on like that. We'd have been ruined when it came out. And it would have come out. Sooner or later."

"So what happened?" Amber asks. Her voice still sounds distant.

"I just told you! He promised me it wouldn't happen again. But I knew it would. I could *tell*. And sure enough, there he was, coming home from school again. *Working late!* I knew exactly what *that* meant. So I went to confront him, at the school. I got there just in time to see a boy leaving, his clothing messed around. So I went inside. I surprised him."

She looks each of us in the eye, and there's a strange expression on her face. Pride. Arrogance.

"Did you shoot him?" Amber asks, breathless.

"Of course not. Where would I get a gun from?" She rolls her eyes and turns to me.

"I pretended there was nothing wrong. I was just passing. I asked him to show me the building works – the new gymnasium, some of the money was coming from my family. And he agreed, mainly because he was feeling guilty about what he'd been doing. And then, when his back was turned, I hit him over the head with a brick. He went down like a sack of potatoes."

"It was easy. I rolled his body in the bottom of the hole and covered it with rubble. The next day they poured the concrete."

Mrs. Jacobs turns and smiles at me.

"And that was the end of Henry."

THIRTY-EIGHT

"TELL ME YOU GOT THAT? Tell me you didn't sit on the phone and stop it recording? Tell me that didn't happen."

We're back in Amber's car, driving back towards school. I don't really know how to describe the atmosphere. We're just… stunned. After Mrs. Jacobs told us about how she killed her husband she went right back to being the sweet scared old lady she'd been before. With the same confused, milky look in her eyes. And when Amber asked her for more details she didn't seem to know who Mr. Jacobs was, let alone what happened to him. I'm not even sure she knew who we were.

I fiddle with the phone, making sure I don't do anything stupid like delete the file. And then I hit play. It's a bit hard to hear with the engine, but you can hear us alright, the two of us getting out of the car and going to the doorstep.

"Come on, let's go back to school," I hear my voice from earlier saying. "She's not going to tell us anything."

I guess Amber can't hear properly, because she turns abruptly into a parking area, off the road, skidding to a halt on the gravel.

"Turn it up," she says.

I do what she says. And then I adjust the slider at the bottom of the screen to fast forward to the part where Mrs. Jacobs confesses.

I killed him. I'd warned him I would. If he kept on with that dirty fiddling he did.

"Wow." Amber says. "Just fucking *wow*."

I don't answer. I just stare out the windshield. The parking area is one of those with a view out over the water. In the distance the mainland is a grey shadow on the horizon. Some way out a container ship is passing by, its massive hull streaked red with rust. Closer still there's a company of gannets feeding in the cold currents, that swirl round the southern tip of Lornea Island, folding up their long thin wings and diving into the water like arrows. I see them, I see it all but I hardly register any of it.

"We have to go to the police." Amber says. I don't answer.

"We *have to*. We know a crime's been committed. A *murder*. We can't not go to the police."

Still I don't say anything. I'm thinking.

"And to think, she put his body under *the fucking gym*! It'll still be there today. I was only in there yesterday for P Ed. That's sick. That's disgusting."

I'm watching the gannets now. They're kind of hypnotic. When they hit the water they can swim down as much as twenty meters. It's like they can fly under that water. I'd quite like to raise a gannet chick one day, but they don't nest on the island, they have these big stacks of rock out to sea where they form massive colonies...

"*Billy!*"

My head snaps around to look at her.

"We have to go to the police."

I open my mouth to reply to her. But I don't say anything. The thing is, I can't get out of my head what happened the last time I went to the police. When Olivia Curran went missing, and I thought that maybe this guy in Silverlea might have kidnapped and murdered her. I actually got a photo of what I thought was him dragging her body out of his house, rolled up in a carpet. Only it wasn't her at all. He was just renovating his house. It was just a carpet.

Without speaking I press play on the phone again. Mrs. Jacobs' voice rings out again. Just from the tone you can tell it's her nasty version.

I killed him. I put his body in the bottom of the hole and covered it with rubble. The next day they poured the concrete...

There's a laugh. I didn't notice it at the time, but it's there on the recording, clear as anything. Only it's more of a cackle than a laugh. Like Mrs. Jacobs is actually a witch.

"Billy? We *have* to go to the police."

I nod. "Yeah. I know."

THIRTY-NINE

ONCE WE'VE MADE the decision, we have to work out how. I mean, you can't just walk into Newlea Police Station and say you've got evidence of a murder. Can you?

Well actually it turns out you can. Or at least, neither of us can think of a better idea. So that's what we do. Instead of going back to school, Amber drives us straight to the police station, the same one where I was interviewed a couple of years ago.

It's weird being back. It doesn't feel like two years since I was last here, and I wonder if I'm going to recognize anyone. But the officer on the front desk isn't familiar.

"Help you?" He narrows his eyes like he doesn't like kids. I'd forgotten how the police are like that.

"We need to speak to a detective," I say, trying to sound firmer than I feel. "We have evidence about a murder."

The cop looks like he's trying to show this happens all the time, but I see his eyebrows going up in surprise.

"What evidence?"

In response I hold up Amber's phone and press play. Mrs. Jacobs' voice rings out inside the quiet of the police station. I stop the recording just after her cackling laugh.

"Who is that?" the officer asks, but I shake my head.

"We need to speak to a detective," I say again.

The officer stares at us for a long time before he does anything. He's obviously pissed, but we need someone more senior.

"I'll find someone you can speak to."

"Thank you."

Ten minutes later the same officer leads us to an interview room. He tells us to sit down and says someone will be with us shortly. It's even more weird being back in here – it's the same actual room I was in last time. It's still got the old fashioned tape-recorders they had before, the ones that actually use tapes. I point them out to Amber, but she frowns at me, like she's not interested.

"They're *analogue*!" I tell her.

She keeps frowning, and then she mutters, more to herself than me.

"This is so fucked up."

Then the door bursts open, and a man comes striding in. He's about to shut the door behind him, when he stops, noticing me. He holds his head still for a few moments.

"*Wheatley!* I knew I remembered that name." Then he closes the door, but he does so slowly, like he's taking the time to remember everything that happened before. I realize I know him too. He was one of the policemen I didn't really get on with when I was here before. Although there were quite a lot I didn't get on with. He sits down opposite us. Before he speaks again he looks carefully at Amber, but then he comes back to me.

"*Billy Wheatley.*"

I don't reply. I don't remember his name. After a while he must realize this.

"I'm Lieutenant James Langley. We met before." He turns to Amber. "And you are?"

While she tells him her name I remember a bit more about him. He was the one who was in charge of the investigation to find the missing girl, but he wasn't very good. He got really angry just because I was trying to help.

"Frank tells me you've got something I should hear." He doesn't start the recorder on the desk, so it doesn't seem like he's got any better at being a detective. I think about pointing this out, but in the end I don't. Instead I re-play the audio of Mrs. Jacobs confessing.

Lieutenant Langley listens in silence with a stern look on his face. When it's finished he scratches at his ear.

"This some sort of joke?"

"*No*." I'm a bit confused by this. Why would I do this as a joke?

Langley thinks for a moment more.

"So who is that?"

"It's someone called Barbara Jacobs," Amber says. She sounds quite nervous. I'd forgotten she hasn't been to a police station before.

"And who's she talking about?"

"Her husband. Henry Jacobs. He was the principal of Newlea High School until 1979. That's when she killed him."

Amber falls silent, and Langley looks at both of us for a while, one after the other.

"1979, you say? That's..."

"Forty years ago," I have to interrupt. I can see him counting in his head.

"Right." He nods, then turns back to Amber.

"How'd you get the recording?"

Amber hesitates before answering. "We've been... We've sort of been investigating what happened to him."

Langley doesn't move.

"Why?"

"Because... We sort of thought... well..." Amber obviously doesn't know what to say, so I interrupt again.

"We started a detective agency," I say. I might as well just tell him. He's going to find out sooner or later.

"Then she hired us. She wanted to find out what happened to her husband before she died, because she's really old. Only it turned out that *she* killed him, and she's forgotten, because she's got dementia."

I feel Langley's eyes resting on my face, like he's sucking in all this information. Processing it piece by piece.

"*Who* did you say started a detective agency?"

I point to myself and Amber. "We did."

Lieutenant Langley's face change now. It stiffens, like he's trying not to show what he's thinking, but he's definitely thinking really hard.

"*You* started a detective agency?"

"That's right."

"You? Billy Wheatley? Started a detective agency?"

"Yes. And then Amber joined in too."

There's a pause.

"Why?"

"I think because she was bored. There's not much happening on Lornea Island and her mom is more interested..."

"No. Why did *you* start a detective agency?"

"Oh," I pause. "Well I didn't really mean to. I was just practicing making a website but then..." I fade out. He doesn't need to know *everything*.

But now Langley looks perplexed. He starts blinking lots. Then shakes his head just a little bit.

"And this lady... This Barbara Jacobs. She actually *hired* you? As a *detective*?"

I glance at Amber, I told her before we got here how we'd end up answering the same questions over and over.

"Yeah."

"Why? What did she want?"

"She wanted us to find her husband."

"The one she admitted to killing?"

I try to explain it again. "She forgot why her husband disappeared, because she's got dementia problems, so she hired us to find out. But then we found out... And, well." I point to the phone on the tabletop.

"And then how did you..." He stops. "*How* did you get this recording?"

"We worked out that she must have killed him, and then decided to get her to confess."

"I worked it out," Amber interrupts.

"Yeah, Amber worked it out." I admit, because that's only fair.

Lieutenant Langley sits silently for a moment, tapping the table with his knuckles. He doesn't look at us. Finally he gets up.

"Wait here."

He gets as far as the door, then turns around and comes back. He snatches the phone from the table.

"You mind?"

Both me and Amber shake our heads.

"I'll be right back."

As soon as he's gone I feel a bit anxious. He's just taken the evidence without giving us any sort of receipt. I think Amber knows this too, so we sit in silence, not even looking at each other.

We end up waiting for ages. Lieutenant Langley comes back several times to ask us new questions, or the same questions again. Sometimes he's on his own, and sometimes he's with other people. At one point the Chief of Police looks in. I met him when I got my medal, so I give a little wave to say hello, but he doesn't wave back, or even say anything, he just stares at us then walks out again.

Then they tell us they need to get our parents here, because they have to do formal interviews. I knew this part was coming, and I wasn't looking forward to it, but it can't be helped. At least Dad is back from the boat, so he's not going to get into trouble for leaving me on my own. And I start to wonder if him having to come to the police station again will remind him how the robbery he's plotting with Tucker is a bad idea. It actually might, and that would be an unexpected bonus.

Amber's step-dad gets here first. I haven't actually met him before. He's wearing a suit and he's really polite to the officers, but he looks super mad with Amber, like she's a pain anyway but this is something else. She has to go with him anyway, and the detective who waits with me explains how they want to interview us separately. They want to check if our stories match up, but I'm not worried because we're telling the truth.

Then Dad comes in. I haven't seen him for over a week. He hasn't shaved on the boat, so he's grown half a beard. It scratches at my face as he hugs me. He looks more worried than mad. He whispers to ask me what I've got mixed up in, but I don't get the chance to answer him, because right away Lieutenant Langley and another detective come in and sit down and begin the formal interview.

FORTY

I HAVE to go over everything I've already told them, all over again. And then when we're finished they want to go back and talk about specific parts of it in more detail, like what I thought the guy at the garage had meant when he told us Henry messed around with kids. It's really tiring, and they keep stopping and pausing the tape, then going outside and we're left there waiting for ages before they start again.

Dad keeps asking when we can go home, but they've always got one more question, until it's really late, and I'm so tired I can't keep my eyes open. Then Dad insists, and in the end they agree, but they say we have to come back first thing tomorrow. Then we get driven home in a police car. I go right to bed, since there's a weird atmosphere at home, with Dad and Tucker and everything. But we have to come straight back to the police station the next morning, and it just carries on like the day before. I sort of zone out of it all after a while, until, about lunchtime, when I get really hungry. Really hungry. I didn't eat last night, and I only grabbed some toast for breakfast. Then finally I say it to one of the detectives. I don't mean to, it just comes out.

"Can I have something to eat?"

It stops them in their tracks. Then one of the detectives, who's kind of looking after us, slaps the table.

"Sure. You like burgers?"

"Yeah."

"Alright then." Then he gets up and leaves.

That was about an hour ago. We've been left alone since then, just me and Dad, and we're not really talking. He's asked me a few questions about the detective agency, and I can tell he's annoyed about it, but he won't tell me off here. He can't.

Then, finally, the door opens and the detective comes back holding a Wendy's take-away bag. It smells amazing. Normally I'm actually not that fond of Wendy's. But right now I'd eat anything.

But then, before I can eat anything, Lieutenant Langley walks back in. He's about the only policeman we haven't seen this morning. In one hand he's holding a plastic folder full of papers. He says something quietly to the other detective, then takes the Wendy's bag from him, and closes the door behind him, so it's just him, Dad and me in the room. He sits down, and pushes the burgers to one side. Then he opens his plastic wallet and pulls out the papers.

"Billy, we need to have a little chat." Lieutenant Langley says.

It's so hard not to stare at the burgers, but I drag my eyes away and look at him.

"I've just got back from speaking to Barbara Jacobs." He looks me right in the eyes, his face not giving anything away. I glance at the burgers, hoping he'll get the idea. But he doesn't.

"She denies killing her husband. She told us he went missing in 1979 and she has no knowledge of what happened to him after that."

Again I look at the burgers. I can talk and eat pretty well. I wonder about saying that to Lieutenant Langley.

"Well that doesn't mean anything," I hear Dad replying. "Not when she's already confessed on the tape Billy made?"

"That recording was made without her knowledge or consent. We can't use it."

"But you're not just gonna drop it?" Dad says. "You heard what she said..."

"I didn't say we're gonna drop it. We're searching records to see if there's any evidence of Henry Jacobs after 1979. On Maui or anywhere else."

"And is there?"

I know I should be following all this more closely, but it's really hard because I'm so hungry. Suddenly my stomach gives a really loud grumble and Lieutenant Langley stops what he's saying and stares at me. Finally he understands, and pulls the burgers back in front of him. He peeks in the bag.

"You hungry Billy?" He says, and I kind of hold my breath. My stomach rumbles again.

He slides the bag across to me. At once I dive in, and pull out a bacon double cheeseburger. It tastes every bit as good as I'd been imagining.

I don't hear much for a few minutes. I'm too busy eating, but when I finish, I realize that Dad and Lieutenant Langley have been talking for a long time, and they're just finishing up.

"So what happens now?" Dad says.

"You take young Billy home is what happens now. And you make damn sure he keeps his nose out of this."

FORTY-ONE

THE REST of the day is a bit like when you get better from having a fever. You're kind of dizzy, and you're not sure what's real and what isn't. I get the sense Dad's not sure how to react either. He feels like he ought to be mad at me, but he doesn't know why, or even if that's the right response at all. After all, it's not exactly a normal situation.

He keeps trying to have a chat with me, but it never really goes anywhere. He keeps shaking his head and asking if I'm alright, but then he doesn't know what to say next. In a way he takes it so well I actually consider telling him I know all about Tucker and what they're planning to do. But that would be a bit much, on top of everything else that's happening. So I keep quiet.

I spend the rest of the day moving Steven. It's actually something I should have done a long time ago, since he's easily ready. I put him outside, in a kind of pen that Dad built. He covered it in chicken wire, so that Steven wouldn't be able to fly off, but I take that bit off, because I actually want Steven to fly away if he wants to. But of course he doesn't. When I go back inside he just comes and sits on my windowsill, I pull the drapes shut so he can't see me. But I know he's still there.

And then I realize I'm actually really tired. Like exhausted. So I go to bed early, and for once I don't go on my computer at all. I just get into my bed and go to sleep.

I'm woken the next day by my phone ringing (I put my own SIM card back in it a long time ago), and I see it's Amber.

"You'll never guess what?" She says, when I answer it.

"What?" I reply. I'm still feeling really sleepy.

"The police have gone into the school. They're gonna dig up the gym."

FORTY-TWO

THEY DON'T CLOSE the school, they just shut off the gym hall. They don't even cancel gym classes, they just get moved out into the school field. In fact, it's almost like there's nothing going on at first – there's just a few police cars parked outside the gym hall, and an officer in uniform standing by the door to make sure no one tries to go in. But then the noise starts.

Deep, rumbling hammering noises, that you can hear from all over the school.

I don't tell anyone about what I know, I just listen to the noises, and rumors that have already started. Some people are saying how it might be Principal Sharpe the police are looking for buried there, which is bonkers when you think about it, but it tells you something about the intellect of some of the students at Newlea High School. Others are talking about how there might be bodies of students there, hundreds of them, murdered by teachers over the years. Like I said, a lot of the pupils here aren't that bright.

Even the teachers are gossiping about it, though they pretend they're not. They say how they just want us to get on with our work as normal, but when a television van turns up with a big satellite dish on the top, and the whole of my science class goes and watches at the window, Mr. Matthews doesn't do anything to stop us until he's had a good look too. So then we get to see this woman in a red dress with her microphone talking to a camera guy, in front of all the police cars. And then someone manages to get her interview streaming live to their phone and we all end up gathering around that, trying to listen.

"...*The Lornea Island Police Department refuse to state at this point why they are interested in the gymnasium of Newlea High School, saying only they are acting on 'credible information'...*"

Then Mr. Matthews does make us all go back to work. But it's impossible to focus, even on science class, with the noise of the concrete breakers. And the rumors keep flying.

I watch the full interview with the presenter in the red dress, later on at home with Dad and Tucker. But there's no actual news as such. Only that the police are looking for something, but they haven't found it yet. It's the same the next day, and the day after that. And then it's Saturday, so I don't go to school, although I keep an eye on the news websites to see what's happening. And then on Sunday night I'm upstairs and Dad calls me down to see something on the TV with him. I almost don't bother, but he says it's important. So I do go down. And this time there is actual news, as in something new.

But it isn't what I expect.

FORTY-THREE

ON THE TV Lieutenant Langley is sitting at a table with the chief of police on one side, and a woman I don't know on the other. There's a load of microphones in front of him on the table.

"What's this?" I ask Dad.

"Local news," he says. "Just came on."

"As you all know," Langley's voice comes through the speakers in a drone. "Over the last few days we've been conducting a detailed search of the foundations of the school gymnasium of Newlea High School. This was in response to credible information regarding the possibility of uncovering evidence related to a possible homicide." Langley pauses, and for a moment he looks at the wrong camera, then he seems to realize it.

"However, that search has not uncovered anything suspicious, and we no longer consider this site to be of interest in this investigation."

Then he starts to make an appeal for information from the public, but I don't really listen to that part.

"What does all that mean?" I ask, when the TV moves on to something else. Dad turns the sound down.

"Does it mean they couldn't find him?"

"No," Dad replies. "It means he wasn't there to find."

* * *

I spend the rest of the day trying to make sense of it. It's possible the police didn't look properly. Or that Mrs. Jacobs was lying to us. Or maybe that she got confused, and she never actually killed Mr. Jacobs at all. But I can't work out which. Then the police want to see me again, which is quite good, because at least they'll explain what's going on.

The patrolman at the front desk leads Dad and me out of the reception area straight away. I expect him to take us to the interview rooms like normal, but instead he goes upstairs where there's a big room full of desks. We follow the patrolman to a little cubicle at the end.

"Lieutenant Langley will be along any moment," the patrolman says. And then he leaves us.

Lieutenant Langley's desk is just like any normal desk, like the ones the secretaries have at school. There's a few neat piles of papers on one side, a coffee mug and a photo frame with its back facing us. I can't quite see it so I lean forward to get a better look.

"Sit still Billy. Don't touch."

"I didn't... I wasn't gonna..."

I don't go on. Dad seems angrier about the whole business today. It's like he was giving me the benefit of the doubt when he thought I might have actually solved a murder. Like he didn't have much choice about that. But now the police are saying there wasn't a body, he's not so sure about it all. I guess I'll have to find that out later though, since right now Lieutenant Langley strides in, wearing the same brown suit he always wears, with his detective badge on his belt. He closes the door on his glass cubicle and nods to Dad.

"Get you a coffee?"

"Sure."

There's a cabinet by the wall with a coffee percolator half full. Langley pours out two cups and puts one in front of Dad. I don't get anything.

"You've seen the news?"

I look at Dad, and he's nodding back.

"We didn't find nothing." Langley shakes his head.

"We pulled up the entire floor. Right down to the bare earth." He glances at me. "Guess you're not gonna have gym classes for a little while..."

"I don't mind that," I interrupt, and he frowns at me, like I wasn't supposed the say anything. Then he sits down behind the desk.

"Listen kid. The reason I've brought you in. We've been here before, and we're not gonna be here again."

He looks at me really seriously, but I don't know what he means.

"This website you made. This *detective agency*..." He stops and sighs.

"You realize you need a license to operate as a private investigator on Lornea Island? Plus you have to be eighteen years of age. You could be looking at a fine of ten thousand dollars. We could lay charges for fraud. If Barbara Jacobs wanted, she could file a civil suit."

I'm not entirely sure what all this means, but it makes me feel nervous. I don't dare look at Dad, but he's the next to speak.

"Does she?"

Langley hesitates. "Not yet she don't."

"And what about you? You said you could lay charges...?"

Langley doesn't answer at once.

"We're not gonna do that either. But we are gonna have this little chat. To make sure we don't find ourselves in this situation again. And I mean ever." He turns to me.

"OK Billy? This ends here. No more inserting yourself into other people's business. No more *detective agencies*. No more... Period."

I open my mouth to speak, but think better of it.

"Cos if this happens again, we're not gonna be having a chat. We're gonna be throwing the book at you."

Still I don't reply.

"You got that?"

I nod.

"I need to hear it Billy."

"Yeah. I got it."

"Good." Lieutenant Langley takes a glug of his coffee.

"So what happens now with Mrs. Jacobs?"

"*Billy!*" Langley sets his coffee cup down. "Did you not understand what just happened?"

"Yeah, I did, I just want to know what's going to happen to Mrs. Jacobs..."

"No you don't. That's not your business. Listen to me, and listen good. The Lornea Island Police Department thank you for bringing this matter to their attention. And we ask you to step away. And if I hear you *don't* do that, I'm gonna personally see to it we file every damn charge we can."

There's a silence, but Dad breaks it this time.

"He understands, don't you Billy?"

Eventually I nod.

"Sure. I get it."

After that, Dad takes me to school. I think he's just dropping me off and I unclip my seatbelt on the road outside, but he keeps going, right into the parking lot.

"What's going on?" I ask. "Where are you going?"

"In to see your Principal." Dad says, swinging into a space too fast.

"Why?" I ask, but all he does is yank on the parking brake hard.

"Why do you want to see Principal Sharpe?" I ask again.

"What makes you think I want to see her?"

And so, for the third time in a month, I find myself summonsed to Principal Sharpe's office. But this time, I'm there alongside Dad.

FORTY-FOUR

SHE'S SUPER MAD. I see it right away. She has to struggle to be polite to Dad, because she's not allowed to shout at the parents in the same way she does to us kids. But she still talks to him in her real tight lipped way that makes it obvious she hates his guts.

"Do you know what this is?" She holds up a folder of documents.

The veins on one side of her neck are sticking out and throbbing.

"Mr. Wheatley?"

It's weird having Dad here. When we came in I thought maybe he would demand answers to what really happened to Mr. Jacobs, but it just feels like he's getting told off too.

"This is the school's insurance policy. I've spent the morning reading it. As well as case law on Section 12 of the 1983 Civil Rights Lawsuits. Do you know why?"

Dad looks at her, and for a moment it seems like he's gonna fight, but then he sighs. "No."

"Well would you like to know?"

Dad kind of waves a hand, like he knows she's going to tell him anyway.

"I've been reading this because the police, over the last week – and thanks to your son's harassment of my mother – have utterly destroyed the school gymnasium. At an estimated cost of..." She stops, and searches for a paper on her desk.

"Over *three hundred thousand* dollars. And apparently neither the police department nor the school's buildings insurance will pay for it. Which means it will need to come out of the school budget. Meaning every single student in this school will have their education suffer as a result."

She drops the folder on the desk.

"Well?"

Dad just shakes his head.

"*Well Mr. Wheatley?*"

"Well what?"

"Well, don't you have anything to say?"

It seems like he doesn't at first. I figure he doesn't want to get in a fight with my school principal. But then he replies, his voice calm and almost casual.

"Cops say they had a warrant. Which means they must've had some reason. So the way I see it, that's hardly Billy's fault."

"Oh yes. Mr. Wheatley. I forgot you're an expert on legal matters. With your background."

She glares at him, but he stares right back.

"What happened to me has nothing to do with this."

"No? You don't think so? Because I wonder if it's part of the problem. It's hardly a stable home life you're giving your son is it? Were you aware Billy was operating an illegal so-called detective agency?"

Dad's eyes flick over to me, then back to Principal Sharpe.

"No."

"I understand from Lieutenant Langley it's an offence to do so without a license. But he won't be pressing charges. For reasons I am unable to fathom, and do not agree with."

There's silence for a long while.

"I've also taken advice on what would be appropriate in respect of Billy continuing to attend this school. As I'm sure you can appreciate, in any normal circumstances what Billy has done is far beyond the threshold needed to expel him from the school. Well beyond."

This makes me glance up. I didn't think you could get expelled if you were a good student like me.

"And I sincerely doubt, if that were to happen, that any other school on this island would take him on."

She glares at me now, like she actually hates me, and I start to feel quite worried. I don't much like Newlea High School, but I do need to get good grades. Otherwise I won't be able to go on and study to be a scientist. And I'll end up like Dad, in dead end jobs. And if I can't even go to school on the island then I don't know what we'll do. We'll have to leave.

"However." And suddenly she looks really disappointed. "I have been persuaded by the state board of education that it might appear inappropriate for me to take any decisions in this case personally, given the involvement of my family." She stares at me.

"I argued strongly against this position as well. But the agreement we came to is this. In this instance the board will take no action. However, if Billy continues his invasion into my, or my mother's privacy, then I shall expel him, immediately, without any further warnings and all the negative repercussions that would bring. Is that clear?"

I look at Dad, to see if he's going to argue against this, but he's looking down at the floor. Then I feel Principal Sharpe's eyes boring into me, and I look up again. She smiles.

"Billy. I want you to listen very carefully."

I don't reply.

"I *clearly* asked you to leave my mother alone. I explained about the illness she is suffering from. Yet you ignored me. In doing so you have caused an untold amount of damage to this school, both financially and in terms of its reputation. Furthermore you have caused a lot of anxiety and stress to an elderly woman who has done nothing wrong.

"Billy, if you step out of line again. If you even think about stepping out of line, I will expel you with great pleasure. And if you go *anywhere near* my mother again you will be pursued in the courts for compensation for the damage you have caused. Is that understood?"

After a little while I nod.

But after that she lets us go. No detention, no nothing. It's weird. I get sent to classes, like nothing has happened. And then the afternoon is just like a normal Wednesday afternoon. Except gym class is held outside on the school field, not in the hall.

FORTY-FIVE

IT'S over a week now since all that happened, though it seems longer. Dad told me again how we had to have a *proper talk*, and how we had to make changes so that nothing like this ever happened again, but then he went out with Tucker, and didn't come back till late. And when they did come back I could tell they were drunk. Then a few days later Dad told me he had another trip on *Ocean Harvest* lined up. And how important it was he went, because he made such good money the last time. And when I asked him who was gonna look after me, he told me Tucker would still be here, and this time he'd make sure he kept a better eye on me. I felt like pointing out how we wouldn't need the money quite so much if he wasn't here, eating all our food, and living rent free. But I couldn't say that. So I just had to bite my tongue.

I haven't seen that much of Amber. She got grounded by her mom, and Principal Sharpe put her in detentions every lunchtime. And she has to register for every class, to make sure she doesn't skip anymore. It's kind of annoying, because I really wanted to see her to work out what really happened to Mr. Jacobs, if he's not buried under the school gym after all.

But then I decided maybe it was for the best. Maybe I should put all this behind me, and just forget it ever happened.

But then something *else* happens. Something pretty bad.

FORTY-SIX

It HAPPENS when I'm doing my homework. Only it's quite boring home-work, so I decide to take a break to have a look through Dad's emails.

You'd think, when someone goes off on a fishing boat, they wouldn't be able to do emails, but actually it's the best way to keep in communication. There's loads of time when they're fishing that they're not actually doing anything, just waiting while the boat goes from one place to another, or when the nets are in the water. And even though cell phones don't normally work that far out to sea, they have this special network where they can bounce an internet signal from one boat to another, up to sixty miles out. But it's a bit like the internet in the old days, you can't stream stuff, but websites and emails work OK.

Anyway, the point is this: Dad uses his email a lot when he's out on the boats. I send him messages all the time, reminding him to take photographs and video if he sees any whales, and to note down his coordi-nates when he sees them.

So, when I look in his inbox, there at the top are the messages from me – some of them not even opened yet. And then there's the usual junk mail. And I'm almost about to close the page when a new email drops – like it's just been sent. It comes from Tucker.

I stare at it in surprise. Tucker is downstairs, right now. Watching base-ball. He called up a while back to see if I wanted to join him. And obvi-ously I just ignored him.

The subject of the email is this:

Fucking Whatsapp keeps cutting out...

Then right beneath that I can see the first few words he's written, even without opening it:

Agreed. Let's go for it...

So now I've got a problem. Obviously I'm curious to know what they've agreed, but to find out I need to click on the actual message. But if I do, the message status will change from *unread* to *read*. And if Dad happens to be looking at his email *right now*, it'll tell him someone else is looking at his emails. Normally that's not a huge problem, as I can change the emails back to *unread* once I've looked at them. But I can't do that if Dad's looking at his messages at this exact moment.

So I wait thirty seconds, to see if Dad opens the email. But nothing happens. That means he's either sailed out of range, or he's not looking at his phone. Maybe they had to haul the nets in or something. So I make a decision, I click on the message. I'll quickly read it, then change it back to unread, and Dad'll never know. But right then, like it sometimes does, our internet decides now is a good time to slow right down. The screen goes blank, and then a box opens on the screen, but without any text in it. It's almost thirty seconds later before the page finally loads, which makes me kinda anxious. When it does so, this is what the message says.

Agreed. Let's go for it day you get back. First thing, before it gets to fucking busy. It'll be way easier than hitting a bank and cash is cash. Don't stress it. We'll be sweet.

Then there's a link, and like before, it's to Carter's Jewelry in Newlea.

I read it twice, to make sure I get it alright. And then hurriedly I close the message and right click to restore it so that it looks unopened. My hand fumbles a bit because I'm nervous, and then the internet times out, making the screen go white, and a message appears in the middle saying:

Aw snap! Something went wrong when displaying that webpage

So then I have to reboot the router, which takes about four minutes, and all the while I'm thinking, I don't know if I managed to set the message to *unread* before it crashed. If I didn't, and Dad logs back on now, he'll see that someone else has already read it. He'll know someone's spying on him.

So when the internet finally comes back, I quickly log back into Dad's Gmail. And I'm right. The message is still there, still marked as read. I'm about it change its status to unread when I notice something else. Now there's a little arrow symbol next to the email. That means that something *else* has changed. Someone's *replied* to the message. That means Dad's seen it and he's replied to Tucker. And I can see the reply too, all I have to do it go to Dad's 'sent items box. And when I do that, this is what Dad's said:

I can't believe I'm saying this. But yeah. Let's do it.

FORTY-SEVEN

LET'S DO IT? Let's do what?

Way easier than hitting a bank? What does he mean by that?

I follow the link again, and there again is the webpage from the jeweler's. This time I don't watch the video of the couple on the beach, but click around the site. Eventually I find a photograph of the front of the store, with its velvet trays of rings and jewelry displayed in the front window. I've never really noticed it before – I'm not really interested in jewelry – but now I see that it's quite a small place, and it's pretty impossible *not* to understand what Tucker means. He's talking about security. Carter's doesn't have all the security of a bank. It doesn't have those metal screens that drop down. It won't have a panic button. It's just a little family business. And that's why Tucker has chosen it. For a robbery.

Let's do it.

And Dad's going help him rob it. My first thought is why? Dad's making OK money at last, aboard *Ocean Harvest*, so why does he need to rob a jewelry store? But as soon as I ask the question, I know the answer. The place on *Ocean Harvest* is only temporary, until the regular crew guy gets better. As soon as that happens Dad'll be back scrubbing out the fish house. And I know how much he hates that.

Even so, you can't just start robbing places. Dad wouldn't even be thinking about it, if Tucker hadn't turned up. He'd just get another job, even thought it's difficult. And I'd help too. I'd get a part time job. Or I'd give up school and get a job. A proper one this time, not chasing around pretending to be a detective. Because look how that turned out.

And look what happened the last time Tucker did a robbery? That guy in the Hounds Beach place got shot and killed. What if the same thing happens here? Half the town already thinks Dad's a criminal. Oh god...

I click back to Tucker's message and read it again. This time I notice *when* they're going to do it. The day after tomorrow, when Dad gets back. I've got two days to work out how to stop him

I suppose I could tell the police. I spend a long time thinking that over. But I can just imagine what Lieutenant Langley would say if I tell them I think my Dad's going to do an armed robbery. He won't listen, and even if he did, it would just mean Dad gets arrested. How does that help?

I think about just telling the police about Tucker? They never did come to arrest him when I activated his SIM card. Maybe I didn't do it long enough? But I don't want to do it again in case that guy – Vinny – rings back.

In the end I phone Amber. She answers right away, and I just blurt everything out. Everything I've found out about Tucker and Dad, and everything I've just said here. When I finish she's quiet for a long time. When she speaks this is all she says.

"Shit Billy."

So I know she can't think of an answer either.

* * *

When I try to sleep it doesn't happen. So I get up. I track Dad's boat with *VesselTrack*, in the hope that maybe they'll run into bad weather and have to go around it, and then they won't get back in time to hit the jeweler's on the day Tucker wants. But that won't even help, because all they'd do is put it back a day. It's not like the jewelry store is going anywhere. And anyway, there isn't any bad weather, and it looks like Dad will get back right on time.

And then, sitting at my keyboard. I realize something I should have seen a long time ago. I think for a second, then I work so fast my fingers can't hit the keys quick enough.

FORTY-EIGHT

SOMETIMES I WONDER if I should actually be a lawyer when I grow up. I reckon I'd be good at it. Or maybe a newspaper reporter. If there still are newspapers when I'm older. Or anything at all. Maybe if we all get flooded by global climate change there won't be any world to be anything in. Maybe that would for the best.

I didn't go to school yesterday. What I was doing was much more important. At one point I heard the phone ringing downstairs, which must have been the school office wondering where I was, but I didn't answer it. And Tucker was out, probably casing out the jewelry store. Well. He can case it out all he likes. Because his plan isn't going to happen. He isn't going to rob anywhere, and neither is Dad.

When I finished working I printed everything out and organized it into three folders. Or maybe dossiers is the right word. I'm never quite sure what a dossier is, but it does sound a very nice word. So that's what I'm gonna call them. Dossiers. And in each dossier I made sure everything was in the right place, and all the images were properly labeled and everything. It took me ages, and that's why I couldn't go to school. I had to have it finished by this evening.

* * *

At seven o'clock Tucker shouts up the stairs to tell me Dad's called, and he's gonna go pick him up from the dock. It's about half an hour, there and back. I use the time to go over everything, but before I know it I hear the roar of the truck's engine in the lane. I'm nervous now. I could easily say I'm tired, or I have to work, and Dad wouldn't think that was odd. He wouldn't even mind, because he probably wants to go through all his plans with Tucker. But I can't do that that. If I just pretend this isn't happening then Dad's gonna rob the jewelry store. And everything we've built here will be ruined.

So I pick up the dossiers, and I walk downstairs.

FORTY-NINE

"HEY BILLY," Dad flashes me a smile as he comes in. He looks tired, I wasn't expecting that.

"You keeping out of trouble?" He gives a little laugh, to show that's a rhetorical question. Or a sort of joke because of everything that happened with the school gym. He dumps his kit bag in the corner of the room. Tucker follows him in, doesn't say anything to me, but goes straight to the fridge and grabs two beers with one hand. He opens them both and hands one to Dad. The remains of our dinner are on the table.

"We left you some," Tucker says. "Not much though, your boy eats a goddamn ton."

I don't answer. It's not my fault if I'm going through a growth spurt.

Dad doesn't reply to any of it though, just helps himself to what's left from the pot in the middle of the table and starts eating.

I've got the dossiers in my arms, folded across my chest. "Did you catch much?" I ask, still standing by the door.

"So so." Dad replies as he swallows a mouthful. "Tough trip though. I'm gonna down this and hit the sack."

He wants to be fresh tomorrow. I have to do this now, or it's not going to happen. I start to hold out the dossier in front of me, then my nerve goes and I pull it back to my chest.

"We should have a little chat before you do," Tucker says to Dad, from where he's leaning against the counter top. "Just go over a few things before tomorrow."

I can't help but feel indignant at how openly he's talking about it.

"What's happening tomorrow?" I keep an eye on Dad as I ask, and sure enough he shoots an irritated glance over at Tucker, like he's a bit pissed at him for bringing it up. It gives me a burst of confidence. But maybe not quite enough, since I find myself still hugging the dossier against my chest.

"Nothing. Nothing important," Dad says, and keeps eating.

I'm still hanging back in the doorway, like I'm expecting to go back upstairs any second. And it's so tempting to do so. To not go through with this. But then if I don't, then Dad is going to do an actual robbery tomorrow, and there's no going back from that. He'll always be a real criminal after that. I have to stop him.

"Dad," I begin.

"Yeah?"

And then I step forward and drop the dossier on the table.

"Dad. I know what you and Tucker are planning to do tomorrow. And I'm not gonna let you do it."

There's a roaring empty silence. Like standing by a waterfall. I can sense how their attention has focused right onto me. Dad's just frozen, his fork loaded with food and half way up to his mouth.

"What's that Bill?" Dad says, his voice is calm, except for a slight waver he can't control.

"I said I know what you're planning to do. At the jewelry store."

Dad lowers the fork back down to the plate. His forehead is knotted in confusion.

"How'd you know?"

"Because I've been spying on you. And on Tucker. So I know he's a criminal. I know he uses a fake name, and that he's on the run from the police. And I know he murdered a security guard in a place called Hounds Beach..." As I say this part Tucker spits out the beer he's drinking, so that it goes all over the floor, and some of it over Dad. But I don't stop. I can't, not now I've started.

"And I know how you're planning to rob Carter's jewelry story in Newlea tomorrow. And I was going to go to the police, but I didn't think they'd listen to me, so I thought the best thing to do was tell you how I know about it and beg you not to do it..."

There's that silence again. But deeper and longer this time. Dad angles round to look at Tucker, like he can't believe I said all this. But then he wheels back to me.

"The *hell* are you talking about, Bill?"

He glowers at me, and then sends a desperate glance across at Tucker. And I can't believe it, because I see he's going to deny it. Only I can believe it, because I knew he would. It's why I had to make my dossiers. So I hand one to Tucker, then give the other to Dad, and then open my copy.

"OK. Page one. When Tucker first arrived he lied about not having a cell phone, and when I checked I discovered he had identity documents in the name of *Peter Smith*. That's the name he goes under now – but he can't use it with you, because you know his real name from when you were kids. So he's not using it now. Page two. Tucker had to keep his phone switched off, because the police were tracking it, so he was breaking into my room to use the internet on my computer. So I installed software that made it record video of whoever used it." I put a full page image of Tucker sitting at my laptop in the dossier. I deliberately chose a not-very-flattering one either, he was picking his nose at the time.

"Page three. These are the websites Tucker was looking at. They're all about a robbery of a jewelry store in Hounds Beach. Why would he so interested in this robbery, if he wasn't involved?" And what I've put on page three are all the articles from the newspapers about what happened to the security guard. The first ones about how he was shot, and then how he'd died later in hospital.

"Page four is..."

"Whoa Billy! What *the fuck* is this? What the fuck are you doing?" Dad interrupts me, and he has to do it really loud because I can't really hear anything too well. I'm kind of getting a bit emotional.

"Page four is..." I try to go on but it's hard to see because there's tears in my eyes.

"Billy stop!"

"...Is another still from the camera on my computer. This one shows Tucker on the *old* phone he pretended not to have. And then you can see on the next page how he smashes it up. And then there's the messages that he got on the phone, which I found when I recovered the SIM card..."

"*Billy that's enough.*"

"...They show... They show this guy called Vinny who's *desperate* to know where Tucker is. And I wondered if he might be Tucker's probation officer or something, only he said wasn't a probation officer when I spoke to him, he sounded more like a gangster or something so..."

"Billy!"

"Then the last page, that's all the messages that Tucker's been sending *you*. About the jewelry store in Newlea, and how you're going to rob it..."

I feel the dossier smashed out of my hands, and the blow knocks me back against the wall.

"Dad, don't do it. *Please don't do it.* If you do it you're gonna get caught, and this time they're gonna be right. All the people who say you're a murderer and a criminal. And they're going to send you to jail.

"And I don't want them to send you to jail."

FIFTY

"Billy you got this wrong. You got this all wrong."

I've stopped crying. At least, mostly I have. I can still feel how wet my face is. And I can feel the edge of the door hard at my back. Dad was right in front of me, but now he's backed off. His face is white, even with the tan he's got from being outside all week. It's like that's just dropped away.

"You've – I don't know how the fuck you've... But you've got this all wrong."

The way he says it, I want to believe him. Dad slowly flicks through his copy of my dossier. It's like he doesn't know where to start, but eventually he goes right to the end.

"This thing tomorrow. It's not a... It's not a *robbery*. I don't know where you... I don't know why you'd even *think* that?"

"Way easier than hitting a bank." I know Tucker's email by heart, so I recite it back to him. "And then you reply. *'Let's do this'*."

"That's... *Jesus* Billy. The fuck are you like? That's..."

He turns away and runs a hand through his hair.

"That's... Look I was gonna tell you. But not until we'd got it in the bag. Because it's such a goddamn long shot on this fucking island where no one gives you a fucking chance."

He breathes hard for a moment. Then turns back to me.

"We aren't gonna *rob it*. We're gonna try and raise a deposit. For a loan."

I try to make sense of this, but it's hard. "A loan?"

"Yeah. Tucker's been digging around, trying to find someone – anyone

– who'd be willing to take some second hand jewelry as security for a loan. It ain't easy to do. When you got no track record, when you're guys like us…"

I screw up my face in confusion. "Why do you need a loan?"

Dad hesitates, then gives a deep sigh.

"For a boat Billy. We're gonna go in together and buy out the *Ocean Harvest.*"

My head is spinning with all this. Is Dad making this up? Just on the spot, to hide what he's really doing? But if so, how come he's thought of it so quick? Dad's not the most imaginative guy you'd ever meet.

"You want to buy *Ocean Harvest*?"

"Yeah. I didn't want to tell you until I was sure we could raise the cash. But Tucker and me, when we were kids, we always dreamed that one day we'd run a boat together. If you have two skippers you can alternate, make sure the boat's always out working. It makes good business sense."

I stare at Dad, I still don't know whether to believe him.

"Billy, I know you don't like it when I'm away, so I thought it would help if Tucker was able to keep an eye on you, when I'm at sea. He won't always be living here. He'll get his own place, soon as we get the boat running and get some money coming in. But he'll be able to look in from time to time. Make sure you're OK."

Still I stare. I realize my mouth's open, but I don't feel able to shut it.

"Come on Bill… You wouldn't believe it, but I got the idea from you. You were going on about that other boat, the *Blue Lady*? That's never gonna happen. I don't have no accounts that a bank can analyze and decide if I'm a good investment. But this Carter's place. They're not so concerned about that. If you can put up something. And I've got a bit saved – and Tucker's got this jewelry - well, they make allowances. You know? They'll charge a bit more in interest. But we reckon we can earn that back. If we get a good run." He puts his hand through his hair again.

"I can't believe you thought I'd… thought I'd try and *rob* somewhere."

I'm silent for a few moments, and Dad is too. You can actually hear the clock ticking on the wall.

"But what about Tucker?" I protest suddenly. "Everything I found out about him. The fake name? The robbery in Hounds Beach? That was real. The security guard *died.*"

"That's…" Dad begins, but then he stops. He turns to Tucker, who hasn't made a sound since spitting out his beer. "Tucker? What *is* that about?"

Tucker doesn't reply, but his eyes are running from side to side. Like he's trying to see a way out of here.

"Tuck? Tell Billy what that's all about. How you had nothing to do with – whatever that is."

Still he doesn't reply, and after a few moments Dad turns right around so he's facing him.

Still Tucker doesn't reply. And then Dad shakes his head.

"Aw shit." Dad says.

"Tucker. What the *fuck* have you done?"

FIFTY-ONE

"I DIDN'T SHOOT THE GUY." Tucker says.

"Aw shit!" Dad drops his head into his hands.

"I didn't. You don't know me well enough I wouldn't shoot anyone?"

"But you were there?"

Tucker is still for a long while, before finally he nods.

"Yeah. I was there."

Dad groans again. He screws up his eyes and presses them with his thumbs.

"Go on," he says finally.

For a while Tucker doesn't, but then he begins speaking in a voice stripped of expression.

"I was working out at Granville, in the steel plant. And that was going alright. But then they made a bunch of us redundant. And one of the guys, who I worked with, he kept going on at me that he had this job we could do, real simple." He stops for a second. "You remember Vincent? Vincent McDonald."

Dad stares. "Tell me you're fucking kidding?"

"I didn't want to do it. Not after I went inside, there was no way I wanted to go back. But Vinny was real insistent. Persuasive. And I had nothing else. I had bills to pay. A guy's gotta live."

"Inside?" Dad pulls him up. "You went to jail?"

"It was nothing. Just a couple of months."

"Why? What the hell d'ya do?"

Tucker hesitates. "I held up a liquor store. Or tried to. Look I needed the money."

"You fucking idiot! Oh man..."

They're both silent for a few seconds.

"Why didn't you tell me?" Dad asks in the end.

Then suddenly Tucker gets real mad. "Tell you? Fucking tell you? How the *fuck* am I gonna tell you? When you've disappeared into thin air like a fucking ghost?"

Dad opens his mouth. Closes it again.

"You know I had to do that. I had to protect my family... What was left of my family."

"And I wasn't family? *Fuck you man...*"

For a long moment they both just stare at each other, both of them breathing hard.

"You left me man. I drove you across the country and *you fucking left me*. And what's worse? You left me because you didn't fucking trust me."

Tucker's breathing now like he's just finished a running race. "So maybe that's why I didn't keep you up to date on everything that happened in my *fucked-up* life."

He turns away. Dad stares at the back of his head, and after a while he speaks. But now he's calmed down. He sounds defeated.

"So what's it about? This business in Hounds beach? What happened."

Tucker turns back. He rubs a hand on his face.

"I told you. I had bills to pay. And Vinny, he made out how he'd found this security guard in a little family jeweler's store out there. Came across him by accident but then began watching him. You see, security guards have to take breaks. They eat sandwiches. They have to go to the bathroom. But what they're supposed to do is vary when they do it. You know, one day go at ten, then next day at twelve, the next day don't go at all. Never get into a pattern. But this guard was lazy. He loved his routine. He *always* took a fifteen minute break at ten thirty. Like clockwork. I went and watched, just to check for myself. And it was just like Vinny said. Ten thirty, he was out the door, leaving this old dear behind the counter, all alone."

Dad's face is expressionless.

"All we had to do was go in there, wave a gun about, and we could walk out with enough gold that we wouldn't have to worry about finding work for a while."

Tucker falls quiet, and Dad gets up. He paces to the sink and runs himself a glass of water. He holds it in the air but doesn't drink any.

"Gold? Am I right in thinking that this gold is what we're gonna put up as security on our loan tomorrow?"

Tucker doesn't answer at first. Then he nods.

Dad takes a sip of the water.

"So when you told me it was left you by your aunt. That was just a crock of shit?"

It's only a tiny movement of his head, but Tucker nods again. Dad rolls his jaw around, like someone's punched it. Then he goes on.

"So what went wrong? In the store?"

Tucker rubs his face with his tattooed hand.

"This guy, Vinny. He's... well, you know what he's like. I thought he'd changed. I thought he was OK. But it turns out he ain't changed at all."

He stops. He can't even look at Dad now.

"Look, we talked it through beforehand. I told him I wasn't interested unless he specifically promised there'd be no violence. I didn't even want to go with guns, but he said we needed to have them, just for show." His tone changes. "Then, once we got in there, he..."

"He what Tucker? What exactly did he do?"

Slowly Tucker shakes his head.

"Everything was going just fine. We got to the store, and just like we planned. There's just the old lady there. The security guy is already away on his break. So we've got fifteen minutes – plenty of time. We get to it. We get the old girl away from the counter, so she can't go pressing any panic buttons. Vinny covers her with the gun. I fill the bags. It's good stuff – gold chains, rings, watches – you've seen it. We work fast, and it's going great. We're gonna be in and out in five minutes. But then the guard just walks right back in. I think he must be fucking short-sighted or something because he just walks right in, on top of us, ten minutes before he's supposed to be there. And he's fucking whistling, like it's the best day of his life... I dunno. Maybe he got served in the sandwich shop easier than normal. I don't know what the hell happened."

"And then what?" Dad asks.

Tucker gives a haunted laugh. "It's such a fucking shame, you know? Even when that guard turned up, you could tell he didn't want no trouble. He wasn't the hero type. He put his hands up the moment he finally saw what was going on. But Vinny freaked out anyway. He started talking how he was gonna execute him. I thought he was bluffing, I was telling him we had to get out of there. And then Vinny shot him. Like it was a game. Like it was nothing."

There's silence for a few moments, and I wonder who's going to speak next. In the end it's Dad.

"Then what?"

"I panicked. I ran. I went outside and jumped in the car. I swear to God I thought Vinny was there with me. But then I saw he was still inside the goddamn building. Still waving his fucking gun about like he's in a movie. So I just drove. I just got the fuck out of there. It was only later I realized I was still holding the fucking bag I'd been filling.

"And then I came here."

FIFTY-TWO

"WHAT A MESS." Dad says what seems an age later. "What a fucking mess."

He flicks through my dossier, on the kitchen table. He comes to the bit about Tucker's fake name. All my research into possible Peter Smiths.

"So how about this? How come you got a false ID?"

Tucker sighs before he answers.

"I don't."

Dad starts to hold up the dossier, but Tucker goes on.

"I don't. It ain't a false ID, I swear it."

"Well you wanna explain why Billy says you do?"

Tucker takes an age to answer.

"I don't have it anymore. I tossed it away. In a trash can in town."

"OK. You tossed it away, but how come you had it in the first place?"

Tucker sighs again and looks down at his feet. Then he lifts he head and looks straight at Dad.

"I stole it. After the robbery. I had nothing on me. No ID, no cash. Just a bag of gold fucking chains that I didn't know what to do with. And I couldn't go home. I didn't know who might be waiting for me there, Vinny or the cops. So I just took a long walk. Tried to figure everything out. That's when I decided to come here. To look you up. But I couldn't get here with no cash. Then I came across this restaurant, this little sidewalk café with tables outside and this asshole sitting there. He's real loud, on his cell phone shouting about some deal. I guess I realized he looked a little like me, even at the time." Tucker gives a rueful smile.

"Anyway, he's sitting there, drinking his frappuccino bullshit, and he's so fucking distracted with his conversation he doesn't notice he's got his wallet just sitting there on the table. I just slid it off and kept walking." Tucker stops.

"Look, I ain't proud of it. I ain't proud of any of it. But I had no choice. You understand that? Don't you?" Dad doesn't reply, so Tucker goes on.

"There was a few hundred bucks in it. Enough to get me here. And there was a driver's license. Look I'm not saying we were separated at birth, nothing like that. But it was enough that I could pass for him if I had too. So I kept it. I thought it might be useful. But then I changed my mind, after you let me stay here. So I tossed it in the trash, like I said."

Still Dad doesn't say anything, but he looks at me, and down at the dossiers, the three of them, spread across the kitchen table and the countertop. I don't know what he's thinking, but I can't get over how I've got it wrong. Everything in them is wrong. Again. Then Tucker goes on.

"You know we can still do it," he says quietly.

"Still do what?"

"We can still go ahead. Buy the boat. Start afresh. They're never gonna come looking all the way out here."

"That's what I thought," Dad replies, not looking at him. "When I came." There's a silence for a while.

"And it worked didn't it?" Tucker says. "They never did find you out here. Not until all the shit happened with that missing girl. And that was just..." He shrugs. "Bad luck?"

Dad doesn't answer. I don't know what he's thinking.

"Who's not?" he says in the end. I see the flicker of confusion in Tucker's eyes.

"Who's not what?"

"Who's not going to come looking?"

Tucker doesn't seem to want to answer this, but Dad's staring at him, so he has no choice.

"The cops. They ain't looking for me. It'll be Vinny they're interested in."

I think back to when I put Tucker's SIM card into my phone. To ry and alert them to where he was hiding. Then Tucker goes on.

"There ain't no one who knows I'm here. And the jewelry's clean. I been researching it, there's nothing that can be traced. I don't see why we can't just go on like we planned. Turn it into cash and put it down on a boat. Like we *always* planned. Like none of this ever happened."

Dad's silent for a while, but in the end he turns to me. "We had this dream," he says. "When we were kids. Tucker and me, we used to sit for hours talking about it. Neither of us had any money. So we used to bait up the crab pots for the fishermen. We'd sit there, slicing up fish heads or smashing up mussel shells, and we'd talk about how one day this is what we'd do for our own boat. We'd catch crab and we'd surf and we wouldn't have to worry about nothing." A smile breaks out on his face.

"I guess I got caught up in that, these last few weeks. I thought here was a chance. My old buddy turns up unexpected, and like a miracle, he's got this jewelry. Some kind of inheritance. I didn't ask the details, because of this even bigger miracle. He wants to buy the boat with it. With me. I thought this is how it was always meant to be. A second chance." Dad shakes his head slowly.

"But there ain't no such thing as second chances." He looks at Tucker.

"Are there Tuck?"

Tucker sounds anxious when he replies. "I told you. We don't have to change anything. We can still go ahead..."

"No we can't. We never could."

"What do you mean?"

"The jewelry. I never really believed you, when you told me it came from some aunt I'd never even heard of before. I just didn't *care*. I thought if I don't know the truth, then it don't even matter where it really came from. But that's not right. It does matter."

"Why? The store's insured. Probably. So no one loses out. And we're going to *build* something with it. We're gonna invest it..."

"Because it's against the law. And because someone got killed when you stole it."

There's another long silence, then Tucker tries again.

"They ain't gonna come, the cops ain't gonna come all the way out here. They're looking for Vinny. And he don't know where I am, thank fuck..."

Suddenly Dad picks up one of the dossiers from the table. He flicks through it for a moment then turns to me.

"Billy, did you say you spoke to this Vinny guy?"

I feel both of them looking at me.

"You did. You said you wondered if he might be Tucker's *probation officer*, but he sounded more like a gangster. What did you mean by that?"

I have to tell them.

"When Tucker threw his phone off the cliff, I climbed down and rescued it. I wanted to know what he was hiding. And then I took the SIM card out, and I put it in my phone." I glance up, wondering if I need to explain how phones work, but it doesn't look like I do.

"And then when all these text messages from Vinny came in, we replied to them." I stop. I didn't mean to say 'we'.

But Dad doesn't seem to notice.

"Go on," he says.

"And I thought he'd maybe just text back, and explain who he was, and why Tucker was hiding from him. But instead he phoned."

"And you answered the call?" Dad asks.

I hesitate. I don't want to explain about how I was thinking it was actually Dad ringing, and how that made me happy because he hadn't rung me the whole time he'd been out on the boat. In the end I nod.

"What did he say?"

I take a deep breath before I answer. "He seemed... He seemed to be trying to find out where Tucker was."

There's a moment of silence after I say this. Tucker gets up. He walks to the window and glances out. It's dark outside, I don't know what he's looking for.

"I didn't tell him," I go on quickly, but I can't not think about what happened with the radio. "But there was..." I stop, swallow.

"What?" Dad says at once. "What happened?"

I have to go on. I have to tell them, so I explain how I wasn't sure if I got to the radio in time, before the presenter said 'Good Morning Lornea Island' in that funny way.

"Oh fucking Jesus," Tucker says, looking out again.

"When was this?" Dad asks.

"About a week ago. Before the thing with the school."

Dad looks at Tucker. He's running his hands through his hair, one after the other.

"Who is this Vinny?" I ask, since neither of them are speaking.

They look at each other. Finally Dad turns to me.

"He's an old acquaintance. We knew him in high school. Never had much to do with him mind, even then it was obvious he was a goddamn psychopath."

He glares at Tucker, who won't meet his eye.

"Who were you running away from? You came right the way out here. Were you running from the cops or from Vinny?

"I dunno, I wasn't necessarily running..."

"Bullshit. You come all the way out here to start a new life. You throw your phone off the cliff. Who were you most scared of? The cops or Vinny?"

"I don't see it matters. Vinny ain't gonna come looking all the way out here anymore than the cops are."

"Then why is he pumping Billy for information on your whereabouts?"

Tucker doesn't have an answer to this.

"Man you *drove away from a robbery without him*. You left him there. You don't think that makes you someone he's gonna want to get even with?"

Tucker gives a half shrug then a little shake of his head.

"But there ain't no way. I mean, even if he heard the name of the island, there's still no way he's ever gonna find me here. No one on the mainland ever even heard of Lornea Island, least not until that girl..."

"Not until that girl went missing, and the whole goddamn country heard about how they were blaming it on me. Think about it. He knows you and me were friends. He knows I disappeared to hide on Lornea Island? How long until he puts it together? Huh? Even Vincent McDonald's gonna work that one out."

There's a long silence.

"Oh fuck." Tucker says at last.

FIFTY-THREE

A FEW MOMENTS later Dad roots around in the kitchen cupboard and pulls out a flashlight. He checks the batteries work, then turns to Tucker.

"Stay here with Billy." Dad says, and moves towards the door.

But Tucker blocks him. "Stop," he says. "Don't."

Dad looks surprised. "What are you doing? I'm gonna go check the yard."

"With that?" Tucker nods towards the light. Then he sighs.

"If Vinny's come all the way out here to find me, you better believe he's gonna come with more than a goddamn flashlight."

Dad doesn't move.

"Don't you have a gun?" Tucker asks, and eventually Dad shakes his head.

"After I got shot I decided I didn't much like them." He hesitates a second, then looks directly at Tucker.

"You did an armed robbery. Where's the gun from that?"

But Tucker shakes his head, "I got rid of it. Tossed it in a river."

There's a silence.

"You could make a gun," I say, without really thinking if that's a good idea.

Dad turns on me at once.

"What?"

"If you had a 3D printer you could make one. I saw a TV program about it. You can download the plans from the internet."

Dad doesn't reply, but Tucker looks interested.

"You got a 3D printer?"

I shake my head.

"No. I wanted one but they're too expensive."

Tucker stares at me for a while, before looking away.

Dad flicks the flashlight on. "I'm gonna take a look outside. Make sure there's nothing out of place. Then we'll figure out what the hell to do next." This time Tucker doesn't stop him.

"Stay here with Billy."

I don't move, but watch the light from the flashlight flicking around outside. Neither me nor Tucker speak at all. I don't know about him, but I'm tensed up, half expecting to hear the bang from a gun. A few minutes later, Dad comes back inside.

"Well?" Tucker says, as Dad locks the front door.

"Nothing," Dad replies. "There's no one there. But we gotta make a plan. We gotta work out what to do."

We go into the lounge, because we don't have blinds for the kitchen window, and I think we all feel a bit nervous with the light on inside and just this black window open onto the night. I've hardly been in the lounge for ages, not now it's become Tucker's room.

"How about the police? Any way you can tell them where he is?" Dad asks.

Tucker's a long time in answering, but eventually he does.

"I don't *know* where he is."

Then Dad doesn't answer for a long while either.

"And how about you? You reckon maybe you should..."

"What?" Tucker says, when Dad doesn't finish his sentence.

Dad sighs. "I don't know. Maybe, go speak to them? Put your side of things. If you weren't involved in this guy getting killed... Maybe you're better off getting ahead of it?"

Then there's a really long pause while Tucker looks around the room. He drums his fingers on the coffee table, then finally scratches at the stubble on his chin.

"I dunno man. I think maybe it's too late for that. I already got a record. And what they gonna do to you? They're gonna want to know where I've been this last month. You really reckon they're not gonna pick you up for harboring a fugitive?"

"So what then?"

Tucker pauses again. "There ain't much choice is there?" He says in the end. "I just gotta leave. I gotta get outta here." His voice nearly breaks as he says it, and I'm shocked, because he looks like such a tough guy, and now suddenly he's nearly choking up.

He squeezes his palm against his eyes, as if trying to force them to stop making any tears, and when he pulls his hands down I wonder if I'm wrong, because there's no water there.

"It wasn't just your dream you know?" He looks at Dad. "The boat. I dreamed about that boat. All the time after you left me. That dream kept me going." His face is tense from where he's trying to stop himself crying.

"But I guess you're right. The idea that guys like us could ever get a break. It just ain't gonna happen."

Dad looks awkward for a moment. But when he speaks he's calm.

"Tomorrow," Dad says. "I'll take you to Goldhaven. You can get a ferry off the island. Find somewhere out of the way and set yourself up... It ain't easy but," he looks around the lounge. "Hell I managed it. It must be possible."

Dad turns to me. "You better get some sleep."

I look at him. "What about Vinny?"

"Tuck and me will take turns staying awake. Chances are he ain't within a thousand miles of here."

I'm not so sure about this, but I am exhausted. But I do feel pretty bad now. I turn to Tucker.

"I'm really sorry," I say. "For messing everything up."

Tucker's face stiffens for a moment, but then it softens into a sad, bitter smile.

"You didn't do nothing wrong kid. I brought this on myself."

"But I told Vinny where you were."

"He would have worked it out." Tucker shakes his head. "Everyone back home knows about your Dad and me. If I disappear, eventually he would have worked it out. It ain't your fault."

FIFTY-FOUR

THE NEXT MORNING I wake up in my bed, and for about half a minute I don't remember anything of what happened last night. Then I jump up and look out the window. I don't know what I'm expecting to see, maybe this Vinny character hiding behind Dad's truck. But everything looks normal. Right down to Steven waiting on my windowsill and flapping up and down when he sees me.

I go downstairs, and find Dad and Tucker already up and in the kitchen, or maybe they never went to sleep. Tucker is making breakfast, spreading peanut butter onto brown toast and throwing it on a plate.

"Here you go kid," he says, sliding the plate in front of me.

"Did anything happen?" I ask. "Did Vinny come?"

Tucker shakes his head. "No. And he ain't gonna come neither. Not when he knows I'm not here. You don't have to worry about that. You shouldn't have to worry neither."

"So what's going to happen?" I persist.

Dad looks exhausted, but he tries to smile. "You're gonna go to school, just like normal."

"And then what?"

"And then there's a ferry tonight that Tucker's gonna be on. So when you get home everything is gonna go back to normal. Just like it was before." He tries to smile again, but it doesn't come out very well. I know why. Everything before was pretty awful.

"But one thing," Dad continues, "You gotta stay in school today. I don't want you going off anywhere on your own, OK?"

I turn to Tucker. I suppose the truth is I've got quite used to having him around.

"Hey don't worry kid. I'm a big boy. I'll look after myself."

"Will we ever see you again?" I ask. "Dad?"

Dad doesn't answer, but after a few moments Tucker does. "You're a pretty good detective Billy. I reckon you'll always be able to find me."

And after that I have to go to school.

* * *

It's super weird being in school. I mean, it's super weird being in school anyway, just with everything that happened with Mrs. Jacobs and Principal Sharpe and the gym, without wondering what Dad and Tucker are doing. But at the same time, it's kind of nice to know that I don't have to worry about Dad trying to rob the jewelry store. I have to lie to my class teacher about why I wasn't in the last two days, but Dad thought of that and gave me a note, saying I was ill. Luckily you only need a doctor's note if it's more than three days.

"Pssst," I need you.

Amber grabs my arms as she speaks, and she pulls me behind the bank of lockers in the main corridor.

"What?"

"Where have you been? I've been looking for you? You haven't been in school for ages."

Oh that. I think.

"And you never answer your phone."

"Sorry. I've been a bit busy."

"Doing what?"

It's lunchtime, so I lead her to the library and when we find a quiet corner I explain everything that's happened.

"*Fuuuccckkk!*" She says, several times, as I tell her. And her eyes go wide and sparkle like they always do when she gets excited.

"So he's on the ferry tonight?"

"Uh huh."

"That means I won't get to see him again," Amber says, and the sparkle dulls a little.

"And they weren't going to rob the jewelry store anyway? They just wanted a loan?"

I don't answer.

"I never really thought they were going to rob it," she says. "He's a nice guy."

In a funny way I think I feel the same way. I mean, he looks scary, and obviously he's an armed robber and not far off from being a murderer, but at the same time, once you get to know him, he's OK. And I think he was quite good for Dad. In a way. I mean sure, Dad should have realized the jewelry was stolen, but at least he made a plan with it. At least he had some ambition. Now what's going to happen? He's just going to go back to scrubbing out the fish warehouse.

I'm so caught up thinking about all this, that it takes me ages to realize that there's something else Amber is worked up about.

"Will you please listen?" She says.

"What?"

"We need to talk about the Mrs. Jacobs case."

I half-hear what she says, but it's really hard. Partly because that all seems a long time ago, and not very important anyway, not compared to Dad. But also, we can't do anything more about it, we'll be expelled. I tell this to Amber now, but she just waves it away like it's nothing. So I tell her again.

"Billy!" Amber waves me away. She's getting frustrated. "Sharpe's only saying that because she's scared. Because we're close to the truth."

I stare at her, like she's gone mad. Then I realize she's right. We have to finish this.

"So what then?" I ask.

Then the twinkle comes right back into Amber's eyes.

"I remembered something. We made a mistake."

FIFTY-FIVE

"RIGHT BACK AT THE BEGINNING," Amber asks. "When we first met with Mrs. Jacobs, do you remember what she said?"

It's a stupid question really, she said lots of things.

"Can you be a bit more specific?"

"She was talking about her husband disappearing. Come on."

I try to remember. "She said it was at Christmas time." I try.

"And..?"

"And... He just walked out? But we know now that he went to live in Hawaii."

"Bullshit. If that was the truth, then why were the police so keen to dig up the gym? Don't you think they would have checked whether Mr. Jacobs was alive and well before making all that mess?"

I've never thought about it in those terms. "Did they say that to you? The police?"

"No. They didn't tell me anything, but it's obvious isn't it? You must have worked that out."

I don't say anything. I'm trying to think if there's a problem with Amber's logic, and if not, why I hadn't thought of it. I'm usually quite good at working things out.

"So what are you saying?"

"I'm saying there can't be any record of Henry Jacobs having ever lived in Maui, at least nothing the police could find. Otherwise they wouldn't have trashed the gym. Which means Principal Sharpe must have been lying."

Again I struggle to find the flaw in her argument, but the more I think about it, the more I see it's quite good logic.

"So what else?" Amber asks.

"What else what?"

"What else did Mrs. Jacobs say?"

I try harder to remember, but it's no good. "I don't know. It's too long ago."

And then Amber pulls out her notebook.

"Then allow me to remind you," she says, opening the book and leafing through the pages. "Here it is." She holds out the notebook for me to see. I can't read half of it because her handwriting is so bad, but I can make out these words:

Before Xmas children excited disappears

"So?" I ask.

"Look again. Don't you see?"

I know how much Amber is loving this, but I don't know what she's showing me. I shrug.

"*Children,*" she says excitedly. "*Plural.* Principal Sharpe had a brother or sister."

I think about this for a moment. I think I already knew that.

"So?" I ask again.

"So! So there's another witness we can speak to. Someone who isn't mad like Mrs. Jacobs or lying like Principal Sharpe."

I wait for Amber to go on, but there doesn't seem to be anything else. I can't help but feel disappointed.

"Is that it?" I ask in the end.

"What do you mean *is that it?*"

"I mean don't you have any more? Like where they are now, this brother or sister?" I don't bother to ask whether they're likely to want to speak to us. Although the answer to that is pretty obvious. But surprisingly, Amber doesn't sound annoyed, she sounds hopeful.

"I've been looking," Amber says, pointing to the computer, but I can't find anything. I lean in to see the screen more clearly. She's got multiple search pages open with terms like *Wendy Sharpe Lornea Island sister,* but none of the results seem to help.

"The problem is, I reckon, we don't know the name to actually search for." Amber goes on, but I stop listening, and read through the search results. One of them, about half way down the list, is for a genealogy website. It sparks something in my mind.

"I was thinking, maybe we could just *ask* Sharpe," Amber continues, and I tune back into her. "But I don't suppose she'll tell us. Not if she's been lying about everything so far."

I sit back. Trying to catch the idea that's forming. Or maybe the half-idea.

"So I know you're quite good at this sort of thing, and I wondered if you had any ideas for how to find them?"

I pull the keyboard towards me and start typing.

"What are you doing?" Amber asks, but I'm too busy to answer.

* * *

Do you remember I told you, my name isn't really Billy Wheatley? Or at least, it wasn't when I was born. My Dad changed it when he took me away after my mom tried to drown me. But since we were technically on the run, he didn't change it properly, not legally. But then, a few months after all that got sorted out, we had to make it legal. And the way we did it, we had to spend ages and ages at the records office, here in Newlea, trying to get all the paperwork sorted. And Dad doesn't really have that much patience for that sort of thing, so once we'd started, I ended up doing a lot of it. Or helping anyway. To be honest, the lady at the records office, Mrs. Richards, did a lot of it. I got to know her quite well.

* * *

"There'll be a birth certificate." I say, as I'm typing.

"You what?"

"If Mr. and Mrs. Jacobs had children on the island, there must be birth certificates for them. They'll be in the records office."

Amber's leans in close enough that I can smell her skin. "See, I knew you were good at this stuff Billy."

I glance across to see her mouth curving up in a warm smile. The light is beginning to dance in her eyes. "I didn't even know there was such a place."

"It's at the town hall. On the first floor, it's right at the back."

Amber grins a goofy smile at me.

"And you can access it from here? You can search it?"

I'm on the website now, Amber leans in, she sounds anxious.

"For some stuff... I'm just checking now." I sit back. "No. You have to go there in person."

"Oh shit. Well can we? Will they let us in?"

I think back to how Mrs. Richards would bake trays of brownies especially for when we had appointments. She'd put one on a plate for me, and then insist I took the rest home in a Tupperware. They were *really* nice brownies.

"I think we'll be just fine."

I start putting my things in my bag, thinking we're going to leave straight away, but then there's a problem. Nothing major, just a hiccup.

"We'll have to go after class," Amber says.

"Why not now?"

"I can't. Sharpe's got all my classes registering if I turn up or not. You know she's looking for any excuse to kick me out of school."

"But the records office closes at four."

We're both silent for a moment.

Amber turns back to the computer, frustrated. "Well how about tomorrow?"

"It always closes at four. It's ten to four, Monday to Friday."

Amber looks irritated. She clicks her jaw.

"Then you'll have to go. You can sneak out now before afternoon classes start."

I don't like this idea, but I don't immediately know why not.

"I'm not meant to miss class either," I remind her.

"Yeah but they're not recording your attendance," Amber says. "So you won't get caught."

I hesitate. If I do get caught, there's a good chance that Principal Sharpe will expel me. But more than that, Dad told me I had to stay in school. I haven't told Amber about Vinny. I didn't want to admit the part where I answered his phone call. And I can't really tell her now.

Amber turns to me and asks in a really pleading voice.

"Come on Billy," She says. "Just go and find out. We've got to know. This could be the key that explains everything."

I tell myself not to worry about things that aren't gonna happen. And I nod my head.

FIFTY-SIX

WE GO DOWN to the main entrance hall together and walk casually through, checking to see if the receptionists are behind their desk or not. Annoyingly they are. So we have to wait in the corridor the other side of the lobby.

"I'll tell you when it's clear," Amber says, then she ducks back into the hall and pretends to read something on the school notice board. I wait, wishing I'd managed to say no to this. I'm going to be finished if I get caught. But then there's a low whistle, and I don't have a choice, so I take a deep breath and step out of the corridor. The entrance hall is unmanned, the receptionists back in their room.

I keep walking, expecting any moment to hear them call out my name. I feel their eyes on my back as I pull open the door and step outside. And then even more so as I walk across the parking lot and out towards the gate. But I don't hear anything, just my footsteps. And then I'm past the gate and out of sight. I breathe a sigh of relief. Then I break into a jog. I want to get this over with as quickly as possible.

* * *

"Well well. If it isn't young Billy Wheatley!"

That's Mrs. Richards. I was a bit worried, as I was walking here, I thought that maybe she might have retired, or died. I didn't think she'd get another job, because apparently she's worked here forever. And I knew she wouldn't forget me.

"Hi Mrs. Richards," I say. "How are you?"

"Oh I mustn't complain Billy. I mustn't complain." she replies. "How are the 'projects?'"

"Good," I say. "How's Arthur?" That's her cat. I used to tell her about my experiments, and she'd tell me about Arthur, like it was sort of the same thing.

"Oh he's just swell," she smiles at the thought. "Naughty as ever. Like someone else I know." She looks expectantly. "Now what brings you here? I thought we had everything settled?"

Then suddenly I'm not sure what to say next. When I spoke to her before I was always getting *my* records. I'm not 100% sure I can get other people's in the same way.

"I'm doing another project now actually," I begin.

"Oh yes?" She smiles, and I think really fast.

"It's like a genealogy thing? For school. We've got to make a family tree of someone important, and..." I hesitate, but just a little. "I decided to do one on the school principal."

"OK." There's a waver in her voice, like no one's ever asked her this before, but it doesn't last long. I suppose, in fairness, I've done odder things.

"So I thought you might be able to help."

"Well..." She makes a big thing about sitting back in her chair. "I can show you anything that's part of the public record. That's the whole point of them!" Mrs. Richards says, and she sounds happy again. "What would you like to know?"

So I ask if she can find Mr. and Mrs. Jacobs, and whether they had any other children, and in no time at all we're both behind her desk, poring over document after document, all about the family.

"OK, so *Henry Arthur Jacobs* and *Barbara June Bennett* were married in 1970, right here in St Richard's Church in Newlea. Then four years later, 1974, we have a birth. A girl named *Wendy Amanda Jacobs*..."

"That's Principal Sharpe," I say out. Mrs. Richards nods, she's getting into this too. "Yes, she becomes Wendy *Sharpe* later on, through marriage." She goes back to the earlier records. "But this is what you wanted to know. Two years after Wendy is born there's another birth. March twelfth 1976, a little boy this time, one *Eric Henry Jacobs*."

I feel a wave of satisfaction and excitement. Amber was right. *Principal Sharpe has a brother, a secret brother*. It's exactly the information I need. And unlike Principal Sharpe he won't have changed his name by getting married, so we should be able to Google him. That's if I can't find out where he is right here.

"Can you tell me if he still lives here on Lornea Island?" I ask.

Mrs. Richards doesn't look at me, she's still scanning the screen. "Maybe, there might be something more recent... Here we go..."

"What is it?"

"There's a linked record for the boy. Eric. Let me just check..."

I wait. Then Mrs. Richards says:

"Oh!"

"What?"

"It's a... It's a death certificate. Dated eighth August 1992."

"Her brother died?"

"I'm afraid so. When he was just..." We can both see her screen, but she's quicker than me in reading the right bit of the records. "Sixteen years old. Oh how sad."

"Does it say how he died?"

"Well there is a cause of death but..." She stops, she looks suddenly worried. "This is a school project you say?"

"That's right." I try and stretch to see around her and onto her screen, but she seems to sense that maybe she shouldn't be doing this now. She leans forward to make it harder for me to see.

"And Wendy Sharpe is the Principal at your school?" Mrs. Richards asks.

"Erm. Yeah," I say.

"Didn't I see something about your school on the news? Weren't there rumors about... With the police digging up the gym? Say, this isn't anything to do with that, is it?"

"No." I reply, still trying to see round her. "Does it say how he died?" I ask again. I'm dying to ask if he was murdered but that might make her more suspicious.

"And shouldn't you actually *be* in school? Shouldn't you have class now?"

"I told you, this is a school project. So I can do it in school time."

But I can tell she doesn't believe me.

"Billy," she says after a moment. "It's lovely to see you here, but I think I should check with your school principal before I give you any more information. Given its personal nature."

"No that's alright." I say as brightly as I can. "There's no need. And anyway, I've got everything I need now."

I smile, because it's true. I've just read on her screen. Eric Henry Jacobs died by drowning.

* * *

On my way back to school I'm super excited. What Amber worked out was useful, but now it's really interesting. Not only did Principal Sharpe have a brother, but he died in mysterious circumstances. Obviously that's bad in the sense it means we won't be able to talk to him, but it's good because there's bound to be plenty on the internet about it. It happened in 1992, and the internet was invented by then, and sixteen year olds drowning is always news. So I need to hurry get back to school right away and get onto the computer.

But then I realize I'm being stupid. I don't have to wait until I get back to school. I've got my phone in my pocket and I can Google from there. So I pull out my phone and start to type in my new information as I'm walking.

I type in *"Eric Henry Jacobs"* and *"drowned 1992"* into Google. There isn't as much as I expected, but right away I see there are some results. The top hit is an article from the *Lornea Island Times*, from the really old version of their website. Walking slowly, with my phone in front of me, I read the first line.

The search for *missing teenager Eric Jacobs was called off today after police revealed he had been...*

But I don't get any further than that, because right then everything goes totally crazy.

FIFTY-SEVEN

I DON'T EXACTLY SEE it happen, because my eyes are on the screen of my phone, but I'm aware of it. A white car mounting the pavement in front of me. It happens so fast I don't even get time to pull my head up before the driver's door is open and a man jumps out. He's much too close to me. I'm about to shout out when he grabs me. He spins me around, and then his other hand is around my neck, cutting off my air so I can't even breathe.

"Come with me," he growls. "We're going for a ride."

I feel a sharp pain below my ribs. It hurts so much I think he might have stabbed me, and I can't help but cry out, but the moment I do his hand covers my mouth. Then something slams into my head. I'm dazed and scared and it's kind of hard to make sense of it, but I see enough to work out it's a gun.

"In the car."

The gun goes back into my ribs, pressing hard and really hurting. I don't even know if I do what he says, or if he just pushes me into the car. I do realize my phone slips from my hand and falls to the sidewalk. I don't pick it up. I don't have time. Then I'm in the car. Behind the wheel.

"Slide across." The man says. For a few seconds I don't even know what he means, but then he raises up the gun so that it's pointing into my face. I can see the hole in the barrel. I can sense the bullet inside being fired and flying out towards me. There's no room to get out of the way, no time to move even if there was.

"Slide across. Now."

I scramble to do what he says. Then he gets in too, pulling the door closed. The motor's still running, and before the door is even shut we're moving. He pulls away from the curb and seconds later we're past the school entrance, heading out of town.

There's a time when we're just driving, a million thoughts running through my head. I think about escaping, just pushing open the passenger door and rolling out, but we're moving fast already. Too fast. I glance across at the man. Right away he looks back at me.

I turn away at once, but try to process what I saw. I'm not good at judging adults ages, but he's kind of Dad's age. He's got short dark hair and stubble, and he's wearing jeans, the gun resting on his leg, still pointed at me. I feel a fresh flush of terror. I've had a gun pointed at me once before, but this is scarier. It feels like we only have to go over a pothole and he'll fire it, even just by accident. I sneak another look. He looks right back again. He's watchful.

"This is a rental. Don't do anything stupid and make me mess it up."

I blink, then I notice the sticker on the windshield. Island Rental Cars. It's the company we used to recommend to tourists.

"Who are you?"

"Shut up." The man says. He keeps driving. Fast, but not crazy fast, and I work out he doesn't want to draw attention to us. We're still going through Newlea, but soon we'll be out of town.

"What do you want."

"I want you to keep quiet so I don't have to shoot you." He resettles his gun in his lap. I wish he would stop pointing that gun at me. Over and over I imagine how it must feel as the bullet enters your body. I can't help it. And then the last moments of your life, in agony, as you actually physically die. It actually hurts just to think about it.

I try to distract myself by keeping track of where we're going. I don't know if it'll help, but I don' t know what else to do. We're past the limits of Newlea now, and there's just a couple of buildings left before the road cuts through the empty part in the middle of Lornea. The gas station whizzes past, and then we're into the forest. There's a couple of bends up ahead and then there's the long straight section that leads all the way down towards Silverlea. But instead of building up speed, the man slows as we get into the trees, and then when we get to a track on the left he pulls into it, and we bump thirty meters off the road, so we're hidden in the woods.

Then he stops the car, kills the motor and turns to me.

"Get out."

I'm too scared to do what he says, so he repeats it. Louder this time.

"Get out. And don't do anything stupid."

This time I claw at the door handle, and I'm surprised when it opens first time. I'd thought it would be locked.

When I'm out of the car he makes me walk further into the woods. It's mostly pine trees here, and they grow pretty thick, so there isn't much light. I stumble a couple of times, and both times I feel the gun pointing into my back to prod me forward. Both times really hard. It's like he wants to hurt me.

"That'll do." He says at last. "Turn around."

I do what he says, and see he's standing a few meters away now, the gun held casually at his waist. I frown in confusion. I don't know why we're here. Surely he doesn't just want to kill me?

"Who are you?" I ask again.

He doesn't answer. Just watches me.

"What do you want? Why have you brought me here?" Maybe he doesn't just want to kill me? I decided I have to get him talking.

"Are you Vinny?" I ask. "You are aren't you? I knew you were coming. You worked out who I was when you heard the radio."

The man finally breaks out into a grin at this. "*Good Moooooooorning Looooornea Issssland!* Yeah. I'm Vinny. That was real nice of you to tell me where to come." He's got really white teeth, like a Hollywood actor.

"But how did you find *me*?" I ask, a few moments later when he goes back to just watching me. It doesn't matter, I don't care. I just need to keep him talking.

It takes him a while, but he does.

"Tucker and your old man were close growing up. And I heard on the news he'd come out here, when he was mixed up in that missing girl case a couple years back. So when I heard Tucker's phone had made it to Lornea Island too, it didn't take much to work out he'd run to his old buddy. So then I flew out here and start asking around. See if I can find anyone who knows where *Sam Wheatley* is living. I met this nice lady in the grocery store. Said she had a kid in the local school that knows Sam Wheatley's kid. Described what you look like. So I've been watching the school. Today you sneaked out for the afternoon. *Lucky me.*"

His voice fades out, but the grin stays on his face.

"So what do you want?"

Vinny doesn't answer. He puts his head onto one side again, and now he lifts up the gun, turns it sideways, and points it at me. Then he screws up his face, like he's not happy with something, and turns the gun so it's on the other side.

"I said what do you want?"

"And I heard you boy." He changes his position again, this time passing the gun to his other hand. He holds it out with his arm straight.

"We're here, in this nice little clearing in the woods, so that you can fully understand the gravity of the situation you're in. Afore we proceed any further. You do don't you? Understand the gravity?"

I don't answer. The way he's talking is freaking me out.

"I mean you could run. You could try and get away from me. Like your buddy Tucker did, but I don't fancy your chances because I will shoot you down."

He smiles at me again, showing his teeth. "You wanna try it? You wanna run?" He lowers the gun, like he's giving me a chance. I stare at him, I move my foot, not even getting ready to run away, but maybe thinking about it. But suddenly his arm locks straight, and before I can even think there's a flash from the barrel of the gun. At the exact same time I feel something cutting the air past my cheek, and then there's a massive explosion that bounces through the pine trees.

I put my hand up to the back of my head, not even sure if I'll feel a hole where I've been shot, but when I pull it away there's only wood slivers. The bullet hit a tree just behind me. It can't have been more than a couple inches from my head.

"But I'm willing to bet I'm a good enough shot to stop you." Vinny goes on, with a little chuckle. He's relaxed his arm again, letting the now smoking gun aim at the forest floor.

"So let's not have any misunderstandings about this, shall we? Because I have other ways to get what I want. If you decide to not cooperate."

I'm too shocked and scared to speak, but slowly I realize he's actually waiting on an answer, so I try to nod, but my neck is so tensed up I can't really do it. If I had thought about trying to run, there's no way I can now. The fear is so thick I can't hardly breathe.

"Good. So now you're going to tell me where your friend Tucker is, and then we're going to pay him a little visit. And then if everything goes according to plan – and only if – then maybe I won't have to shoot you. How's that plan sound to you?"

Again he waits, and again I manage to force my rigid neck into something like a nod. I try to actually answer him too, but it comes out as just a noise.

"Good." I see the teeth again. They're like the teeth a movie star has, but for some reason they make him even more terrifying.

"So get talking." Again he straightens his arm, and the pistol is aimed right at my face. His arm is super steady, it's like it's mounted on a vice.

"One...Two..."

He doesn't wait. He doesn't give me any time, and I still can't get any words out.

"Three."

FIFTY-EIGHT

"HE'S AT HOME." I blurt the words out.

I don't even have time to think about lying or tricking him. I'm too scared. I don't even get to think if what I've just said is *true*. Dad and Tucker might have left for the ferry already.

"Where's home?"

"Littlelea." There's a flash of irritation on Vinny's face at this, and I take something from it. I don't know what exactly.

"Where or what is *Littlelea*?" He asks.

"It's where we live. It's in the south of the island. Overlooking Silverlea Beach. You just follow the road we were on before to get there."

"How nice." The white smile comes back now. "And is Mr. Nolan expecting any company, do you know?" As he speaks he waggles the gun to tell me to start moving back toward the car. When I do so he falls into step behind me, the muzzle pressing into my back. I struggle to think what to say. What's best to say. What's even the truth.

"I don't think so." I manage in the end.

"Well let's hope not. For your sake."

We walk until we're back at the car. Vinny unlocks it with the remote.

"Get in," Vinny says, pulling open the passenger door, so I do so. There's a moment as he walks around the back of the car when I realize he doesn't have the gun trained on me. I could do something, I could escape even, but I can still hear the sound of that gunshot, still feel the bullet whipping past my ear. So I don't. Then suddenly he's in the driver's seat again and he has the gun pointed at me, resting on his thigh.

"So let's go to Littlelea," Vinny smiles.

We rejoin the main road, and I desperately try to think. I wish I had my phone, maybe I could tap out a message, but it fell to the road when Vinny grabbed me. Maybe someone will find it? Maybe they'll work out I was taken? But even if they did, they wouldn't know who took me, nor where he's taking me.

Maybe Amber will work out I've taken longer in the records office than I should? Maybe she'll work out what's happened? But that's no good either. I glance at the clock on the dashboard of the car, she'll still be in class. And there's no way she could work out where I am anyway. Not in time to do anything.

"So how'd you get hold of Tucker's phone?" Vinny asks suddenly and I'm jerked back to the present.

"I found it," I hear my voice answering. I stop myself from explaining about how he threw it down the cliff.

"He had it switched off and hidden but I found it. I wanted to find out why he was here."

"Oh yeah?" Vinny smiles. "Well lucky old me once again. It seems I owe you big time." He falls silent for a few moments before going on.

"And did you? Find out why he was here?"

I hesitate. I'm aware that he's getting information from me, when I meant it to be the other way around. But there's no way not to answer him.

"I know about the robbery."

Vinny turns sharply towards me and studies me for a long while.

"And you know what he did?"

I want to say I know what *he* did, what Vinny did, in shooting the security guard, but I'm too scared to say that.

"I know he drove off and left you there." I say in the end.

"Yes he did." Vinny says, and then he's silent, and the silence unnerves me so I keep talking.

"But he didn't mean to. He panicked. After you..."

Vinny looks at me and arches one eyebrow.

"That what he told you?" He says.

I don't answer, instead I just nod.

"Didn't look to me much like he panicked. Looked more like he decided to leave me there to get picked up by the cops." He grins again. "But what he don't know is, I've got a good set of lungs on me. I had to run my way out of there, but I made it." Then Vinny's voice turns dark.

"What else'd Tucker say he did?"

I think for a moment, not understanding. But then I work it out.

"He took the jewelry. That you stole from the store in Hounds Beach."

"Yes he did that too." Vinny turns to me. "And now I'm going to get it back."

Right now we get to the turn off for Littlelea. I think that maybe I could just ignore it and we'll drive right past. But then we'll end up in Silverlea so that's no good. And anyway the turn off is clearly marked with a sign.

"Littlelea," he reads. "Should I be taking this turn?"

I nod.

I have a sudden idea. I don't know if it's a good idea, I don't have time to even think about it. The words come out of my mouth before I get the chance.

"I know where the jewelry is." I say.

For a second I think that maybe Vinny didn't hear, and I'm actually relieved because, obviously I don't know where the jewelry is, nor how it would even help much if I did. But then he turns to me, his eyebrow arched again.

"How's that then?"

And now he's said that I have to go through with it.

"He hid it. I saw him hide it. In the rocks, down by the beach where we live. When he first got here. That's why I was suspicious of him. That's why I took his phone."

Vinny seems to think about this for a long time, so I keep going. I'm still not sure exactly where this is going, but I'm committed now.

"I can take you to it. Tucker will never tell you where it is. If you kill him, you'll never find it. But you can have it, you can have it now." I point in front of us, at the road that leads down to the Littlelea end of Silverlea beach. It's at the foot of the cliff where our house is. There's nothing there but a dirt parking lot and the beach.

"I can make Tucker talk easy enough."

"Yeah but you don't need to. I can take you to the jewelry now. It's gold, I've seen it." Obviously I haven't, but I remember Tucker saying what it was. The mention of gold seems to work.

"He hid it?"

"Yeah. I guess he didn't think it was safe to keep it in the house."

We're almost at the turning now, and I think that Vinny is going to drive right by. Suddenly I'm desperate for him not too. It's not much of a plan that I've got, but it's better than nothing, and right now, nothing is the alternative. But it seems he senses it's a trap. We're level with the turning, and then we drive right by, his head cocked over, looking at me. But then he slows down.

"You better not be messing with me Billy. Like I said, I can find Tucker with or without you. I don't need you alive."

He stops the car, and then very calmly he slips it into reverse and backs up till he's level with the turn again. Then he looks at me again, a questioning look. I just nod. Then he turns the steering wheel and we set off again, rolling down towards the parking lot at Littlelea beach.

I try to think through what I'm doing. It wasn't a whole *plan* exactly, to bring him here. It was just a sense of something, I'm not sure what. Then I kind of work it out. It was when he didn't know where Littlelea was. He doesn't *know* the island. He doesn't *know* the beach. And I do. I know it better than anyone. So if I can get him onto the beach, then maybe I can lose him there. If I can get him into the rocks. I know every boulder, every crack of our cliffs. Quickly I decide where I'll pretend Tucker hid the jewelry, and then work out the quickest way from there up the cliff. If I'm lucky I'll be able to catch Dad and Tucker before they leave for the ferry. We can all get away. And work out what to do after that.

"Seems quite a public place to hide a bag of gold chains." Vinny says. He's stopped the car just before the entrance to the parking lot. It's empty, but there's space for maybe forty cars when it gets busy mid-summer. He taps his fingers on the steering wheel.

"Not really." I reply. "Hardly anyone ever comes here." I can feel my body filling up with adrenalin, getting ready for when I run. I'm desperate for him to let me out.

"Just park at the front. We have to walk to get there."

I feel him staring at me for a long time, suspicious as hell, but then we roll forward again and he parks where I said. Then he's first to get out. He looks around, scanning the little river that runs by the parking lot. At the steep cliff behind it. It's easy to cross the river since it breaks up into multiple streams when it hits the beach, each one studded with rocks. That's where we'll cross, I decide.

I get out the car too. Trying to make myself sound confident.

"It's this way. Down by the beach."

I sense he's more cautious here than he was in the car or the woods. He moves close behind me, and I feel the gun press into my back again. But he's doing it differently now, like he's trying to hide it, in case we see anyone. But that's unlikely this late in the season.

"So where we headed?"

. . .

I point about a third of the way down the beach, where hundreds of rocks of all sizes lay piled about and half-buried in the low-tide sand. I know every last one of them.

"Over there," I say, and keep walking. Vinny doesn't reply.

I lead him across the river, jumping across from one flat stone to another. Sometimes when tourists do come here they dam the river, or storm waves move the rocks, so that it's hard to cross, but I always come and put them back afterwards. I hear Vinny behind me swear, and turn to see him put a foot into the water. It gives me a jolt of confidence. He doesn't know the beach. I can lose him here.

Once over the river there's just a short stretch of sand before we get to the base of the cliff. You can't see my house from here, it stands too far back from the cliff top, but it's just above us now. I make a silent prayer that Dad hasn't left already.

"Kid are you messing with me?" Vinny asks. "'Coz if you're messing…"

"No, I'm not, I promise. It's just up ahead. He had to hide it above the high-tide line," I interrupt him. I turn a little so that I'm heading back up the beach, towards the area where short grasses partly cover the rocks. The sea never gets in here, but you still get cliff falls, so there's lots of boulders scattered around. I aim for the middle of them and prepare myself to run.

But now that I'm here, my idea doesn't seem so clever after all. I assumed that Vinny would just be following behind me, but actually he's actually holding me, with one hand on my shoulder, and the gun still pressed into the small of my back. I thought that when I got here I'd be able to run, and do it quickly enough so that I could shelter behind a rock before he could shoot me. Now I realize that's impossible. I try to shake him loose, just a little bit, making out I need his weight off me to help me balance, but he just grips me tighter.

We reach the rock I was aiming for. We start to walk behind it. My plan was to run from here, but there's no chance.

"So?" Vinny says when I stop. "Where is it?" I can tell from his tone he's almost at the point of flat-out not believing me, so I look around, desperate for anything that's going to help. I see stones on the floor, maybe I could pick one up and hit him with it? But he's twice the size of me, with a gun pressed into my kidneys. It's not going to work.

Then I see something – a piece of dried seaweed. It's not a lot, but it gives me a half-plan.

Casually I turn the piece of seaweed over with my foot. "I got it wrong," I tell him. "It's not this rock, it's that one." I point a little further down the beach, this time towards one of the bigger and most distinctive rocks structures on the beach, a sheer-faced slab that connects the cliff to the sand at forty five degrees, like a tennis court that's been tipped on its side. I hold my breath, praying he won't see what I'm thinking. "I'm sorry."

He doesn't react at first, but then I feel myself spun around, and he jabs the gun into my face.

"Last chance Billy boy," his teeth flash white in the sunshine, but it's a grimace now rather than a smile. "Or you're gonna be fish food."

We walk on, with Vinny gripping me even tighter than before, so there's no way to escape. I realize now he saw this coming. But this time I lead him more purposefully. The rocks we're headed to was one of my favorites, growing up. I used to have a rope tied to the top, so I could climb up, pretending to be a famous rock climber. Only it was difficult in some parts because you get so much seaweed growing on the rock. Actually you get different types of seaweed as you go higher, because the tide covers the lower part for longer. Some of the seaweeds are easy to see, but others are translucent, so you can't see them. But they're just as slippery.

We get to the base of the rock now where it disappears under the sand. At the top, where it connects into the cliff, there's a shelf of grass. It's actually not that bad a place to hide jewelry. I can sense Vinny's interest in it.

"It's up there." I say, pointing at the ledge. For a second he releases me, and I wonder if this is my moment, but I'm not quick enough, and the gun is pressed into my stomach.

"You have to climb up," I continue.

"Well OK then." Vinny says.

So I turn and put one foot carefully on the bottom of the rock slope.

"It's slippery," I tell him. "Be careful." But I don't tell him how to climb it.

The lower part of the slope is covered with bladderwrack. The best technique here is to find the limpets. They grip onto the rock like little pyramids, and you can use them as footholds and handholds. My feet find a couple now, almost automatically, and I scale the first bit easily. I turn to see Vinny is coming up behind me, but he's struggling trying to hold the gun and see what he's doing. I move a bit faster, accelerating higher and away from him. The limpets don't reach higher up and the bladderwrack gives way to the translucent seaweed. Its real name is Ulva something or other, but I used to call it *Witches Paper seaweed* because it's white when it's dry and nearly invisible when it gets wet. You can only really climb the dry bits, and I'm lucky because there's just enough patches of white left for me to climb to the top.

The other thing I used to do, when I was a kid, is slide down on the

Witches Paper. You need a bit of rock that doesn't have barnacles or limpets, because otherwise you can really hurt yourself, so I never did it right here. But that isn't going to stop me now. I look back down the way I've just climbed. I'm ten meters up from the sand now, and nearly at the ledge where I'm pretending the jewelry is hidden. But I can't let us reach it, because if we do it'll be obvious I've been lying and there's nowhere else to go. So I take a deep breath. Vinny is about five meters below me, just getting to the top of the bladderwrack part of the slope, and he seems to be concentrating more on the climb than he does on me. If I'm going to do it, it has to be now.

With a scream that I don't intend I suddenly launch myself back down the slippery translucent seaweed and right towards Vinny. He looks up, and I see him raise his arm, not to shoot, but just to protect himself as I come sliding down towards him, but he doesn't have time. I hit him with my feet and then we're both falling and sliding the remaining way down the slope. I feel sharp pains as I'm dragged over patches of barnacles and the limpets. And seconds later we're tangled back together on the beach.

Vinny starts to shout something but I don't wait to listen. I'm already on my feet and running.

FIFTY-NINE

WHEN I HAD this plan I envisioned myself running so fast it would feel like flying, but now it's happening it's more like running in slow motion. I can't make my arms and legs move properly, and I feel this paralyzing terror that I'm going to be cut down by a bullet any moment. But it doesn't come, and when I turn a corner I get some relief. There's solid rock between me and Vinny, with his gun.

I *feel* the protection it gives me, cutting off the murderous bullets. I keep running, my legs pounding over the sand, and I speed up now. My feet start dancing over the rocks as I come to them. I've clambered these rocks so many times I know every angle, every solid step and every rock to avoid walking on because it moves or because it's coated in slippery weed. My leg hurts, and I glimpse red – blood – from where I must have caught it on something sliding down the rock face. But I don't care. I don't feel any pain.

I keep moving, my feet a blur, towards the cliff path. It's been closed for years because the steps cut into the rock have collapsed in places, but I've always used it. It's *my* path. It comes out at the top right by our house. The bottom of the path is fifty meters away. I'm going to get there.

But to my amazement, and horror, I'm not leaving Vinny behind like I thought I could. He's fast, *really* fast. At first I hear him shouting, but then he goes silent and I just catch the occasional hit of feet on sand or the splash as he jumps through the rockpools. Twice I glance behind me and I'm shocked at how close he is. I see the look of hard concentration on his face. I turn back, and try to run faster still, nearly at the base of the cliff path now. And for a moment there's near silence, just the sounds of the two of us panting and running through the rocky shore.

When I get to the path I can hear he's closer. Just a few meters behind me now. I realize he could stop at any moment and line up a shot, and I think the only reason he doesn't is because he knows he's going to catch me. Up ahead the path cuts up the cliff in a series of stepped zigzags, and there's no shelter at all, not until higher up where brambles offer some protection. I flash past the sign saying *Danger, path closed*. I wonder for a second if that might slow him down, but I know it won't.

When I hit the slope I slow, you can't help it when you start going uphill, and Vinny closes still further until we're both climbing, him only an arms' length below me. He's so fast, it's moments before he's going to catch me. But in my haste to climb I'm loosening stones and small rocks and sending them cascading down the cliff behind me. And now Vinny has to deal with those as well as scrambling up the uneven steps. I do my best to loosen more as I go up, and for a few seconds the gap between us even widens a little. But then I hear Vinny let out a roar of rage. Then he must accelerate again because I sense him, getting closer and closer behind me. I'm not even a third of the way up the cliff before I feel his hand catching on my leg. I try to shake it off, but it tightens around me, pulling me to the ground. Gripping me hard.

I roll onto my back, and dig my hands into the dirt trying to stay where I am, and then I arch my foot to release it, and for a second he's left holding my shoe, and he slips a meter down the slope with it. Then he growls again, and he tosses the shoe. I see it bounce down the slope below him.

Then I see Vinny start moving up towards me again, but this time I'm ready for him. I push my palms into the earth to anchor myself, and tense my legs. As Vinny reaches me I kick out, hitting his face with my one remaining shoe. I see his chin jerk to the side as I connect, and he yells out in rage. I try to do it again, but miss this time, so instead I kick at his hand with my foot, while I scrape earth into my hands. He slips back and I crawl backwards up the cliff a few more yards. For a moment we both stop.

"You fucking little shit," he snarls, feeling his jaw. "You're dead." And then he awkwardly pulls the gun up in front of him. There's no hesitation, but his face changes as he goes to pull the trigger, but as he does I scream and fling the handful of grit and stones from the path towards his eyes.

I don't wait. I hear him scream, and as I'm turning I see the dirt spraying into his face. But then I turn and again, upwards towards the top of the cliff, my house, and to where I'm praying my Dad hasn't left yet.

SIXTY

THIS TIME I open out a lead. When I scramble over the top of the path, onto the cliff top, I can't even see him behind me. I feel my leg hurting, and now my shoulder too, but the adrenalin is strong enough that they're hardly slowing me. Below me, not far below, I hear him coming again.

I only have one shoe on now, and my sock slips on the grass, giving me a lopsided limp. I'm exhausted. I want to stop to get some air, but I daren't. I stumble along the cliff top towards the house, and there, I see Dad's truck is still parked in the driveway. They haven't left yet. I feel a massive rush of relief. I try to shout out but I have no breath.

And then I see the front door of the house open and Dad step out. He's carrying Tucker's bag, and he swings it into the back of his truck. Then he turns back to the house.

"Dad!" I try to call out, but I'm so short of breath, no sound comes out. He doesn't hear me. It's like a bad dream. I start to feel the space behind me, where I know Vinny will appear at any moment. I have to cross open ground before I get to the house, there's no shelter to protect me from bullets.

But then something makes him turn – maybe the movement of me waving my arms – and he sees me. His face is confused. He waits a few beats, as I close the gap towards him, desperately waving my arms at him.

"Billy? What the hell are you doing here?" He steps forward, to get to me, moving himself out into the open.

"He's here. Vinny's here. He's got a gun!" I try to say, but the words don't come out loud. I so out of breath.

"I'm just taking Tucker to the ferry," Dad says, moving forward still further, half-smiling in confusing. "Why aren't you in school..?"

I wave my arms again, trying to make his step back. Finally he notices that something's wrong. "Hey? What happened to your leg? You're bleeding..."

I reach him now and just crash into him, pushing him back so at least we're behind the truck. Vinny must have got to the top of the cliff by now. I can feel him lining up a shot. But Dad resists me. I try to speak again, desperately sucking in air so I can form the words.

"We've got..." I pant. "Move... We've got to..."

"The hell are you saying?" Dad cuts in, starting to sound alarmed now. I still can't get more than two words out I'm so short of breath.

"The hell is it now?"

But before I can try again to explain there's another gunshot. I feel a huge flare of panic, and for a second I'm sure it hits me, square in my back, but then I realize it hasn't, it's just the way I've tensed up, in a spasm of panic.

I see snatches of Dad, trying to make sense of what's happening. I see his face, the emotions flowing across his features. Surprise, shock, fear. I hear more shots. Two. Three. I can't even tell how many. As I watch I can almost see the back of Dad's head explode and blood bursting out, I expect it to happen so much. I'm so freaked, it takes me time to see that this doesn't happen. I realize I'm screaming, and the only thing that stops me is a boot, a few moments later, struck hard into my ribs.

SIXTY-ONE

"Shut the *fuck* up."

I'm still so short of breath, it doesn't take much for me to do what he says.

"Get on your knees, hands behind your head."

It's Vinny, speaking through great panting lunges of breath. It takes me a second to see it's not me he's talking to now, it's Dad. I turn to look, still not sure if he's been shot or not, but I can't see any blood. Our eyes meet. I try to make him see I'm sorry. That I tried to tell him what was happening.

"Get on your *fucking* knees and put your hands behind your head." Vinny snarls a second time. He's got his gun held in both hands, pointed right at Dad. His eyes slide to me though now, like he's covering both of us. Slowly Dad does what he says, dropping one leg and then the other until he's kneeling in the dirt of our drive. I feel certain that as soon as he does, Vinny is going to shoot him. Execute him. It's like when he led me to the forest.

"No!" I call out, putting my hand on Dad to try to stop him.

"You too, you little shit." Vinny turns to me, aiming the gun at me now. It's amazing the power of it. It makes me freeze, imagining again the death it can deliver, with just a twitch of his fingers.

"*Kneel.*" Vinny says. I'm shaking, but I do what he tells me. Then Vinny steps carefully around. I see him glancing around, at the house, at the surrounding land, but there's no one around. Our closest neighbors are half a mile away.

"Well well. If it isn't Jamie fucking Stone. So this is where a rat like you goes to hide," Vinny says. He gives a nasty smile.

"Vinny," Dad replies. "Let the boy go. Whatever this is about, he's got nothing to do with it."

"Shut up," Vinny snarls. And Dad takes a breath of air, like he's going to say something else, but then does what he's told. Vinny looks around again.

"Where the fuck is he?"

Dad takes a second to answer this, and then when he does, his voice sounds weird. Cautious. Tense.

"Who?"

And then, so quick I don't really see it happening, Vinny has an elbow wrapped around my neck, and the barrel of the gun pressed against my temple.

"Where the fuck is your buddy Tucker?" Vinny spits out the question this time, I can feel flecks of saliva hitting my face.

I see Dad tense, on the verge of jumping forward, but stopping himself when he sees there's no chance.

"Tucker Nolan? I haven't seen him in years."

"Oh yeah? Well how come your boy already told me he's been living here. Two fucking rats. Now where the fuck is he?"

Dad's quiet for a second.

"OK, he was here. He got off the island this morning. There's a boat in an hour. If you go now you can get after him..."

"*Bullshit*. The truth or I blow the kid's brains out."

I screw my eyes closed, wondering whether I'll hear the bang, or my brain will explode before the sound hits it. It's weird how that's what you think about at times like this.

"OK," Dad's calm, trying to reassure Vinny. "He's in the house. He went to the bathroom."

I feel the hold around my neck loosen, and open my eyes. But I'm just in time to see Vinny's arm extend, and then he brings the gun crashing down onto the front of Dad's head. It's so quick, there's nothing he can do about it, no time to move out of the way. There's a sickening crack of metal hitting bone, and Dad slumps backward. Then, because of the way he's kneeling, so he can't actually fall backwards, instead he rocks, and then falls to the side. I don't know if he's unconscious or dead. I guess I must scream out again, because the next thing I know Vinny is shouting at me to shut up too.

"Unless you want the same?" He snarls, and lifts the gun to threaten me.

I'm quiet again. I look at Dad. He's lying on his side across the driveway. He's not moving, I can't see if he's breathing, but there's blood seeping out of a wound on his forehead. I turn to look at Vinny again, my eyes wide in terror.

But Vinny doesn't seem interested. He stabs the gun into the small of my back again, and forces me to move, half dragging me so that Dad's truck now stands between us and the front of the house.

"I know you're in there Tucker," Vinny calls out loudly. He's almost ignoring me now, but he keeps the gun pressed hard against me, and he's strong. He's unbelievably strong, his forearm wrapped around my neck, restricting the air I can get in. I think for a second that maybe I could drop my head down and bite his arm, but my chin is in the way, stopping me from moving. And then he changes his grip, tighter again, so that it's impossible.

"Tucker you *motherfucker*. Get your sorry ass out here."

Then we both wait, watching the front door. It doesn't move. I don't even know if I want it to. I just suddenly know I was wrong to lead Vinny here. I thought it would save me, but it hasn't helped. Not at all.

"Tucker... Don't make me come in after you," Vinny shouts now. Then suddenly he takes the gun from my neck and aims it at the house. He fires off three shots, shattering the kitchen window and then the windows of the lounge. The noise of it rises up and booms around the clifftop. Then when the echoes die out, nothing's changed.

"Tucker. Get out here now or the kid dies." Vinny shouts into the silence.

Nothing moves in the house. Dad's still lying still. I begin to wonder if maybe Tucker has escaped out the back. It's what I'd do. At least. I think it is.

"You know I'll do it Tuck. I'm gonna count to three."

I feel my eyes start to flick about, desperate for a way out of this. But he's gripping me tight. The gun is pressed against my temple again. Vinny forces me to my feet, so we're visible from the house. If anyone's there to see.

"One."

What if he's not there? What if he's gone? I don't want to die. Not like this.

"Two," he calls out. Then he speaks to me.

"Say goodbye boy."

He takes a deep breath. I struggle, but he tenses and stops me, it doesn't seem to take any effort.

"Three."

SIXTY-TWO

MY EYES CLOSE. I don't expect to ever open them again. But when I do, I'm not dead. Instead I see my house. The front door is open, and Tucker's standing there. He's got his hands raised, and at once, Vinny aims the gun at him.

"You armed?" Vinny shouts.

"No." Tucker replies.

"Bullshit. Lift up your shirt."

But the second Tucker begins to move his hands, Vinny shouts again.

"*Slow down.* Do it *slowly.*"

Then, moving his hands very deliberately, Tucker does what he's told, unbuttoning, and then pulling open up his shirt until we can see his tattoo.

"Take it off. Drop it on the ground."

Tucker slips the shirt from his shoulders and lets it fall.

"Now turn around. Do it slowly."

So he does, turning a complete circle until he's back facing forwards. There's no gun, or any weapon on his torso.

"Now drop your pants."

"What?"

"Drop your fucking pants."

I see a dark look pass over Tucker, but he begins to unbuckle his belt, and then pushes his jeans down his legs. They get down to his knees so he's just standing in his underpants.

"All the way off. Shoes too. Do it slowly."

Tucker is slow to respond. But I guess he had no choice, because then he reaches down and pulls off one shoe and then the other. As he does so he slowly pulls out a kitchen knife out that he must have put into his sock. He holds it up, handle first, so that Vinny can see it.

"Toss it away." With his eyes Vinny indicates the direction he wants Tucker to throw it, away into the yard.

I watch as the knife traces a little arc and lands in the grass. I wonder if there's any way I can get to it, but Vinny is still holding me, and even if he wasn't, I don't know what I'd do with a knife. I try to imagine using it, but I can't.

"Keep going," Vinny says. His attention hasn't moved from Tucker. And as I turn back, Tucker is continuing to undress, until he's standing there just in his underpants.

"This ain't got nothing to do with the kid," Tucker begins. He sounds strangely calm, like this isn't that different from a normal conversation. "Nor Jamie neither."

"You made it to do with them. By hiding out here."

Tucker doesn't reply. He looks like he's about to, but then doesn't have the words.

"You knew I'd come for you. That's why you ran. You choose to hide here."

I stare at Tucker as Vinny says this, and for a second he looks back at me. But he turns back. I see him shake his head, very slightly.

"I didn't run. Least. I didn't mean to run. We were finished in there. It was going just like we planned it. It ain't my fault you decided to shoot the guy."

"He would have come after us. I was just doing the job properly. *Like we fucking planned.*"

Even from here I can see Tucker's nostrils flare in frustration. He doesn't have an answer again.

"Whatever dude. I don't think we're ever gonna agree on that one."

"Step forward." Vinny says, and Tucker hesitates.

"I said step forward." Vinny repeats.

"If it's the stash you've come for, it's in the truck. You can take it."

"Oh I will," Vinny says. "But you know I didn't come all the way out here just for a few gold chains. I can get that anywhere I want. There's a principle here. You don't split like that. Because there's consequences..."

I feel Vinny tighten the grip around my neck even more. He still has the gun pointed at Tucker. His arm outstretched now. I see in Tucker's face how the sight of the gun is affecting him. He can't even move his eyeballs.

I guess it's because he knows this guy. He knows exactly what he's capable off.

"Now kneel." Vinny says. The atmosphere has changed. It's like we all know there's no more talking to be done. Tucker takes a long time to do anything, I can see him looking at his options. If he kneels down, Vinny is going to shoot him. But if he doesn't Vinny is going to shoot him. I suddenly realize I'm going to have to watch. I'm going to have to see Tucker's head burst open and his brains spray out. And then what's going to happen to me?

But then I suddenly notice another pair of eyes watching what's going on. Uncertain eyes. Nervous, almost reptilian eyes. I blink, not sure if I can trust what I'm seeing. But I can. I try to make contact with the eyes. I try to send a message. But the eyes are only watching.

"Kneel motherfucker," Vinny shouts out now. "And maybe I leave the kid alive."

I sense Tucker's turning to me, but I'm not looking at him now. I'm totally fixated on the other pair of eyes. The eyes belonging to a juvenile herring gull, sitting on the top of the house watching the whole scene unfold. A herring gull that doesn't like it when he sees me being threatened. I stare at Steven, desperate for him to understand. In front of me Tucker slowly kneels in the dirt. Vinny grips my neck tighter still and drags me forward, so that the tip of the gun is just a few yards from Tucker's head, bowed down, like he can't face looking at it.

"Mmmmmmmmm," I suddenly say, as loud as I dare. "Hmmmmmmmm-mmmmmmm."

Vinny shakes me. "Shut the fuck up kid."

But I don't.

"Hmmmmmmmmmmmm. Mmmmmnnnggg." I'm louder this time, and I see the reaction it has in Steven. His head stills, and I see him lean forward where he's perched, like he's contemplating taking off. Considering if I'm in trouble. But he doesn't do it. He still just sits there. I know I have to make Vinny hurt me. It's the only way to make Steven move.

So I moan again, and I push against Vinny, knocking his aim off Tucker for a second. It's not long enough for Tucker to react, but it annoys Vinny. He has no idea what's going on. He responds by shaking me, harder.

"Fucking keep it down kid. Unless you want me to shoot you first?"

"Mmmmhhhhhmmmggghhh" I shout it this time, and I struggle even more, and this time Vinny loses it. The side of the gun makes contact with my head, but it's more of a push than a blow since there's no backswing.

Even so I see Steven's reaction to it. He steps forward from the ridge of the roof, his wings opening as he does so.

I don't hesitate. I know exactly what's coming, and I try with all my might to shake myself free from Vinny's grip. For a second it's easy for him to keep me overpowered, and I realize he's had enough. He's turning the gun now, to shoot me first, to rid himself of this pest. But right at that moment a flashing brown-grey-white creature smashes into him. He doesn't have time to even let out a cry before he's hit by five pounds of bird, slashing with his beak and the three claws on the end of each of his webbed feet.

Then everything happens so quick it's hard to make out. I feel I'm free, and I roll back. For a moment I see Steven all over Vinny's face, as he's lying on his back on the ground. And then Tucker is in there too. And I see a horrible moment when Steven's wing is caught at a horrible angle, and Vinny rolls on top of him, crushing him beneath his bodyweight. But when he's clear of the bird, his face slashed and bleeding.

But by then Tucker is standing over him with the gun.

SIXTY-THREE

IT'S JUST A FEW SECONDS, but everything has changed. I blink at the new reality in front of me. Tucker is holding the gun with both hands, and I can see them shaking. Steven is squawking and calling loudly, and he's dragging one wing behind him over towards his old pen.

I rush over to Dad. For a second I don't want to touch him, I don't know why, it's like I'm scared I'll find his skin cold. But that's stupid, even if he was dead, he wouldn't have had time to cool down. Then I don't have to think about that anymore because I see his chest is moving. I can hear the breaths, he's rasping as he sucks air in and out. There's a gash on his head, but it's like he's sleeping.

"He OK?" Tucker shouts to me.

I look up. He's keeping Vinny sat on the ground, the gun trained at his head. Vinny's bleeding from a gash to his cheek.

"I think so."

"Get him on his side." Tucker shouts again, but I already know. I've been to lots of talks at the Silverlea Surf Lifesaving Club about how to help people who've nearly drowned. I know all about the recovery position, and I roll Dad into it. It's harder doing it with a real person than it is with the plastic dummies we practice with.

When I can't do anymore I run back to Steven. He's sitting still now, one wing folded, the other laid out on the ground. It's clearly broken, and he's obviously in pain, but animals often make a lot less fuss than humans.

I let him nudge my hand and talk to him in a quiet soothing voice. I tell him I'll fix it, that he'll fly again.

"Is that your seagull Billy?" Vinny calls out to me, still watched by Tucker. "Your trained seagull?" He laughs, like he can't believe the question he's just asked, or what's just happened. I don't answer him.

"Cos that is fucking weird," he goes on. "To be training fucking seagulls."

I still don't answer him, but I look over this time.

"At your age you should be going out getting laid. Not training fucking seagulls."

There's something about Vinny's voice that still scares me. A confidence. I look at Tucker, just as he resettles the gun in his hands that are trembling visibly now. I realize this is isn't quite over. I feel myself wishing Tucker would just shoot him. Just in the legs or something. Not because I want Vinny to die, it's just I'm still scared of him. Still terrified. It's like I can see what's going to happen. I don't know how, but somehow he's going to get the gun back. Vinny is the only one of us who's still calm. Composed.

"You got any more animals I should know about?" Vinny goes on. It's like he's enjoying himself. "A... I dunno, a ninja fucking rabbit?" He laughs at the idea, and I see him beginning to pull his legs underneath him, like he's preparing to get up.

"Don't move." Tucker says, but his voice wavers. He doesn't sound in control.

"Oh I'm just getting comfortable. I ain't gonna cause no trouble." Vinny slows his movement but he doesn't stop. He's testing Tucker, and since Tucker doesn't stop him, he fails the test.

Shoot him, I want to call out, but I don't. I begin to understand Tucker's problem. Now he has the gun, he's got a problem. If he shoots Vinny, he's shooting an unarmed man. There's consequences for that. Consequences that last forever. I can see the doubt in Tucker's face. I can see it in his arms, they're shaking now. I begin to think that, even if he did pull the trigger, he might actually miss.

Vinny stops moving now. He's moved his attention from me and Steven onto Tucker. He has all his attention on Tucker. I can see he's looking for an opportunity, and I'm terrified he's going to get it.

He glances sideways, at where the knife Tucker had lays discarded in the grass. Tucker doesn't seem to even register this.

"So," Vinny seems to have come to a decision. He's got a plan. "You've got my gun. But are you gonna use it? Because the way I see it. Those are your only options."

Tucker doesn't answer him. He just holds the gun on Vinny, like he's waiting for something. I don't know what.

"And it seems to me, the longer we sit here, the less chance you've got of using it. You know what I mean?"

Still Tucker doesn't answer. He just waits, not saying anything.

"Oh we can sit here as long as you like. Nice view and all. But sooner or later you're gonna have to make a decision." Vinny smiles again, he's getting more confident with every passing moment. He starts to move his legs again.

"Uh huh," Tucker says at once, and this time Vinny stops. But only for a second.

"You ain't gonna shoot me are you? You ain't got it in you."

"And you can't call the cops, because how would you explain all this? The bag of gold in your truck. So you gotta make a decision Tucker. Shoot me. Or don't shoot me. And if you don't, I'm just gonna get up and walk out of here."

"Stay on the fucking ground."

But this time Tucker looks away. In the distance there's a new sound. I can't place it at first.

"I already made a decision." Tucker says. And Vinny looks confused. He's heard the sound too, and at the same moment we both work out what it is. The sound of a car, maybe more than one car.

"I was gonna catch the boat today," Tucker says. "Keep running, but when you turned up just now, I changed my mind."

And then two marked police cars appear from round the bend and skid to a halt. Two police officers leap out of the first car, sheltering behind the open doors, their guns drawn and trained on Tucker. They shout out, screaming at Tucker to drop his weapon.

He looks at Vinny, and gives a bitter laugh, then lets the gun swing down and fall to the ground.

"You thought I couldn't call the cops. Well you got that wrong. Cos I already called them."

SIXTY-FOUR

THE POLICE RUN FORWARD, shouting, and before I know what's happened Vinny is leaning over the hood of Dad's truck with handcuffs on his wrists. Then they shove Tucker next to him. He keeps his eyes on Vinny all the time, and I can see him smiling. Vinny isn't smiling though, he looks super mad, like he'd have preferred it if Tucker had shot him after all.

Then they take them away, towards the cars. As they push Tucker into one he calls out to me.

"Tell 'em everything you know Billy. Tell 'em the truth."

Another police officer is crouched down by Dad, talking on his radio. I want to go over there, but I'm still sitting with Steven, stroking his feathers keeping him calm. Some time later a woman police officer comes over and starts asking me questions about what happened, and whether I'm alright, and why I'm sitting holding a seagull. There's an ambulance here by then too. The medics wheel a trolley over to where Dad's lying, and before too long they take him away. I want to go with him, and the police officer says she'll take me in her car to the hospital, but then she doesn't want me to take Steven. In the end she agrees that we can take him, but only as far as the vets in Newlea. I know the Newlea vets quite well, so that's OK. I know they'll look after him.

Then by the time we get to the hospital Dad's awake and they let me see him. But that's a bit worrying, because he's really groggy, like he's super tired, or drunk, but the doctors say that's normal and I don't need to worry. They've done scans and they don't think there's any serious damage, he just got hit really hard and knocked out.

Then I have to give an interview, right there in the hospital, in someone's office, and talking into a video camera. I have to explain everything that happened to me, right from the moment Vinny grabbed me from the side of the road, until the police came and arrested him. It's hard at first, because they interrupt me every now and then to ask questions about how I know Vinny, and how I knew he was looking for jewelry, and I have to remember what Tucker said, about being honest. I don't really know if it's the right thing to do or not, but once I start I don't really have any choice.

Then, because it's late by then and I can't go home, I get taken to a hotel with a lady called Gill. She's from the Child Protection Services. I already know quite a lot about them. She gets us rooms next to each other, with a connecting door, and she starts to explain how she's going to sleep right there and how I don't have to worry, but I just want her to go away so I can order dinner from the room service and eat it on the bed watching TV.

The next day Gill takes me back to hospital, and Dad's a lot better, he's sitting up and eating. They don't let him go home yet though, because they still want to observe him in case he gets concussion. So I spend a really long day just hanging around the hospital with Gill, answering the same questions over and over and over.

Finally Dad gets discharged and Gill lets me go home with him. We take a taxi but we don't talk much on the drive. I don't think either of us want to say anything that the driver will overhear.

It's strange getting home. Dad has to put boards up to cover the broken windows in the house. And while he does that I look at his truck. It has actual bullet holes in the sides. Some of them go all the way through one side and come out the other.

I wonder if Dad will want to talk, but instead he cooks us some food, and when we're finished eating he washes the dishes and tells me I should go to bed and get some rest. So I do, and I must be pretty tired, because it doesn't take me any time at all to get to sleep.

SIXTY-FIVE

WHEN I WAKE the next morning Dad's already up and he's set the table for breakfast. It's only cereal and toast, and a carton of long life orange juice from the back of the cupboard, but he's still put a knife and a spoon and bowls and plates on the table. The thing is, it suddenly seems weird that there's just two places. After Tucker being here for such a long time.

"Morning Billy," Dad says. He sounds choked up too. I wonder if it's for the same reason.

They haven't told me anything about what's happening to Tucker. I kept asking – Gill, and the police officers – I asked whether he'll go to prison and if so, for how long. But they either didn't know, or they wouldn't tell me. But I know he will. You could tell from their faces, if nothing else.

And that makes me feel really guilty, because it's all my fault, when you think about it. If I hadn't interfered with Tucker's phone then Vinny would never have found out he was here on Lornea Island. Then Vinny wouldn't have come looking for him and then Tucker would never have had to give himself up to the police. Actually it's worse than that. If it wasn't for my interfering, Dad and Tucker would have got their loan by now and they'd be buying the *Ocean Harvest* already. They'd be setting up together in business just like they always wanted to ever since they were kids. Sort of like I wanted Dad to do, right at the start of all this.

I want to say something about all this, but it's all so big. I don't know where to begin.

"Morning," I say, in the end. And I sit down. For a moment I don't do anything, and then I pour myself a bowl of Cheerios, feeling uncomfortable because Dad's watching me. Then he gets up and makes a pot of coffee. I can hear him, pouring the water and getting a cup. Finally I can't take it anymore.

"I'm really sorry," I say, putting the spoon down. "I'm sorry I messed everything..."

"Stop," Dad interrupts me, his voice firm.

"You don't have a single thing to be sorry about." He takes the seat opposite me. He's holding his mug of coffee, squeezing it tightly with both hands, but even so I can see his hands are shaking.

"I'm the one who needs to apologize."

I don't really understand.

"But if I hadn't used Tucker's phone, then Vinny wouldn't have known he was here."

Dad takes a deep breath in.

"And you'd have got your loan. You'd be buying *Ocean Harvest*."

But Dad shakes his head now.

"You know, spending two days in a hospital bed gives you a little time to think." Dad begins, and I realize I need to stay quiet. I need to let him speak.

"I've let you down. A lot." He pauses, like he's choosing his words carefully. "Tucker's a good guy, at heart. But when someone like him turns up, unannounced, with a bag full of pearl necklaces and gold chains, saying how he wants to use it to make a new start... You've gotta wonder. You've gotta ask, where does that come from? And I didn't ask. I didn't ask because I didn't want to know the answer.

"But you did. You asked Billy. You asked me, and I wouldn't tell you, so you found out for yourself. Just like you always do."

He stops talking, but for a long time he keeps looking at me. I start to feel a bit self conscious. I didn't even know there *was* any gold.

"But I still messed everything up. Tucker's still going to go to prison because of the way I did it."

It takes a few moments, but in the end Dad nods.

"Yeah. And that's what should happen too. *He* made the decision to rob that jeweler's store. No one told him too. And with a guy like Vinny too. I hope he's not there too long, but he needs to spend a little time reflecting on that."

There's a silence for a moment. It's funny, Dad's laid out this breakfast but neither of us are eating any of it.

"And what was his alternative? Being on the run? That's no life."

I think for a few moments, until something strikes me. "But you went on the run," I say. "How come that was right then, but isn't now?" I think it's the first time I've ever actually asked Dad about this, what happened with mom and everything when I was a baby. He watches me, his eyes level.

"That was different. We went on the run because we didn't do it. Tucker would have been on the run because he did."

I consider this for a few moments. I suppose I see the logic of it.

"Eat up. I'll run you to school. But we gotta go somewhere on the way." I look up, surprised.

"Where?"

"Eat up. You'll see."

* * *

I get my bag and climb into the truck. You can see all the way through the bullet hole in my door, and there's a dent in Dad's door on the other side, so that bullet must be stuck inside the driver's door. I might try and get it out later.

"Where are we going?" I ask again, but Dad won't answer.

So I have to try to guess. We take the road towards Newlea, but then, instead of going all the way to school, we turn off towards the Holport where Dad works. It's also the road to where Mrs. Jacobs lives, so I start to feel a bit nervous. But when we get to the junction Dad takes the road that winds down towards the port itself. I look across at him, confused, but he keeps his eyes forward and doesn't say a word.

We stop on the hard, parking up above the basin where all the boats are moored up. I want to ask again why we're here, but there's a man waiting for us. A young guy in a suit. He's holding a plastic folder, closed, so I can't see what's in it. He shakes Dad's hand, and then he looks at me, and hesitates for a second until I put my hand out too. Then he leads us down onto the pontoon, and I start to get an idea where we might be headed.

But I still don't really understand it.

SIXTY-SIX

"I GOT TO THINKING," Dad says suddenly. He doesn't seem to care that the other guy can hear him. "If I can buy one boat with Tucker and get into fishing, then maybe your plan wasn't so crazy after all."

Up ahead of us the *Blue Lady* sits tied up, just like the last time I saw her.

"She's thirty nine feet long," the man starts to read from his clipboard. "Inboard diesel engine. She's not the fastest but she'll cruise at twenty knots. And with excellent MPG as well. Feel free to step aboard folks."

The guy holds out his hand to help Dad onto the boat, I guess he sees Dad's limp, but Dad ignores him and steps across on his own. Then he reaches out an arm for me to come over too.

"Come on Billy. You can show me around."

I don't know what to think, so I just listen as the salesman reels off all the specifications for *Blue Lady*, but I'm really impatient for him to open the door. I've seen the pictures on the inside so many times, but I've never actually *been* inside. I've never quite worked out how it all fits together.

"So you looking for personal use or..?" The salesman says, as he pulls out a set of keys. They're on a piece of string with a paper tag attached, the name of the boat written on it. "Or you looking to set up some fishing charter business?"

"Neither," Dad says, looking at me. "I was thinking about maybe running some whale watching trips. You know, run some tourists out there?"

"I gotcha," the salesman says. I think he's going to say that's a crazy idea but he doesn't. "My sister just got back from vacation in Florida. She went on one of those boats they have down there. She can't stop going on about it."

Just then another boat motors past and a small wave rocks the *Blue Lady* in her berth. I feel her, moving from side to side under my feet and I hardly listen to Dad or the sales guy any more.

"Are you serious?" I ask Dad, as the salesman unlocks the cabin door. "What about the money?"

"I definitely ain't promising anything, we gotta do a lot of work on that business plan of yours, and I still gotta speak with the bank. But I didn't think it could hurt to take a proper look." He hesitates and looks around.

"And she's a nice boat."

Dad climbs the ladder to the flying bridge, and the sales guy follows him up. So I go into the saloon on my own. It's light inside, since she has big windows. There's the little navigation area like I saw before, and then steps leading down into the cabin proper. I descend carefully, letting my fingers brush against the varnished woodwork. Up above I can hear Dad and the sales guy talking, but I can't hear what they say. I don't even want to though. Right away I'm lost in my own world. I'm down here while we're out at sea. I'm explaining to a group of tourists, super excited, about how we might see humpback whales, or minke, or fin whales, or sperm whales or even blue whales, or even maybe orca. I've only seen orca one time, from the top of the cliff. But that's only because I've never had a boat before. I've never had a way to get out to where they like to be, off the continental shelf.

It's warm down here, and there's a smell. It's a bit musty I suppose, but it's probably only because no one's had the *Blue Lady* open for a while. I hear a sudden sound below me, and I'm confused for a second, but then I realize it must be Dad and the sales guy turning on the engine to check it runs. There's a faint smell of diesel too, but overall I like it. It's nice. I sit down on the bed, right at the front of the boat, and I imagine what it must be like to sleep here, while the engine powers the boat along, cutting through the water, miles away from the land.

SIXTY-SEVEN

"WHAT HAPPENED THIS TIME BILLY?"

That's Amber. I'm back at school now, and she's just grabbed me in the corridor. She doesn't seem to be in a very good mood.

"You go out to find out whether Principal Sharpe's had a brother or sister, then I don't hear for you for *three whole days?*"

"I got kidnapped," I say, quietly, because I don't want the whole school to know.

"Yeah right. By aliens I bet."

"No, it was Vinny, Tucker's friend."

She stares at me, her head tipped right over on one side.

"You got *what?*"

She says that really loudly, and she's blocking the whole corridor now, her hands on her hips.

"Come with me," I say, walking towards the canteen.

"Why?"

"Because it's a long story, that's why."

I lead her to a table where no one can overhear, and I explain everything that happened. From when I was taken, on the way back from the records office, right up to when the police came and arrested Vinny and Tucker. Amber listens, only interrupting a few times where there are parts she doesn't understand. I don't know what I'm expecting when I'm finished, but it's not the reaction I get.

"I don't believe it," she says.

"You don't believe me?"

"Oh no, I believe it alright. I just don't believe how all the exciting stuff happens to you, *again*."

I can see she's joking, at least a bit, but it still annoys me. I guess I'm tired of the way Amber always thinks it's just a game.

"It wasn't *fun* Amber. I got kidnapped. I got shot at, I nearly got killed. I thought I was going to die."

"Yeah you said. Several times."

She turns away from me, her arms crossed over her chest.

"So what did you find out anyway?"

I don't follow this.

"What do you mean?"

"Did you even find anything out? In this records office of yours."

"Oh that. It isn't *my* records office."

"Oh, *whatever* Billy. I only asked if you found anything there?"

I feel my forehead start to wrinkle like it does when I get a bit annoyed.

"Yes," I say. "I found out that Principal Sharpe had a younger brother. He was born three years after she was, and his name was Eric."

From the look on her face, I'd say Amber would have preferred it if I'd not found anything out.

"And I suppose you've already talked with him have you?"

I look at Amber, feeling my forehead scrunch up even more. "Haven't you been listening? I was kidnapped, driven around at gunpoint and then stuck in hospital telling everything to the police over and over again. When exactly would I have had time to do any work on the case?"

"Oh here we go again."

I look away in frustration. I'm really not sure what her problem is.

"And anyway," I tell her. "I can't because he's dead."

"He's *what*?"

"He's dead. Principal Sharpe's brother drowned."

"*Drowned*? Fucking hell Billy. I cannot believe you didn't tell me this!"

I sigh, really loudly. "Amber I got kidnap..."

"How did he drown?"

I stare at her. "Give me your phone." I say in the end. She looks at me, openly suspicious.

"Why?"

"Because I need to search the internet, and I lost my phone when I was kidnapped at gunpoint." I reach across and grab her phone from the table in front of her. And then I open up her web browser, peer down at the little screen, and retype the google search I made for Eric Jacobs. It doesn't take long before I pull up the article I found, moments before I was taken by Vinny.

"Here you go." I angle the phone so we can both read it. "We can find out together."

The search for missing teenager Eric Jacobs was called off today after police revealed he had been suffering from depression in the days before his disappearance. It's believed Eric swam out into Lornea Sound in the early hours of last Tuesday morning near to his family home and leaving a pile of clothes on the rocks. It's now understood that Eric spoke to his family repeatedly in the days and weeks before, and seemed very low. Speaking on behalf of Lornea Island Police Department, Lieutenant Dale Collins said: "The Coastguard and volunteers have worked day and night in this case, but with the fierce currents off the southern tip of the island, it's now highly unlikely that Eric's body will be recovered. Our thoughts are with the family at this difficult time.

Amber looks at me once we've both finished reading. She's still pouting. "So what does that mean?"

I scroll down the screen a bit. "Look. It gives a number to ring if you're in need of help. For the Samaritans."

"So he killed himself?" Amber shakes her head. "Well that's a fat lot of use."

I don't reply, in fact I hardly hear her. I'm thinking instead about Eric. He would have been about my age. Thinking about it, he would probably have gone to this school too. He would have sat right here in this same cafeteria. He would have seen the same things I see, and yet, he chose to kill himself. He decided he preferred to swim out into the cold waters of Lornea Sound and let himself sink into the deep. That's terrifying.

"I wonder why he did it?" I start to say, but then I'm interrupted by Amber talking again.

"Or maybe he didn't? Maybe he was murdered too? Think about it... If he found out what happened to his dad, then maybe the old lady bumped him off too? To keep him quiet. I bet Principal Sharpe knows about it too, that's why she never told us she had a brother...."

"*Oh shut up Amber. Why don't you just shut up?*"

I don't mean to shout at her like that. I've just had enough.

"What? What's *wrong* with you?"

"Nothing's wrong with me, what's wrong with *you*? She didn't hide the fact she had a brother, we just never asked. And her brother's dead. He *killed himself*. You just don't know what it's like!"

"What what's like?"

"When bad things happen to your family. You just don't get it!"

Amber shoots me a funny look, but it's gone in a flash, then her face hardens again.

"Unless he didn't. Unless he was killed, because he was going to reveal what really happened to his dad."

"Just stop it! I told you, this isn't a game. It's people's lives. It's Principal Sharpe's *life*. We should never have gotten involved. It's not our business."

Amber stares at me. I shove her phone back across the table to her. Then I grab my bag.

"This whole thing, we got it wrong. We got it all wrong. It was never a big mystery, it was a tragedy. All along."

Amber's face is white with rage now, her eyes dark and sunken under her brows. I glower at her, wanting to keep fighting. But then I'm too angry. I stand up and stalk. I feel her eyes on me as I go.

I'm so wound up, I just walk at random round the school, which I never do normally, because there's lots of places I can't go. Or shouldn't go. Like the part of the school grounds at the back of the science block, where the basketball courts are. I don't like basketball, or any sport really, but that's not why I normally avoid it here. It's because this is where James Drolley and his friends usually hang around at lunchtime. And they do it because none of the teachers like coming back here, so they can do whatever they want. But I'm so annoyed with Amber's reaction to what happened to poor Eric Jacobs that I'm not thinking straight. And that continues when Drolley spots me.

"Hello Wheatley!" I actually nearly bump into him before I realize who it is. "You come for your daily dead arm have you?" He's got into this habit of punching me in the arm every day. He seems to think it's a kind of game we're playing, almost like we both enjoy it. I sort of told you about it.

"Which one do you want to do? Left or right?" He grins at me, and I can smell he hasn't cleaned his teeth in days.

Normally I'd talk to him, but I don't think I can today. I try to push past, but he steps in my way, blocking me.

"Where'd ya think you're going *Wheatley*? I ain't seen you all week. I must owe you three days worth of punches. Maybe four." He begins to roll his sleeves, and his friends abandon their game and gather closer to watch what's going to happen.

But today I'm just not in the mood.

"Let's do both arms shall we Wheatley?" Drolley grins again, and he lines up a punch. He's kinda got me trained so I don't even move, just to get it over and done with.

But then I don't know what happens. It's definitely something that's never happened to me before. I feel my hand tighten into a fist, and I pull it back behind me. Then, while Drolley is still grinning like an idiot, I spin myself around, and throw my arm forward with all my might. Dad tried to teach me once, how to throw a punch, and I kinda remember now, how you're not supposed to aim at the target, but through it. Behind it. That's what I do now. Then there's a massive, sudden pain in my knuckles as they smash into Drolley's face and keep going. And then I hear this shouting, and it's me. Yelling at Drolley, even though he's not standing there any more, he's sprawled on his back on the ground.

"Why don't you just stop it? Why don't you just *get lost*? I'm so fed up with you. You're just an *idiot*. Wasting everyone's time. People who are trying to be sensible. Trying to work in class or do useful things. Why don't you just...?"

I stop. I'm about to swear at him, and I don't want to, because that would be wrong. And I'm shocked by the scene around me. I'm panting like I've been running hard, and Drolley is still on the floor. His nose is split and gushing blood over his mouth and chin.

"Oh shit," someone says. I don't know who. "Wheatley's broken his nose."

"I didn't want to hit him," I say to his friends, they're all staring at me now, their mouths hanging open. "I don't want to hit anybody. I've just had enough of violence. I just want him to leave me alone."

And then I pick up my bag and walk on.

SIXTY-EIGHT

As soon as afternoon classes begin I know what's going to happen. First of all everyone's staring at me, and then a girl who's never even spoken to me before comes up and asks if it's true that I punched out James Drolley. I don't know what to say, so I explain that I didn't really mean to, it just happened. But instead of having a go at me, like I expect her to, because James Drolley is a much more popular kid than I am, she doesn't.

"I'm so glad someone's finally done that," she says instead.

I stare at her in amazement.

"He's such a jerk. Him and his stupid friends. They're always picking on me. No one ever does anything about it."

And then more people come up and tell me the same thing. Even Paul, who *is* one of his stupid friends, whispers to me that he's glad it happened. It's weird.

But from the moment Mr. Matthews, the teacher, comes in, I know I'm not going to get away with it.

"Billy Wheatley? Mr. Evans would like a word with you. Right away please."

Mr. Evans is the Deputy Principal. If I'm being sent there, it must mean Principal Sharpe isn't in today. That's something I suppose, but even so I feel my face flush hot with the injustice of it all.

* * *

"I assume you're familiar with the school policy on fighting?" Mr. Evans says, when I'm standing in front of his desk. And actually I'm not, since I've never had to consider it before.

"I suppose you're probably not allowed to do it?"

"No you are not. This school does not tolerate violence. Not in *any* circumstances." Mr. Evans replies. Then he fixes me with a stare and holds it until I have to look down at my feet. Then he waits what feels like a full half-hour before going on.

"However, I understand from several of Mr. Drolley's associates that he himself threw the first punch, and that you were merely responding to provocation. Is that correct Billy?"

I look up again, confused.

"No, he didn't..." But I don't get any further because Mr. Evans interrupts me.

"*I said*, Billy, that my understanding is that Mr. Drolley initiated the violence, and that you were simply defending yourself. And if that's the case it would certainly influence how I view your role in the matter. Now can you confirm, that is indeed what happened?"

I squint at him, really confused now. I'm pretty sure Drolley didn't actually hit me this time at all.

"If you say so."

"Good. Violence is never the answer Billy. Never." He keeps his eyes on me. "Not even when it seems that maybe it is the answer. It isn't. Are we on the same page?"

I don't know how to answer this. I don't know what page we're on at all.

"So if you have any more trouble with Mr. Drolley, you come directly to me. Rather than taking matters into your own hands. Is that understood?"

If I'm honest it isn't, but I nod anyway.

"Good," Mr. Evans says again. "Excellent. Now I have lots to do this afternoon, so I suggest you go back to class and we make sure this is the end of the matter. OK?"

And that's the end of it.

SIXTY-NINE

THERE'S some good news when I get home. Someone's posted my phone back to me. It had my name and address on a sticker on the back, so I was hoping this might happen, but I still think that's quite lucky because a lot of people would have kept it.

Then I sit down with Dad, he wants to go through the spreadsheet I made, about the whale watching business. So we check through every figure I used, like for how many people we could fit onto the boat, and how much we could charge them, and how much we'd need to spend on fuel. He makes me change loads of the figures, and then redo all the calculations, and with every little change the business ends up costing a little bit more to run, or making a little bit less money. So at the end it's all a bit depressing. Dad tries to stay positive, but I can see he's worried about it.

Then I go upstairs, and I can't stop myself thinking about my fight with Amber. I don't really argue with people, but with Amber it's hard not to. I decide her problem is she thinks everything's about *her*. That's why she's always dyeing her hair new colors - to make people look at her. She's desperate for attention. And she's not even a good detective. She jumps to conclusions too quickly. Like seeing conspiracies where there aren't any. And she just thinks everything is a game, for her entertainment.

But it's not a game. Not to Mrs. Jacobs. Not to Principal Sharpe, and it definitely wasn't a game to Eric Jacobs.

I think back to when this all began. I knew then we shouldn't have got involved. I knew we could never have actually found out what happened. We were never real detectives, and the only reason Mrs. Jacobs hired us was because she was too crazy to notice we were just kids. But even so we should have known we were messing around with *real* people, with real feelings, and real lives.

I think about how we told the police about Mrs. Jacobs 'confession'. I think I feel the most guilty about that. It wasn't ever a real confession. It was just a mad old lady getting confused because her memory was going. I feel my chest heat up with shame.

Then I remember the check.

The five thousand dollars from Mrs. Jacobs. I took it, but told myself I'd only pay it in if we actually found out what happened to Mr. Jacobs. I guess we never will now. I rummage around in my desk drawer until I find it. I look at the spidery handwriting. Five thousand dollars written out in black ink. I should tear it up. I'm about to do it too, when something stops me. It's the thought that she's got loads of money.

I'm not thinking of cashing it. Honestly it's the opposite of that. I'm thinking how she's got so much money, she probably hasn't realized that we *didn't* cash it in the first place. There'll be so many thousands in her bank account, she won't notice five thousand either way. Which means she'll think we've ripped her off. She'll think we tricked her into telling the police she killed her husband, and stole a load of her money.

I can just imagine how that would make me feel. If I was a little old lady I mean, and my husband had run away and my son had killed himself. I'd definitely feel even worse about all that if I also thought I'd been conned by some private investigators who were just kids.

So I know what I have to do. I slip the check into an envelope and put it into the pocket of my shorts.

So I'm all ready for tomorrow.

SEVENTY

I'M ON MY BIKE, cycling down to the southern tip of Lornea Island. There is a bus, but it doesn't go all the way to Mrs. Jacobs' house. It's quite remote where she lives. It's actually further than I realized though. And the hills are bigger too. But I'm nearly there now.

Last night my plan was to actually speak to Mrs. Jacobs. To apologize for everything we did - recording her without her knowing about it, and then getting the police involved and everything. But now I'm not going to do that. I'm just going to slip the check through her letter box and cycle home. She'll understand - well she won't understand, because she's mad - but what I'm saying is it won't make any difference if I speak to her or not.

It's a nice sunny day when I'm cycling, but then just as I arrive a cloud slides over the sun and makes it feels colder. It makes the house look spooky too. I didn't really see it when I came before, but it actually looks like one of those houses in horror movies, a bit run-down. Mrs. Jacobs has all the drapes across the windows, so that anyone could be in there, looking out, and I wouldn't see them. Thinking about that, I don't even know if *she's* home. I try to think back to whether there was ever a car here when I came before. I can't think though, and that makes me realize again that I was never actually very good at being a detective, since I'm not very observant. I get off my bike and I lean it against a tree. I feel quite uncomfortable now, with Mrs. Jacobs' big house towering over me.

I try to walk up to the front door confidently, listening to the crunch of stones under my feet. Then I can't find the letterbox, and I wonder if maybe she has one of those box ones at the edge of her property, that I didn't notice. But then I see it, a slim, cast iron slit right at the bottom of the door. I pull the envelope out of my pocket. I wish I'd written a note now, to explain why I'm returning the check. But she'll work it out. Or maybe she won't, but I'll know I've done the right thing.

I bend down and try to push the envelope through the letter box, but it's flimsy, so I have to use my fingers to push the metal plate back, and feed the paper through. And I'm just doing that when I suddenly feel my fingers gripped by the metal, tight against my knuckles.

I leap back in shock, but my hand is trapped. Then I realize what's actually happening. It's just the door opening. She must have heard me. Or maybe she *was* standing by one of the windows, watching.

I get my hand out now, and get back to my feet. And I see Mrs. Jacobs peering out at me from behind the front door.

"Mr. Billy?" She says. "What on earth are you doing here?"

SEVENTY-ONE

SHE BLINKS at me from the darkness inside the hallway. There's a trickle of blood from where the letterbox scraped at my finger.

"Mr. Billy?"

I want to just hand her the envelope and climb on my bike and cycle out of here. But I know if I do, she'll feel hurt again.

"I came to... erm..." I hold out the envelope.

"Oh – your hand! It's bleeding."

"It's nothing, it's just a scratch, from when..."

"Oh that wasn't me? When I opened the door? I am *so sorry* Mr. Billy. Let me fetch you a band-aid."

"It's alright..."

"Nonsense," she opens the door wide, and before I do much about it, I'm ushered inside. "Come through to the garden and I'll see what I can find."

So I swallow, and do what she says.

Her patio looks just like the first time I came here, with Amber, full of enthusiasm for investigating her mystery. Only this time I notice how she has a view of the water. Lornea Sound, the stretch of the coast where her son swam out to drown himself.

"Here you go dear," Mrs. Jacobs comes out holding a tray. On it there's a zip-up first aid kit, bright red with a white cross on it, and a pitcher of iced tea with two glasses. She sets it down, then sits and opens the first aid kit, finally pulling out a single band-aid. Then she takes a long while to get the band-aid from the little sleeve they come in, with her long wrinkly fingers shaking as she works. The cut on my finger isn't bad, I've already sucked off the blood and there's no more coming out. But even so, I take the band-aid when she finally holds it out to me, and wrap it around. She looks happy about it.

"So," she says, sitting down opposite me. "Mr. Billy, what brings you all the way out here?"

I think before I answer. About the check, which I've put back in my pocket now, about all the trouble I caused her by going to the police. About how she must look out every single day and see the swirling waters of Lornea Sound.

"I wanted to say I'm sorry," I tell her. I watch her for a second but then I can't. I lower my eyes.

"Sorry? What on earth for?" Mrs. Jacobs replies.

"For everything really. You see," I hesitate. I don't know if it's even worth me explaining, but so far today she hasn't done anything obviously crazy, so maybe she's having a good day. "We were never proper detectives. Amber and me," I tell her. "We thought we might be, but actually the world is a lot more complicated than we understood. We're just kids really."

Mrs. Jacobs responds by reaching forward and pouring out two glasses of iced tea. I watch to see if she's going to pour it all over the floor like last time, but she ends up with both glasses exactly three quarters full.

"You're rather clever kids," she says.

I don't know how to respond to this, so I sort of half-smile at her and take a drink. It's nice after all the cycling I've done, and the sun's come back out. I drink a bit more.

"And I think you've proven to be rather a good detective Mr. Billy." She says.

Again I've got no idea what she means by this, so I try to go on with what I came here to say.

"I wanted to say sorry about the police."

That makes her pause, just for a second, as she's lifting her glass to her cracked, thin lips, I see the withered definition in the muscles of her arm. It must be weird to be old, and have your body decaying all around you. And your mind.

"I rather brought that upon myself. I do sometimes get carried away, stuck out here all on my own, I get muddled." She takes a tiny sip then puts the glass down. There are coasters on the table and I notice how she puts it precisely in the middle of the one in front of her. I straighten my glass too, so that it's not overhanging the coaster she put for me.

"The doctors tell me I have *dementia*." She screws up her face at the word. "It's such a bore – I do hope they'll have found a cure before you get to my age. It makes me forget things. When I first called you I had quite forgotten what happened to Henry. I had myself in a right pickle about it."

She stops, so I ask her. "But you remember now?"

"Oh yes."

I want to ask her if he went to Maui, but I don't know if it's the right thing to do, to remind someone that their husband ran away.

"I remember where I buried him now."

* * *

I know you won't believe me, but at that exact moment another cloud goes over the sun, a really big, thick one this time, and everything really does go dark this time. Or maybe it's just feels like it because, sitting out here with Mrs Jacobs and no one else for miles around, is a little bit scary.

"Pardon?"

"I remember now where I buried him."

I swallow carefully. "Where?" I ask, because what else *can* I ask?

But then she starts talking about something completely different, so I wonder for a moment if I imagined what she said.

"You know, when Wendy and Eric were little they used to love it out here. They would play all summer long. Water fights, they used to love water fights. Do you enjoy water fights Mr. Billy?"

I open my mouth then close it again. Eventually I shrug.

"Not much."

"Eric loved it like nothing else. He would get himself soaked. And Wendy was very much a serious child, but that was one thing that made her loosen up." She's lost for a moment, absorbed by her own memories. I try to remind myself that, whatever she says, it's just the madness speaking. She doesn't *really* remember where she buried him, because she didn't bury him. They're just words.

"That's why I told you Henry was under the school gym. Because that's what I always told Wendy, when she was little. I thought it would be strange for her, the idea of playing out here otherwise."

Mrs. Jacobs looks around the garden, and then she smiles.

I know they're just words, but I can't help myself try to work out what they mean.

"Why would that be strange?"

Mrs. Jacobs waits until she sees my eyes fix onto hers, and then she glances down to the ground. It looks very deliberate.

"Oh come now Mr. Billy," She slides her eyes down a second time, and this time I follow them, and then notice the ground beneath my feet for the first time. It's made up of large stone slabs, each a half-meter square, their tops bleached by the sun.

"It would have been strange, don't you think? To grow up playing out here, knowing your father was hidden right beneath your feet?"

I don't believe her. Or maybe I don't want to believe her. "He's in Maui. Or he went to Maui, that's what Principal Sharpe told us."

"Because that's what we told everybody who asked. Not that many people *dared* to ask. You didn't in those days. It was more a hint here, a nudge there, to all the gossips on the island. Just enough that everyone knew *where* he'd gone, but no one felt able to talk about it." She laughs suddenly. "Do you know I even travelled to Maui? I posted back birthday cards, so they'd have the correct post mark, in case the police ever became suspicious. But they never did. Not until you got involved of course."

I don't reply.

"You don't believe me? Or, you're not sure what to believe any more?" She looks sad now. "You came here to apologize to me Mr. Billy, but it's me who should be apologizing. For everything *I've* done."

"Look at me Mr. Billy, tell me what you see?"

I do what she says, the first part at least. I see a frail old woman, with flesh that droops from the bones on her arms. The skin flakey and cracked.

"Tell me!"

I jump, shocked by how fierce she sounds. "An old lady?"

She smiles at this, then slumps back a little in her chair.

"An old lady who has lied her whole adult life. Do you know what that's like? A life of deception? I've plotted and schemed and connived and covered up, always believing myself and my children on the brink of a terrible peril if the truth were ever to come out. But do you know what's worse than being found out?" She looks away suddenly, and I see water forming in her eyes. When she looks back she's smiling through tears.

"*Not* being found out. Left to fade away, alone, and realizing that no one ever really cared. Mr. Billy, I *murdered* my husband and I hid his body and I made it my life's work to get away with it. Until I found out, I never *wanted* to get away with it. Not forever."

There's no way I can't not believe her now. I don't know what's happening to her, but it's not madness. Not craziness. She's telling me the truth now, I'm sure of it. I just don't have a clue what to do about it.

Mrs. Jacobs begins tapping her foot now, like she's getting impatient. "There's a shovel. In the shed over there," she points. "Would you be a darling and go fetch it?"

I don't move.

"Why?"

"Because I've put you in a pickle. You know where Henry is, but you can't tell anyone, not after going to the police once with your story of him being under the school gymnasium. No one will ever believe you without proof. "

I don't answer, I just listen.

"I'm sure you have one of those cell phones on you? They're all young people seem to look at these days. With a camera?"

I nod.

"Well then. A strong young man like you can easily prize up these slabs, and then you can get your proof. I don't suppose there'll be much left other than bones by now. But you can take a photograph. And then you won't have to worry about not being believed."

Still I don't move, but she just stares at me with a weird, horrible smile on her face. And even though I don't want to, I find myself slowly climbing to my feet.

SEVENTY-TWO

THE TOOL SHED is cool and dark. Neatly organized. It smells of cut grass from a big petrol mower that takes up most of the space. I find the shovel easily enough, leaning up inside the door. I pick it up, feeling its weight. I walk back with it, and I wait for more instructions.

"You might need to lift up a few slabs Mr. Billy," Mrs. Jacobs says. She's put the tray with the drinks on the lawn, and she's dragged the table over to one side. "I think you should start with this one."

I don't though. Not for a long time. I just stand there, with the shovel in front of me, wondering how I got into this, and how I can get out of it. I want to throw the shovel down, run back through the house and get as far away from here as I can. I could too. I don't suppose Mrs. Jacobs could do much to stop me. But if I did that, I still wouldn't know for sure. And even after everything I've been through, I do want to know the truth.

"If you put the edge between the slabs here, you should be able to lever them up." She comes towards me. I can see how frail she is. It kind of gives me the confidence to do what she says. I step forward and scrape away at the dirt that's built up between the paving slabs.

"That's it Mr. Billy. That's it."

I put my foot on the top of the shovel and force it down between the slabs. I lean back on the handle, pushing my weight into leveraging up the first slab. It resists, but only for a moment, then it breaks free, cracking the mud all around it. I get a glimpse of yellow sand underneath before the weight of it pulls the slab back down. I think I expect to see something horrific there, but it's just sand.

"You'll need to get your hands underneath it dear. Then you can drag it onto the grass." There's enthusiasm in her voice. A weird enthusiasm.

I lift the slab again, and this time I put my foot on the handle of the shovel, keeping the blade under the concrete so that I can get my fingers under each side. It's heavy, but not too heavy. I manoeuvre it away to the side and drop it onto the lawn. Then I look back. Now there's a glaring square hole in the patio. Squashed flat sand. Cut into it are channels dug out by ants, they look like a river seen from space.

"You'll need to lift a few more, and then dig down. Just a little." Mrs. Jacobs says.

With the first one gone it's easier, and the square of yellow sand quickly doubles then quadruples in size. I have to concentrate so hard on moving the slabs I can almost trick myself into not knowing why I'm doing it. But when I have six slabs moved she tells me to stop. I remember then.

"Now dig the sand out. Carefully mind."

I grab the shovel again, and gently scrape at the sand, cutting through the ant runs. I make myself think about them, instead of what I'm actually looking for. They're old runs, fortunately, I'm not disturbing an actual live nest...

"Come on Mr. Billy, put your back into it. He's further down than that."

Her words bring me back. I stop for a moment, but then I try to empty my head completely, and I crunch the shovel properly into the sand. I balance a load on the shovel, then lift it out. I start a pile on the patio. It's years since I made a sandcastle, but that's what I think of now. Summer days with Dad, when I was little.

Quickly the sand builds up. A couple of times I unearth a stone, and get a jolt of panic that it's something else. I can hardly look at the hole I'm digging. I'm expecting to see a ghastly death mask of Henry Jacobs, with flesh still falling from his face, and I wish now I hadn't started this. But it's hard to stop. Then my shovel hits something hard.

She claps her hands together and leans right over me.

"I think you've found him. Scrape the sand off Mr. Billy. Careful now."

I do what she says, revealing something buried in the hole.

The color is the off-white that bones turn when they're old. I know it well enough from identifying animal skulls I've found in the past. And from the shape I can tell this is a skull too. The back of it, although I've never seen a human skull before. Very carefully I insert the shovel to one side, and gently extract more sand so that more of the bone is revealed. I do this a couple of times more, until it's quite clear what I'm looking at – the rounded back of a skull, and part of a jaw bone. Then I stop and look at Mrs. Jacobs.

She's standing by the hole, watching what I'm doing, and she's got her hands clasped against her chest. And she's crying again.

"Oh Henry," she says, then she gives me a goofy look.

Then I put down the shovel and pull out my phone to take a photograph. I'm a bit worried when I do this, that she might try to stop me, but she doesn't even seem to notice. I pull the phone from my backpack, I frame a photo so that it's clear what it is, and I press the shutter. Then I take another shot, this time pulling back to get the hole and Mrs. Jacobs' house in the background – so the police know exactly where the body is buried. Then, since Mrs. Jacobs is still ignoring me, I attach the photo to a text message for Amber. I quickly type out the words.

You were right. Sorry.

"I'm going to go now Mrs. Jacobs." Again I'm half-expecting her to try something to stop me. But I guess she knows I'd be stronger and faster than her. So she just gives me a smile.

"Not yet dear," she says.

I don't know what she means by this.

"Why not?"

"She'll be here any second."

"Who will?"

And then a voice calls out from inside the house. The last person I was expecting to see.

"Mother?!"

SEVENTY-THREE

PRINCIPAL SHARPE MOVES QUICKLY, like a spider when a fly lands in its web. She puts herself between where I'm standing and the door. I look around, there's no other obvious way out.

"Wendy, how nice of you to arrive so promptly," Mrs. Jacobs says. Then she turns to me.

"Wendy installed a panic button. She said I had to use it if you or that girl ever came to harass me again. That was the word she used: 'harass'. I did tell her you've only been perfectly polite, every time we've spoken. But I did press it Mr. Billy, all the same. I pressed it when you first arrived." She tilts her head onto one side, and goes back to gazing into the hole.

Principal Sharpe takes in the scene. She's holding a purse, and she suddenly starts rifling through it, and I don't know what she's going to pull out, but then I'm shocked, and I guess maybe a bit weary to see it's a gun. It's only a small one, much smaller than the one that Vinny had, but it's still a gun. In my school principal's hands. She points it at Mrs. Jacobs for a second, but then she points it at me. I see the barrel wobble with how her hands are shaking,

"What's going on? What on earth is going on?"

"I wanted to introduce young Billy here to your father," Mrs. Jacobs says. She seems to be standing more upright now. Principal Sharpe puts her free hand over her mouth. Then she leans forward, looking into the hole I've dug.

"Oh Christ," she says. "Mother. What have you done?"

"I did tell you Wendy," Mrs. Jacobs says. She sounds totally calm. "That Henry was here. After they dug up the gym I told you. Don't you remember?"

Principal Sharpe doesn't answer, she just takes in big gulps off air, like she's struggling to breathe.

"And now I've decided to do the right thing."

"The right thing? This isn't the right thing." Principal Sharpe turns on her and snaps. "You stupid woman. *You stupid, crazy, deranged old woman.* The right thing was keeping your mouth shut."

Her eyes are crazy, swiveling this way and that.

"You're so *selfish*. You think you can excuse your part in this, so *you* get to disappear with a clear conscience. But you don't think about others, you never did!"

The gun isn't pointing at me anymore. Principal Sharpe is waving it all over the place, and her attention is on Mrs. Jacobs. I look behind her, at the door. If I can slip behind her I can run. Maybe I can lose her somewhere in the house.

"Have you considered it might be *you* I'm thinking about?" Mrs. Jacobs voice rises up now, like she's not calm anymore. "You think you can keep this hidden your whole life. But believe me, you don't *want* to keep it hidden."

"Oh right? You know what I want do you? You know best? I'll tell you what I wanted, I wanted you to stay on the fucking medication and not embark upon this absurd..."

"*Language!*" The tone of Mrs. Jacobs voice makes Principal Sharpe stop at once. It makes me freeze too, just as I'm about to sneak past Principal Sharpe's back.

"I did not bring you up to have cussing in my house."

"Mr. Billy," Mrs. Jacobs turns towards me. It makes Sharpe notice me as well, and she snatches her arm across so the gun is pointing at me again.

"We should really explain all this, since you've found yourself witness to an awkward family argument."

Principal Sharpe actually looks at me now, I mean actually looks at me. I think she realizes she's pointing a weapon at one of her students. That's not normal for school principals. It's hard to get back from that. There's a moment when she seems to acknowledge it with a twist of her lips. Then Mrs. Jacobs goes on speaking.

"Wendy here was just a girl when it happened. She was unlucky enough to interrupt Henry doing what he did with her brother. I don't have to tell you what that was, do I Billy? I don't like to speak about things like that."

I don't reply. I don't take my eyes off Principal Sharpe.

"I knew of course. About Henry and his *tastes*. I knew it was happening with some of the children at the school, but he always promised me it would stop, or that they liked it. Or that he'd be discreet – or whatever he thought I needed to hear. And times *were* different then. People didn't make such a fuss as they do these days."

"Mother!" Principal Sharpe's voice is a warning to Mrs. Jacobs to stop, but the old woman carries on.

"I confronted him about it, and... Well, you can see for yourself what happened." She gestures towards the hole in the patio, where the skull of Mr. Jacobs is still partially uncovered.

"Eric was too young to know what had happened. I told him that Henry had gone away, just the same as I told everyone else. But that was never going to work with Wendy. So I made it our secret. I said her father had been so naughty, I'd had to put him under the school gym, and no one could *ever* know. And you might think a little girl wouldn't be able to keep such a secret, but Wendy did. She sucked it inside herself. She absorbed it. That secret *became* her. She even decided to become a teacher, so as to take a job at Henry's old school, and make sure the gym was never dug up. It was a little late, by then, to tell her that he was never there in the first place."

Principal Sharpe glares at Mrs. Jacobs at that, and the hurt is visible in her eyes.

"And that might have been the end of it," Mrs Jacobs continues. "But then Eric started asking questions. Awkward questions."

"Be quiet mother!" Principal Sharpe warns again. But again it has no effect.

"He wanted to know where Henry was in Maui. Why he'd stopped writing birthday cards – Oh I couldn't keep disappearing to Hawaii. I should have had him move somewhere more convenient." She smiles.

"It became an obsession with poor Eric. This wondering about his father. And he sensed there was something - something between Wendy and myself, that we weren't telling him. I don't know, perhaps a part of him remembered what happened when he was little?"

"Mother, I'm warning you. I will use this thing." Principal Sharpe stops pointing the gun on me now and aims it at Mrs. Jacobs.

But the old woman either doesn't see or doesn't care. "Of course by then, Wendy was a young woman. She'd grown up with our secret, and the belief it had to be kept whatever the cost." She stops for a moment, looking sad.

"I argued to bring Eric into the secret. That he would keep quiet about it once he knew the truth, but only when he knew the truth. Wendy argued something different. Didn't you dear?"

I watch Principal Sharpe, her long, narrow chest heaving in and out.

"Eric was weak. He wouldn't have kept quiet. He couldn't have."

"You don't know that dear. You wouldn't give him the chance."

The two of them stare at each other. And then I notice something. In the darkness of Mrs. Jacobs's lounge there's a movement. A subtle, careful movement. I glance at Sharpe and Jacob's eyes, but they haven't seen it. They're too busy glaring at each other. So I look back, and try and make it out. And now I see it properly, and my breath catches in my throat. It's a figure, somehow familiar. A person, moving, with their back to the wall, sliding slowly and cautiously towards the door. And then the figure reaches the door. The light catches on purple hair.

It's Amber.

She stops. Her eyes meet mine and she raises a finger to her lips. I have to work hard not to stare. I look around her, hoping to see other figures, the police maybe, but there's no one. She's alone. Amber flicks her eyes to Principal Sharpe and back, warning me not to give her away.

"We agreed that Wendy should be the one to explain it to him," Mrs Jacobs continues, oblivious to what I've just seen. "So she took him for a walk, just at the bottom of the garden here, along the clifftop. Perhaps you'd like to explain what you did next, dear? What you did to your little brother?"

Principal Sharpe doesn't say anything. And after a few moments, Mrs. Jacobs continues.

"I don't know why she's gone coy about it. She was cool as a cucumber afterwards. Ever so matter of fact." She smiles tightly at me. "We have a boathouse, just around the corner, so we were able to tow his body out into the sound and weigh it down. And then pretend it was all a great tragedy, that poor Eric had been unhappy for some time, though that part was true enough…"

"He was like Dad," Principal Sharpe says suddenly. "Eric would have turned out like Dad."

"And you turned out rather like me." Mrs. Jacobs cuts her off.

I look from one of them to the other. They're not looking at me, so I glance again at Amber, to see what she's doing. I see now she's holding the poker from a fire set in one hand. I suppose she's planning to use it to smash the gun from Principal Sharpe's hand. I nod, trying to give her the message that I understand.

"What are you doing?" At once I snatch my eyes back to Principal Sharpe. She must have been watching me after all. She turns around, and Amber's there, in full sight. She's not close enough to swing the poker. Amber freezes, caught.

"Drop it!" Principal Sharpe says. "Drop it on the ground."

For a second Amber doesn't, and I feel my breath thicken. I know what Amber's thinking, about rushing forward, to try and take on Sharpe, and I'm desperate for her not too, because I know what guns can do. She'll get one step and then she'll die, right in front of me.

"Drop it!"

Amber does what she says. There's a clang as the metal poker falls to the ground.

"Get over there with the boy."

All of Principal Sharpe's attention is on Amber now. And I realize that maybe *I* could do something. But what? If I try to rush her, then she'll shoot Amber, or swing the gun and shoot me. And there's no weapons I can get. Nothing near to where I'm standing. And then the moment is gone, and Amber is next to me, her hands raised in the air. I hear her breathing, short and fearful.

"You will not win, either of you. I told you to stay away from my family and you ignored me but *you will not win.* You might think it'll be hard to explain your disappearance, but we'll find a way, won't we mother? That's what we do in this family."

She turns to Mrs. Jacobs now, and I realize that we've all taken our eyes off the old woman. Because now everything's changed. At some point Mrs. Jacobs must have picked up the shovel, and readied herself to swing it like an axe. Because at that moment that's exactly what she does.

It flashes in the light, as it cuts through the air.

SEVENTY-FOUR

THE BLADE of the shovel is turned sideways, so that it knifes through the air. It lands with a thud in the back of Principal Sharpe's head. Her snarl slackens and then droops away, and then something white passes behind her eyes. Then her knees buckle, and she flops to the ground. Through her hair a black-red line fills up and leaks blood onto the floor. It puddles out around her.

I think Amber screams, or it might be me. I'm not sure. But the next thing I know is Mrs. Jacobs has reached down for the the gun. She feels the weight of it, like she's selecting vegetables at the supermarket.

"Well that was easier than I thought," Mrs. Jacobs says. Her voice is calm, almost happy. "I'm sorry you had to see that, but I'm afraid Wendy's had it coming for a very long time." She steps forward and, slowly, she bends down to feel for a pulse at Principal Sharpe's neck.

"Where did you come from?" I ask Amber.

"I was following Sharpe," she says. "I was doing a stake-out outside her house. She drove here so fast I could hardly keep up with her. Then I saw your message."

"Did you call the police?"

Amber hesitates, but then she shakes her head. I screw my eyes shut.

The next moment there's an explosion of noise. My eyes open just in time to see Principal Sharpe's body jerk on the floor, and then the gun jump in Mrs. Jacobs hands. The noise of the shot bounces back off the house. Then she turns to us.

"Just making sure," she says.

The tip of the gun is still spewing smoke, like water flowing from a pipe, only rising instead of falling. I stare at it, transfixed. Then she points it at us, somewhere in the middle of where we're both standing, and I wonder which one of us she'll shoot first. And which one I want her to shoot first. It's weird how you think about things like that. How that matters. But then, awkwardly, she lets the barrel fall down and turns the gun handle first towards us.

"Well?" She says a second later. "Which one of you is going to take it?" She steps forward, holding out the gun in front of her.

"I've called the police," Amber stammers.

"I should hope so. This is definitely a police matter." Mrs. Jacobs smiles. Then she makes a decision. She hands the gun to Amber and then she steps back and looks at the body of her daughter, and at the hole where her husband lays buried.

"Would anyone like some more iced tea while we wait?"

Amber calls the police while she fetches it.

EPILOGUE (1)

We played Scrabble while we waited for the police. I was winning too, and I had a really good word lined up when they finally got there with all their guns and the shouting and everything. So I never got to put it down.

I found out later on that they never stopped investigating Mrs. Jacobs. Even after they dug up the gym and didn't find anything, they still believed she'd killed him because there were no records of him in Maui or anywhere else. They probably would have gotten around to arresting her even if she hadn't murdered Principal Sharpe. But that certainly sped things up.

It's amazing how quickly things move on in schools though. Everyone was really excited for a few days, but even just a week after it all happened, most people were more interested with who was going out with who, and where the next party is going to happen.

But by then I'd already moved on anyway. I was back looking at the whale watching business with Dad. And soon we got past the stage of just planning it, and went to the next stage. Dad rang all the banks on the island, and finally one of them agreed to discuss a loan. They want to actually do a meeting though, so we can lay out exactly what we need the money for, and how we're going to pay it back. I wanted to come along to show them, only Dad said it would be better if he went to the meeting without me, on account of me being just a kid and it looking a bit strange if I went through all the figures. So that's why I'm waiting outside the bank now. In Dad's pick up, with the bullet holes still in the sides. And hopefully when he comes out we'll be all set. It's pretty exciting.

* * *

"So? How did it go?" I can tell right away that Dad's trying to prank me, because he looked really unhappy walking out the bank, with his shoulders slumped down, and his new suit looking all uncomfortable.

"They didn't go for it." He gets in beside me.

"Don't wind me up. They must have." I can't stop smiling

"No Billy, they really didn't."

I can tell from his eyes. He's really not joking after all. "But, we can pay it back, it says so on the spreadsheet!"

Dad closes the truck door, then just sits there, not moving. Eventually he speaks.

"They're not prepared to lend the amount we asked for. They will give us less, but it's not enough. It doesn't buy us the boat." He stares out through the windshield, then he turns to look at me.

"I'm sorry kid…"

"But why?"

"Because we're… Because we're not their kind of people. I did tell you Billy. I got no financial history. No influential backers. No contacts. I did warn you this might happen." He puts his hands on the wheel, grips it hard.

"Well how much are we short?"

"Enough. Enough that it ain't gonna happen." Still he doesn't start the engine.

"But what if we spend less on the marketing? All that insurance stuff you added, maybe we don't need that? Maybe we can…"

"They liked the idea." Dad cuts me off. "Generally, they liked it. They said the business plan was solid. Well thought-out. But they don't make the decisions any more. They just go with what the computer says. And with my credit history. There's a limit. And it just ain't high enough." He turns to look at me.

"Look, we can try again, in a year or two, when I've put some cash away."

"But what about the *Blue Lady*? Someone else'll buy her. We won't be able to do it in a year."

Dad shakes his head. "I'm sorry kid, I really am."

"I can get it. I can get five thousand dollars."

"Billy, where the hell are you gonna get…"

"Is it enough? Is five thousand enough?"

Dad hesitates. In the end he shrugs. "If you really could, it would make a start."

Then he fires the engine. And without another word he drives me back to school.

* * *

I don't go to my lesson though. I've got much more important things to do. I go straight up to the library, and get on the nearest computer. But then I don't know what to search for. It's not exactly a common problem, is it? Trying to work out who Mrs. Jacobs' five thousand dollar check actually belongs to. I mean, first of all, she's just committed first degree murder in front of two witnesses, and admitted to another murder, so I don't know if the police will seize all her money. And then even if that doesn't happen, we were never quite a legal detective agency when she gave it to us in the first place - we never had a license to operate. And then even if that doesn't matter, then half of the money is Amber's. It's super-complicated. But in a funny old way, I'm quite good at super-complicated things.

EPILOGUE (2)

Amber comes round early. She's really excited about everything, and she's picked up Steven from the vets for me, because she's got a car and I haven't. His wing is healed, and the vet didn't charge anything, which was really nice of them, because vets are really expensive.

"They said they don't want to see or hear from you ever again."

"You're joking aren't you?"

"No. They said you cost them a fortune, you never leave them alone, and your bird is the messiest, most vicious animal they've ever worked on. I think they meant it."

I hardly listen, I'm too busy feeding sprats to Steven. His soft brown eyes are almost totally yellow now. He does look quite frightening these days.

"I'm just making sandwiches, do you want to finish off for me?"

"Where's your Dad?"

"He's finalizing things at the bank. He's going to meet us there."

"Well let's go then."

* * *

Amber parks on the edge of the harbor, midway across two spaces, and only moves the car when I point this out to her. Then she takes the cool box from the trunk, and I take Steven, and we walk over to the gate that leads out onto the pontoon. I see the security guard hurrying over, and I know what he's going to say, but he doesn't get a chance because Amber asks if he wouldn't mind holding the gate so she can get the cool box through. Then he just watches us walk down the pontoon like he doesn't know what to say. And even if he had tried something, the next thing is Dad turns up.

It wasn't that hard in the end. I found this website which was all about what happens to prisoner's money when they go to jail. Apparently it's only in some financial crimes like fraud where the police can seize your assets. So even though Mrs. Jacobs did murder Henry Jacobs, because the money they had came from her family, it's still her money. It was a bit more difficult to unravel the problem of the detective agency not being exactly legal. It meant that the terms and conditions we had on the website weren't 100% legal either, which in the end was handy, because there were still a couple of mistakes that we hadn't noticed, and I had to contact Mrs. Jacobs, in a prison on the mainland where she's on remand, to get her to say whether we had to give the money back, but then she said...

"So where's this boat I've invested all my money in?" Amber interrupts me, as we walk down the pontoon.

Mrs. Jacobs insisted that we'd done exactly what she'd paid us for, and that the five thousand was only ever an upfront payment. So she wrote a second check and insisted that Amber should have it. And then Amber said...

"Wow - that's beautiful. Didn't I tell you an island detective agency needs to have a boat as well as a car?"

Well, it turned out 5000 dollars wasn't quite enough for the bank after all, we needed almost double that. But you can probably figure out what Amber said.

* * *

It's a really lovely day for it. There's not much wind, and it's really bright sunshine. And Amber and me carry the cool box into the galley area, and we put all the food and drink into the fridge, which Dad gets himself used to the controls. Then, when we're ready, he starts the engine, and tells Amber and me how to untie the ropes. It's pretty fun, clambering on the deck and on the pontoon, following Dad's orders, and feeling how the boat dips under our weight as we clamber around. And smelling the tang of diesel in the air and feeling how the boat is humming, like it's just as excited as I am.

"Cast off bow line," Dad shouts to me, and I let go of one end of the rope. I pull it, so that it runs through the ring on the pontoon, and the front of the boat is untied then. Dad shouts to Amber at the stern, and she does the same, and then I get a tingle inside me as the engine note deepens, and there's a rush of bubbles coming out behind us, and then we start moving. I kind of miss the first bit because Dad gets me to bring all the fenders in and stow them away, in case it gets wavy out to sea, but I kind of see the rock breakwater pass by as Dad steers us out of the harbor and out into the actual sea.

"Billy, go and grab a beer from the fridge will you?"

I do what Dad says. Down below she's really stable. And there's this comforting throbbing sound from the motor, but you can still hear the sound of water splashing down the sides of the boat. And you can see it too, strikingly blue through the porthole windows. I take a beer and a couple of cans of soda from the fridge, then I take it back outside. I climb the ladder, to where Dad is sitting steering, with Amber beside him. I open the drinks and pass them around. Then Dad takes a sip.

"So Billy," he says to me, as we clear the last bit of the breakwater. "Where do we find these whales of yours?"

The End

A SHORT MESSAGE FROM THE AUTHOR

Thank you for reading *The Lornea Island Detective Club*. I really hope you enjoyed it!

I never intended to write this book. When I published *The Things you find in Rockpools* in February 2018 it was a standalone mystery thriller. But it quickly became my most popular book, selling 50,000 copies in just one year. It was also my favourite book, and this is mostly down to the character of Billy. I think this more than anything encouraged me to wonder what might happen next if I went back into his world.

However, it was also one of the more difficult books I've written. Most protagonists in fictional mystery series are cast as actual detectives, making it (reasonably) plausible that they keep stumbling upon exciting and dangerous mysteries to solve. It's literally their job. It's rather less plausible that the same should happen to an eleven year boy. So before I even began I needed some way of making it (reasonably) believable for a whole new mystery to come and find Billy, and hence the Lornea Island Detective Agency was born.

But I also realised that fresh-faced Billy's had an advantage over all those battle-scared alcoholic-divorcee detectives out there solving mysteries in other books. Billy was just 11 in *Rockpools*, but since a new story must logically take place after the first, he would therefore be older. And that gave me the opportunity to explore how Billy might have changed as he grows from a boy into a young teenager.

And as soon as I realised that, I also realised I could take this even further. How would Billy look at sixteen? At eighteen? I genuinely wanted to know, which is always helpful when you have to sit down for hour upon hour typing out a story.

Therefore I'm really pleased to announce that the third book in the Rockpools series (probably called *The Appearance of Mystery*) is already well under way, and will be published in early(ish) 2020.

If you've enjoyed Rockpools and this book, I do hope you'll stick around to find out what comes next. If you're not already on my mailing list, it's the best way to stay in touch. Not only will you be treated to my occasionally amusing emails, I'll also send a free copy of *Killing Kind*, a novella I wrote in 2018. (The blurb is over the page)

To sign up, all you have to do is type the following into any web browser. Then follow the onscreen instructions.

www.greggdunnett.co.uk/free

And just in case occasionally amusing emails just aren't your thing, you can unsubscribe at any time. 24 hours a day. Even on Christmas day, if that's how you roll...

Thank you again for reading. I really appreciate it. ☺ And if you're looking for another read right now, then might I recommend *The Wave at Hanging Rock*? It's my first novel and I still think it's got the best twist of any I've written. Keep turning the pages to find out more...

Gregg Dunnett
December 2019

READ 'KILLING KIND' FREE

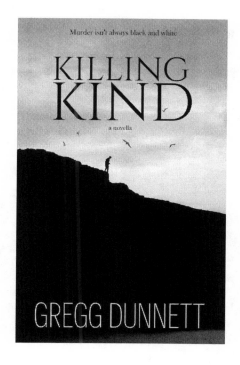

A killer is leaving notes on London's park benches, confessing to their lifetime of crimes.

A detective has the chance to solve cases that have baffled her colleagues for decades.

But only if she can work out who he is, before he gets to her.

Because - in a story where not everything is what it seems - not even murder is black and white.

Killing Kind is a tense novella with a twist that will stay with you.

Read free by typing the following link into any web browser and following the instructions:

greggdunnett.co.uk/free

THE WAVE AT HANGING ROCK

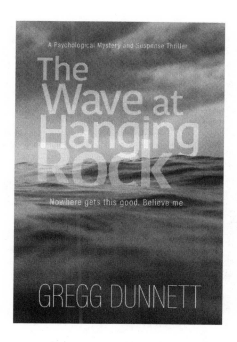

Natalie, a young doctor, sees her perfect life shattered when her husband is lost at sea. Everyone believes it's a tragic accident. But a mysterious phone call prompts her to think otherwise. She sets out on a search for the truth.

Jesse, a schoolboy, is moved half way around the world when his father is blown up in a science experiment gone wrong.

Two seemingly unconnected tales. But how they come together will have you turning the pages late into the night. And the twist at the end will leave you reeling.

The Wave at Hanging Rock is Gregg's debut novel, released in 2016. With over a quarter of a million downloads it quickly became an Amazon bestseller and was shortlisted for the Chanticleer Award for Best Mystery or Suspense novel of the year.

The Wave at Hanging Rock is available on Amazon as an ebook and paperback, and as an audiobook from all good bookstores.

ABOUT THE AUTHOR

Gregg Dunnett is a British author writing psychological thrillers and stories about travel and adventure, usually with a connection to the coast or to the oceans. Before turning to novels he worked as a journalist for ten years on a windsurfing magazine, briefly owned a sailing school in Egypt, taught English in Thailand, Portugal, Turkey and Italy, taught sailing in Greece and Spain, and also had several rather duller jobs along the way.

His brother is the adventurer Jono Dunnett who in 2015 windsurfed alone and unsupported around the entire coastline of Great Britain, and who is currently windsurfing around the coastline of Europe.

Gregg lives in Bournemouth on the south coast of England with his partner Maria. They have two young children, Alba and Rafa, for whom the phrase "Daddy's working" has absolutely no effect.

Gregg's debut novel was an Amazon top 100 best seller in the UK and was downloaded over a quarter of a million times across the world. His third novel was an Amazon bestseller in the UK, US, Australia and Canada.

Gregg on why he writes:

"I've always wanted to do two things in life, to write, and to have adventures. When I was a kid I imagined grand affairs. Kayaking across Canada, cycling to Australia. Whole summers in the Arctic. Did it happen? Well, partly.

I've been lucky, I spent some years abroad teaching English. I worked in sailing schools in Greece and Spain. I really lucked out with a job testing windsurfing boards for the magazine I grew up reading. I made a questionable decision (OK, a bad decision) to buy a windsurfing centre on the edge of the Sinai Desert. I've also done my fair share of less exciting jobs. Packing and stacking potatoes on a farm, which got me fitter than I've ever been in my life. A few years in local government which taught me that people really do have meetings that result only in the need for more meetings, and they really do take all afternoon. I spent a pleasant few months in a giant book warehouse, where I would deliberately get lost among the miles of shelves unpacking travel guides and daydreaming. I've done a bit of writing too, at least I learned how to write. *Boards* Magazine isn't well known (it doesn't even exist today) but it did have a reputation for being well written and I shoe-horned articles in my own gonzo journalism style on some topics with the most tenuous of links to windsurfing. But the real adventures never came. Nor did the real writing.

Then, in 2015, my brother announced he was going to become the first person to windsurf alone around Great Britain. I don't know why. Apparently it was something he'd always wanted to do (news to me.). It was a *proper* adventure. It was dangerous, it was exciting. Before he even set off he got on TV, in the papers. Some people thought he was reckless, some thought he was inspirational. Lots of people thought he'd fail.

But he didn't. He made it around. He even sailed solo from Wales to Ireland, the first to make the crossing without the aid of a safety boat. I was lucky enough to be involved in a superficial planning level, and take part in a few training sails, and the last leg of the trip. But he did ninety nine percent of it on his own. One step at a time, just getting on with it. That was quite inspiring.

In a way it inspired me to pull my finger out. I'd been writing novels - or trying to write novels - then for a few years. But it was touch and go as to whether I was going to be one of those 'writers' with a half-finished novel lost on a hard drive somewhere, rather than someone who might actually manage to finish the job.

I've now got two lovely, highly demanding children, so real adventures are hard right now. I still try to get away when I can for nights out in the wilds rough camping, surf trips sleeping in the van, windsurfing when the big storms come. I love adventures with the kids too.

I hope in time to get around to a few real adventures. I want to sail across an ocean. I want to bike across a continent. I definitely want to spend more time surfing empty waves.

But for me, for now at least, the real adventures take place in my mind. In my real life I'm too chained-down with the mortgage to travel the world at the drop of a hat. But when I'm writing I'm totally free. When I write, that's me having an adventure."

For more information:
Sign up to Gregg's mailing list

www.greggdunnett.co.uk
hello@greggdunnett.co.uk

Copyright © 2019 by Gregg Dunnett

All rights reserved.

No part of this book may be reproduced in any form or by any electronic or mechanical means, including information storage and retrieval systems, without written permission from the author, except for the use of brief quotations in a book review.

Cover design by Coolwatercreative.co.uk

Made in the USA
San Bernardino, CA
07 July 2020

75050716R00188